The Solar Pons Companion

#7

The Solar Pons Companion

#7

Based on the characters and series created by August Derleth

Basil Copper

& Stephen Jones

DIP

Solar Pons colophon by Gary Gianni.

2 4 6 8 10 9 7 5 3 1

FIRST DIP EDITION

ISBN 978-1-786361-78-3

Design & Layout by Michael Smith
Printed and Bound in England by T.J. International

PS PUBLISHING LTD
Grosvenor House, 1 New Road
Hornsea, HU18 1PG, England

editor@pspublishing.co.uk www.pspublishing.co.uk

Contents

Editor's Note

The information included in the 'Introduction' is taken from correspondence between Basil Copper and Arkham House Publishers, Inc., as contained in a series of letters dating from July 22nd 1976 to February 29th 1980. No other letters pertaining to Basil's relationship with the publisher—either regarding Solar Pons or other projects—has been found amongst his personal files at this time.

'Plots of the Stories', 'Characters in the Novellas' and 'The Sayings of Solar Pons' were compiled by Basil Copper between 2000–2005 and were discovered in an envelope amongst his correspondence marked "Complete definitive typescript" dated July 1, 2005. They have been edited and slightly reformatted for their first appearance here, which also includes additional material not originally in the author's version of The Solar Pons Companion.

SJ.

JAMES TURNER, U.S.A.

WITH PARCEL OF TYPESCRIPT.

THE SECRET FILES OF SOLAR PONS.

COPY.

19/10/77.

Dear James.

Here, as promised, is the typescript of the third Solar Pons collection, THE SECRET FILES OF SOLAR PONS.

I hope you will like it; this note is very brief as I have already covered the contents etc., in another letter air-mailed to you today and which you will undoubtedly receive much earlier than this parcel, as I'm not exactly sure when I will be able to get it packed up and off to you.

I'd appreciate a line just as soon as it arrives safely.

All best wishes.

Sincerely.

Basil

Introduction: Once A Pons a Time

"An omnibus on the lines you suggested would be possibly the most satisfying single publishing event of my career."

—Basil Copper, May 1978

ALTHOUGH HE IS best remembered for his Lovecraftian novels and macabre short stories (the latter collected in the companion volumes *Darkness, Mist & Shadow,* also from PS Publishing), Basil Frederik Albert Copper was also a popular author of detective and mystery fiction.

Born in London in 1924, Basil served in the Royal Navy for four years during World War II before resuming a career in journalism. He made his debut as a fiction writer with 'The Spider' in *The Fifth Book of Pan Horror Stories* (1964) and, around the same time, he began writing his first novel while working in a newspaper office. Published in 1966, *The Dark Mirror* launched a series of hard-boiled thrillers in the Dashiell Hammett/Raymond Chandler mode, featuring Los Angeles private investigator Mike Faraday.

Basil had been reading horror novels and pulp magazines since he was a teenager, so he was very aware of American writer and editor August Derleth, who was also the co-founder and publisher of the influential small press imprint, Arkham House Publishers, Inc.

Having begun to establish a solid career as a professional writer, on impulse Basil decided to write to Derleth, asking if there was any possibility he would consider publishing some of Basil's macabre tales. "He replied in most cordial terms," recalled the author, "asking to see my work. Some of my tales had already seen publication in Pan Books and I was astonished to learn that he had already heard of me. His encouragement, long and enjoyable letters, and his patronage when he offered to publish my first American hardback under the imprint of his famous Arkham House, formed one of the warmest and most delightful strands of my writing life."

Although August Derleth was enthusiastic to introduce Basil's work to an American audience through his anthologies, it was only after Derleth's sudden death in 1971 at the age of sixty-two that Arkham House would publish the British author's first collection—*From Evil's Pillow* (1973).

"Unfortunate indeed that our correspondence was to last only five or six years," lamented Basil, "for his chats on paper, in which he was incredibly frank about his financial and other difficulties, were a constant example to me of honesty and courage in the face of great odds, which bolstered my own resolution in times of discouragement and financial difficulty."

Following Derleth's death and the brief return of original co-founder Donald Wandrei, James Allen Turner took over editorial operations at Arkham House in 1973, where he remained for more than twenty years.

While editor at Arkham, James Turner expanded the imprint's range of authors and helped put the company on a more established financial footing.

Turner would eventually publish a further three books by Basil—the collection *And Afterward, the Dark* (1977), and the novels *Necropolis* (1980) and *The House of the Wolf* (1983). However, before that happened, he made the British author an offer he couldn't refuse.

In the late 1920s, August Derleth had begun writing a series of stories about consulting detective Solar Pons (whose name in Latin literally means "Bridge of Light") after he received a letter from Sir Arthur Conan Doyle stating that there would be no further tales of Sherlock Holmes.

Derleth's Pons was closely modelled on Doyle's character—he lived at 7B Praed Street, not far from Paddington Station; his own Dr. Watson was Dr. Lyndon Parker, and Mrs. Johnson was their long-suffering landlady. Eight volumes of these Holmes pastiches were published between 1945 and 1973 under Arkham House's specifically created companion imprint Mycroft & Moran.

Unfortunately, Derleth had never visited Britain, and his research was necessarily limited. As a result, the Pons stories were riddled with factual and typographical errors and inaccuracies.

Basil himself had undertaken a similar process when writing his Los Angeles-set Mike Faraday books. Although critics admired the author's authentic descriptions of the City of Angels, Copper had in fact never been to California. All his knowledge was gleaned from watching old movies and referring to maps. In fact, the series was so popular that it eventually spawned fifty-two volumes over twenty-two years, often at the rate of two or more books a year, until it ended in 1988.

Basil Copper and James Turner embarked on a voluminous (sometimes daily!) trans-Atlantic correspondence, during which Basil pointed out the errors in Derleth's Pons stories. As a result of these gentle criticisms, Turner eventually commissioned him to revise and edit the entire Pontine canon for *The Solar Pons Omnibus*.

For Basil it was a real labour of love and, for almost eighteen months between other writing assignments, he corrected around 2,000 mistakes in the seventy short stories and one novel, also arranging them in their internal chronological order, rather than by the date they were published.

"It was undertaken as a tribute to August's memory and due to my affection for the man," he later recalled in a 1995 article, "and I did not wish any payment for the work, but Arkham eventually insisted that I accept a fee, which was entirely in keeping with their scrupulous business ethics.

"Those many thousands who now read the definitive texts will find it very hard indeed to detect even one fault of usage or terminology," Basil continued in the same article. "It was the least I could do in tribute to August in undertaking the work."

Unfortunately, the entire venture proved controversial from the beginning.

In 1966, the Praed Street Irregulars had been founded by bookseller Luther Norris as a Solar Pons fan club, along the same lines that the better-known Baker Street Irregulars were devoted to Sherlock Holmes. Basil himself was admitted into this group in 1976 under, as he described it, "the somewhat dubious title" of 'The Late Mr. Faversham'.

Many people in the PSI regarded what Basil was doing as

"tampering" with the original texts, in much the same way that these days scholars of H.P. Lovecraft, Robert E. Howard and Clark Ashton Smith insist on reinstating the original text—whether or not that was the authors' original intention—and thereby ignoring the often diligent editing of people like Derleth and others.

"Incidentally, there have already been rumbles on the Pons front, regarding our new corrected edition," Basil informed Turner in a letter dated July 28th, 1976. "I had a letter from Luther Norris this morning... On the reverse was a splenetic letter from one Jon L. Lellenberg ('Ebenezer [sic] Snawley') fulminating against the sacrilege done by me and Arkham on August's sacred text. He thinks it 'absolutely appalling' etc. 'An impertinent action that can scarcely be justified on any literary grounds... Incredible that they would do this!'. I must confess that such early reaction fills me with foreboding and horror."

"August himself was quite disarming about the errors," Basil pointed out to Turner in a letter dated October 8th. "He would have been the first to agree to corrections and, as you know, he employed people in England in earlier years to correct extensively (though they obviously failed to do so). If August himself was not too proud to take advice and let others revise, surely the enthusiasts should be grateful that all the howlers have been removed and that such a scholarly edition exists. I thought your Anglicisation of the text particularly valuable. As I pointed out earlier, Conan Doyle made mistakes, but not of locale, social usage, police procedure etc."

Turner firmly reminded Basil that "the Irregulars remain a factor which must be reckoned with—it is a strategic element in the entire Solar Pons phenomenon" and, more importantly, that their support "would be invaluable in launching your new series."

As part of his attempts to generate more money for the struggling Arkham House, James Turner had overseen a rights deal for all of August Derleth's Solar Pons books to be published in paperback by Andrew Ettinger's Pinnacle Books, who were based in New York City at the time.

These reprints had been quite successful but in 1976, after seven volumes, Pinnacle had exhausted all the original Derleth material and asked Turner if he could recommend someone to continue the series.

He naturally suggested Basil Copper.

Basil had always had a great love for Sherlockian mysteries and he was, of course, more than familiar with the entire Pontine canon thanks to his work on *The Solar Pons Omnibus*. Now facing some financial difficulties of his own as a freelance writer, Basil readily agreed to the deal which involved the author and Arkham House splitting all income derived from the books on an equal basis. Turner also intimated that, eventually, Basil's Pons stories would be collected together in permanent hardcover volumes under the Mycroft & Moran imprint.

"Eventually they will publish a massive, illustrated hardback edition of my new Canon, comprising some four to six volumes," Basil optimistically wrote to Luther Norris for the Irregulars' newsletter *The Pontine Dossier*. "This will be, of course, after the paperbacks have appeared."

Things began well, and in mid-1976 Basil plunged into writing his "pilot" Solar Pons story, 'The Adventure of the Perplexed Photographer', which he sent off to Arkham House as soon as it had been retyped by his secretary, Marion Pender.

James Turner, who was still making his own and Basil's corrections to *The Solar Pons Omnibus*, was impressed with this initial submission and responded in a letter dated July 22nd: "'Perplexed Photographer' is surely a capital effort (as Solar would say) and splendidly maintains the long Pontine tradition." He then went on to make several editorial points (including a discrepancy in the spelling of "Edgware Road") and raised the question of any proposed Arkham editions being able to keep up with the Pinnacle schedule, before concluding: "Such administrative details can always be resolved later—the significant point at the moment is that the perpetuation of the Pontine series has been triumphantly reasserted by the 'Perplexed Photographer', and I am certain that this alone commands for you the heartfelt gratitude of everyone at Arkham House and Pinnacle."

"Naturally, I was thrilled and delighted at your enthusiastic reception of 'The Perplexed Photographer'," Basil replied on July 31st. "I was naturally rather worried and anxious as to how you would receive it and I am so glad it has come up to expectations."

Arkham House's lawyer, Forrest D. Hartmann, submitted the story to Pinnacle in early August for approval, and Turner advised Basil that he should "finish the entire first volume and then send me the completed manuscript" while they waited for the paperback imprint to come up with contractual terms. "I frankly never doubted your ability to carry on the Pontine Tradition with vast aplomb and finesse," he added.

Meanwhile, Hartmann wrote to Basil to assure him that even if Pinnacle decided not to proceed with a paperback edition, Arkham House would still want to bring the collections out in hardcover. He was prepared to draw up a contract that would cover all the new stories, with a royalty of 10% on any Mycroft & Moran editions and an 80/20 split in the author's favour on the Pinnacle editions against an initial advance of $500.00.

The author thanked him, adding that: "it would be an enormous help at a somewhat difficult time." As usual, Basil was concerned about his cash-flow situation, having estimated that he had lost around £3,000 over the previous decade in money owed to him by various publishers.

He asked Hartmann if, instead of paying the proposed advances due upon publication, Arkham House could pay "on submission of an acceptable typescript", as he was concerned that the books might not be published by Mycroft & Moran for several years.

"This would mean that I would not see any financial return perhaps for three or four years and I am currently devoting a great deal of time and effort into producing the new Solar Pons stories and giving them the maximum craftsmanship, detail, atmosphere etc."

Upon completion of 'The Adventure of the Perplexed Photographer', Basil had immediately begun work on the remaining five stories in the book. As he revealed: "Some of the new Solar Pons stories are strong on horrific atmosphere, as I hinted, with spiders and sinister goings-on in ancient mansions... I am thoroughly enjoying this task, which doesn't seem like work at all; lots of winter atmosphere, old houses, fog, and creeping tarantulas and deadly snakes! Plus some in-jokes which I think will be appreciated; for example, 'Ipi Idol' is really Pons' own version of 'The Speckled Band', though the plot is much more complicated than Doyle's fairly short story; at the end, Pons makes a reference to his 'illustrious predecessor'."

The Dossier of Solar Pons was completed by the end of October. The manuscript ran for 266 typed pages and comprised the stories 'The Adventure of the Perplexed Photographer', 'The Sealed Spire Mystery', 'The Adventure of the Six Gold Doubloons', 'The Adventure of the Ipi Idol', 'The Adventure of Buffington Old Grange' and 'The Adventure of the Hammer of Hate'.

In a covering letter to Arkham House dated November 1st, Basil explained: "I have taken a good deal of trouble with them and they are well varied and well sprinkled with Gothic and macabre elements, though, as already notified, I have included one or two lighter moments."

He went on to describe it as "a pretty solid book", while also revealing some interesting insights into his working methods: "Not bad going when one considers I worked for an hour a day, four days a week for ten weeks on this particular project. I didn't rush it at all and, in fact, I usually find that one spoils things that need good craftsmanship if one spends more than an hour at a time on any one project. Which is why I usually work on three or four books at once, so that I can switch to something fresh."

Basil had earlier explained to Turner that "I am also, with your permission, doing what ACD [Derleth] did and not limiting the titles to 'The Adventure of' in each case; for example, Doyle has these standard titles interspersed with others such as 'The Disappearance of Lady Francis Carfax' and 'His Last Bow' etc. and I am hoping to do the same, as I think this breaks up the format a little and avoids monotony. I hope you agree."

He also went on to observe: "Incidentally, I am setting all this first volume firmly in the 1920s, as Pons would have been in his prime then i.e. in his early forties. I think August forgot this as some of the stories were obviously set in the 1950s, when Pons would have been in his late seventies!!!"

James Turner acknowledged receipt of the manuscript in a letter dated November 14th, in which he explained that he had not yet had time to look at it as he was finishing off an urgent proofing assignment. However, he did reveal (somewhat despairingly) that one of the editors at Pinnacle had complained that 'The Adventure of the Perplexed Photographer' was "rather long".

Two weeks later he had read the typescript, as he revealed in his letter of the 28th: "I had a grand time reading the *Dossier* several days ago. The fact that this series is now being written by an Englishman is distinct and unmistakable, and there is no point in pretending that it doesn't count heavily in these stories: the names, places, even the food served by Mrs. Johnson, all seem startlingly authentic."

Turner went on to praise the repartee between Pons and Parker, noting that "this dry, understated British humour is probably something that only a native could handle properly." He also had a few "piddling" editorial comments, which for the most part Basil was happy to go along with. However, there was one small sticking point over how Inspector Jamison would properly address Solar Pons.

"There is a serious objection to this," Basil responded in his letter of December 6th: "See my notes in editing the Solar Pons omnibus. It may seem strange to American ears but there is, and would have been, particularly in the 1920s, an enormous social gap between a man like Inspector Jamison and a distinguished person like Pons. In fact, Jamison would normally have called him "Sir", and not "Mr. Pons", let alone "Pons"!

Even in these days the police are enormously polite over here (even if corrupt!) and even a university-educated Police Inspector, for example, would normally call a person he was questioning "Sir", or "Mr.", even if the person addressed was of quite humble class. This is one thing about Derleth's work which stands out like a sore thumb to the British reader: the crude Jamison airily addressing his social betters as "Pons" or "Parker". However objectionable this may appear in the light of today's democratic society it is a fact of life over here and in the 1920s, when modes and manners were preserved as in aspic, jars considerably. I take it by your remarks that you have, in fact, removed the "Mr." from my suggested text for Derleth's Pons Canon, and I would ask you, in fact, to think about this in the light of what I have said, as it does seriously damage the veracity of the text in British eyes. It would jar as much as if Lestrade addressed the Great Detective as "Holmes". No doubt you have observed that all these police characters address the Master as "Mr. Holmes". And quite right too. Adrian Conan Doyle fell down badly when trying to follow his father and made the same mistake as August. But it won't do."

James Turner grudgingly acquiesced to Basil's demands, but jokingly added: "I'll go along with your position—so long as you answer the mail when the Irregulars start squawking!"

He had already used the new Pinnacle series to deflect continuing criticism from amongst the Irregulars towards *The Solar Pons Omnibus*. "I would prefer to have them pester me with anticipatory queries regarding the forthcoming *Dossier of Solar Pons*," he wrote.

The year ended with Basil already hard at work on a second volume, *The Further Adventures of Solar Pons*, but with still no sign of a contract for the first one from Pinnacle Books.

By the beginning of 1977, Basil was almost halfway through the second Solar Pons collection, despite having not received any contracts or payment for his efforts so far. In his first letter of the year to James Turner, he expected to have the third story, 'The Adventure of the Baffled Baron', finished by the end of the first week in January.

He had already explained to Turner that the first story in the book, 'The Adventure of the Shaft of Death', was set in Bath: "A magnificent Georgian city (which HPL would have love . . .) and which I've just visited for the first time. I've used the experience to advantage but this novella runs to sixty pages. It is right for the narrative, as I think you will agree, when you read it, but I can just imagine Pinnacle's comments. I hasten to add that other tales will be shorter and that there will be a basic content of six, at least. But I feel that at least forty-fifty pages is necessary to bring out the nuances of atmosphere, characterisation."

On January 19th, James Turner finally got the go-ahead from Forrest Hartmann to send a copy of *The Dossier of Solar Pons* to Pinnacle. Braving the snowstorm that was blanketing Illinois, he drove to his local library where he photocopied the manuscript, which he mailed to New York the following day.

A day later, Basil finally received two copies of the contract for *Dossier* from Arkham House, along with a cheque for $500.00. Also enclosed were two copies of a Memorandum of Agreement that allowed for further payments of the same amount for each subsequent book in the Solar Pons series.

"This has made a great difference to the current financial situation," Basil admitted to Hartmann in a letter written that same day. Two weeks later he revealed to Turner that outstanding payments from other publishers had "temporarily cleared all my financial problems". He also announced that he was already "sketching out" a third volume of Solar Pons stories.

Basil completed the second volume on April 1st and mailed the completed manuscript of *The Further Adventures of Solar Pons* to Arkham House three days later. The manuscript ran to some 286 pages and, in his covering letter, Basil mentioned that *The Adventures of Solar Pons* could be used as an alternate title for the collection, being under the impression that it had not been previously used by Derleth.

This second volume contained 'The Adventure of the Shaft of Death', 'The Adventure of the Frightened Governess', 'The Adventure of the Baffled Baron', 'Murder at the Zoo', 'The Adventure of the Surrey Sadist' and 'The Adventure of the Missing Student'.

Still without any news about the Pinnacle deal, Basil also started straight in on the next collection, *The Secret Files of Solar Pons*, with a story entitled 'The Adventure of the Haunted Library'.

In a letter dated April 8th, James Turner confirmed acceptance of *The Further Adventures of Solar Pons* but advised the author that he might want to "await some firm commitment from Pinnacle before proceeding to the *Secret Files*", adding that if the paperback deal fell through then it might take three or four years before Arkham House could bring out the first two books in hardcover editions.

However, Basil was not to be dissuaded. "It may be that if I stop production I may not be able to get back into stride again," he wrote back eleven days later, "so I am going great guns with Solar Pons and have planned the first six volumes, being already well into the third."

He reiterated the point in a letter dated May 2nd: "Please

don't worry about the Solar Pons books I am writing. It will take me years to write them all and I'm sure that things will have sorted themselves out long before that. But I don't think you need be afraid of having dozens of volumes stock-piled."

The following day Turner sent back a short list of editorial comments and suggestions (including changing the name of the chief villain in 'The Adventure of the Baffled Baron' from "Baron Ennesfred Kroll" to "the Doctor", in keeping with August Derleth's affectionate pastiche of Sax Rohmer's insidious Dr. Fu Manchu). This also necessitated a change in the title of the story.

"I read the *Further Adventures* over the weekend and thought it to be even more successful than its predecessor," wrote Turner, "while *Dossier* contains a couple of thinly-plotted episodes, the new manuscript maintains a uniform standard throughout, especially in terms of capturing the flavour of the Doylean originals."

Turner also told Basil that, unless a paperback deal was forthcoming, he would have to suspend work on the series after *Secret Files* as "it is just impossible for a small firm like Arkham House to stockpile manuscripts on the basis of projected commitments".

In a letter dated June 10th, Basil asked James Turner what he thought of this opening from a tale initially entitled 'The Adventure of the Agonised Actor', the first story in the third Pons volume:

> "You cannot mean it, Pons!"
>
> "I was never more serious in my life, Parker."
>
> Solar Pons looked at me with tightly compressed lips. We were sitting by ourselves in a first-class

> railway carriage passing through the rolling countryside beyond Dorking. It was a cold winter's day and frost sparkled in the tangled grass of the fields, yielding diamonds in the hard light of the pale, wintry sun.

The author admitted, "God knows what happens after that. Though no doubt it will come to me before publication day."

Basil went on to reveal: "I'm really enjoying the Solar Pons series and I think some of this enjoyment must come through in the writing; keeping up the Gothic and macabre atmosphere well, as I think the reader really enjoys this type of ambience in the period detective story."

Meanwhile, Turner had suggested that they might be able to sell first serial rights to some of the Pons stories to *Ellery Queen's Mystery Magazine* or *Alfred Hitchcock's Mystery Magazine*, which Basil had no objection to. Unfortunately, the directors of Arkham House did not agree, and they turned down his proposal.

By the summer of 1977 Basil was in financial difficulties again—with around £4,000 in royalties owed to him by various publishers around the world, he found himself £300 away from breaking his *new* overdraft limit at the bank.

However, as usual, things soon began to look up again. Basil finally received the contracts for *The Further Adventures of Solar Pons*, along with a cheque for $500.00, from Forrest D. Hartmann at the end of July. That payment, along with a couple of others from his UK publisher, helped see Basil through another difficult period.

He was also once again optimistic about the future, telling Hartmann: "If all goes well with Pinnacle, I plan at least six [volumes] and could go on as long as you require, from a long-term view, and I am sure Pinnacle would be able to sell them in large quantities".

Meanwhile, *The Solar Pons Omnibus* had been delayed due to concerns over the health of illustrator Frank Utpatel, who was in his seventies and suffering from severe emphysema, and also ongoing financial problems at Arkham House. Despite this, in August 1977 Basil was given a "Praed Penny Award" by Luther Norris' Praed Street Irregulars for his work editing the book (which was somewhat ironic, given the continued sniping against the project in *The Pontine Dossier*). Science fiction author A.E. Van Vogt accepted the prize on his behalf at the annual dinner in Los Angeles.

Unfortunately, as Basil confided in a letter to James Turner, when it arrived the following month, it was not quite what he had been expecting: "In my naïvete I had imagined that the impressive-sounding Praed Street Award, the 'Irregulars' highest honour' etc. was at least a bronze medal in a nice velvet-lined case. What I got was a cardboard certificate with my name spelled wrongly!!!"

Basil sent it back with a polite note asking if they could correct the mistake. He never had a reply from them or ever received his amended certificate.

The author finally completed work on the third collection, *The Secret Files of Solar Pons*, towards the end of September 1977. The longest manuscript so far, at around 300 pages, it included the stories 'The Adventure of the Haunted Rectory', 'The Adventure of the Crawling Horror', the retitled 'The Adventure of the Agonised Actor', 'The Adventure of the Singular Sandwich', 'The Adventure of the Ignored Idols' and 'The Adventure of the Horrified Heiress'. It was mailed to James Turner on October 19th.

"I do honestly believe that these books represent some of my best work," Basil explained, "and I'm sure you understand that I'm modelling them directly on the Holmes Canon, though at the moment I dare not read either Doyle or Derleth, lest I should copy plot details direct."

Meanwhile, after a delay of almost two years, things were finally moving ahead with the Pinnacle Books deal. Just not in the way that anyone had quite expected...

In a letter dated November 6th, 1977, James Turner told Basil that Forrest Hartmann had finally received a contract for *The Dossier of Solar Pons* from Pinnacle Books, who had recently relocated from New York City to Los Angeles, California. However, because new clauses differed so markedly from the earlier agreements for the August Derleth material, Hartmann had swiftly rejected the contract and given the publisher—who had a reputation as being a poor payer—an ultimatum to either stick to the previously-agreed terms or else Arkham House would offer the new series elsewhere.

By the beginning of the following month, Pinnacle had revised its initial agreement to a paperback-only deal. Now the copyrights to the stories would, as they should, remain in Basil's name and not Pinnacle's, and the publisher would not control any film rights.

In a letter dated December 1st, Turner gushed: "*Secret Files* is a positively smashing collection, easily the equal—if not superior—to *Further Adventures*, with not a weakish story in the entire manuscript". He singled out 'The Adventure of the Crawling Horror' for special praise, "possibly because of the supernatural adumbrations, but also because 'Silas Grimstone' is one of the best-delineated secondary characters in any of the ninety-odd Pons adventures written thus far"; he went on to compare the story to "a head-on collision between Conan Doyle and Charles Dickens".

"I do, as you know, put a great deal into them," Basil replied eight days later, "and I feel myself that 'The Crawling Horror' is one of my best; atmosphere or *stimmung*, as the Germans call it, means almost everything to me as a macabre writer and it is useless trying to thrill the reader without it."

Turner had also included a handful of editorial notes in the earlier letter, and it is obvious from their correspondence that author and editor worked well together:

"Let me firstly just go into the matters of style etc. you raised on the last Solar Pons volume," wrote Basil. He then went on to point out that in the UK "it is perfectly correct to speak of 'the Rev. Brown' or 'the Rev. Smith' etc. though of course we do not use the term without the prefix 'the'. I have no objection at all if you wish to speak of 'the Rev. Mr. Smith', though I feel myself that as they are both titles, the duplication is superfluous . . . if it makes you uneasy please amend the text."

In the same letter, Basil went on to explain his use of the term 'heterogeneous'—"it merely means diverse in character; in the context didecais [sic] are different from tramps"—while also readily accepting a number of other changes that Turner had suggested. He admitted that he had described the character of Inspector Jamison more like Conan Doyle's Inspector Lestrade than Derleth's original—"I fully agree with your comments, of course, and it is essential to reconcile the description with August's".

It is obvious from their numerous exchanges that their "literary partnership"—as Basil referred to it—was a success, and that they shared an equal respect for each other's talents: "I am more pleased than I can properly convey at your appreciation of this series," Basil wrote; "I am more concerned at satisfying you and Forrest as well as the Derleth family, which is why I am trying to make the new series of as high a quality as possible. Unlike August, I am not harried out of my life and having to write every hour of the day and night in order to keep vast commitments—such as Arkham House—going, and thus can give these tales the detail, depth and atmosphere that they cry out for. Your approbation means a great deal to me and I am extremely happy that we are so perfectly in accord on all these literary matters, both in the Pons series and in the macabre field. I think we both are concerned only at the *quality* of the finished product which is as it should be, but so rarely obtains in the rat-race of ordinary commercial publishing."

Perhaps the most surprising thing about the letter was that Basil also revealed that he was working on a *fourth* Solar Pons collection: "Perhaps I ought to explain at the outset that I'm already on volume four; I had decided to write six volumes, principally because I fear that if I get out of the mood, I may never be able to get quite back into it again. However, I intended to say nothing and was merely going to stockpile the material at this end as I did not wish to embarrass Arkham in the matter of advances etc. through the mere fact of my being so prolific."

James Turner had also suggested that it might be better to let Pinnacle publish *The Further Adventures of Solar Pons* as the first book, as Basil had "become ever more adept at writing these pastiches as you have gained experience".

Basil was having none of it: "I would be grateful, however, if you could see your way clear to letting Pinnacle publish the volumes in the order in which they were written; i.e. by commencing with the *Dossier*. I make the suggestion because I feel that the *Dossier* is of good quality for a debut and it would surely be wrong to commence on a high note and then to let people feel that there was a drop in quality—however slight—for the later instalments of the series. Of course, they are all as good as I can make them, and the variation to which you draw my attention is undetectable to me, but then I am probably much too close to the material.

"I feel it is much better to start with a good quality volume and then to top them as the series continues, so that the reader is (we hope) more pleased as he goes on with them, rather than feeling that they are tailing off."

As it turned out, such discussion would be a moot point anyway.

The year 1978 began with the death of Luther Norris, founder of the Praed Street Irregulars, at the age of seventy-five, and more uncertainty about the deal with Pinnacle.

Just as the contract for the new Pons series had almost reached the signing stage, the editor on the project, Roger Elwood, left the company and was replaced by science fiction author Robert Silverberg.

Basil had known Elwood from when the latter had published the author's story 'Cry Wolf' in his 1974 anthology *Vampires, Werewolves and Other Monsters*. He was also aware of who Silverberg was, and wondered "what the function of an editor on such a series would be".

By the end of January, Forrest D. Hartmann had finally grown tired of Pinnacle's endless delays and wrote to Andrew Ettinger requesting a reversion of rights on August Derleth's original Solar Pons stories so that Arkham House could offer the entire series to a different publisher.

Pinnacle's response was to immediately request to see copies of Basil's *The Further Adventures of Solar Pons* and *The Secret Files of Solar Pons*.

In early April Ettinger was insisting that royalties should be paid only on copies sold rather than the entire print-run, a not unreasonable request that Arkham House reluctantly agreed to. However, by the end of the month Hartmann's ploy had paid off, and on April 24th he wrote to Basil informing him that contracts had finally been signed with Pinnacle for *The Dossier of Solar Pons* and enclosing a cheque for $675.00, representing a half-share of the first advance, with an equal amount to be paid when the book was published in December.

By now, Basil was worrying about not seeing proofs of his Pons series: "Do you think the texts will be accurate?" he asked James Turner in May 1978. "What will they be printing about me (if anything) on the jacket?... I hope they won't put August's name in gigantic letters on the cover and my name inside in microscopic type, as though it were a ghosted sort of thing."

In another letter, Basil hoped that the paperback publisher would not "tamper with the stories in any way", and he reiterated to Forrest Hartman that Turner would be "keeping a highly expert eye on textual matters etc. when the time comes".

Unfortunately, he would be in for a shock.

As Turner had warned him in May: "I wish it were true that Arkham House would be in a position to review the proofing on this series, but for some reason paperback firms (at least in America) never make galleys available to authors, even for paperback originals."

He also reminded Basil that Pinnacle only held photocopies of the original stories and that the original typescripts remained at his home in Collinsville, Illinois, "piled on my dresser".

That same month the author also received the belated Arkham House contracts for *The Secret Files of Solar Pons*, along with the usual cheque for $500.00 from a suitably contrite Forrest Hartmann.

Basil continued to keep James Turner up-to-date with his progress through his prolific letter-writing. Back in January he had mentioned that he was working on a new Pons tale called 'The Adventure of the Phantom Face' and joked: "This one is especially for Dr. Lyndon Turner as you liked the 'Crawling Horror' so much . . ." In another letter, dated March 10th, he continued: "'The Phantom Face' turned out to be one of the best, I think; came out at novella length, about seventy-three pages, and I was extremely pleased with it."

He also added that he was writing another new Pons story "tentatively entitled 'The Lead Egg' but which will undoubtedly be changed to something more alliterative before long".

At the end of May he explained that he was "about halfway through the third story in Vol. 4 which promises to be a good one; shades of Chesterton's Father Brown in some ways, though only in an echo of the plot. Poor old Jamison is really up the creek this time, arresting the wrong man and having to climb down!"

He continued: "I've already, this morning, worked out a lost love for Pons. I've given her the name of Lady Georgina Peel. How does that grab you? She would be rather like Diana Rigg in *The Avengers*."

By early August he revealed that he was "well on with the fourth tale in the fourth volume, which promises to be a cracking good one, set in the Scottish Highlands in the depths of winter, with a murderous rifle duel for the finale, between Pons and Colonel Alistair McDonald, 'the third most dangerous man in Europe' and author of *The Dimensions of Ecstasy* (1923). I think you'll like this one."

In October, having apparently forgotten their earlier discussion, Basil was asking Turner if he wanted the typescript when it was completed for the fourth Arkham House volume "in order to keep the flow to Pinnacle going". He also mentioned that he was working on 'The Adventure of the Cursed Curator', "all about horrific happenings in an Egyptian Museum", and was also "Thinking about doing a final story for this collection set against a railway background, which could be fun".

By early December he had almost completed the book: "It's a good collection and one of which I am proud," he wrote.

In the meantime, Pinnacle Books had been undergoing something of a corporate reorganisation: Robert Silverberg had been let go and his proposed SF list cancelled, and the company was now concentrating on "series" novels. They had already enquired about the fourth Pons volume when, in November, they requested permission to split *The Further Adventures of Solar Pons* and *The Secret Files of Solar Pons* (which they still had not yet contracted for) into three smaller volumes by extracting two stories from each volume and creating an additional fourth, as-yet-untitled, collection. They were also now proposing $2,000 for each of the new volumes.

Even though this would play havoc with Basil's carefully-constructed series, James Turner pointed out that "three shorter volumes will reap greater royalties than two books" and recommended that they accept the proposal.

Basil was clearly not happy with Pinnacle. "The brutal truth is that over the past two to three years (I am now taking in the time since I started work on the project) they have paid Arkham only $675 and they have paid me only the same amount," he wrote to Turner on December 12th. "This is simply not good enough and I feel we must start getting commercial and hard-nosed like these people."

However, he was surprisingly willing to go along with the new publishing plan: "Strangely enough, I was thinking on these lines myself recently as the Pons *oeuvre* has been growing and expanding and each tale is now novella length," he continued in the same letter. "The proposal, as put, would probably mean nine or ten paperbacks in toto, which would involve me in little more work than the proposed six volumes of six stories each." He concluded, "This is entirely satisfactory to me... The reader will still be getting excellent value with the four long novellas in each volume."

The new year began on a more positive note than the previous one. Forrest Hartmann wrote to Basil on January 8th, 1979 with two pieces of good news—the contracts for the next three Pinnacle paperbacks had been signed and returned, and *The Dossier of Solar Pons* had been published. He also enclosed a cheque for $1,350.00, representing the author's share of the initial advance on the three new Pons volumes, which once again saved Basil from financial crisis.

It seemed as if things were finally looking up.

The "extra" Pinnacle collection would now be titled *Some Uncollected Cases of Solar Pons*, and that would be followed by *The Exploits of Solar Pons*.

Basil wrote to James Turner again on January 9th to let him know that he had almost completed the (new) sixth volume, *The Recollections of Solar Pons*, which was now creeping up towards 400 pages. "I'm so well into the mannerisms and atmosphere now that I just let the stories take me on," he explained, "the plots are well-structured, I believe, but I let the atmosphere and descriptive passages run on, as I believe that will pay and they do, for me at least, make the stories live. I simply can't believe in the non-Sherlock Holmes type of deductive stuff (*à la* Agatha Christie) which is almost all dialogue and no descriptive atmosphere at all."

Things were also becoming somewhat complicated keeping track between the Pinnacle editions featuring four stories and the proposed Arkham House volumes containing six: "Incidentally, I'm sending on to you the complete new volume of Pons, containing six stories," continued Basil. "That way a proper Arkham contract can be drawn up and you can then split up the volume in the manner planned, in order that the next four-story collection can be sold to Pinnacle. Then, I will send you another two long stories in due course, which will make the sixth Pinnacle collection, but another Arkham contract will not mature, of course, until you receive a further four stories from me to make up an original (Arkham) volume. Providing we keep our records straight and don't get our stories (and various titles!) muddled up, all should be well."

Even before the first volume had been published, the marketing department at Pinnacle had contacted Hollywood producer Herbert J. Wright, who had turned Basil's story 'Camera Obscura' into an episode of *Night Gallery* in 1971. Wright, who went on to co-produce *Star Trek: The Next Generation* (1987-94), had written to Basil in August 1978, suggesting that they might try to "get something going" at Warner Bros. with the character. Wright had also been talking up a film version of Basil's novel *The Great White Space* and several other projects, none of which ever came to fruition.

As Basil candidly confided to James Turner in a letter written in April 1978: "I just laugh; it's silly really, for a writer to expect anything of film deals or Hollywood prospects. Mine came out of the blue and it was great to get something I never expected; I am content with that but don't expect anything else. If it comes it's a bonus."

Pinnacle Books finally published *The Dossier of Solar Pons* in January 1979. To establish it as part of a continuing series, they retained the logo design from the August Derleth editions and renowned cover artist Ben Stahl. The volume was also numbered #8 and, contrary to Basil's fears, his name was displayed slightly bigger than Derleth's. Also, as agreed, it contained all six stories in the order that the author had originally intended, although it was the only time that this would happen.

However, there was a bigger problem brewing. As far back as October 1976, James Turner had reassured Basil not to worry about Pinnacle tampering with his texts ("this company did not even have the sense to correct the typos appearing in the Mycroft editions!"), yet when Basil received two advance copies of the book on January 15th, he discovered that his worst fears had been realised.

While he acknowledged that it was "very nicely produced" and that "the cover drawing was nice", he also pointed out in a letter written to Turner that same day: "I noticed when I opened them, that what you had warned me about had come to pass. Some clown in their editorial department has been subtly at work.

"Firstly, the 'Explanation' had been put in front of the book, slightly altered and in quotes, as though it were part of the blurb. All my carefully engineered English text had been changed to American usage. Well, that's fair enough, I suppose, though it does jar and detract from the English atmosphere, just as would English usage in a Raymond Chandler novel.

"However, some idiot has been quietly at work 'improving' my material. The first page I turned to spoke of 'lawyer Chadburn Bradshaw'. It seemed reminiscent of Russian practice: 'tractor-driver Vokshov and artist Koslowsky spoke against'. My text read, of course, '*the* lawyer Chadburn Bradshaw'. I groaned in horror at the second random page I opened. The passage read, 'he was out at dawn as I was scrubbing the stove'. This is Mrs. Johnson speaking and the piece would draw howls of mirth from English readers.

"As you know stoves over here are and were made of cast iron, and 'scrubbing' such a piece of equipment would find them eaten up with rust in a few weeks. My original text read 'black-leading the stove' and is the correct procedure, which preserves them from rust and brings them up in a dull glow, like pewter. This converts what I am trying to do into a nonsense.

"I would be grateful if someone could convey to Pinnacle that the efforts of this editorial clown are not appreciated by me and that his 'improvements' to my text merely make the author look like a fool. In view of their glowing eulogy of my work on the back cover it seems odd, to say the least, that they should attempt to demolish it editorially within the covers."

There had been better news the previous week when Forrest Hartmann sent Basil a cheque (via his agent, Kirby McCauley) for *Necropolis* before contracts had even been completed. The author revealed in a letter to Hartmann that it "has knocked a huge chunk out of my overdraft and will, I'm sure, put me on an even keel for 1979". However, Basil also noted that he was still owed $675.00 as his share on publication of *The Dossier of Solar Pons*.

Basil also reiterated to Hartmann his disappointment at the changes to his text: "Unfortunately, someone at Pinnacle has done his best to devalue the new series by drastic updating of the text...it's a pity, really, as it's destroying the atmosphere I've laboured so long to carefully build up. But I'm sanguine about it as I have the hardback texts from Arkham with their definitive texts to look forward to eventually."

Unfortunately, Basil would eventually be disappointed on that front as well.

None of the subsequent Pons volumes had been published by Pinnacle by early May 1979, when James Turner wrote to Basil to tell him that *Further Adventures* was not on the publisher's summer schedule. "If only they would advertise Pons widely and aggressively promote the new series, the whole Pontine phenomenon would begin to gain momentum," he grumbled.

Turner went on to speculate that because Pinnacle didn't hold "sufficient rights" in the material they were not prepared to promote it as well as they should, and he also again raised the prospect of trying to place some of the unpublished stories with the digest mystery magazines in the hope that such action would prompt Pinnacle to release the books at more frequent intervals.

To this end, towards the end of July he mailed a copy of 'The Adventure of the Cursed Curator' to Davis Publications, publisher of *Ellery Queen's Mystery Magazine.*

Meanwhile, Basil was still awaiting his ten author copies of *Dossier*, which had been published four months earlier. In fact, it transpired that the books had been sent to Arkham House's Los Angeles agent for the Pons material, Florence Feiler, and her involvement in the Pinnacle deal also explained Basil's missing funds.

In early June Turner discovered—completely by chance, while visiting his local bookstore—that *Further Adventures* was scheduled for release in August. Pinnacle had simply not informed anybody. The publisher also finally requested the typescript for *Exploits*.

Following completion of 'The Adventure of the Mad Millionaire' in the summer of 1979 (it "turned out quite nicely" the author told Turner), Basil was "back in the macabre, fog-bound vein" as he started work on 'The Adventure of the Devil's Claw' in August.

That same month Basil received a batch of advance Pons material from Pinnacle Books forwarded on by Arkham House: "So far as the new Solar Pons volumes are concerned," he wrote to Turner on the 28th, "the jackets, which are bright and inventive, are the best things about them.

"As always, I screamed when I turned to the text. The first tale I opened was 'The Adventure of the Missing Student' and I screamed when I saw that my careful English prose circa 1926 had been mangled by the insertion of such Americanised anachronisms as "the gas-tank" and "the convertible". I am determined this time to look no further and will reserve my uncontrollable joy until the Arkham texts appear. But those jackets are really good."

However, while commenting on one of the cover proofs he had received from Pinnacle, the author noted that they had "altered the title of *Some Uncollected Cases* to *The*," but he went on to admit that he "particularly liked the gorilla".

In his lengthy reply of September 3rd, Turner revealed that #9 *The Further Adventures of Solar Pons* had indeed been published in mid-August, as promised, and that #10 *The Secret Files of Solar Pons* was scheduled for October.

The new collection contained 'The Adventure of the Shaft of Death', 'The Adventure of the Defeated Doctor', 'The Adventure of the Surrey Sadist' and 'The Adventure of the Missing Student'.

As previously noted, 'The Adventure of the Defeated Doctor' had originally been entitled 'The Case of the Baffled Baron', but was changed after James Turner had suggested a small, but crucial, modification to the ending.

"So far as *Further Adventures* is concerned," Turner wrote, "I retrieved the original ms. and began to compare typescript with printed text . . . I reached a point at which you had written 'interrogatively', which Pinnacle had duly amended to 'questioningly", and I was afraid to read any further. The cover painting, at least, is a nice one, better than *Dossier*.

He was also of the opinion that as Pinnacle had even bothered to send them some pre-publication material it showed that the company was finally taking Solar Pons seriously as a financial concern. Turner also added that editor Eleanor Sullivan at *Ellery Queen's Mystery Magazine* had turned down 'The Adventure of the Cursed Curator' because it was nearly twice as long as the stories the publication usually featured.

Basil finally received his share of the additional advance due on publication of *The Further Adventures of Solar Pons* in early October from Forrest Hartmann but, with Pinnacle still owing money on the remaining books already in their possession, he was forced to temporarily suspend work on the Pons series so that he could knock out a new 60,000-word Mike Faraday novel in just ten days to earn some quick cash.

A week later Turner mailed the author his copies of *The Secret Files of Solar Pons*. The volume contained 'The Adventure of the Crawling Horror', 'The Adventure of the Anguished Actor', 'The Adventure of the Ignored Idols' and 'The Adventure of the Horrified Heiress'.

In an earlier letter to Arkham House, Basil had revealed that 'The Adventure of the Anguished Actor' had originally been entitled 'The Adventure of the Agonised Actor', which he had forgotten to change on the Contents page and copyright information of the book manuscript.

"I think you will be pleased with Pinnacle's apparent new attitude to your texts," Turner wrote optimistically, "they still observe US spellings, but in all other matters are scrupulously honest."

Unfortunately, Basil did not agree: "The cover is the best thing about it," he wrote on October 22nd. "Despite both our pious hopes, as expressed in your and Forrest's letters, this diabolical firm has done it again and from the most brief and cursory examination of the text, I would say this is about the worst example of their flagrant disregard of our wishes in the matter, that I have so far come across. It gives me such acute pain to look at these productions that I daren't delve any more deeply than my first rifflings.

"I opened the book with high hopes but the most cursory examination revealed such illiterate ineptitude on the part of the oaf who is butchering our texts, that I found myself unable to go on. The first page I opened substituted 'railroad' for 'railway'. The next said 'flashlight' for 'torch'. I was struck dumb by the third example in which Hardcastle the actor is descending the steps of his mansion, 'a pack of Irish wolfhounds at his heels'.

"I ask you! I had written 'brace' which, as you well know, means two. A pack would be at least two dozen couples, which means something in the order of fifty hounds! The asinine insanity is compounded by the unknown blurb writer responsible for the jacket material. Not only has he now omitted all references to the author on the jacket, he now writes with authority on the 'charming, chilling *fin de siècle* London'. As you know the book is set firmly in 1922-28!"

To be fair to Pinnacle, the latter quote actually only appeared on the promotional material and not on the actual book itself, but no doubt Basil was blinded by his anger and disappointment at this stage.

"I really daren't trust myself to speak of the sloppy, inept, vulgar and ignorant treatment which has been given to my work throughout by Pinnacle," he continued, "who seem determined to cheapen and distort everything that I've striven so hard to do . . . I really must stop before I choke and foam at the mouth, but I simply daren't look any further in case of even worse horrors."

He concluded, "Would they treat Conan Doyle's texts like this? Probably they would. He's dead and even more impervious to such atrocities!!!"

The following day, Basil also confided in a letter to Richard Fawcett, editor of the *August Derleth Society Newsletter*: "Glad you like the Solar Pons series; between ourselves, they are being ruined by fatuous and anonymous editorial revisions but I look forward to the definitive texts from Arkham."

James Turner wrote again on November 9th and admitted that it had been "devastating" to receive Basil's report on *The Secret Files of Solar Pons*. He admitted that he had only been able to make a "most cursory" comparison between the published text and the original manuscript before leaving for the World Fantasy Convention in Providence, Rhode Island, and concluded that "the editors at Pinnacle simply cannot desist from tampering with your work, to the point at which the paperback versions resemble a 'Solar Pons for Junior Readers' series".

December arrived on a more positive note as Forrest Hartmann finally sent Basil a cheque for $450.00, being his share of the additional advance from Pinnacle due on publication of *The Secret Files of Solar Pons*. The author was once again in dire financial straits—writing four Mike Faraday novels in just eight weeks—so at this point anything helped.

Hartmann mentioned in his covering letter that there had been "a rather significant management change" at Pinnacle, which he thought might be for the better as they were apparently expanding their publishing programme. He also added that *Some* [sic] *Uncollected Cases of Solar Pons* would soon be published and that there would, again, be an additional payment due upon publication.

In the meantime, Hartmann forwarded Pinnacle's belated royalty statement for the first volume, *The Dossier of Solar Pons*, for sales through to June 30th, 1979. This revealed that the book had gross sales of 39,251 copies, with 14,036 returns. At an 8% royalty against the advance of $3,000.00, the book had earned $933.54 in royalties. However, with the publisher holding a $1,000.00 reserve against further returns, the statement showed an unearned balance of $66.46.

Hartmann acknowledged that it was "very difficult to draw any conclusions from this statement because one can reasonably expect book returns in the future". However, he did declare himself to be "pleased with the preliminary results" before going on to recommend that Basil shouldn't be in too much of a hurry to complete the stories he was working on as "the economic rewards from Solar Pons may be very slim during the next six to twelve months".

James Turner's final missive of the year confirmed that the fourth Pons volume was scheduled to be published in January and, like Hartmann, he cautioned Basil to complete the sixth volume when his schedule reasonably permitted, but to then await further developments before proceeding with any more.

As things turned out, it was prescient advice from both men at Arkham House.

At the beginning of 1980 Basil was elected Vice-Chairman of the Crime Writers Association of Great Britain, taking over the Chairmanship for the 1981-82 period. He revealed this news to Forrest D. Hartmann in a letter dated January 11th, having already explained that he had come to the same conclusion regarding the continuation of the Solar Pons series.

"The Pons series will have to be left in abeyance until we find our way through the wood," he wrote, "and commence publication of Pons through other hardback and paperback firms, which will make us independent of Pinnacle's whims."

He went on to add: "Of course, Pons remains amongst my most important work, together with my macabre output, and I do put a great deal into the series, so far as time, effort, craftsmanship and the delineation of atmosphere is concerned. I am sure that this will pay off in due course."

Pinnacle did, indeed, publish #11 *The Uncollected Cases of Solar Pons* in January, but it was the last Solar Pons book that the company would do. The volume contained 'The Adventure of the Haunted Rectory', 'The Adventure of the Singular

Sandwich', 'Murder at the Zoo' and 'The Adventure of the Frightened Governess'.

The opening story had originally been called 'The Adventure of the Haunted Library', but Basil changed it when he realised that title had already been used by August Derleth.

Sales were not as high as expected, possibly because the company—as James Turner had so succinctly put it—"apparently has done nothing on behalf of this series save send their typo-ridden editions out into the world to fend for themselves".

Pinnacle limped on for another five years before declaring bankruptcy and being dissolved. The imprint was revived in 1988 when its assets were purchased by the Windsor Publishing Corporation, which in turn was merged with the Kensington Publishing Corporation seven years later.

Suffice to say that neither Arkham House nor Basil Copper made very much money off the new Solar Pons series, despite their initial high hopes.

After numerous delays—mostly caused by financial concerns—*The Solar Pons Omnibus* was eventually published in 1982, when it appeared from Arkham House/Mycroft & Moran as a 1,300-page, two-volume slipcased set, with an Introduction by Robert Bloch and illustrations by Frank Utpatel (who had passed away in 1980). Limited to 3,031 copies and priced at a hefty $39.95, August Derleth's carefully corrected stories were arranged by their internal chronology.

Unfortunately, the Pons aficionados—who had been hostile to the project from the very beginning—vociferously denounced the volume, and all Basil's meticulous work was undone in 2000 when *The Original Text Solar Pons Omnibus*, edited by Peter Ruber and Jean-Pierre Cagnet, was published in two volumes by the revived Mycroft & Moran imprint being used by Canadian publisher George A. Vanderburgh. The text reinstated all of Derleth's numerous mistakes and re-ordered the stories into their initial date of publication.

Even more regrettably, James Turner's plans for Arkham House to publish Basil's Solar Pons stories in "a series of uniform editions, possibly the same or slightly longer than [Lovecraft's] *Selected Letters* volumes, and each with a number on the spine or some other such signification of an ongoing set of releases" eventually came to nothing, as did any hint of a Hollywood film.

Turner continued to oversee editorial operations at Arkham House until 1996, when he left the company over creative differences with co-owner April Derleth. He immediately set up his own World Fantasy Award-winning imprint, Golden Gryphon Press, and went on to publish the same kind of books he had done at Arkham until his premature death just three years later.

Meanwhile, as the copyrights in his own Solar Pons stories remained with the author, Basil Copper continued to attempt to get the original versions of his work into print.

He initially thought that he had found the answer in Academy Chicago Publishers who, in 1987, not only reprinted his first volume *The Dossier of Solar Pons* in a supposedly definitive paperback edition but, that same year, also issued *The Further Adventures of Solar Pons* containing four corrected novellas from two of the earlier Pinnacle volumes. Unfortunately, the author's bad luck continued when new errors were introduced into the text and any promised royalties failed to materialise.

All was not lost, however, and in 1993 Minneapolis small press publisher Fedogan & Bremer issued *The Exploits of Solar Pons* in a handsome hardcover edition illustrated by

Chicago artist Stefanie Kate Hawks. The book contained four previously unpublished novellas, which had originally been written back in the late 1970s for Arkham House: 'The Adventure of the Verger's Thumb', 'The Adventure of the Phantom Face', 'Death at the Metropole' and 'The Adventure of the Callous Colonel'.

Not only did the publisher also issue the volume in a 100-copy signed edition in slipcase, but it also arranged for the author to make his first trip to America for the 1993 World Fantasy Convention held in Minneapolis, where it launched the collection appropriately on Halloween with a party held at Sherlock's Home, a restaurant, pub and brewery in Minnetonka, Minnesota.

Two years later, Fedogan & Bremer published *The Recollections of Solar Pons*, again illustrated by Stefanie K. Hawks. This new hardcover volume contained three previously-unpublished stories from the 1970s, 'The Adventure of the Mad Millionaire', 'The Adventure of the Cursed Curator' and 'The Adventure of the Hound of Hell', while 'The Adventure of the Singular Sandwich'—which the publisher also issued as a special promotional chapbook—appeared for the first time in its definitive text.

Basil's final Solar Pons story, 'The Adventure of the Devil's Claw', eventually saw print in 2004 from the Welsh publisher Sarob Press under the title *Solar Pons Versus the Devil's Claw*, with an Introduction by Sherlock Holmes expert Richard Lancelyn Green. "Basil Copper is the equal of August Derleth," he wrote, "and both are worthy heirs of Sir Arthur Conan Doyle."

The story had never been completed with the cancellation of the Pinnacle Books deal, but Basil was able to piece it together from his original story notes and even expand it to short novel length. It was published as a stand-alone hardcover and a deluxe limited edition of fifty copies signed by the author and dust-jacket artist Les Edwards.

The following year Sarob Press released *Solar Pons: The Final Cases*. It contained corrected versions of four previously published stories, with the name of the eponymous client from 'The Adventure of the Anguished Actor' inexplicably changed from 'Elijah Hardcastle' to 'Cedric Carstairs' by the author. Also included was the first appearance of Basil's original draft of 'The Adventure of the Baffled Baron', which reinstated his intended ending, identifying a different character as being the villain. As a bonus, the volume also collected Basil's Sherlock Holmes pastiche, 'The Adventure of the Persecuted Painter', which itself quite possibly began life as an idea for an intended Solar Pons story.

With that volume, after a quarter of a century of uncertainty and continued disappointments, all of Basil Copper's Solar Pons stories had finally been published by various imprints, although the author continued to disown some editions after unauthorised re-writing by in-house editors.

Basil never had the pleasure of seeing all his Pons stories collected in a definitive omnibus edition. However, before his death in April 2013 at the age of 89, he and I started working on these two volumes. I also wanted to collect all his macabre fiction together and, with the help of PS Publishing, we did just that in 2010. Two years later we collaborated again to publish Basil's Gothic novel *The Curse of the Fleers* in a version that the author originally intended.

Although it saddens me that he never lived to see this handsome presentation of his entire Solar Pons Canon from the same imprint, I'm also heartened to know he was aware that we were working on it.

It has taken forty years but here, finally, are *The Complete Adventures of Solar Pons* by Basil Copper. Once again prepare to be plunged into an idyllic English countryside or the chill and foggy streets of London, as that great city's second most famous consulting detective—ably supported by the reliable Dr. Lyndon Parker—uses his "ratiocinative" powers of logical deduction to solve murders both mysterious and macabre...

—Stephen Jones
London, England
April, 2016

Foreword

IT SHOULD BE noted that the entire canon of my own Solar Pons stories following the series written by the late August Derleth was commissioned and authorised by Arkham House USA back in the mid-1970s but, for various reasons, were withheld from publication and are only now appearing in their original form after many years in limbo. Over the decades a number of editions with altered and mutilated texts have appeared. The definitive texts of the remainder of my canon can be found in the following:

The Further Adventures of Solar Pons (Academy Chicago, USA, 1987 pbk)

The Dossier of Solar Pons (Academy Chicago, USA, 1987 pbk)

The Exploits of Solar Pons (Fedogan and Bremer, USA, 1993 hbk)

The Recollections of Solar Pons (Fedogan and Bremer, USA, 1995 hbk)

Solar Pons Versus the Devil's Claw (Sarob Press, Wales, 2004 hbk)

Solar Pons: The Final Cases (Sarob Press, Wales, 2005 hbk)

—Basil Copper, 2005

The Solar Pons Companion

For my Beloved Parents
ETHEL MAUD COPPER and
EDGAR GERALD COPPER,
both of whom, sadly, died before
they could see any of my books in print.

—Basil Copper

In The Footsteps of Sherlock Holmes

This article was discovered as a rough draft amongst Basil Copper's papers. There is no indication as to where it was intended to appear, but author annotations and internal evidence suggest that it was written October 27th–28th, 1998 for publication in the UK the following year. So far as I am aware it was never revised or polished, and I have only lightly edited it for publication here. SJ.

IT WAS IN the early 1920s when a young student at the University of Wisconsin, who was interested in becoming an author, wrote to the great Sir Arthur Conan Doyle in England and asked if he intended to write any more Sherlock Holmes stories. Sir Arthur replied that he did not. The young man then wrote back to ask if the famous writer would mind if he himself wrote some more Holmes tales. The answer was in an emphatic negative.

Unfazed, the young man sat down to write his own Sherlockian pastiches. He called his detective hero Solar Pons—he once explained the derivation of the name to me as "Bridge of

Light"—and his Watson counterpart Dr. Lyndon Parker, tenants of rooms in 7B Praed Street, London, where they are looked after by their motherly landlady, Mrs. Johnson, the counterpart of Holmes' Mrs. Hudson.

The student was August Derleth, a name that was to become celebrated in his own country, but little-known in Europe and the other English-speaking nations of the world. He eventually got some of his Solar Pons stories published in the USA in 1929 and was later active in an amazing diversity of roles. For he was a polymath, a giant in stature, in energy and in the esoteric world he had chosen to make his own.

A man of enormous appetite for life, for the good things like food, and for his literary labours. He took on a workload that endured decade after decade, and that would have crippled any ordinary human being and which, tragically, finally ended his life at the age of 62, after heart complications.

August was a poet, an essayist, co-founder of the world's most celebrated macabre and fantasy publishers, Arkham House, and its associated imprint Mycroft & Moran; a Hollywood scriptwriter, newspaper columnist, author of several hundred books, some of them published by such distinguished New York houses as Scribners, but the majority issued under his own Arkham House logo; and thousands of newspaper and magazine articles; university lecturer; public speaker, and he also recorded his own poems on discs and wrote forewords for other writers' work.

In addition to all this he had assembled perhaps the world's largest collection of comic strips; had written the Judge Peck novels, lengthy regional novels written against the historical context of his beloved Wisconsin, where he spent weeks tramping the woods in search of his great culinary delicacies, morels, a type of mushroom much favoured by connoisseurs; had written eight volumes of Solar Pons adventures, issued in hardback under his own imprint; books on Catholic themes which gained him the Apostolic Blessing of Pope John in 1959, and he had also been awarded a Guggenheim Fellowship in 1938.

August was highly gratified at being praised by such a distinguished author as Sinclair Lewis, which must have sustained him in many bleak years of toil in which, he once told me, he worked against sixty-day promissory notes in order to support his family of two young children, his aged mother and the beautiful home he had custom-built, Place of Hawks, where his own library and Arkham book stocks were kept. He was a passionate book collector, amassing a library of some 12,000 volumes; a chess enthusiast; a strong swimmer; a writer of children's books; a devoted father and family man; oversaw films of his tales made for TV; and he had written hundreds of macabre short stories and novellas, many of which have become classics in the genre. As if all this were not enough, he edited volumes of ghost stories which have appeared in both hardback and paperback on a world scale, and almost single-handed thrust the great horror writer H.P. Lovecraft, the recluse of Rhode Island, into international fame with his patronage and tireless promotion of the former's work through publishing all of his novels and short stories under the Arkham imprint.

And with this list I have by no means exhausted all the range and scope of his activities in the literary world. A Renaissance man, then, as I have often described him, both in print and in lectures.

My own association with August Derleth began many years ago when, as a newspaper editor, I was at the same time embarking on a career as a professional author of crime novels,

Gothic novels, macabre short stories and novellas, essays, film scripts and non-fiction works. I had written to him to see if there was any possibility of him publishing some of my macabre fiction, and he replied most warmly. He had already seen some of my horror stories in the famous Pan Books series and, as I have recorded elsewhere, his encouragement, long and enjoyable letters and his patronage when he offered to publish my first American hardback under the aegis of Arkham House, formed one of the warmest and most delightful strands of my writing life.

Regretfully our relationship, conducted entirely on paper, was to last only some five or six years, but during that time August emerged as a man of great probity, courage and generosity. His death in 1971 at the early age of 62 was a staggering blow to his host of friends and literary colleagues and a world-wide loss in the publishing field. A brilliant editor, James Turner, then took over the running of Arkham and he published a number of my macabre story collections, as well as major Gothic novels of mine. But one day I wrote to him after he had sent me some copies of August's Pons volumes and I pointed out a number of errors in the texts. The upshot was that Arkham then commissioned me to revise and edit the entire Pontine Canon—some eight volumes, eventually published by Arkham in a handsome two-volume slip-cased edition as *The Solar Pons Omnibus* in 1982.

This definitive work collected together everything August had ever written about Pons and the contents of the two volumes, running to over 1,300 pages with fine illustrations by the late Frank Utpetel and with a Foreword by Robert Bloch, brought together *In Re: Sherlock Holmes—The Adventures of Solar Pons*, *The Memoirs of Solar Pons*, *The Return of Solar Pons*, *The Rem-*

iniscences of Solar Pons, The Casebook of Solar Pons, A Praed Street Dossier, the novel *Mr. Fairlie's Final Journey* and *The Chronicles of Solar Pons.* A veritable feast for Pontine enthusiasts, bringing together as it did some seventy short stories and a novel together with the fine and appreciative Foreword by Robert Bloch. Many of the stories achieved much wider circulation and some were republished in both hardback and paperback on both sides of the Atlantic.

The editing of the Pons Canon was carried out as a labour of love and was a most enjoyable task which occupied me for almost a year and a half, between other writing assignments. It was undertaken as a tribute to August's memory and due to my affection for the man I did not wish any payment for the work, but Arkham eventually insisted that I accept a fee which was entirely in keeping with their scrupulous business ethics. It was some while after this that James Turner asked if I would like to carry on the Pons series myself. Of course, I accepted immediately and over the next two years I wrote some six volumes. These were *The Dossier of Solar Pons, The Further Adventures of Solar Pons, The Secret Files of Solar Pons, Some Uncollected Cases of Solar Pons, The Exploits of Solar Pons* and *The Recollections of Solar Pons*, together with a half-completed novel, *The Devil's Claw* which, incidentally, I managed to piece together from original plot-notes rediscovered in my files, and successfully completed some seventeen years after it was begun.

All the stories in my own Pontine Canon are of novella length, some running to over seventy pages, which gave me much greater scope for character, plot development and all those macabre elements of atmosphere which are so dear to my heart. They were received with great enthusiasm by James Turner but unfortunately they had a chequered history over the years as paperbacks by imprints which completely destroyed the 1920s British atmosphere by rewriting and inserting crass and stupid alterations, one went bankrupt and others did not pay. Fortunately I now have splendid American publishers, Fedogan and Bremer in the personas of Philip Rahman, a computer expert with a group of Minneapolis hospitals; and his partner, Dennis Weiler, a surgeon.

They produced a magnificent hardback edition of my Gothic novel *The Black Death* which was launched with great success when I was Guest of Honour at the World Fantasy Convention in Minneapolis in October-November 1993. Then followed two equally sumptuous hardback collections of my mostly unpublished novellas, *The Exploits of Solar Pons* and *The Recollections of Solar Pons*, all three volumes being superbly illustrated by my close friend and collaborator, the American artist, Stefanie Kate Hawks. All these books, both slip-cased and signed, and the "ordinary" editions have sold in astonishing quantities and have been hailed by both the Solar Pons organisation, known as the Praed Street Irregulars, and by Sherlockians on both sides of the Atlantic.

Apart from other volumes of mine planned by Fedogan and Bremer, they intend eventually to publish a four-volume omnibus edition containing the authentic texts of my remaining four collections, which will appear in a huge slip-cased edition along with the first two volumes. One of my most atmospheric Pons novellas, 'The Adventure of the Crawling Horror', is due to appear in the Fedogan and Bremer hardback anthology *Dark Detectives*, edited by my old friend the author and anthologist, Stephen Jones. Another, 'The Adventure of the Callous Colonel' has appeared in the USA in a Barnes & Noble hardback collection entitled *Murder Most Scottish*.

My own stories, which were both longer and more atmospheric than August's, as I have noted, were firmly based on Holmes and Watson, of course, but at the same time adhering firmly to August's original depiction of Pons and Parker, so that Pons still tents his long fingers before him or pulls thoughtfully at the lobe of his ear. Critics and long-time followers of Derleth's *oeuvre* have pointed out to me that his stories were more like outlines for stories than finished works. I agreed but this is not to denigrate August. He often wrote Pons tales in a room crowded with drinking students while doing stints as a university lecturer in Wisconsin and it is not surprising, given these circumstances, that his stories were somewhat sketchy.

In all there are about 2,000 errors of British usage which had to be corrected. For instance, he would write, "the cars were switched to the loop line", whereas railway terminology in Britain would be "the carriages were shunted on to a siding". Or he would have Pons and Parker driving along in the middle of London "toward the Chiltern Hills", which is rather like, on a much larger scale, having someone driving along Hollywood Boulevard towards New York. August, of course, knew there was something wrong with his texts—like Lovecraft before him, he had never visited Britain—and he asked another author to revise the texts, but I found that little or no work had been done in that respect. In undertaking this task it was the least I could do in tribute to August's memory.

What of my own texts? I had time, quietness and the leisure to write my own novellas. I do not intend to go into too much detail of the plots or *dénouements* of my own work in this field as that would spoil the reader's pleasure—I hope it can be called that and, judging by the comments made to me in letters from the USA and this country, and by learned members of the Sherlock Holmes Society in London, I have not been unsuccessful in following in the footsteps of Sherlock Holmes.

A number of notable Sherlockian scholars have given their approval and have noted, accurately, that my stories were rooted firmly in the Conan Doyle mould, but as I have noted, I have also kept faithfully to August's own ambience and to the true aspects of his own creations.

This has been widely recognised in America and the Praed Street Irregulars have twice honoured me with their awards, while in 1979 the Mark Twain Society of America inducted me as a Knight of Mark Twain in succession to the late Henry Williamson "for your contribution to modern fiction".

I like to think that I have been faithful to the memories of both Conan Doyle and August Derleth in the traditional detective field. Time alone will tell.

Plots of the Stories

The Adventure of the Perplexed Photographer. When Bruce Beresford, principal of a leading London photographic agency, brings an apparently trivial series of events to Pons' consulting room—the smashing of his glass photographic plates, culminating in an attack on him in Soho one night, when more glass plates are destroyed—Pons and Parker little realise that Beresford's misfortunes will help to entrap a cunning murderer. For Inspector Jamison of Scotland Yard enlists Pons' help to solve the horrific murder of Professor Mair, a distinguished academic, pinned to the floor of his locked study with a javelin thrust into his body. But with the aid of Beresford's photographic expertise Pons is able to unravel an intricate and apparently unconnected series of events to bring the killer to book.

The Sealed Spire Mystery. Dr. Glyn Campbell, the Rector of Shap in Surrey and Rural Dean of Stapleford, is in dire distress when he seeks Pons' help. He appears to be going mad because of a number of inexplicable happenings, ranging from many articles in his house which go missing, the mysterious persecution persisting for months, until its culmination at an important lecture, when Campbell produces from his briefcase, not the expected sheaf of notes but the corpse of a colleague's favourite cat. On top of all this there is a sealed spire at St. Mary's Church, about which many wild legends have accreted. An eccentric old woman in the village, Mrs. Grace Harbinger, is vociferous in urging the Rector to open the Sealed Spire, which she is convinced contains the Scroll of Thoth and other treasures which may affect the future of the world. But the spire contains an even more sinister secret as Pons unravels a history of church intrigue and a plan to prevent the Rector's preferment to high office.

THE ADVENTURE OF THE SIX GOLD DOUBLOONS. Pons and his devoted colleague and biographer, Dr. Lyndon Parker, are taking a stroll in a London park on a beautiful summer's day when their old friend Superintendent Stanley Heathfield brings a singular problem to their attention. The murder of Elihu Cook Stanmore, blackmailer, forger, swindler and thief, as Pons describes him, has been found with multiple stab wounds in the back and with six gold doubloons on the desk in front of him. The problem seems insoluble and there are dozens of suspects in the case as the society blackmailer's files name people of high rank. To make matters even more complex a post-mortem reveals that Stanmore suffered a heart attack and had died before the murder. The trail leads to such prominent people as Lady Mary Hawthorne and the Duke of Leinster and, in a surprising finale, Parker learns that no one is a villain after all.

THE ADVENTURE OF THE IPI IDOL. Colonel John d'Arcy, a retired District Commissioner in East Africa, inherits The Briars, an old mansion on the Essex marshes, from his uncle,

Silas Renfrew, who had also lived in East Africa in earlier years. He was in fear of his life after discovering a carved African idol on his desk. According to him it portended death, and was the work of Africa devil worshippers. Renfrew's son, Adrian, went out one night after a disturbance in the grounds and was stung by something venomous which led to an agonising death within three days, despite all the efforts of the doctors. The Colonel has received a similar idol through the post, which brings him to Pons' door. An enormous spider and a deadly snake are among the sinister forces threatening the Colonel and his fiancée, but in an horrific finale, Pons unmasks the evil agent endeavouring to get hold of the Colonel's fortune.

The Adventure of Buffington Old Grange. Bruce Oldfield, a Berkshire accountant, buys an ancient house, Buffington Old Grange, into which he moves with his wife and two young children, after it has been completely renovated; but the property has a bad reputation and there are stories of hauntings, and a miser, the former owner, who was found hanged in the attic. Oldfield, an extremely frightened man, comes to Solar Pons with a bizarre story of mysterious events at the house culminating in an attempted murder, when his wife is pushed down some steep cellar steps by an unseen force. But Pons has more mundane but no less frightening explanations, leading back to an evil conspiracy some twenty years earlier. Although he has at first no explanation for the "grey, corpse-like face" which had so frightened Mrs. Oldfield, he has a shrewd idea of motive after going through old newspapers in the local library. Eventually, he arranges with the family to leave the house on a supposed holiday, while he and Parker bait the trap and wait for sinister events to unfold in the cellar.

THE ADVENTURE OF THE HAMMER OF HATE. Eustace Fernchurch, a young apprentice architect in Yorkshire, is accused of murdering his hated rival in love by dropping a heavy mason's hammer on his head from a high tower which is undergoing repair. He evades the police, travels to London and bursts into Solar Pons' sitting room in a dramatic manner, a hunted man, who implores the help of the great consulting detective. Despite the overwhelming weight of the evidence, Pons immediately sees a number of flaws in the police case and agrees to take up the young man's defence. Pons and Parker travel to Yorkshire, where the former works with Inspector Robert Fitzjohn of York C.I.D. Fernchurch had been engaged to a somewhat fickle young girl, Evelyn Smithers, who lives with her father, Professor Smithers, who is Curator of the ancient building involved in the murder. Fitzjohn is at first convinced of Fernchurch's guilt, but Pons thinks otherwise and eventually solves the case when one of his most astonishing theories is proved to be the truth. But Pons has already come to some conclusions about the young man's fiancée and observes to Parker that if the marriage takes place he will be extremely surprised. And so it proves…

THE ADVENTURE OF THE SHAFT OF DEATH. [*Note: Basil appears to have inadvertently left this story out of the manuscript when he was compiling his plot descriptions of the Solar Pons stories.* SJ.]

THE ADVENTURE OF THE BAFFLED BARON. When the murdered body of the world-famous sculptor, Romaine Schneider, is found with his skull crushed in his Hampstead studio, the crime seems unsolvable. Because the studio was locked and the murdered man had the only key to the door. There were no other entrances or exits from the studio, which was over the top of a garage and the skylight was some twenty feet from the studio floor, and in addition firmly screwed shut. The mystery seems absolutely baffling, especially to Inspector Jamison of Scotland Yard, who is in charge of the case. Untypically, he enlists the help of Solar Pons and Dr. Lyndon Parker, and it soon becomes clear to the former that the person who killed the sculptor must have been of gigantic stature, as the single death blow was delivered squarely to the top of the head. And there are plenty of people who might have wished Schneider dead, including his equally famous arch-rival, the sculptor Sir Hercules Kronfeld. In solving this apparently unsolvable crime, Pons also uncovers a plot which has world-wide ramifications.

The Adventure of the Surrey Sadist. It is a mild day in early April when Pons is consulted by Emil Rawnsley Colefax of the Clarendon Court Hotel in Surrey, who brings a bizarre problem to Pons' consulting room. The young man comes from a troubled background, his domineering father having twice forced him to break off his engagements to be married. In addition, though Colefax wanted to be a commercial artist, a profession for which he had some talent, his father had again intervened, insisting that he become an architect, like himself. Colefax had finally broken with his parents, his mother dying shortly afterwards. He had then become a commercial artist, earning a precarious living, but one day he had read in a newspaper that his father had died, leaving a fortune of two hundred thousand pounds. A short while later he saw the apparitions of his dead parents in the garden of the hotel. The terrified young man then seeks the help of Pons, who tells him, "As I have remarked previously on more than one occasion, this agency stands four-square behind the natural laws of physics, Mr. Colefax. I do not believe in ghosts and Parker and I, together with the occasional assistance of the doctor's revolver, have disproved them in a number of cases". Pons and Parker take up the challenge and unmask a devilish plot to get hold of Colefax's fortune.

THE ADVENTURE OF THE MISSING STUDENT. Silas Rillington, a neighbour of Bancroft Pons in St. John's Wood has been reduced to a nervous wreck by a series of weird incidents. He is a retired merchant with connections in the East, who has been able to assist the Foreign Office in delicate matters of diplomacy for some time, which is why he had asked Bancroft's help. He had been sent a note saying if he wished to see his son alive again, he should leave £15,000 in used banknotes at the left luggage counter at Charing Cross Station. Later he received two packages, each containing a severed finger, reiterating the original threat and that he should leave the package containing the money addressed to Adam Bede, the central character in George Eliot's novel. A reclusive man, Rillington had merely locked the packages in his safe. When questioned by Pons, he says he has no son! Parker is appalled at this, but Pons soon discovers that there is another Silas Rillington, an immensely wealthy man, who is the head of a vast financial empire. When Pons tactfully approaches him he obviously knows nothing of the matter and says his son, Rodney, is on holiday in Spain. So Pons and Parker leave a heavily sealed package at Charing Cross Station and when the pair keep watch in the stationmaster's office high above the concourse, a heavily disguised man collects it. He drives away, followed by Pons and Parker in a hired car. Their quarry leads them to a lonely farm building in Ashdown Forest in Sussex, where the kidnapper is unmasked and the young man rescued unharmed.

The Adventure of the Crawling Horror. Old Silas Grimstone, a wealthy City man who nevertheless has miserly habits, is terrified by a weird apparition bathed in blue fire which rises from the edge of a marsh near his remote house on the lonely Gravesend marshes. In bitter winter weather Pons and Parker set out to hunt the phantom down, which involves them coming across a number of outwardly suspicious characters about the area. An old man is found dead in the ice at the edge of the marsh and the miser, who lives in a rundown mansion with his daughter acting as housekeeper, is further terrified by a ghastly face which appeared at the window late at night. Pons and Parker hunt down the phantom of the marsh and in so doing the former unravels a complex story of ancient wrongs and revenge, culminating in a horrific finale in the depths of the marsh when death again strikes and a logical explanation emerges for a series of disparate and seemingly disconnected events.

The Adventure of the Anguished Actor. Solar Pons has seldom been called upon to unravel a sinister plot involving murder on stage, when Cedric Carstairs, a famous matinée idol, seeks his help. A steel-shafted arrow is the intended weapon as Carstairs is acting out the part of a strangled murder victim, appropriately enough, in his new play, *Death Comes to Thornfield*. Pons and Parker are soon plunged into a vortex of fear and suspicion backstage, as they begin their investigations. There are many suspects in the jealous, overheated world of egotistical actors and actresses, but Pons finds his way unerringly through the tangle which leads to a tremendous real-life finale on stage. The murderer, disguised as a member of the theatre orchestra, is quietly slipping away, apparently unseen, but Pons' sharp eyes, which miss nothing of the dramas playing out both on stage and in real life, brings the villainous perpetrator to book.

THE ADVENTURE OF THE IGNORED IDOLS. In one of his most celebrated cases Pons again crosses swords with Charles Brinsley LaFontaine, a daring master thief who has warned a major London museum that he will steal the priceless gold Baku Idols on display, some of the institution's most treasured possessions, which attract many visitors. But among the hundreds of people thronging the museum every day LaFontaine is able to move about undetected. Is he one of the attendants with a black moustache, a blind man with a beard or a distinguished professor, a world-famous archaeologist? And are the Baku Idols really the objective of this gifted master thief? But the museum authorities had under-estimated the greed of multi-millionaire collectors. Despite all the difficulties, Pons and Superintendent Stanley Heathfield of Scotland Yard are able to trace the stolen property to a high-ranking and distinguished personality who is persuaded to give up the treasures while given immunity from prosecution. But LaFontaine has slipped through their fingers, though Pons views his exploits with grudging admiration.

THE ADVENTURE OF THE HORRIFIED HEIRESS. Pons and Parker are enjoying a peaceful break in their chambers in Praed Street when the bull-like figure of the sadistic Edmund Roseacre bursts in and threatens them and warns Pons to stop interfering in his affairs. When he tries to strike Pons with his stick, the detective breaks it in half and hurls it back into the bully's face, cutting his chin. He then warns the man he will throw him downstairs if he doesn't leave immediately and Roseacre beats a hasty retreat. Later, Roseacre's niece, a young girl called Evelyn Brentwood, arrives in great distress. She is heiress to a considerable fortune and lives with her uncle in a gloomy mansion called The Priory, in a small village near Godalming. Sinister events surrounding her had included the hanged body of the family solicitor, Mr. Marcus, which crashes against her bedroom window. She faints but when she recovers Roseacre tells her she has been the subject of a nightmare. But then the hanged body of Marcus is found in his London house. From this tangled skein Pons and Parker must try to discover the gruesome truth, which leads to a horrific climax worthy of *Grand Guignol.*

The Adventure of the Haunted Rectory. Miss Elizabeth Stuart of The Old Rectory, Grassington, brings a strange tale to Praed Street, which seems to bear all the marks of the supernatural. Some years before, her father, The Rector of Grassington, had died of shock when a savage, bearded face had appeared at his library window. Now, Miss Stuart has also had a number of frightening experiences, when another evil intruder has appeared at the open French windows in bright summer weather. Books in her father's study have been examined and thrown to the floor. When Pons and Parker come to stay in Grassington, the former finds the focus of the manifestations seem to turn on an old Bible containing a slip of paper with corrupt Biblical references. The quotations contain a cipher which leads Pons to the ancient church adjoining the Rectory. Here he sets a trap for a cunning and vicious criminal which culminates in a murderous encounter in the church at dead of night.

THE ADVENTURE OF THE SINGULAR SANDWICH. Lyndon Parker is appalled to read in his morning *Times* that his old friend Aramis Tregorran, a famous painter, has been arrested for murder, after strangling his estranged wife Sylvia, who was sitting for her portrait. The studio was locked and no one could gain access as the key was inside and when the door was broken in by household staff, the artist was found in a dazed and incoherent condition. The case against him seems hopeless, but owing to Parker's heartfelt plea on behalf of his old friend, Pons agrees to look into the matter. Inspector Jamison is jubilant at his open-and-shut case but Pons notices some strange circumstances which do not seem to add up. In one of the most brilliant schemes involving murder and revenge, Pons is finally able to get to the heart of the matter, and though Tregorran is technically guilty of strangling his wife, Pons is able to clear him of murder and reveal the identity of the person whose twisted hatred planned such a diabolic scheme.

MURDER AT THE ZOO. A series of weird happening at Regents Park Zoo in the heart of London have been intriguing the population for some months, following the exploits of a prowler who has been releasing dangerous animals from their cages at dead of night. Following the release of a Bengal tiger from the Lion House a man's body is found in a gorilla's cage. Solar Pons, working closely with Scotland Yard, knows that gorillas are vegetarians and immediately sees something far deeper in a disconnected chain of events, in his efforts to clear the name of a young keeper, who has been wrongfully accused of releasing animals at the Zoo. High-ranking rivalry has erupted between two distinguished members of the Zoological Society of London. How Pons, ably assisted by Dr. Parker, finds his way to the heart of the matter, brings to a successful conclusion one of his most absorbing cases.

The Adventure of the Frightened Governess. Lyndon Parker is roused from his bed at 6:00 a.m. by Solar Pons, who tells him they have pressing affairs before them—"a matter of life and death" no less. Their client, Miss Helen Jane Helstone, a tall, fair young lady, has been engaged as governess by Mr. Clinton Basden, master of a huge mansion in Surrey. Though there are dozens of applicants for the lucrative post of governess, she is accepted almost on sight, to take charge of two strange young children, who cannot even speak English. Even more bizarre is the fact that she is required to dress in a certain way and her only duties seem to be those of accompanying the children on long rambles in the floodlit grounds at night. But one night someone tries to shoot her and, terrified, she escapes from the estate, takes an early morning train and begs Pons to help her. He soon discovers that even more extraordinary events are involved; including representatives of an Eastern European state; a royal lady; an eminent British surgeon; and a gang of international terrorists. With the aid of his brother Bancroft, a powerful figure at the Foreign Office, obscure happenings become clear as Pons brings the highly dangerous case to a successful conclusion.

The Adventure of the Verger's Thumb. Taking a rare holiday in Norwich in brilliant summer weather, Pons and Parker's tranquil sojourn in the ancient city is interrupted by an urgent summons from the Dean of Norwich himself. There have been strange occurrences in the cathedral, which began with the verger having his thumb "bitten" by a gargoyle; messages being left in the cathedral; rough-looking men whispering in the pews; and a disturbed tomb in the crypt, where renovation work is taking place. None of this makes sense to Parker, but Pons begins to see a pattern emerging and his deductive powers lead to an exciting climax at night when a vicious criminal gang try to escape down river on a motor launch toward the sea.

The Adventure of the Phantom Face. The small village of Tidewater, near London, is being haunted by a mysterious and terrifying apparition with a weird mummy-like face. But when a wealthy landowner, Mr. Charles Boldigrew, collapses and dies when this evil apparition appears at his study window on a dark night, matters become even more sinister, though a local doctor diagnoses heart failure as his patient had long suffered from a serious heart complaint. But his nephew, Michael Balfour, who lives with his uncle at Bredewell House and is the sole beneficiary under his uncle's will is not satisfied and enlists Pons' help. Parker is inclined to suspect a rather strange character who runs a local toyshop whose stock includes grotesque carnival masks, but his friend has other ideas. Pons works with Detective Inspector Horace Cunliffe, an astute police officer stationed in Essex, and tackles the case on entirely different lines. Aided by the apparently innocuous incident of a child's air pistol and a carnival mask being stolen from a doctor's waiting room, he brings a cunning murderer to justice, at the same time revealing the motive.

Death at the Metropole. An old soldier who lost an eye in the First World War and now works as a porter at the Metropole Hotel in the Strand brings a tale of murder and deception to Pons and Parker's sitting room. A strange foreigner with dark glasses, a muffler and heavy overcoat, despite the hot weather, arrived at the hotel the previous night and has now been found strangled. Inspector Jamison of Scotland Yard, with his usual obtuseness, has arrested the manager, Mr. Hibbert, on the flimsy grounds that the key to the murdered man's room was on the table, while the only other key was hanging at the night porter's desk in the hotel lobby. Pons disabuses him of this ridiculous notion and attempts to solve an outwardly incredibly complex situation. Otto Voss of Hamburg, another guest, Esau Thornton of Surrey, and a gang of international bank robbers are all involved and Parker plays a leading part in a tremendous *mêlée* at the hotel when the killer is unmasked.

The Adventure of the Callous Colonel. In one of his most sinister encounters, Pons and Parker thwart the plans of Colonel McDonald, "the third most dangerous man in Europe", who is in process of floating a gigantic land swindle. McDonald's agents, led by the gigantic figure of Mungo Ferguson, have been trying to force Miss Jennifer Hayling to sell her late parents' small Scottish estate, so that the scheme by the Scottish Land Trust can go ahead. Pons, who has already been sent a deadly gadget by the Colonel, which could have killed him, takes up the challenge and he and Parker travel with Miss Hayling to Scotland where even more horrific incidents await them; which include a venomous spider sent to their client at an Edinburgh hotel; an epic fight between Pons and Mungo Ferguson; and a final deadly encounter on a Scottish crag between Pons and the Colonel, using high-powered sporting rifles.

The Adventure of the Cursed Curator. Horatio Biggs,

Curator of the Egyptian Museum in London, intrigues Pons with a bizarre tale of mysterious events at the Museum, culminating in a ghastly image with a wrinkled mummy face staring at him from behind a gap in his bookshelves. An attempt was later made on his life when an enormous earthenware pot pushed from an upper floor of the Museum narrowly missed crushing him to death. Biggs has recently returned from an archaeological expedition to the Valley of the Kings and the Egyptian authorities assign an intelligent man named Achmed to accompany him to London. Pons believes him to be Inspector Achmed of the Cairo Police, but doubts arise after the man is murdered by being pushed under a London bus. The mystery deepens still further when the real Chief Inspector Achmed of the Cairo Narcotics Squad is found floating in the Nile. Inspector Jamison of Scotland Yard thinks a murderous gang of thieves is attempting to steal treasures on loan to the Egyptian Museum, but Pons eventually proves otherwise and brings the criminals to book.

THE ADVENTURE OF THE HOUND OF HELL. In one of his most baffling cases Solar Pons is faced with what appears to be an absolutely unsolvable crime. A miserly but immensely wealthy old woman, Miss Emily Schneider, has been strangled on a bleak winter night in a lonely woodshed in a neglected corner of the grounds of her mansion, The Pines, in Essex. There is thick snow and the most extraordinary thing about the case is the old lady's footprints are indented in the snow as one would expect but the murderer's, though they go to the shed, never return. There is no other exit from the structure which is set on the edge of a steep drop to an icy cold stream, so no one could have got out that way. A young solicitor, Rollo Watling, who was present at the house that evening and who was the old lady's heir, is suspected of the murder but his fiancée, Miss Eunice Chambers of Fulham, begs Pons' help in clearing him. Inspector Stanley Rossiter of Colchester C.I.D., though an intelligent officer, sees Watling's position a hopeless one. But Pons has other ideas. He is convinced of the young man's innocence. He feels that a number of people who were owed money by the miserly recluse must come under suspicion. And by a brilliant deductive feat he solves the mystery of the "invisible man" and brings him to justice. The Hound of Hell is a monstrous silver effigy which is supposed to bring bad luck to the person who owns it, and Mr. Watling was in possession of it; a rare gift from his aunt.

The Adventure of the Mad Millionaire. An encounter between Lyndon Parker and a former neighbour, Colonel Mortimer, ushers in one of Solar Pons' most extraordinary cases, that of the millionaire financier, Hugo Foy, whose apparently insane actions are underlaid by a sinister secret. Foy drove his Rolls-Royce stark naked in the moonlight, wears white drill trousers with a dark City suit and uses a billiard cue to hole out his ball on the golf course. And that is not all, for he brings down the Colonel with a flying rugby tackle, drinks champagne with ginger beer as well as pelting Mortimer with eggs. "Capital!" says Pons, who has already sensed a method in Foy's madness. The case culminates in a tense climax involving corruption in high places, kidnapping and assassination attempts engineered by an evil South American warlord, "Tiger" Marceau of Paragonia, and an equally corrupt Ambassador, Arpad Krish.

THE ADVENTURE OF THE DEVIL'S CLAW. Originally written in the 1970s, after being commissioned by Arkham House, the material was rediscovered in the early 1990s, and prepared for publication, thus completing the Canon. A young schoolmaster, Hugh Mulvane of Chalcroft Manor in Buckinghamshire, is heir to a vast fortune but brings a tale of brooding horror to Pons and Parker's cosy sitting room. He is in great fear and lurid reports in the popular press tend to cast suspicion on him, following the death of his reclusive uncle, Simon Hardcastle, whose body has been found in the lonely private graveyard at the Manor. Mulvane had followed him there to find out why he should frequent this grim place at dead of night, but had been knocked unconscious by an unseen assailant. At first it appears that Hardcastle had suffered a heart attack but a post-mortem reveals that he had apparently been naked on a bitterly cold winter night and had been stabbed by some very thin metal instrument which had penetrated the heart. Round the body were strange claw marks like those of no beast known to science. Earlier, a tramp had been found dead in the woods with the same marks round the body, which had revived the ancient local legend of the Devil's Claw, leading to the national press reporting "a reign of terror" in the area. When Pons and Parker arrive on the scene of the crime they are plunged into a maelstrom of deception, murder and bizarre happenings, with a large number of possible suspects. Eventually, Pons sets a trap for a cunning criminal, culminating in a sinister vigil at the top of an ancient tower on the estate, leading to the unmasking of the perpetrators.

Characters in the Stories

(Together with Animals and Certain Inanimate Objects)

A

Abernathy, Roscoe. Forger and murderer who lived above a cooked meat shop in North London. "'I fancy Roscoe Abernathy will be out of his stride by the appearance of Scotland Yard officers with warrants in the early hours of tomorrow morning.' 'What had he been up to, Pons?' 'Forgery and murder among other things, Parker. Undone by a child's pinafore button. One would hardly credit it, given the nature of the man.'" [*Parker*]
The Adventure of the Devil's Claw

Abrahams, John. Secretary to the famous stage and film actor Cedric Carstairs. "A tall, slim young man of about thirty with dark, bushy hair . . . He was a good-looking, personable young man who might have made an excellent actor himself." [*Parker*]
The Adventure of the Anguished Actor

Achmed. Real Chief Inspector Achmed of the Cairo Narcotics Squad, assigned to guard Horatio Biggs, Curator of the Egypt-

ian Museum in London, who is transporting treasures from the Valley of the Kings for a major exhibition at the Museum. Inspector Jamison of Scotland Yard is later informed by the Cairo Police that the real Inspector Achmed's body has been recovered from the Nile and an impostor, also later murdered, had taken his place.
The Adventure of the Cursed Curator

Achmed, Police Inspector. Educated Arab who spoke perfect English, assigned by the Egyptian government to Horatio Biggs, Curator of the Egyptian Museum in London, to act as secretary and general factotum on an archaeological dig in the Nile Valley. A gigantic man over six feet tall who is in reality an officer of the Cairo Police sent to guard Biggs and the museum treasures. Later murdered by being pushed under a London bus. In reality an impostor who has taken the real Inspector's place.
The Adventure of the Cursed Curator

Amsden, Lionel. City stockbroker, living on his uncle, Professor Mair's money, at The Poplars, Highbury, who crosses swords with Pons when the latter questions him about Professor Mair's murder. A blond giant, well over six feet tall, handsome in a brutal way in which coarseness and sensuality fought for supremacy in his features. Addicted to horse racing and gambling which had greatly depleted his income.
The Adventure of the Perplexed Photographer

Armitage, Clifford. A man who handled the financial affairs of Professor Mair, a distinguished academic brutally murdered in his locked study at his mansion in Highbury. "A slim, open-faced young man with a shock of brown hair. Dressed tastefully

and quietly in a light grey suit . . . He cut a slender, dapper figure, his blue eyes gazing intently as he was introduced to the distinguished detective." [*Parker*]
The Adventure of the Perplexed Photographer

Armstrong, Sir Idris. Distinguished surgeon at Charing Cross Hospital and an acquaintance of Pons, whom the latter consults in the course of his inquiries into the whereabouts of one of his students, young Rodney Rillington, son of a wealthy industrialist.
The Adventure of the Missing Student

Aurelius, Marcus (Marcus Aurelius Antoninus). Real name M. Annius Verus. Born April 26th A.D. 121. Roman Emperor-Philosopher, author of *The Meditations*. Quoted by Pons in the following terms: "'The philosophers counsel patience, Parker. In the mind that is once truly disciplined, as the good Marcus Aurelius has it.'"
The Adventure of the Singular Sandwich

Ayres. Business manager of the famous stage and film actor Cedric Carstairs, who is playing the lead in a new thriller, *Death Comes to Thornfield*, at the Negresco Theatre in London, after the actor has received threats that he will be killed on stage during the play.
The Adventure of the Anguished Actor

Ayres, Sir Clifford. Distinguished surgeon of Harley Street, called in to attend a royal patient at a mansion in Clitherington, Surrey. "A tall, cadaverous man in a frock-coat of sombre colour . . . [he] made a little gobbling noise like a turkey cock and stepped forward with white features." One of the country's

leading specialists in heart diseases and strokes, Parker tells Pons.
The Adventure of the Frightened Governess

B

Backer, Dr. Erik. Buckinghamshire Coroner who adjourned the inquest on Simon Hardcastle of Chalcroft Manor in the village of Chalcroft, who was found dead near the estate's ancient family burial ground under suspicious circumstances.
The Adventure of the Devil's Claw

Balfour, Michael. A young man living at Bredewell house in Tidewater, Essex, who is haunted by the apparition known as the "Phantom Face", which is terrorising the area. His uncle, a wealthy landowner, Charles Boldigrew, with whom he lived, died in mysterious circumstances after seeing the face at his study window one dark winter night. "A frank-looking, open-faced young fellow of about twenty-eight, smartly but sensibly dressed in a checked overcoat which he took off at my companion's invitation to reveal a belted Norfolk jacket, worn over thick tweed trousers. His fresh features were reddened and roughened with the wind and his thick black curly hair much blown about and tousled, for he was hatless." [*Parker*]
The Adventure of the Phantom Face

Barker, Mr. Savile Row tailor, partner in the firm of Barker and Fromset who had removed the premises to Regent Street at the behest of their wealthy client, the Duke of Porchester.
The Adventure of the Haunted Rectory

Barlass, Kate. Heroine of a dramatic poem quoted by Pons in

praise of a very strong and brave keeper at London Zoo who had put his arm through iron brackets to act as a door bar, so preventing a tiger from escaping from its cage. Kate Barlass was a serving maid who had performed the same act to prevent armed men from coming through the door, thus allowing their intended victims to escape.
Murder at the Zoo

Basden, Clinton. A man who advertises the position of a governess at a large mansion in Surrey at such a high salary that dozens of girls apply for the post, but only Helen Helstone is given the position with nothing following a cursory interview with Basden. She had a suspicion that Basden was not the master of the house and observes to Pons, "He was quite an ordinary little man, an Englishman obviously, and rather ill at ease, I thought, among the foreign-sounding employees among his retinue."
The Adventure of the Frightened Governess

Bavaria, King of. "'The King of Bavaria was unusually lavish in that little matter in which I was able to assist him, Parker.'" [*Pons*]
The Adventure of the Shaft of Death

Bede, Adam. Title of a novel by George Eliot used as an alias by a criminal collecting a parcel of money from the left-luggage counter at Charing Cross Station.
The Adventure of the Missing Student

Belding. White-faced thin man, an associate of Colonel Gantley, acting as the Colonel's supervisor in the drug trade in the

East End of London. Captured by Pons and Parker, who realise that the big fish has escaped them.
The Adventure of the Baffled Baron

Beresford, Bruce. Head of a photographic firm in the Strand, one of London's best known agencies. "A tall, heavily bearded man on whose thick-checked ulster raindrops glistened in the light of the room." [*Parker*] He has been plagued by a series of bizarre incidents, involving the smashing of his photographic plates, theft of materials and an actual physical assault on his person. An experienced and distinguished photographer whose collaboration with Pons leads to the unmasking of a cold-blooded murderer.
The Adventure of the Perplexed Photographer

Bevan, Mrs. Housekeeper at The Priory, Pease Pleasance in Surrey, the estate of the evil-tempered Edmund Roseacre, a brutal character who has designs on the estate of his young niece, Miss Evelyn Brentwood. "A tall, angular, middle-aged woman with a good-natured face." [*Parker*]
The Adventure of the Horrified Heiress

Biggins, Mrs. Housekeeper to the murdered sculptor Romane Schneider in a locked studio in Hampstead. When Pons and Parker, on the track of drug dealers, called at the house they are told, "The housekeeper, Mrs. Biggins, is resting in her room."
The Adventure of the Baffled Baron

Biggs, Horatio. Curator of the Egyptian Museum in London. A small, mild-faced man, dressed in a plaid check overcoat. A man of Welsh extraction and a distinguished academic, recently

returned from an archaeological dig in Egypt. "'For example, he is a member of the Coronel Club, a bachelor, a keen enthusiast for the cinema, widely travelled, has recently returned from Egypt and is devoted to the music of Bach.'" [*Pons*]
The Adventure of the Cursed Curator

Biggs, Mr. Postman in the village of Stonecross in Essex where one of the people on his round was Miss Emily Schneider, who was found strangled in her woodshed in bitterly cold, snowy weather. Though a postman he also carried out shoe repairs for people in the area to supplement his small salary. A tall, stringy individual with a morose face, Biggs told Pons, "Miss Schneider owed me thirty pounds for work and materials, which is a lot of money to me... But I would not have killed her for it, if the amount had been three thousand pounds."
The Adventure of the Hound of Hell

Billings. Under-keeper at London Zoo, who had been slightly injured when a night-time prowler let dangerous animals loose in the Zoo grounds.
Murder at the Zoo

Blakeney. Escaped convict frequenting Norwich Cathedral while receiving messages from his associates, who hope to retrieve a large sum of stolen money. A huge man with close-cropped head and sullen face.
The Adventure of the Verger's Thumb

Boldigrew, Charles. Wealthy landowner of Bredewell House in Essex, who has collapsed and died after apparently seeing a "Phantom Face" at his study window one dark winter night.

But suspicious circumstances lead the dead man's nephew, who also lives at Bredewell House, to seek Solar Pons' help.
The Adventure of the Phantom Face

Bolton, Miss Annabel. Friend of famous research chemist Celia Thornton, sharing a house with her in St. John's Wood. A woman "of striking beauty" . . . her flashing "brown eyes were shrewd beneath the masses of lustrous dark hair." [*Parker*]
The Adventure of the Singular Sandwich

Bracegirdle, Mrs. Pregnant patient of Dr. Parker who has a difficult confinement. "'When you come in looking irritated, your hair hanging over your eyes and your waistcoat buttoned crudely, at least two buttonholes out of alignment, it is no great matter to deduce that you had to off-coat and buckle to and that the confinement had been a trying experience.'" [*Pons*]
The Sealed Spire Mystery

Bracegirdle, Mrs. Housekeeper to Charles Boldigrew of Bredewell House, Tidewater, in Essex where her master was obsessed with the security of the premises, but died after seeing a horrible-looking face at his study window one dark night. A tall, distinguished-looking woman with greying hair, faded grey eyes and a well-modulated voice. "The housekeeper, who was dressed in a dark tweed suit with a touch of white at the throat bowed courteously." [*Parker*]
The Adventure of the Phantom Face

Bradshaw, Chadburn. The family lawyer of Colonel J.R. d'Arcy of The Briars, Essex. "A thickset man with a silver moustache and hair thickly powdered with white strands . . . very

white teeth and a faint tan on his lean face. His voice had a Scottish accent as he wrinkled his brows in concentration 'Mr. Pons? Not the famous consulting detective?'" [*Parker*]
The Adventure of the Ipi Idol

Brentwood, Evelyn. A young girl who arrives at Pons and Parker's quarters in Praed Street in mortal fear of her life. She is terrified of her brutal guardian, Edmund Roseacre, and with good reason. "The slim, fair girl who came into our chamber at the heels of Mrs. Johnson looked so pale, so cold and so wretched that my heart went out to her . . . Her long blonde hair was all wet with the clammy breath of the fog and she had such a white, set expression on her sensitive features and such fear and lurking uneasiness in her troubled eyes that I at once led her to a warm place by the fire." [*Parker*]
The Adventure of the Horrified Heiress

Brewer, Professor John. High-ranking scholar at the London Library who assists Pons on the telephone, by giving him details on legends and in particular on the old folk tune, *The Devil's Waltz*, while Pons is investigating the bizarre murder of millionaire Simon Hardcastle near an ancient graveyard on his estate of Chalcroft Manor in Buckinghamshire.
The Adventure of the Devil's Claw

Brice. Bookmaker in Buckinghamshire who is owed a considerable sum of money by Andrew Peters, estate manager at Chalcroft Manor in Buckinghamshire. ". . . a coarse-looking man with a heavy moustache, and dressed in a thick overcoat of glaring check." [*Parker*]
The Adventure of the Devil's Claw

Brown, Amos. Farmhand on Chalcroft Manor estate in Buckinghamshire who was responsible for saving the life of the estate manager, Andrew Peters, when he dragged him from an icy pond, after he had been savagely attacked from behind. An elderly man with a white moustache "...who stood with his hands thrust deep into the pockets of his corduroy jacket." [*Parker*]
The Adventure of the Devil's Claw

Bryant. Racehorse trainer whom Pons suspects of doping the favourite from his stable, Mulcallah, which has failed in races three times in a row.
The Adventure of Buffington Old Grange

Buckfast. C.I.D. Inspector investigating the murder of the world-famous sculptor Romane Schneider in his locked and secure studio in Hampstead. A thin, sandy-haired man in a dark brown suit, with a worried expression on his face. "His faded blue eyes looked curiously at us." [*Parker*] "This business gets stranger every minute," he tells Inspector Jamison.
The Adventure of the Baffled Baron

Buckley, Mr. *Nom de plume* of a cunning international thief, Charles Brinkley Sheridan, who collected his ill-gotten gains from a bank messenger at Croydon Airport in the early hours of the morning, once again eluding Solar Pons' clutches.
The Adventure of the Ignored Idols

Bulstrode, Sebastian. The largest builder in the small town of Maldon in Yorkshire, who steals the fiancée of Eustace Fernchurch, a young architectural apprentice with the firm of

Truscott and Sons in the some town. Described "an absolute bull of a man," fearless and brutal he is killed by a hammer dropped from a tower under renovation, which hits him squarely on the head. Fernchurch is the only person on the tower and arrives at Pons' consulting room on the run as a wanted murderer. But is he? Pons thinks otherwise.
The Adventure of the Hammer of Hate

C

Campbell, Dr. Glyn. Rector of Shap in Surrey and Rural Dean of Stapleford. A life-long bachelor in receipt of a private income, who is being persecuted by a series of bizarre and inexplicable events which are making his life a misery. He is due to present an important paper before a distinguished gathering of high church dignitaries and is afraid of losing his mind. He is also being pestered by an eccentric woman parishioner who is urging him to open the sealed spire in his church. But Pons sees something far more sinister beneath what appears to be a series of stupid practical jokes. "His broad, red features were roughened with the cold and his faded blue eyes wept behind his gold pince-nez. His old-fashioned clothing had a slight greenish tinge, as though it was not only old but mouldy, and the scanty white hairs on his head were dishevelled and much whipped about by the wind." [*Parker*]
The Sealed Spire Mystery

Carpenter, Jethro. Rare book dealer who calls at The Old Rectory, Grassington, near Haslemere, in answer to a curious advertisement Pons has placed in an evening newspaper in order to trap a dangerous criminal. "A small, dapper gentleman,

impeccably dressed in a dark suit and wearing lavender-coloured gloves." [*Parker*]
The Adventure of the Haunted Rectory

Carstairs. Junior keeper at London Zoo who tackled a Polar bear which had been released from its enclosure by a sinister night marauder. "'With commendable courage . . . he attempted to corner it with a pitchfork, but it attacked and savaged him. The attendants managed to keep it at bay, penning it with rope, hurdles and netting and when my own people arrived they had to shoot it.'" [*Superintendent Stanley Heathfield*]
Murder at the Zoo

Carstairs, Cedric. Distinguished stage and film actor whose life is threatened by a series of sinister messages forecasting his death on stage, in a new play called *Death Comes to Thornfield.* "And indeed, the handsome, somewhat florid figure of the former matinée idol was descending the steps toward us, a brace of Irish wolf-hounds at his heels . . . he seemed even taller and broader than I remembered. He must have been over fifty by now but was still handsome in a fleshy way and had tremendous 'presence', as those in the stage profession call it. His eyes and his flashing smile were his greatest features and though his complexion was ruddy and florid, indicative to me of a long indulgence in alcoholic spirits, he was still a fine figure of a man and would pass for a good while yet, with skilful make-up and stage lighting." [*Parker*]
The Adventure of the Anguished Actor

Castleton, Dr. Cedric. Assistant Curator of the Egyptian Museum in London. "A tall, distinguished-looking man with a

black beard flecked with grey…" [*Parker*] A leading Egyptologist, who had written a number of interesting accounts of his explorations, in the national press.
The Adventure of the Cursed Curator

Chambers, Miss Eunice of Fulham. "Her thick, fair hair hung down in swathes on either side of her pale, oval face and the snow crystals glittered on its disarray. She had been crying, but even her reddened eyes could not disguise the beauty of the features or their distinction and breeding. She wore a thick, tailored overcoat which clung to her slim figure and she took a quick, vibrant step forward, which gave the scarf round her neck a wavering, agitated movement." [*Parker*]
The Adventure of the Hound of Hell

Chang. Gigantic Chinese chauffeur in the employ of Colonel Gantley of Hampstead, a criminal masquerading as an antique dealer. Exceeding his instructions, he murdered the distinguished sculptor Romane Schneider with a crushing blow to the top of the head. Wounded by Parker as he tried to attack the doctor and Pons.
The Adventure of the Baffled Baron

Chatterton, Police Sergeant Cedric. "He had a keen, alert face, now much reddened with wind and his thick black moustache gave him a forbidding aspect." [*Parker*] "'Sergeant Chatterton, unless my senses deceive me? We last met on that Whitechapel business some half-dozen years ago.'" [*Pons*]
The Adventure of the Hound of Hell

Chetwynd. Young medical student and the best friend of

Rodney Rillington, a fellow student and millionaire's son who has been kidnapped and held to ransom. But Chetwynd has moved from Charing Cross Hospital to St. Wilfred's Hospital in North London, where Pons and Parker find him. "A large-boned, cheerful individual with an open, pink-cheeked appearance which made him look like an overgrown schoolboy. In his white coat, with stethoscope peeping from one pocket, he appeared, in fact, like a choirboy engaged in some mischievous errand." [*Parker*]
The Adventure of the Missing Student

Colefax, Edward. Uncle of Emil Rawnsley Colefax of Surrey. "Taller, thinner, and quite bald" compared to his brother. "'Have you any other relatives?' 'Nobody really close, Mr. Pons. There is only my uncle, Mr. Edward Colefax. He is my father's brother, but I have not seen him for years. He lives at Eastbourne. My family came from there.'" [*Emil Colefax*]
The Adventure of the Surrey Sadist

Colefax, Emil Rawnsley of Clarendon Court Hotel, Oxhill, Surrey. "A thin, sensitive-faced person of about thirty-eight years old... neatly but rather shabbily dressed. His overcoat, though of good quality and cut, had seen better days, and I could see that his shoes were much scratched and worn, the laces broken and retied." [*Parker*] He had "fair hair and a frank, open face". "I will not beat about the bush, Mr. Pons. I fear for my sanity, if not my life. You will hardly believe my story." [*Emil Colefax*]
The Adventure of the Surrey Sadist

Colefax, Mrs. Emil Colefax's mother. Long dead, but seen as

an apparition by her son in the garden of his hotel, the Clarendon Court in Oxhill, Surrey.
The Adventure of the Surrey Sadist

Colefax, Senior. Stern, architect father of young Emil Colefax, a tyrannical parent. "'The discord between myself and my parents got worse as I became older. It culminated in a terrible row over a young lady to whom I became engaged. The engagement was broken off as a result. I became bitter and never forgave my father.'" [*Emil Colefax*]
The Adventure of the Surrey Sadist

Conyers, Miss Jean. Niece of murdered Professor Mair in Highbury. "A tall, slim girl with dark hair whose sombre clothing and haggard features proclaimed her grief." [*Parker*]
The Adventure of the Perplexed Photographer

Cornfield, Clive. Well-known Essex farmer who called at the home of Mrs. Emily Schneider in Stonecross, a small Essex village, to discuss the state of the fencing between their adjacent properties, the same day the old woman was murdered. "A smart, military-looking figure dressed in riding breeches and a heavy tweed overcoat had hurried across to us . . . He was limping slightly." [*Parker*]
The Adventure of the Hound of Hell

Cornish. Attendant at the Mentmore Museum in London, which is being threatened by an audacious criminal who intends to steal precious gold artefacts. A tall, spare man with a black moustache, dressed in a neat grey uniform with a peaked cap.
The Adventure of the Ignored Idols

Coutts, Angela. Young maidservant at the mansion of the late Simon Hardcastle, Chalcroft Manor, near the village of Chalcroft in Buckinghamshire. "A pretty clear-complexioned girl whose downcast eyes and timid demeanour could not conceal her innate vivacity or her attractive exterior." [*Parker*] She had a well-modulated, refined voice. A slim, modest girl who tells Pons that the old man had made indecent suggestions to her.
The Adventure of the Devil's Claw

Crathie, Angus. Cantankerous old Scottish gardener at the home of Miss Emily Schneider, a miserly but wealthy old woman, who lived at The Pines at the lonely village of Stonecross in Essex, who was later murdered in the gardener's woodshed. Crathie, who had died some years earlier, "'...was as cantankerous as Miss Schneider. They both respected one another and the sparks always flew when they were discussing how the garden should be laid out and such matters. But they got on fine together!...They were two of a kind, really.'" [*Mrs. Hambleton, housekeeper at The Pines*]
The Adventure of the Hound of Hell

Cresswell. 1st Baron of Cresswell Manor, Surrey, family seat of the Cresswells. "'Well, we do not require all that ancient history.'" [*Pons*]
The Adventure of the Haunted Rectory

Cresswell, Sir Roger of Cresswell Manor, Surrey, last of the line. Served in the Grenadier Guards. Killed in action in the First World War. Unmarried, therefore no issue. His seat, the empty Cresswell Manor, was burned down in a mystery fire in the same year as his death.
The Adventure of the Haunted Rectory

Cubitt, The Rev. Dr. "'In the end I confided in the Rector of Peas Pleasance, the Rev. Dr. Cubitt. He said that Mr. Solar Pons was the most famous and most successful consulting detective in England and gave me your address.'" [*Miss Evelyn Brentwood*] "'A wise man, your Rector.'" [*Parker*]
The Adventure of the Horrified Heiress

Cummings, Mrs. Housekeeper to the Duke of Leinster at his Sussex mansion. An elderly woman with "... pleasant, motherly features." [*Parker*]
The Adventure of the Six Gold Doubloons

Cunliffe, Inspector Horace of Essex Police. Officer who is investigating the mysterious death of wealthy landowner Charles Boldigrew at his home, Bredewell House, in the village of Tidewater after seeing a "Phantom Face" at his study window. A grizzled, thickset police officer with grey eyes; a veteran of fifteen years of C.I.D. work, whose bluff manner conceals a shrewd, intelligent brain. "'As I surmised before we ever came to Essex, Parker, he is an extremely shrewd and capable officer.'" [*Pons*]
The Adventure of the Phantom Face

Cust, Miss. Professional nurse with forty years' experience, standing guard over the kidnapped son of Hugo Foy, a multi-millionaire industrialist in a mansion in a remote part of Surrey. A grey-haired woman with an intelligent face, dressed in the uniform of a nurse.
The Adventure of the Mad Millionaire

D

Dabson, Isaac. Young secretary of Dr. Glyn Campbell, Rector of Shep in Surrey. Pale-faced, hook-nosed man with wild eyes. "'A cool customer, our Mr. Dabson.'" [*Pons*]
The Sealed Spire Mystery

Daniels, Police Constable. A gigantic figure of a man, aged about thirty, encountered by Pons beneath a gas lamp in Hampstead. He had found the murdered body of the famous sculptor Romane Schneider in his studio in Hampstead in the early hours of the morning. "Nasty business, Mr. Pons... I have not seen you, sir, since that murderous affair in Paddington. Right on your own doorstep." What Daniels found inside the studio "made him so sick that he had to come out again for air," said Inspector Jamison.
The Adventure of the Baffled Baron

d'Arcy, Colonel John H. Former District Commissioner of Urundi in West Africa, who retired in 1921 when the members of the Planters' Club presented him with an ornamental engraved walking stick, from which Pons deduces, rightly, his background in the Colonial Service. "Colonel d'Arcy was indeed an enormous man, more than six-feet tall and proportionately broad. He wore a large checked overcoat against the bitter cold outside and carried a black homburg in his hand. His open, bearded face had a deep tan, and piercing blue eyes looked first at me and then at my companion." [*Parker*]
The Adventure of the Ipi Idol

Dartmouth, Mr. "One of the principals of Swettenham and Fuggle, estate agents of Highbury, for whom I had done a great

deal of work, telephoned these premises to seek my help." This is what Bruce Beresford, proprietor of a major photographic business in the Strand, tells Solar Pons. The former had been engaged to take pictures of a mansion in Highbury called The Poplars, though he did not know that its owner, Professor Mair, who intended to sell the property, had just been murdered.
The Adventure of the Perplexed Photographer

Dass, Ram. Wealthy head of a high caste Indian family who lives with an entourage of servants at a mansion known as The Grange, near the village of Tidewell in a remote area of Essex, where sinister events have taken place. Has been involved in a boundary dispute with the owner of an adjoining property. "A tall, impressive-looking gentleman with a black beard and cruel eyes which looked like a hawk's in his brown features, he was yet courteous and reserved. With his impeccably cut tweeds he could have been mistaken for an English country gentleman at a distance. His voice, when he spoke, was low and cultured." [*Parker*]
[*See also "Ram Dass Society of Bombay"*]
The Adventure of the Phantom Face

Dawkins. Servant of the murdered blackmailer, Elihu Cook Stanmore, who lives at the suite of a West End hotel rented by his master. Had been with Stanmore for fifteen years and was devoted to him. "A small, subdued-looking man, with dark hair going silver at the temples. He was lean, with a prominent Adam's apple, aged about fifty, and wearing discreet, not to say sombre, clothes . . . There were traces of shock still on his features and the redness of his eyes indicated that he had been weeping." [*Parker*]
The Adventure of the Six Gold Doubloons

Dermot, Angus. Geologist and mineralogist of Culzean Lodge, Inverness, who has been employed by Colonel Alistair McDonald "the third most dangerous man in Europe" who is the brains behind the Scottish Land Trust, to carry out a survey of land in the district in order to float a fraudulent company. "A trim, short man of about thirty with dark, tousled hair and a good-natured face. His eyes expressed surprise behind his steel-framed spectacles... With his thick brown tweed suit he looked out of place in the room, as though farming were his natural vocation." [*Parker*]
The Adventure of the Callous Colonel

Devil's Claw. A popular superstition which is terrorising the small village of Chalcroft in Buckinghamshire, where a wealthy recluse, Simon Hardcastle, has been found dead in the ancient graveyard of his estate. Round the body were six-toed claw-marks which could have been made by no animal known to science, due to their curious configuration.
The Adventure of the Devil's Claw

Devil's Waltz. A strange and sinister tune whistled at dead of night at the ancient family graveyard of Chalcroft Manor in Buckinghamshire. Solar Pons identifies it as an old Irish folk tune, after consulting the curator of a London museum.
The Adventure of the Devil's Claw

Dobbs, Jethro. A small, rather roughly dressed man, a former employee of Sebastian Bulstrode, a wealthy building contractor of Maldon, near York, who had a tremendous row with his evil-tempered employer a short while before the latter's mysterious death. "I'm one of the best masons in the business and I should

think I know my work," he told Pons. He had just finished a section of wall with all the skill of a master craftsman at the base of an ancient tower when Bulstrode arrived in a terrible rage and tore all his work to pieces with a crowbar and hammer and sacked him on the spot.
The Adventure of the Hammer of Hate

Dollond, Carstairs and Digby. Three ecclesiastical colleagues of Dr. Glyn Campbell, Rector of Shap, in Surrey, who were killed in the First World War. "'Though they were even then in their fifties, they volunteered to serve as chaplains. A terrible waste, gentlemen.'" [*Dr. Glyn Campbell*]
The Adventure of the Sealed Spire Mystery

Dresden, Mrs. Dark-haired, pleasant woman who is housekeeper to Mr. Clinton Basden of The Priory, Clitherington in Surrey.
The Adventure of the Frightened Governess

Dunlop and Flinton. London bankers who employ a young man called Gear who was asked to collect a pouch for one of the bank's Swiss customers and deliver it to Count Ferzetti.
The Adventure of the Ignored Idols

E

[*Note: There are no characters whose surnames begin with "E" in the whole of Basil Copper's Solar Pons canon.*]

F

Falkner, J. (John) Meade. English novelist (1858-1932) who wrote two fine adventure stories, *Moonfleet* (1898) and *The Nebuly Coat* (1903), much admired by Pons, who commends his plotting ingenuity to Parker when the pair are trying to work out a coded message.
The Adventure of the Haunted Rectory

Fawkes, Reginald Ashley. Thief and fraudster involved in a plot to murder and also secure the estate of Miss Evelyn Brentwood, the niece of Edmund Roseacre of Godalming in Surrey. "'Fawkes was not only down on his luck; an adventurer like Roseacre, but a skilled forger and an unscrupulous criminal who had already served one prison term.'" [*Pons*]
The Adventure of the Horrified Heiress

Fellows. Medical student at Charing Cross Hospital, a friend of Rodney Rillington, a fellow student who has been kidnapped and held to ransom. A dark-haired young man, dark-bearded and dark-browed. Bad tempered, sullen and angry and with a violent temper, he threatens Pons with violence and tells him that he is the middleweight boxing champion of the medical school. Pons coolly warns him that if he crosses swords with him he might need medical attention himself and he stalks away enraged.
The Adventure of the Missing Student

Ferguson, Mungo. "President" of the Scottish Land Trust, a dummy company set up by master criminal Colonel Alistair McDonald, as a means of floating a gigantic swindle. A huge,

red-bearded bully who is bested by Pons in a physical encounter much to Parker's satisfaction. Later found dead in a ravine, the work of his employer when Ferguson's activities become too dangerous so his schemes.
The Adventure of the Callous Colonel

Fernchurch, Eustace. A young man, a former mason now taken on as an apprentice architect, living and working in a small town near York, accused of murdering his rival in love, Sebastian Bulstrode, by dropping a heavy mason's hammer on to Bulstrode's head from a high tower which was undergoing renovation.
The Adventure of the Hammer of Hate

Ferzetti, Count. Italian millionaire in London for an international conference. The world's greatest expert on certain areas of Chinese porcelain. "A broad, graceful-looking man with a well-trimmed black moustache, was about fifty years of age . . . fully dressed except for his jacket, he wore a red-silk dressing gown and Oriental-style slippers . . . He wiped his fleshy lips fastidiously with his napkin." [*Parker*]
The Adventure of the Ignored Idols

Fitzjohn, Inspector Robert of York C.I.D., the officer in charge of the murder inquiry into the death of Sebastian Bulstrode, a wealthy builder of Maldon, near York, of which a young architectural apprentice, Eustace Fernchurch, is accused. "A tall dark man impeccably dressed in a tweed suit and raglan overcoat." [*Parker*] He put the arrest warrant for Fernchurch in his pocket and said, "Let this unpleasantness rest for a moment . . . A few informal words over a drink would not be out of place."
The Adventure of the Hammer of Hate

Fosdyke. Sandy-haired young man with a fair complexion. A medical student at Charing Cross Hospital. He had a frank, open face and a pleasant disposition. Bubbling with good humour he laughs as Pons puts his ill-tempered colleague Fellows to flight.
The Adventure of the Missing Student

Foster, Conrad. Secretary to Sir Clive Mortimer, President of the Zoological Society, based at London Zoo. "A thin, young man with sandy hair." [*Parker*] At Sir Clive's instructions he takes notes as Superintendent Heathfield of Scotland Yard and Pons interrogate members of the Zoo staff regarding bizarre and dangerous incidents at the Zoo involving animals being let loose from their cages at dead of night.
Murder at the Zoo

Foy, Anthony. Young son of multi-millionaire industrialist Hugo Foy, who has been kidnapped in order to force his father to comply with the wishes of a South American dictator. "'A bright-faced, fair-haired child...He is the fulcrum around which this whole case revolves.'" [*Pons*]
The Adventure of the Mad Millionaire

Foy, Hugo. Millionaire living at The Boltons, Kensington, whose weird antics—which include holing out his ball on the golf course with a billiard cue; driving his Rolls Royce naked in the moonlight; and drinking ginger beer with champagne—has caused consternation at his company meetings and serious repercussions in the City. But Pons senses a purpose behind his apparent madness. First seen by Pons and Parker dressed in blue overalls in his vast garden, operating his large-scale steam railway, which is one of his principal hobbies. "He had frank, open

features, with the square, firm jaw often found in captains of industry; strong white teeth and lines of concentration at the corners of the mouth. He was an energetic, not to say dynamic figure, but I fancy I saw signs of sorrow and strain in the depths of his brown eyes and beneath the façade of his good manners." [*Parker*]
The Adventure of the Mad Millionaire

G

Gantlet, Colonel. Tenant of a mansion called Cheneys in Hampstead, where the adjoining studio was the scene of the brutal murder of the world-famous sculptor, Romane Schneider. "A tall, fussy-looking man in his early sixties with whitening hair and a frayed silver moustache. He had deep furrows at the corners of his mouth that made his yellow face look like something out of one of those plays set on tropical islands which were becoming the vogue in the West end. He wore a lightweight drill suit with military-style buttons and his brown eyes twinkled benevolently from behind silver-rimmed spectacles." [*Parker*]
The Adventure of the Baffled Baron

Garratt, Dr. Police surgeon, called in to examine the body of Elihu Cook Stanmore, a wealthy blackmailer murdered by multiple stab wounds in his Westbourne Grove flat. A tall, black-haired man wearing gold spectacles. "'. . . I should imagine few would mourn Mr. Stanmore's passing. In my duties as a police surgeon I have seen many things, but I cannot say I shed any tears during my examination this morning.'" [*Dr. Garratt*]
The Adventure of the Six Gold Doubloons

Gear. Young, slim, frightened man with a black moustache, employed by the bankers Danlop and Flinton. Wearing a dark suit. "'I was asked to collect this pouch from one of our Swiss customers and deliver it to the Count.'" [*Gear*]
The Adventure of the Ignored Idols

George. "A little, wizened man wearing a dark overcoat and a battered check cap was standing in a gap in the hedge. He hastily put the carcass of a rabbit in his pocket as we drew abreast." [*Parker*]
The Adventure of the Hound of Hell

Glaister, Detective Inspector of Scotland Yard. "A door in the far corner of the room opened and a tall, frosty-haired man came in. He looked incuriously at the Superintendent…'I would like you to take a statement from Mr. Hardcastle here. He is the man we wish to question in connection with this business at the Zoological Gardens. He is the client of Mr. Solar Pons, whom I believe you know.' The Inspector smiled and came over to Pons and shook his hand cordially. 'Glad to see you again, Mr. Pons.'" [*Parker*]
Murder at the Zoo

Glida and Company. Theatrical costumiers of Bond Street, London, where Pons consults the management on disguises while investigating a murder.
Death at the Metropole

Goodman, Mrs. Theodisia. Housekeeper to Jabez Kemp, a 73-year-old merchant who hanged himself in an attic in his mansion in Berkshire in 1902.
The Adventure of Buffington Old Grange

Gore-Willoughby, Captain Nigel. British Army officer escorting Miss Evelyn Smithers of Maldon, Yorkshire, through York Station on a weekend trip to meet his parents. "The tall man with angry eyes and a clipped moustache, dressed in a captain's uniform, looked at us with well-bred indifference." [*Parker*]
The Adventure of the Hammer of Hate

Grace. Parlour maid in the service of Horace Oldfield, a Berkshire accountant at Buffington Old Grange; a nervous girl, much given to worrying about legends of hauntings and suicide in the old house. But despite this she has seen nothing of the sinister incidents surrounding the Oldfield family.
The Adventure of Buffington Old Grange

Granger, Jocelyn. Secretary to Septimus Grimpton of Penderel Lodge, Penderel Parva, near Bath. A thin, sandy-haired man with even white teeth. "He had an alert expression on his face and his body was coiled like a tense spring so that he reminded me of nothing so much as a wire-haired terrier." [*Parker*]
The Adventure of the Shaft of Death

Grieves, Sir James. Deputy Curator of the Mentmore Museum in London. Distinguished archaeologist who unearthed precious Chinese porcelain, now housed in the gallery at the Museum which bears his name. "A tall, spare man in a black frock-coat with a gold eyeglass in his right eye . . . With his old-fashioned white stock; silk cravat; and red carnation in his button-hole he looked like a startled stork." [*Parker*]
The Adventure of the Ignored Idols

Grimpton, Ephrosina (1780-1855). Grandmother of Septimus

Grimpton of Penderel Lodge, Penderel Parva, near Bath, interred in a mausoleum in the grounds of the estate, where a former convict, Abel Stokoe, had been murdered. The inscription on her tomb was a quotation from Fitzgerald's translation of *The Rubáiyát of Omar Khayyám*: Turn Down An Empty Glass.
The Adventure of the Shaft of Death

Grimpton, Septimus. A wealthy landowner of Penderel Lodge, Penderel Parva, near Bath, who is plagued by sinister occurrences at his estate, culminating in a brutal murder. "He was a man of some seventy years of age, though of vigorous aspect and with a rosy complexion almost like that of a child. He had snow-white hair which hung over his forehead in careless wisps, and his tufted eyebrows waved in comic manner behind his gold pince-nez as he talked. One of the most striking things about him was his vivid blue eyes which made his face come wonderfully alive." [*Parker*]
The Adventure of the Shaft of Death

Gimpton, Thaddeus. Younger brother of Septimus Grimpton, wealthy owner of Penderel Lodge, near Bath. A man of about sixty ". . . dressed impeccably in a grey suit with a blue bow-tie. The family resemblance was striking and I was not surprised when our host introduced him as his younger brother, Thaddeus . . . and though his thick hair was liberally sprinkled with silver, he exhibited none of the scholarly traits of his brother." [*Parker*] When being introduced, he told Pons, "I shall find it fascinating to watch so distinguished a practitioner of the forensic art at work."
The Adventure of the Shaft of Death

Grimstone, Jethro. Brother of Silas Grimstone, a wealthy but miserly recluse of Grimstone Manor, a lonely house on the Gravesend marshes. Former business partner of the City firm owned by the two brothers. Jethro objected to his brother's miserliness and they quarrelled. Silas Grimstone announced to the City that he had bought his brother out of the firm and that the latter had emigrated to Australia.
The Adventure of the Crawling Horror

Grimstone, John. Young man who returns from Australia to avenge the murder of his father by his treacherous business partner. A pleasant young man from abroad, staying at The Harrow Inn at Stavely, on the Gravesend marshes under the name of Norman Knight, while carrying out a masquerade to terrify the real murderer.
The Adventure of the Crawling Horror

Grimstone, Silas. Wealthy but miserly City businessman of Grimstone Manor on the Gravesend marshes in Kent. A man of about seventy with a face lined with deep furrows and dressed in a mildewed overcoat and had his shoes tied with string. "His mouth had a cadaverous and lopsided look. I found out later that this resulted from his wearing a set of second-hand dentures which did not fit him properly. As Pons had so properly observed, few men had ever existed with such miserly habits. His rimless pince-nez had evidently been garnered from the same source as the dentures…Altogether, he was one of the most remarkable specimens I ever beheld and the more I saw of him the more my initial impression of unpleasantness and shiftiness were reinforced." [*Parker*]
The Adventure of the Crawling Horror

Grimstone, Miss Sylvia. Niece of miserly millionaire Silas Grimstone, who acts as his housekeeper at Grimstone Manor on the lonely Gravesend marshes. A highly-strung, grey-haired woman, interested in flowers, plants and nature. A woman with "…a square, strong face and her features were quite pleasant when she smiled, which she did briefly at the introductions." [*Parker*]
The Adventure of the Crawling Horror

Grunwin, Ebeneezer. Murderer, who had beaten a man to death, mentioned *en passant* by Pons to Parker when the latter is astonished to find his friend belabouring a bolster with a walking stick, in order to prove the man's guilt. "'The East End is well rid of another scoundrel.'" [*Pons*]
The Adventure of the Phantom Face

H

Hambleton, Mrs. Housekeeper and companion to Miss Emily Schneider, a wealthy but miserly old woman at The Pines, near Stonecross in Essex, who is murdered one dark, snowy night when she went out to replenish her firewood at a potting shed in her garden. She "…had a rather fine, but sad face, as though she had found life disappointingly short of her expectations." [*Parker*]
The Adventure of the Hound of Hell

Hamilton. Plain-clothes ex-police officer, a burly former ex-boxer, who helps Pons and Parker, together with other police officers, to tackle a murderer in the foyer of the Metropole Hotel in the Strand.
Death at the Metropole

Hannah. Old Housekeeper to Mrs. Stuart and her daughter, Miss Elizabeth Stuart, who live in the Rectory at Grassington, near Haslemere in Surrey, which is disturbed by bizarre and mysterious manifestations, which had apparently caused the death of the Rector, the Rev. Stuart. "A cheerful, middle-aged woman with her hair scraped back in a bun." [*Parker*]
The Adventure of the Haunted Rectory

Harbinger, Mrs. Grace. An imposing-looking woman of about seventy with snow-white hair and rouged cheeks. "The effect was bizarre against the whiteness of her complexion. She wore a strange-looking gown, mauve in colour, belted in at the waist like that of a mediaeval chatelaine. Around her neck was suspended a gold chain bearing a curiously shaped gold locket." [*Parker*] For years she has been writing letters to Dr. Glyn Campbell, the Rector of Shap in Surrey, urging him to open the sealed spire above the bell chamber of his church of St. Mary where she asserts that the Scroll of Thoth is hidden, the contents of which could save the world. "'Her mind is a little affected, I think. The thing is a confounded nuisance, and a national newspaper got hold of the story some years ago.'" [*Dr. Glyn Campbell*]
The Sealed Spire Mystery

Hardcastle, Hezekiah. Ancestor of murdered millionaire Simon Hardcastle who was found near the ancient family graveyard on his estate in Buckinghamshire, a short distance from the tomb of Hezekiah.
The Adventure of the Devil's Claw

Hardcastle, John. Underkeeper of the Lion House at London Zoo, suspected of being the mysterious intruder who opens

cages at the zoo at dead of night and lets dangerous animals loose. "A young man of about twenty-eight entered, with tousled fair curly hair. He was roughly-dressed in a dark blue uniform but there was an air of such honesty and decency about him, notwithstanding his haggard and distraught expression, that I warmed to him immediately." [*Parker*]
Murder at the Zoo

Hardcastle, Simon. An immensely wealthy man with a great estate, Chalcroft Manor, in Buckinghamshire, but mean and reclusive, as though afraid of something in his past. He is found dead near the old family graveyard on a bitterly cold winter's night and at first it is thought he died of heart failure, but it turns out to be murder. The mystery is even more complex as it transpires that a thin needle-like instrument has penetrated his heart without passing through his clothing. In his sixties he could still tear a pack of cards in half with his bare hands. "A formidable customer, Parker." Pons observes. Despite his years he could pass for a much younger man with his jet-black hair sprinkled with grey.
The Adventure of the Devil's Claw

Harewood, Mrs. Housekeeper to millionaire financier Hugo Foy at his mansion in The Boltons. "A middle-aged woman with greying hair and with a manner of great dignity and authority almost glided into the room." [*Parker*]
The Adventure of the Mad Millionaire

Hawthorne, Lady Mary. Socialite engaged to be married to the Duke of Leinster, who is being blackmailed by a man called Elihu Cook Stanmore, a cunning criminal who is later found stabbed to death in his London flat. A beautiful, dark-haired

woman with an imperious manner which was marred by her state of agitation. "For all her poise and the fact that she was in her own house she reminded me of nothing so much as a small animal menaced by a snake." [*Parker*]
The Adventure of the Six Gold Doubloons

Hayling, Miss Jennifer of Wortley Hall, Norfolk and Inverness. "A tall, fair-haired girl of about twenty-five, whose pink cheeks and flashing eyes bespoke some degree of agitation." [*Parker*] An orphan, whose parents were killed in an "accident" engineered by a master criminal. She wore a thick jersey dress which clung to her full figure. On her head she wore a West End milliner's version of what passed in the South for a Scottish lady's tam-o'-shanter with a knitted bobble.
The Adventure of the Callous Colonel

Heathfield, Superintendent Stanley of Scotland Yard. Immaculately groomed, military-looking figure, with a clipped grey moustache and well manicured hands. A gentleman police officer of the old school. "He looked more like a dapper Army officer than ever." [*Parker*]
Murder at the Zoo

Helstone, Miss Helen Jane. A tall, slim, blonde girl who is engaged as a governess by Mr. Clinton Basden of The Priory, Clitherington in Surrey, where she becomes the centre of bizarre and frightening events, involving murderous foreigners who attempt her life; a secluded wing of the mansion from which she is barred; and two very strange children who do not seen to understand English.
The Adventure of the Frightened Governess

Hibbert. Manager of the Metropole Hotel in the Strand where a savage murder has been committed. Arrested by Inspector Jamison of Scotland Yard on suspicion of having committed the crime. A large man with glossy black hair and wearing elegant clothes.
Death at the Metropole

Higgins, Judson. Rare book dealer who visits the Rector of the late Rev. Stuart at Grassington, near Haslemere in Surrey, where a sale of the late incumbent's library is being held. "A short, bearded man with a pronounced limp... Though well dressed in expensive clothes and wearing white gloves, there was something sly and furtive in his appearance which I didn't take to. He had cold grey eyes beneath his whitening eyebrows and his thick hair was liberally dusted with silver. He had a high, mincing pedantic voice and was engaged in a shrill altercation with his companion." [*Parker*]
The Adventure of the Haunted Rectory

Hobbs, Jethro. Escaped convict who is helping to recover a large sum of money, the proceeds of a major robbery at a Norwich bank three years earlier. Hobbs and his fellow criminal Blakeney are using Norwich Cathedral as a dead letter drop, part of a scheme headed by master criminal Karl Kramer and his wife Elise.
The Adventure of the Verger's Thumb

Hodgson. Keeper of the more dangerous animals at London Zoo. "A thickset, amiable-looking man in Zoo uniform, evidently the person with the keys." [*Parker*] The man in charge of the staff locker room and recreation area at the Zoo. A picture

of his "young lady" falls from his locker and Pons congratulates him on his choice.
Murder at the Zoo

Hooper. Press photographer from the Shap and Stapleford *Chronicle*. A thickset man wearing a black homburg hat and carrying a heavy plate camera. "'Where is this sensation you promised us, Mr. Dabson?'" [*Hooper*]
The Sealed Spire Mystery

Horrabin, Godfrey. Secretary to the murdered sculptor Romane Schneider at his Hampstead studio. A dark-haired man of about thirty "...with an ashen-white face and full lips from which the colour had now fled...He was of an enormous height, well over six feet tall." [*Parker*] Horrabin had been the sculptor's secretary for the past five years. He says of his employer, "Like most artists he was extremely temperamental. He had been involved in some tremendous arguments and on occasion in actual physical violence."
The Adventure of the Baffled Baron

Hoskins. Gardener at the estate of Septimus Grimpton of Penderel Parva, near Bath, who is able to assist Pons in his inquiries into the death of Abel Stokoe, a former convict, found murdered in the grounds. "A middle-aged, stolid sort of person with a fringe of greying whiskers which gave his face a nineteenth century aspect." [*Parker*]
The Adventure of the Shaft of Death

Hugo, Duke of Leinster. An aristocrat engaged to Lady Mary Hawthorne, who is implicated in the murder of Elihu Cook Stan-

more, who is blackmailing the Duke's fiancée for a cache of stolen love letters written during the First World War. A tall, distinguished-looking man, wearing a handsome Van Dyke beard, he had on a green baize apron over his light grey suit, while cleaning ancient weapons in his gun room as Pons is questioning him.
The Adventure of the Six Cold Doubloons

Hound of Hell. Family heirloom of Miss Emily Schneider, a miserly but intensely rich old woman of The Pines, near Stonecross in Essex. "A large silver effigy, exquisitely fashioned, of an enormous dog, standing on its hind-legs, savaging a man who is attempting to climb a tree. It is engaged in tearing his throat out and is a rather dreadful and terrifying ornament, though of superb craftsmanship, and believed to be of Eastern European origin." [*Parker*] But it brought bad luck to Miss Schneider, who is found murdered in a potting shed in a remote corner of her garden one dark winter's night.
The Adventure of the Hound of Hell

Housekeeper. Unnamed servant to Andrew and Sarita Peters at a mediaeval manor house, Yeomans, on the estate of Chalcroft in Buckinghamshire. "The housekeeper, a motherly-looking woman in her early fifties, had strong nerves and was a great support to her mistress." [*Parker*]
The Adventure of the Devil's Claw

Housekeeper. Unnamed servant of the Rev. George Neville Stoner, Rector of Chislington. "The elderly woman looked at us doubtfully. She wore a thick, quilted dressing gown and had evidently been on the point of retiring." [*Parker*]
The Sealed Spire Mystery

Hoxton Builder. "'Might there be some notes for me in this business, Pons?' I asked. My companion smiled. 'I fear not, Parker. It is too mundane for your chronicles and though "The Adventure of the Hoxton Builder" might raise considerable expectation in the reader, I fear it would fall far short of your best efforts in the field. Though Scotland Yard will be glad to learn that Mr. Wilson is in the net.'" [*Parker*] [*See also under "Wilson, Jabez"*]
Murder at the Zoo

I

Ironside, Mr. Stationmaster at Charing Cross station, who assists Pons and Parker by providing an office high up in the building where they can survey the left-luggage counter where a kidnapper will be hoping to claim a parcel containing £15,000.
The Adventure of the Missing Student

J

Jamison, C.I.D. Inspector of Scotland Yard. Ineffectual small man who appears in many of Pons' cases, usually critical or dismissive of the great detective's theories but usually ends up baffled and sometimes has to enlist Pons' help in particularly difficult cases. However, he has his uses, Pons tells Parker on more than one occasion "'I thought the deductive reasoning behind it too brilliant for Jamison.'" [*Parker*]
The Adventure of the Hammer of Hate

Jeffries. A tall, black-bearded man, an imposing figure. "He

was dressed in a suit of shaggy tweeds and he looked at us in a most unfriendly manner from beneath beetling black brows." [*Parker*] Barrel-chested servant to the Duke of Leinster, suspected of being implicated in the murder of a blackmailer.
The Adventure of the Six Gold Doubloons

Jeffries, Gordon. A member of the Council of the Zoological Society of London. A tall man in a dark frock-coat and "... with the white mane of hair which made him look like a musician bowed stiffly." [*Parker*] Choleric character who is outraged by the activities of the so-called "Phantom of the Zoo", as newspapers dubbed him, who is causing damage and releasing dangerous wild animals from their cages during the night. "'A detestable man, Mr. Pons... But brilliant in his field. He has many enemies,'" Sir Clive Mortimer, President of the Zoological Society, tells Pons.
Murder at the Zoo

Jenkin, Mrs. Housekeeper to Dr. Glyn Campbell, Rector of Shap in Surrey. "A pleasant, middle-aged woman with a worried face." [*Parker*]
The Sealed Spire Mystery

Jenkins, Gaffer. An old gypsy living in a caravan near Penderel Parva, near Bath. He dies, his fellows at the encampment burning his caravan and all his belongings; but one member of the band, Mordecai Smith, who throws a knife Jenkins had lent him into the river Avon, is suspected of murder by Bath Police.
The Adventure of the Shaft of Death

Jessel, Tobias. Old man found dead on the Gravesend Marshes

in suspicious circumstances. Much addicted to drink and a patient of Dr. Strangeways of Stavely who told Solar Pons, "'He is far too frequently in the four-ale bar of The Harrow and I told him so.'" [*Dr. Strangeways*] "A bright-eyed old man whose red nose and broken-veined eyes bespoke long indulgence in liquor . . . He had a fringe of white beard and his nautical-style peaked cap and thick blue clothing gave him the look of a seaman." [*Parker*]
The Adventure of the Crawling Horror

Johnson, Horace. Pseudonym for Solar Pons who wishes to meet millionaire financier Hugo Foy, whose strange conduct is so alarming his shareholders that Foy's neighbour, Colonel Mortimer, has asked Pons to investigate.
The Adventure of the Mad Millionaire

Johnson, Mrs. Pons and Parker's amiable landlady at 7B Praed Street, whose "well scrubbed face" often appears round the door of their chambers, bearing a tray containing nourishing delicacies, or announcing a stranger who has a dark tale of bizarre or murderous happenings, which often plunges them into dangerous situations. After a particularly good meal Pons remarks, "'You have excelled yourself, Mrs. Johnson.' The good-humoured features of Mrs. Johnson relaxed in a broad smile. 'Good of you to say so, Mr. Pons,' she murmured." [*Parker*]
The Adventure of the Surrey Sadist

K

Karswell, Mrs. Housekeeper to Colonel d'Arcy at The Briars on the Essex marshes. "A middle-aged, stately woman with

reserved manners which concealed great warmth of character." [*Parker*]
The Adventure of the Ipi Idol

Kellaway. Manager of the Royal George Hotel in Norwich, where Pons and Parker are staying for a brief holiday before being involved in a bizarre mystery.
The Adventure of the Verger's Thumb

Kellett, Dr. Medical man called in by Bath Police to ascertain the cause of death of Abel Stokoe, a former convict found murdered in the grounds of Penderel Lodge, Penderel Parva, near Bath. "'A massive wound over the heart... Apparently inflicted with some semi-sharp instrument wielded with considerable force. Dr. Kellett said it was incredible Stokoe had survived so long.'" [*Septimus Grimpton*]
The Adventure of the Shaft of Death

Kemp, Jabez. "The Squire of Buffington Grange", a miserly old man found hanging in the attic of the mediaeval mansion in 1902. The 73-year-old former tea merchant had always shunned his fellow townsfolk.
The Adventure of Buffington Old Grange

Kemp, Major Alan. Tall, fair-haired former Army officer, a friend of Miss Elizabeth Stuart of The Old Rectory, Grassington, near Haslemere in Surrey. "With his sandy moustache, faded blue eyes and fresh cheeks he seemed the very epitome of the retired military man. A red setter slouched on the tiled floor at his feet. Kemp wore a suit of well-cut tweeds, his dark blue shirt, open at the throat, adding an informal touch, while his

right hand toyed casually with a leather dog leash as we talked." [*Parker*]
The Adventure of the Haunted Rectory

Knight, Norman. A pleasant, fresh-faced, broad-shouldered young man staying at the Harrow Inn at Stavely on the Gravesend marshes in Kent. "A Colonial gentleman, I believe," the elderly waiter tells Pons. "He has been here some time and goes daily to business in Gravesend." He has strained a ligament in his leg walking about the countryside and walks with a limp.
The Adventure of the Crawling Horror

Koch, Karl of Stuttgart. A tall, bearded man in his forties, staying at the Royal George Hotel in Norwich, where Pons and Parker are taking a brief holiday. But in reality he is a master criminal planning the retrieval of a large sum of stolen money. [*See "Karl Kramer of Zurich", which is his real identity*]
The Adventure of the Verger's Thumb

Kramer, Elise. Wife of Karl Kramer, master criminal staying at the Royal George Hotel in Norwich, under an assumed name. A slim girl, with a white, strained face, carrying a heavy black suitcase when she is apprehended. "Her eyes were burning savagely as she stared at Pons." [*Parker*]
The Adventure of the Verger's Thumb

Kramer, Karl of Zurich. Master criminal staying at a Norwich hotel with his wife Elise, under an assumed name while attempting to recover a large cache of stolen money with the aid of his wife and two escaped convicts, the latter being the only people who know Karl and Elise attempt their escape

aboard a motorboat down the River Yare at night. [*See "Koch, Karl of Stuttgart", which is his assumed name*]
The Adventure of the Verger's Thumb

Kranko. Balkan terrorist shot dead by Lyndon Parker, as he attempted to shoot the doctor and Pons in the grounds of The Priory, Clitherlington, Surrey, in a night raid on the house in an attempt to assassinate Princess Sonia. "'You need not distress yourself, Dr. Parker. Krenko was one of the most murderous scoundrels who ever walked in shoe-leather. You have done Dresdania a great service tonight, doctor, for which she cannot thank you enough.'" [*Prince Mirko*]
The Adventure of the Frightened Governess

Krish, Dr. Arpad. Paragonian Ambassador in London, implicated in a plot involving kidnapping and extortion by a terrorist called "Tiger" Marceau, shot dead by Dr. Parker in a siege of a locked room in a Surrey mansion. Following Pons' intervention, Krish is declared *persona non grata* and deported from the country.
The Adventure of the Mad Millionaire

Kroll, Baron Ennesfred. Master criminal who is the great enemy of Solar Pons. He works quietly behind the scenes and sends Pons a message through the post, unsigned and in block capitals: MR PONS—YOUR ROUND I THINK. WE SHALL MEET AGAIN. "Solar Pons sat back at the table and lit his pipe. 'He is the most dangerous man in Europe, Parker. I would give a great deal to have netted him.' And his eyes looked beyond the homely commons of our room and gazed bleakly into the void." [*Parker*]
The Adventure of the Baffled Baron

Kronfeld, Sir Hercules. Famous sculptor, a deadly rival of his fellow sculptor Romane Schneider, murdered in his Hampstead studio. After a number of heated arguments, the two men had actually attacked one another's sculptures and demolished portions of them. "A gigantic figure with a beard heavily flecked with grey. Contrary to my expectations he was elegantly dressed in a light grey suit and blue bow-tie and his fresh complexion and careful grooming completely belied the conventional picture of the artist. He was leaning carelessly against a winged female nude, evidently one of his own works, while he carried on a murmured conversation with an elegant young man with patent leather hair and a soulful expression 'My accountant...All the same these young fellows nowadays. They seem to think we're in this for art's sake... It is always interesting for a master in one field to meet a *maître* in another, Mr. Pons.'"
[*Parker*]
The Adventure of the Baffled Baron

L

LaFontaine, Charles Brinsley. Forger and all-round master criminal, who has thrown down a challenge to Scotland Yard, warning them that he will break into the Mentmore Museum in London and steal the famous Baku Idols, a set of gold effigies which are worth a fortune. "One of the most consummate scoundrels who ever lived yet his audacity is so unbounded and his villainies perpetrated with such style that one cannot help admiring him," Pons tells Parker. "We have crossed swords only once and on that memorable occasion he escaped." LaFontaine is a master of disguise and Pons continues, "He is a considerable artist, seldom uses violence, robs only large institutions and

organisations which can well afford it and I must confess I have a grudging admiration for him."
The Adventure of the Ignored Idols

Leibnitz. Portrait photographer in the Strand, London. "'On our visit to Chapel Court Jamison showed me a scrap of one of the photographs. It bore a few fragments of lettering and I was able to identify it as the cipher of Leibnitz, the portrait photographer in the Strand. Jamison went there and their records clinched the matter.'" [*Pons*]
The Adventure of the Horrified Heiress

Lennard, Mr. Night receptionist at the Metropole Hotel in the Strand, where a murder has taken place. "... a thin, sallow man with silver hair cut *en brosse*. He wore a faded blue suit and somehow looked all of a part with the Metropole. His gold pince-nez hung by a frayed velvet ribbon from his lapel and he peered anxiously about him ..." [*Parker*]
Death at the Metropole

Loder, Colonel Francis. Curator of the Mentmore Museum in London where a set of rare Baku Idols is in danger of being stolen by a consummate thief and forger, Charles Brinsley LaFontaine. The Colonel is "a handsome, silver-haired man in a well-cut grey suit with a wine-red bow-tie hanging like a bright butterfly beneath his chin ... He was both courteous and brisk and I formed a very favourable first impression of him." [*Parker*]
The Adventure of the Ignored Idols

Lovelace, Wednesday. Son-in-law of Jethro Stringer, "The Mad Corinthian of Netherhampton", who had presented a set of

special pipes to Solar Pons for his work on his father-in-law's case. Mentioned by Lyndon Parker, who is complaining about the smoke emitted from one of the set.
The Adventure of the Six Gold Doubloons

M

Mackney, Johnnie. Young boy living in Tidewater, Essex, where murders have been committed. His mother was angry because she thought he had lost an expensive air pistol and a carnival mask in a local doctor's surgery, but the items had been stolen by the murderer.
The Adventure of the Phantom Face

Mackney, Mrs. Mother of Johnnie Mackney, whose air pistol and carnival mask have been stolen by a cunning murderer while the pair were sitting in a crowded doctor's surgery. But his mother is angry because she believes he had been careless and lost them.
The Adventure of the Phantom Face

Mair, Professor. Distinguished savant brutally murdered "in the most sickening circumstances" in his locked study at his mansion in Highbury. An expert in Chinese ceramics, he had retired from the British Museum some years before. Mair, a man of about seventy, with a snow-white beard, suffered from arthritis and intended to sell his house and move to a country with a drier climate. He had been killed with a steel-tipped javelin, wielded with tremendous force, which had pinned his body to the floor.
The Adventure of the Perplexed Photographer

Mainland. Lawyer's clerk in Lincoln's Inn, who was telephoned and told to dispose of the practice by a criminal called Reginald Ashley Fawkes, who had assumed the murdered man's identity.
The Adventure of the Horrified Heiress

Mandlville, Mrs. Elderly housekeeper to Aramis Tregorran, famous society portrait painter of Chelsea, who is accused of murdering his wife when she was sitting for her portrait in his studio.
The Adventure of the Singular Sandwich

Mannering, Captain. Estate manager for Silas Grimpton, a wealthy scholar of Penderel Lodge, Penderel Parva, near Bath. A huge, red-faced man with a yellow moustache, dressed in a hairy tweed jacket and riding breeches. Violent tempered, addicted to drink as evident from his bloodshot blue eyes.
The Adventure of the Shaft of Death

Mantalini, Madam. Circus performer, described as "The Woman with a Thousand Talents!", who performed at Melton in Berkshire in the earlier part of the twentieth century. Billed as a strong-woman, acrobat, clever mime and ventriloquist. "'She was a lady of many parts, Pons.'" [*Parker*]
The Adventure of Buffington Old Grange

Marceau, "Tiger". Terrorist who is normally resident in the South American republic of Paragonia. "'About the most dangerous man in South America . . . A born adventurer and saboteur, the son of a French father and an American Indian woman. He has been behind nine-tenths of the mischief in that unhappy corner of the world for the past dozen years or so.'" [*Pons*]
The Adventure of the Mad Millionaire

Marcus. London solicitor who is in charge of Miss Evelyn Brentwood's late parents' estate at The Priory, Peas Pleasance, in Surrey. "'Though Uncle Edmund was my guardian, Mr. Marcus had control of the estate in trust for me when I became of age . . . My father owned a rubber plantation in the East and there was money in the family before that. I suppose there is a good deal of money coming to me, one way or the other, but I have never thought much about it.'" [*Evelyn Brentwood*]
The Adventure of the Horrified Heiress

Masterson, Miss Sybil. Fiancée of Hugh Mulvane, nephew of Simon Hardcastle and heir to his murdered uncle's vast estate at Chalcroft Manor near the village of Chalcroft in Buckinghamshire. "A tall, slim girl whose fair hair hung down almost to her shoulders . . . with steady grey eyes, fine teeth beneath the full, sensuous lips and an agreeable way of laughing which I found engaging . . . she wore a long, semi-formal gown which suited her full-breasted figure and she presented a picture of animation . . . her hair flying as she directed her gaze first in one direction and then another as the conversation went round." [*Parker*]
The Adventure of the Devil's Claw

Matthews, Sergeant. Officer of Chalcroft Police in Buckinghamshire, set by his superiors to guard Hugh Mulvane, the heir to a vast estate whose life may be in danger.
The Adventure of the Devil's Claw

McDonald, Colonel Alistair. "'Explorer, big-game hunter, stalker, collector of esoteric objects, he also has regrettable criminal tendencies which have made him a good deal of money. At

the present time I should class him as the third most dangerous man in Europe . . . In fact he has twice tried to kill me, the most recent occasion being yesterday . . . Oh, yes, the Colonel has a great deal to him . . . He is as much at home among the shelves of the library and the higher philosophy as he is at a rough shoot or on one of the crags of his native heath.'" [*Pons*] McDonald lives at Ardrossan Lodge, about twenty miles from Aberdeen. A scholar who has written, among other studies, *The Dimensions of Ecstasy*. A tall, military figure . . . "A smartly-dressed but almost emaciated old man with a gaunt face, hook-nose and iron-grey moustache. The only things alive in the dead white face were the burning yellow eyes which were fixed unwinkingly upon Pons . . . 'Well, Mr. Pons,' he said in a low, soft voice. 'We meet at last.'" [*Parker*]
The Adventure of the Callous Colonel

McMurdo, Mr. Proprietor of a large toyshop in the village of Tidewater in Essex, which sells, among its stock, hideous carnival masks similar to a bizarre "Phantom Face" which has been frightening people in the neighbourhood late at night, culminating in at least one death. A short, bearded man with a helpful attitude to his customers, both children and adults alike.
The Adventure of the Phantom Face

Meakins. One-eyed former Willesden plumber who works as a porter at the Metropole Hotel in the Strand where murder has been committed. An old soldier, he had a wound ribbon on the jacket of his uniform. "He was indeed a pitiable sight, dishevelled and out of breath, his white hair fallen over his eyes, his dark blue uniform only half-buttoned . . . He had a gaunt, rugged face in which deep lines, either of suffering or caused

by some disease, ran from his nose down to the corners of his mouth. As Pons had surmised, he had something wrong with his right eye for the eyelid was all puckered down over what I suspected to be an empty socket." [*Parker*] "'Though I was well over the age for the Army, I lost my eye at Ypres, doctor . . . It is a poor substitute but I wear the ribbon just the same.'" [*Meakins*]
Death at the Metropole

Mecker, Dr. Registrar at Charing Cross Hospital. "A thin, pleasant-looking man with a small black goatee." [*Parker*]
The Adventure of the Missing Student

Metcalfe. Chauffeur to Colonel John d'Arcy of The Briars, Essex. "'I have taken the liberty . . . of begging the loan of one of your cars from your chauffeur round at the stable wing. He seems an amiable fellow and readily agreed, with the proviso that I obtain your authority.'" [*Pons*] "'Certainly, Mr. Pons . . . Metcalfe is a stickler for protocol, I am afraid.'" [*Colonel d'Arcy*]
The Adventure of the Ipi Idol

Miggs. Head Verger at Norwich Cathedral where strange happenings have perturbed the church authorities, leading Miggs to seek out Pons and Parker, holidaying in the City, to convey the Dean's request for help. "A short, rather shabby-looking little old man in dark clothes" who tells Pons he had a terrifying ordeal in a side chapel of the cathedral when a gargoyle "bit" him in the thumb, drawing blood. A former shoe repairer who had been in service at the cathedral for many years. "'He has a great sense of propriety and is one of the most zealous

guardians of the Cathedral and its fabric... but... has odd little ways.'" [*Canon Howard Stacey*]
The Adventure of the Verger's Thumb

Mirko, Prince of Dresdania. A tall, bearded man with brown eyes and an imperious manner. A high-ranking member of the government guarding H.R.H. Princess Sonia in a Surrey mansion, where she is being treated for a heart condition by a leading Harley Street specialist.
The Adventure of the Frightened Governess

Moffat, Clarence. Private secretary to Professor Mair, a distinguished academic murdered in a locked room at his mansion in Highbury. "A thin, fussy-looking, middle-aged man in a rusty black frock coat and striped trousers... thin strands of black hair shaped carefully across but not concealing the baldness of his head." [*Parker*]
The Adventure of the Perplexed Photographer

Mooney. Senior C.I.D. officer in charge of preliminary investigation into the murder of famous Sculptor Romane Schneider in his studio in Hampstead. The door was locked and there was no key. There were no signs of forcible entry and the locked skylight was twenty feet from the floor, Mooney tells Pons. Mooney's "heavy black moustache which stood out like a great bar of shadow on his alert, intelligent face." [*Parker*]
The Adventure of the Baffled Baron

Morgan, Inspector of Bath C.I.D. called in to lead the police hunt for the murderer of a vagrant found dying with his chest crushed in, near a mausoleum on the estate of Silas Grimpton

of Penderel Lodge, Penderel Parva, near Bath. Pons says Morgan comes from the Rhondda Valley, is a member of the Metropolitan Police Hockey Club and still remains a member; that he formerly served in the Metropolitan Police, was an enthusiastic rugby player in earlier years when he had his nose broken twice. All facts verified by Morgan himself.
The Adventure of the Shaft of Death

Mortiboys, Horace of Epping. Murderer who carried out the crime in Epping Forest with the sound of the gunshot muffled by a cushion, mentioned *en passant* by Pons. "I fancy my theory will stand up in court. Sufficiently, I trust, to put paid to the unspeakable activities of the abominable Mr. Horace Mortiboys of Epping."
The Adventure of the Callous Colonel

Morticott. Gigantic seven feet tall Head Attendant at the Egyptian Museum in London. Wounded in the 1914-18 war, he walks with a limp. "The smart blue uniform he wore seemed only to emphasise his lop-sided appearance as he shuffled along the corridor toward us, dragging his lame left foot. His enormous hands dangled limply and the sardonic face looked particularly sinister because of a partial paralysis of one side, which pulled the muscles down; no doubt the result of his wound. Yet the entire impression of this giant was one of enormous power." [*Parker*]
The Adventure of the Cursed Curator

Mortimer, Miss Claire. An Essex landowner's daughter who becomes engaged to Colonel John d'Arcy of a nearby estate known as The Briars, and who supports him admirably when

d'Arcy is faced with a dangerous scheme to control his estate and fortune. "A slender, dark-haired girl with wide blue eyes." [*Parker*]
The Adventure of the Ipi Idol

Mortimer, Colonel. Peppery, retired Army officer living close to a millionaire financier, Hugo Foy, with whom he has invested a great deal of money in the latter's companies. He brings a bizarre tale to Pons and Parker's cosy sitting room, involving the millionaire's mad antics verging on insanity; which include driving his Rolls-Royce naked in the moonlight; playing golf with a billiard cue; and drinking champagne with ginger beer. Mortimer fears a market crash but Pons senses far more sinister causes behind the millionaire's apparent madness.
The Adventure of the Mad Millionaire

Mortimer, Mrs. Mother of Claire Mortimer. "A matronly lady with greying hair." [*Parker*] Almost as handsome as her daughter "despite her seniority".
The Adventure of the Ipi Idol

Mortimer, Sir Clive. President of the Zoological Society of London. Fiery little man who glares belligerently at people. He has a pink face ". . . almost like a child's, with feathery white hair and a thin smear of moustache like lather. With his old-fashioned frock-coat, his dark raincoat and the black wideawake hat he carried in his hand, he resembled an illustration out of a nineteenth-century volume by Dickens or Wilkie Collins." [*Parker*]
Murder at the Zoo

Moules, Dr. Hugo. Berkshire coroner who returned a verdict of suicide on Jabez Kemp, a miserly recluse who hanged himself in an attic at his mansion, Buffington Old Grange, in 1902.
The Adventure of Buffington Old Grange

Mullett. Head gardener at Kew Gardens, arrested for murder. Pons had kept watch for the hardened criminal so that he could be apprehended. "'Croci already out at Kew...Ah, Parker, if you had been communing with nature as I have been recently, you would not think it quite so remarkable. My vigil in the Paxton glass-houses and my subsequent apprehension of Mullett have made me more appreciative of the extraordinary flora of this planet.'" [*Pons*] "'I thought the deductive reasoning behind it too brilliant for Jamison.'" [*Parker*]
The Adventure of the Hammer of Hate

Mulvane, Hugh of Chalcroft Manor in Buckinghamshire, where murder and mysterious events have terrified the local population. A teacher at Chalcroft College and the only beneficiary of his murdered uncle, the immensely wealthy Simon Hardcastle. A burly man with a bald patch around the crown of his head, the centre of a fringe of sandy-coloured hair. He wears thick pebble glasses and is dressed in country tweeds and smokes strong cheroots. "'You are an artistic and some-what impractical man, though you have a very practical streak; you are in your early thirties though you look older; you have been a pupil or are almost certainly a teacher at Chalcroft College; I should incline to the latter due to certain obvious indications; you are a heavy smoker; have charge of the College library in addition to your other duties; ride a bicycle about the countryside a good deal, though you could

certainly afford a car; and do your own photographic developing.'" [*Pons*]
The Adventure of the Devil's Claw

N

Nazreel Pasha, Achmed. Distinguished archaeologist at the Cairo Museum. Mentioned *en passant*, who assigned a high-ranking Egyptian police officer to accompany Horatio Biggs, Curator of the Egyptian Museum in London, to guard treasures from the Valley of the Kings on loan from Cairo for a major exhibition in London.
The Adventure of the Cursed Curator

O

O'Hara, President. Head of the state of Paragonia. Corrupt dictator who employs terrorist "Tiger" Marceau in his criminal activities to increase his wealth at the expense of his people. He and the Paragonian Ambassador in London, Arpad Krish, were both sent to prison awaiting trial.
The Adventure of the Mad Millionaire

Oldale, Inspector George of Melton C.I.D. in Berkshire, an efficient officer who adds his authority to Pons and Parker in capturing two cunning criminals in a deserted mansion. "A tall, vigorous man in his mid-forties with jet-black hair and an alert, terrier-like expression." [*Parker*]
The Adventure of Buffington Old Grange

Oldfield, Dulcie. Small daughter of a Berkshire accountant,

Horace Oldfield and his wife, who is frightened by an apparition which appears to her when playing in the attic of their ancient home, Buffington Old Grange.
The Adventure of Buffington Old Grange

Oldfield, Horace. The owner of Buffington Old Grange in Berkshire, which he is convinced is haunted. "Tall and thin, he was immaculately dressed in a fur-collared overcoat and a smart check suit, but the effect was marred by his wild, staring eyes, dishevelled hair, and generally distraught demeanour . . . He was a man of about forty or forty-five years of age; of a studious aspect, with gold-rimmed pince-nez. His features were regular and would have been pleasing had it not been for his agitated expression. He had a thin wisp of fair moustache on his upper lip, and his teeth were regular and even. His sandy-coloured hair was receding a little; his grey eyes wore a sad expression as he gazed at us." [*Parker*]
The Adventure of Buffington Old Grange

Oldfield, Mrs. Wife of Berkshire accountant Horace Oldfield. A pretty, fair-haired woman, who narrowly escapes death when a sinister character with a "hideous visage, grey corpse-like" pushed her down some steep cellar steps.
The Adventure of Buffington Old Grange

Oldfield, Sally. One of two small blonde daughters of accountant Horace Oldfield and his wife, who live in an ancient house in Berkshire where sinister incidents have taken place.
The Adventure of Buffington Old Grange

P

Parker, Dr. Lyndon. Devoted friend and biographer of Solar Pons. A middle-aged and extremely busy general practitioner in the middle of London, sharing chambers with his friend at 7B Praed Street, where the pair are looked after by their amiable landlady Mrs. Johnson. An expert shot whose revolver has frequently extricated them from extremely dangerous situations. Despite being so busy on his medical duties and chronicling his friend's experiences, he is always ready to take leave and travel with Pons to remote areas of Britain to assist in bizarre and seemingly insoluble cases. The late Sultan of Turkey once described Pons as "a prince among detectives" and in turn Pons has often praised Parker, on occasion referring to him in the following terms: "You are the supreme catalyst, Parker. You put your objections to the matter under discussion so simply and clearly that I have no difficulty in eliminating the dross, which facilitates my going to the heart of the matter... You underestimate your gifts, my dear fellow. I derive a good deal of benefit from the homely summings-up of the little problems that come my way from time to time."
The Sayings of Solar Pons

Parker, Mr. Persona adopted by Dr. Lyndon Parker who poses as a fellow antique dealer while assisting Pons in solving a mystery involving the sealed spire of St. Mary's Church in Shap, a small village in Surrey.
The Sealed Spire Mystery

Pattenden, The Rev. The Rector of Channock in Yorkshire, appalled during a sermon at St. Mary's Church in Shap, Surrey,

when the Rector of St. Mary's, the Rev. Dr. Glyn Campbell, produces the corpse of his favourite cat, Sheba, from his bag. It had been strangled with wire and the congregation breaks up in uproar. A sinister person is persecuting Dr. Campbell who tells Pons, "I was almost assaulted by Pattenden; sadist and murderer were among the terms flung at me."
The Sealed Spire Mystery

Penrose, Charles. A tramp turned away from The Pines, a large mansion in the village of Stonecross in Essex by the rich but Miserly Miss Emily Schneider when he comes to beg for food and a little money. He falls under suspicion when the old lady is later murdered. "A pathetic, bearded figure in threadbare clothes, who sat with his red face hunched over his tea, as though the room and its shabby surroundings were the most luxurious *milieu* he had ever known. Even without the shaking hands and the red-rimmed eyes his cirrhosed complexion would have denoted the alcoholic." [*Parker*]
The Adventure of the Hound of Hell

Pennyfeather. A grocer from Stonecross in Essex, who is owed money by a wealthy but miserly woman, Miss Emily Schneider, who is strangled one dark night in a lonely potting shed in the grounds of her mansion.
The Adventure of the Hound of Hell

Peters, Andrew. Estate manager at Chalcroft Manor in Buckinghamshire, where murder has taken place. A dark-bearded man with very white teeth and vivid blue eyes. "With his smart hacking jacket; riding breeches; leather boots; and the silk scarf pinned in at the neck, he looked every inch the estate manager.

His hands in their lemon-yellow gloves held the reins gently but firmly." [*Parker*]
The Adventure of the Devil's Claw

Peters, Mrs. Sarita. Beautiful, slim, dark-haired woman of South American ancestry, married to Andrew Peters, estate manager of Chalcroft Manor in Buckinghamshire. Strong, dashing personality, she rides a white horse at reckless speed about the estate. "She had the very faintest accent but anyone could tell by the dark mass of hair and the vivid configuration of the beautiful, sensual face that she hailed from the Latin countries . . . I should have said she was about thirty or thirty-two and her well-cut riding habit was spattered with mud as though she had ridden her mount through the shallows of one of the ponds." [*Parker*]
The Adventure of the Devil's Claw

Petter. Official of the Mentmore Museum in London which is under threat from an international thief who goes under the name of Charles Brinsley LaFontaine who has already carried out a number of audacious thefts on the Continent without ever being caught.
The Adventure of the Ignored Idols

"Phantom of the Zoo". Sensational phrase used by the popular press to describe a mysterious intruder who breaks open cages at London Zoo in the dead of night, to allow dangerous animals to escape. "'Pschaw, Parker,' said Solar Pons, interrupting me rudely. 'Pray spare me the rubbishy fulminations of the popular press. This is all very well for the romantic shop girl or the more lurid manifestations of the cinema, but we continue to apply

the ratiocinative processes at 7B. As I have observed before, this agency stands foursquare upon the ground.'" [*Parker*]
Murder at the Zoo

Pilkington, Miss Helen. Private secretary to Horatio Biggs, Curator of the Egyptian Museum in London, in charge of the Museum staff records and general correspondence. "A tall, slim, fair girl with a slightly flushed face." [*Parker*]
The Adventure of the Cursed Curator

Pip. Small dog belonging to Miss Evelyn Brentwood, the niece of Edmund Roseacre of The Priory, Peas Pleasance, near Godalming in Surrey, found poisoned by her vindictive guardian and buried in the rose garden.
The Adventure of the Horrified Heiress

Pons, Bancroft. Foreign Office official of high rank, brother of the more celebrated Solar Pons but one who wields much more power behind the scenes. His analytical brain is even more powerful than that of the former. He features in a number of Solar's adventures and is able to exert a great deal of influence while remaining incognito. In contrast to Solar, Bancroft is a massively built man and while seemingly sedentary he can be extremely agile when the occasion calls for it. Pons defers to his brother in a number of ways and though he rarely visits Pons and Parker at Praed Street, when he does it is obvious that his presence heralds something extraordinarily important.

Pons, Solar. Private consulting detective, almost as celebrated as his great predecessor, sharing rooms at 7B Praed Street with his friend and biographer Dr. Lyndon Parker, who has chronicled all his most important cases. Lean, feral-featured with crisp, incisive manner. A heavy pipe smoker, occasionally "fumigating" his old friend when concentrating on a particularly difficult case. Extremely powerful and athletic, with a tremendous handclasp and adept at single-stick and a first-class amateur boxer, who has often bested sinister opponents three times his weight and size.

Porchester, Duke of. Seen by Pons and Parker dancing about on the opposite pavement in Regent Street on a brilliant June day, "He was a little, peppery, red-faced man in formal clothes and with a silk cravat. He carried a stick and from the opening and closing movements of his mouth, he appeared to be muttering imprecations of some sort." [*Parker*] "'It is a fairly common occurrence, Parker. The Duke of Porchester has been having a little altercation with his tailor.'" [*Pons*]
The Adventure of the Haunted Rectory

Postgate. A milkman in the Village of Stonecross in Essex, who was owed £40 by the wealthy but miserly Miss Emily Schneider, who is later murdered, causing him to become one of the suspects.
The Adventure of the Hound of Hell

Poynter, Mr. A tall, elegantly dressed dark-haired man staying at the Clarendon Court Hotel, Oxhill, Surrey. "'He has been here some weeks. I understand he is a manufacturer from the Midlands who is currently resting for his health.'" [*Emil Colefax*]
The Adventure of the Surrey Sadist

Prendergast. Attendant at the Egyptian Museum in London.

"A tall, broad-shouldered man with an alert, intelligent expression." [*Parker*]
The Adventure of the Cursed Curator

Q

[*Note: There are no characters whose surnames begin with "Q" in the whole of Basil Copper's Solar Pons canon.*]

R

Ram Dass Society of Bombay. A secret organisation which, in earlier years, had threatened Simon Hardcastle, millionaire owner of Chalcroft Manor in Buckinghamshire, later found murdered near the old family graveyard on his estate. But Pons says he knows a good deal about the secret societies and cults of this world and he has never heard of them.
[*See also "Dass, Ram"*]
The Adventure of the Devil's Claw

Relph. Valet-butler to world-famous portrait painter Aramis Tregorran of Chelsea. "A tall, thin man with careworn features." [*Parker*]
The Adventure of the Singular Sandwich

Renfrew, Adrian. Cousin of Colonel John d'Arcy, formerly of West Africa, son of Silas Renfrew who went in fear of his life when living on his Essex estate, The Briars. Young Adrian Renfrew had died "under mysterious circumstances" and the estate had passed to Colonel d'Arcy.
The Adventure of the Ipi Idol

Renfrew, Silas. The eccentric uncle of Colonel John d'Arcy who comes to Pons with a bizarre tale of strange events in which he has become involved, after his uncle left him his estate in Essex, worth £100,000 and a similar sum in cash. Pons sees at once that this is the pivot on which the sinister plot surrounding the Colonel revolves.
The Adventure of the Ipi Idol

Richmond, Dolly. Actress mistress of Cedric Carstairs, distinguished stage and film actor, who has engaged Pons to solve the riddle of death threats he has been receiving. Richmond is co-starring with Carstairs in a new play, *Death Comes to Thornfield,* in the West End of London. She is addicted to expensive jewellery, fur coats and toques. An imperious woman. "I had an impression of icy beauty; of upswept blonde hair; and a manner close to tears beneath the anger . . . and her blue eyes blazed as she swept past us." [*Parker*]
The Adventure of the Anguished Actor

Rillington, Rodney. Medical student at Charing Cross Hospital, who has been kidnapped and held to ransom in a remote area of Sussex. He had told his fellow students he was going on holiday to Spain so no one had missed him. A very pleasant young man who would make a very able doctor, was the Charing Cross Registrar's considered opinion.
The Adventure of the Missing Student

Rillington, Silas. Reclusive, retired merchant, a neighbour of Bancroft Pons in St. John's Wood, who has received packages containing severed human fingers with notes demanding a ransom of £15,000 if he wishes to see his son alive again. But

Rillington has no son and Bancroft enlists his brother's aid. Rillington is a thin, cadaverous man with the deep yellow complexion often caused by a life spent in the tropics. "He watched us with unwinking, bird-like eyes and extended an emaciated claw to Pons." [*Parker*]
The Adventure of the Missing Student

Rillington, Silas. So-called "Copper King", multi-millionaire financier and the namesake of another Silas Rillington, who lives in St. John's Wood, London. Rillington's son has been kidnapped and held to ransom but Rillington is unaware of this as the ransom note has gone to the Rillington who lives in St. John's Wood. So Pons decides to keep silence without distressing the father, while he and Parker attempt to track down the kidnapper. The father is a distinguished-looking man of about fifty with a silver-grey moustache. He has a mansion in Park Lane, a villa on Capri and runs a network of businesses world-wide.
The Adventure of the Missing Student

Roberts, John. Hardened criminal convicted with his partner Ezekial Walton to hard labour at Reading Sessions by Mr. Justice Strange before the First World War. Roberts and Walton carried out thefts in Berkshire but the money was never found. Parker described Roberts as a formidable man, built like a boxer. He had fair hair and appeared to be fairly young. "He had a white, set face in which his eyes burned like tiny sparks of fire." [*Parker*]
The Adventure of Buffington Old Grange

Roseacre, Edmund. A gigantic bull of a man who bursts into Pons and Parker's sitting room, intending to threaten them for

interfering in his affairs. He lives at The Priory, Peas Pleasance in Surrey with his niece, Miss Evelyn Brentwood, heiress to a considerable fortune administered by Roseacre, who is her guardian. She is terrified of his outbursts. A sadist and a murderer, he is a huge, bearded man with pig-like eyes. Earlier in his life he had lived in the East where he habitually bullied his servants, often physically. Addicted to drink and with an uncontrollable temper. When he attempts to hit Pons with his thick walking stick, the detective breaks it in half and throws it in his face, whereupon he retreats downstairs in a blind rage.
The Adventure of the Horrified Heiress

Rose, Miss. Cook at The Pines, near Stonecross in Essex, where her mistress Miss Emily Schneider, a rich and grasping old woman, has been found strangled in a shed in a distant part of her garden.
The Adventure of the Hound of Hell

Rossiter, Inspector Stanley of Colchester C.I.D. "A stout, impressive figure with a waxed moustache and his jacket had obviously been let out to accommodate his corpulence" [*Parker*] "'An extraordinarily shrewd brain behind a stolid exterior, Parker. He will go far, mark my words... However, he has an undisciplined mind at present, which he is not using to its best advantage. He is entirely upon the wrong track in this instance.'" [*Pons*]
The Adventure of the Hound of Hell

Rutherford, Mr. *Nom de plume* adopted by Pons who poses as an antique dealer who has come to appraise some of the rarer

pieces of Dr. Glyn Campbell, Rector of Shap in Surrey, while investigating the bizarre events surrounding the Rector and the sealed spire of his church.
The Sealed Spire Mystery

S

Sainsbury, George. Family lawyer of Mr. Michael Balfour of Bredewell House, a lonely mansion near Tidewater in Essex, where his uncle, Charles Boldigrew, has died under mysterious circumstances after seeing a hideous face appear at his study window late at night. Sainsbury himself was murdered just as Pons was about to question him about the family will.
The Adventure of the Phantom Face

Salmon, Mrs. Housekeeper at Buffington Old Grange in Berkshire, the home of accountant Horace Oldfield, in which a series of bizarre and ghastly happenings occur. A striking-looking woman of about fifty with jet-black hair, smartly dressed in a tweed suit, she courageously helps her employer to tackle a mysterious fire which had broken out in the kitchen of the mansion. But she is not all she seems, Pons eventually discovers.
The Adventure of Buffington Old Grange

Sanders, Professor. A blind man walking with a stick, elegantly dressed with a well-trimmed beard, making his way through the Mentmore Museum in London and kept under observation by Pons and Parker in case he might have been a daring thief who had warned the authorities that he was about to commit a major robbery there. "He went across to one of the large stone idols set into a niche and moved one delicate hand across its features,

almost caressingly." [*Parker*] He had carried out important excavations in Mesopotamia. The last thing he achieved before his tragic accident.
The Adventure of the Ignored Idols

Schneider, Miss Emily. Rich but miserly old woman found strangled in a lonely potting shed on a snowy night when the murderer's footprints went to the shed but apparently never returned, leaving a baffling problem for the local police and Solar Pons. Miss Schneider's nephew and sole heir, Roland Watling, who was in the house on the night of the murder is accused of the crime but his fiancée, Miss Eunice Chambers, implores Pons to look into the matter. Miss Schneider owed money to a great many local tradesmen, which sets Pons' mind in a different direction.
The Adventure of the Hound of Hell

Schneider, Romane. Internationally acclaimed sculptor, currently having an exhibition of his work in London, murdered in his Hampstead studio. Killed by one of his own mallets used for his sculptures. Described as the greatest Sculptor Britain had ever produced. "'I have seldom seen a more pointless sort of crime, Mr. Pons. There was no robbery as far as we can make out; no one had a motive; and the studio had not been broken into.'" [*Inspector Jamison*]
The Adventure of the Baffled Baron

Scott. Attendant at the Egyptian Museum in London. "A small, almost weedy man with a defeated face in which a ragged moustache was the greatest distinguishing feature." [*Parker*]
The Adventure of the Cursed Curator

Scott-Green. Benefactor of the Mentmore Museum in London, threatened by the depredations of an internationally renowned criminal. The Scott-Green Gallery in the Museum, visited by Pons and Parker, is his memorial.
The Adventure of the Ignored Idols

Sealed Spire. A spire above the bell chamber of the Norman church of St. Mary's at Shap, in Surrey, which has been sealed for a long time and around which a number of sinister legends had accreted. An old lady in the village, Mrs. Grace Harbinger, had repeatedly written to the Rector, Dr. Glyn Campbell, asking for the sealed spire to be opened, a venue in which she is convinced that the Scroll of Thoth is hidden. "'It has become rather like Joanna Southcott's Box, Mr. Pons. Open the sealed spire and all the problems of the world will vanish.'" [*Dr. Glyn Campbell*]
The Sealed Spire Mystery

Serafis, Nicodemus. A large, bearded man from Bulgaria, a fellow guest at the Clarendon Court Hotel, Oxhill, in Surrey, seen by Parker acting suspiciously outside Emil Colefax' room at the hotel. He occupies Room 16 but Parker is convinced that his beard is false. "'An entirely implausible name, Pons. Most likely completely fictitious.'" [*Parker*] He carries out his threat to pull the man's beard with disastrous results.
The Adventure of the Surrey Sadist

Setton. Fellow actor in the play *Death Comes to Thornfield*, who warns the star, Cedric Carstairs, that his liaison with his wife, Dolly Richmond, will have to end or there will be drastic consequences. "'There are other ways than physical violence.

Just remember what I have said. Leave Dolly alone!'" [*Setton*]
The Adventure of the Anguished Actor

Sheba. Cleric's pet cat whose strangled corpse is produced from the briefcase of the Rev. Glyn Campbell at an important gathering of churchmen, which causes an uproar which almost ends with blows being exchanged. Dr. Campbell is the victim of a sinister persecution which brings him to Pons and Parker's sitting room, culminating in the unmasking of the culprit behind the bizarre events. *The Sealed Spire Mystery*

Sheffield, Eugene. Pseudonym of Dr. Lyndon Parker, masquerading as a famous large-scale steam railway expert so that Pons can get acquainted with millionaire Hugo Foy, who is the subject of his latest inquiry.
The Adventure of the Mad Millionaire

Sheldon. Postmaster in the small village of Chalcroft in Buckinghamshire, who runs out of the building and calls Pons to take an important telephone call from Chalcroft Manor where murder and attempted murder have taken place on the estate. "A portly middle-aged man in a faded grey suit." [*Parker*]
The Adventure of the Devil's Claw

Sheldon, Mrs. Sidonia. Postmistress at Chalcroft, which she runs with her husband. She first came to the attention of Pons and Parker when they read an account in a national newspaper of the bizarre events taking place in the village. Mrs. Sheldon was quoted by a reporter as saying that footprints found near a body were neither human nor animal tracks.
The Adventure of the Devil's Claw

Sherlock, Dr. Oldest friend and adviser to Charles Boldigrew of Bredewell House, Tidewater, in Essex, who has died under mysterious circumstances. The doctor was "…an amiable, sandy-haired man in his early sixties with gold pince-nez perched on the end of his nose and a rather fussy manner…Dr. Sherlock's faded blue eyes stared at me ingenuously." [*Parker*]
The Adventure of the Phantom Face

Shipton, Mrs. Housekeeper to the wealthy bibliophile Septimus Grimpton of Penderel Lodge, Penderel Parva, near Bath.
The Adventure of the Shaft of Death

Simmons. Butler to Silas Grimpton of Penderel Lodge, Penderel Parva, near Bath. A grave-faced man with a fringe of white hair at the temples.
The Adventure of the Shaft of Death

Simmons. Surrey postman who delivers parcels containing effigies and death threats to the mansion of the famous stage and screen actor Cedric Carstairs.
The Adventure of the Anguished Actor

Slater, Munro. "'Late of H.M. Prison, Dartmoor. Known to us as Jethro Carpenter, rare book dealer.'" [*Pons*] "A hard-faced, crop-headed man with battered features like a boxer, now reddened and perspiring…" [*Parker*]
The Adventure of the Haunted Rectory

Smith. A bald-headed man who bought a powerful slide lantern from a photographic dealer in Oxhill, Surrey.
The Adventure of the Surrey Sadist

Smith, Mordecai. Gypsy suspected of the murder of Abel Stokoe, an ex-convict found dead in the grounds of a large estate near Bath. A dark-haired, thickset man, sullen, roughly dressed and in handcuffs. "'I did throw the knife in the river, sir, but it had nothing to do with Stokoe. One of our band, old Gaffer Jenkins, died three weeks ago and we burned his caravan and all his possessions, as is the Romany custom. But I remembered that some months ago he lent me the knife. It was bad luck to keep it, sir. I couldn't burn it because it was made of metal, handle and all. So I got rid of it by throwing it in the river and that's the truth.'" [*Mordecai Smith*]
The Adventure of the Shaft of Death

Smithers. Estate foreman at Chalcroft Manor, near the village of Chalcroft in Buckinghamshire, who hands Pons a pair of enormous shears on the instructions of his employer, Hugh Mulvane. "A tall, broad-shouldered man with mutton-chop whiskers . . . His piercing grey eyes looked at Pons with intense curiosity." [*Parker*]
The Adventure of the Devil's Claw

Smithers, Evelyn. Flighty 25-year-old daughter of the Curator of the Castle Museum in Maldon, a small town near York. Tall, with blue eyes and long golden hair, open and good-natured on the surface but who had no compunction in abandoning her fiancé, Eustace Fernchurch, when he is accused of murdering his rival for her affections.
The Adventure of the Hammer of Hate

Smithers, Professor. Curator of the Castle Museum in Maldon, Yorkshire, father of Miss Evelyn Smithers, fiancée of

Eustace Fernchurch, a young architectural assistant suspected of murdering a local builder, Sebastian Bulstrode. A cadaverous, sour-faced individual in a rusty black frockcoat, "Professor Smithers . . . came toward us blinking short-sightedly. He shook hands with Pons and myself in a distinctly chilly manner." [*Parker*]
The Adventure of the Hammer of Hate

Smithers, Professor Adrian. Keeper of the Papyrus Department at the Egyptian Museum in London. Enormously tall savant, gaunt almost to emaciation, who wears a frayed goatee beard slightly stained with nicotine. He had a shambling walk and "his hand was cold and damp to the touch". [*Parker*]
The Adventure of the Cursed Curator

Smithson. Gardener to the Oldfield family at Buffington Old Grange in Berkshire.
The Adventure of Buffington Old Grange

Smithson, Miss Anna. Receptionist at the Metropole Hotel in the Strand, where the brutal murder of one of the guests takes place. A tall, slim girl with fair hair. "The young lady smiled, revealing perfect rows of teeth." [*Parker*]
Death at the Metropole

Society of Dodgers. Part of a nightmare Lyndon Parker experiences when involved with Pons in the terrifying events surrounding the Devil's Claw, where murder and what amounts to a reign of terror has taken place in the small village of Chalcroft in Buckinghamshire. He is relieved to be wakened from his disturbing dream by one of his host's servants at

Chalcroft Manor.
The Adventure of the Devil's Claw

Sonia, Princess of Dresdania, who has come to England with her entourage in secret, for medical treatment for a heart condition by Sir Clifford Ayres, an eminent Harley Street specialist. She is guarded by a high-ranking member of the government, Prince Mirko. Pons and Parker become involved when an English governess looking after children in the Surrey mansion narrowly escapes death when terrorists break into the grounds and start shooting.
The Adventure of the Frightened Governess

Stacey, Canon Howard. Dean of Norwich who consults Pons on mysterious occurrences in the Cathedral, "Tall, distinguished-looking man in the neat grey suit . . . a man of about sixty-five, with a pleasant, open face and an unlined complexion though, like his wife, he still bore a deep tan. His silver hair rose in thick waves on his head so that it almost resembled an eighteenth-century powdered wig. His white, even teeth gleamed in a welcoming smile but I could see anxiety and doubt in the steady brown eyes." [*Parker*]
The Adventure of the Verger's Thumb

Stacey, Mrs. Winifred. Wife of the Dean of Norwich. "A regal, grey-haired woman whose features bore the dark tint that skin acquires after long years of exposure to tropical sun." [*Parker*]
The Adventure of the Verger's Thumb

Stanmore, Elihu Cook. Resident in Westbourne Grove, London, with a West End hotel suite and two country houses, but

who is "One of the greatest blackguards in London" as Pons describes him. Swindler, forger, blackmailer and thief, he has been found with multiple stab wounds in his back and with six gold doubloons lying on the desk in front of him. He was "a man of about sixty-five years old, with a shock of white hair which stood out around his head like thistledown." [*Parker*] A piece of white pasteboard on the desk before him bore the legend: REVENGE IS SWEET. But the post-mortem reveals that he had died of a heart attack before he was stabbed.
The Adventure of the Six Gold Doubloons

Stanwell, D'Arcy. Unfortunate actor who was killed on stage by a steel arrow supposedly fired from an empty stage box at a Liverpool theatre during the performance of a thriller called *The Arrow of Fate*. He had been mistaken for the play's leading man, a famous actor called Cedric Carstairs.
The Adventure of the Anguished Actor

Stapleton, Inspector. Officer of Buckinghamshire Police, called to the scene of the murder of millionaire Simon Hardcastle near the ancient family graveyard on his ancestral estate, Chalcroft Manor.
The Adventure of the Devil's Claw

Stebbins, Norman. Head Keeper at the London Zoo. A man of enormous strength, he held the main door of the Lion House closed despite the efforts of a Bengal tiger to escape, by putting his arm through the retaining clamps in place of the metal door bar. A thickset, muscular man in his early forties, with a bright, intelligent face, bisected by a heavy brown moustache.
Murder at the Zoo

Stedman, Mr. Elderly patient of Dr. Parker, who had a heart attack, resulting in the doctor being called out in the middle of the night; he then called an ambulance from a public telephone box, saw the old man in to hospital past the crisis and returned to Praed street in time for breakfast.
Death at the Metropole

Stevens, Mr. Gardener to wealthy Charles Boldigrew at his lonely estate near Tidewater in Essex. "A decent, kindly old man with silver hair which looked as though he were himself powdered with frost." [*Parker*] He had been terrified when "a horrible face . . . all green fire, with glowing red eyes" came at him out of the shrubbery.
The Adventure of the Phantom Face

Stillwood, Sandra. Famous stage actress, wife of the even more celebrated matinée idol, Cedric Carstairs. Hostess of a huge Surrey mansion. "A striking looking blonde woman of about thirty-eight . . . shadow passed across her handsome features as she led the way into a huge drawing-room which contained many oil paintings and drawings of herself and her husband in their various stage and screen roles . . . The blonde woman's eyes flashed and I saw for a brief moment the dynamic beauty that had flowered to such remarkable art in innumerable films and plays." [*Parker*]
The Adventure of the Anguished Actor

Stokesby, The Rev. Isaac. Rector of Grassington, near Haslemere in Surrey. A huge, black-bearded man with red-rimmed eyes who was ". . . clad in a black surplice and a silver cross glittered on the chest. The atmosphere was one of veiled hostil-

ity though the voice was civil enough." [*Parker*] "'There have been some strange goings-on in the village these past months and I always keep a careful eye on strangers.'" [*Stokesby*] "'He had the ribbon of the Military Cross on his surplice, Parker. He obviously served in the late war and the M.C. does not come up with the rations. If I mistake not the Rev Isaac Stokesby has seen some heavy trench fighting.'" [*Pons*]
The Adventure of the Haunted Rectory

Stokoe, Abel. Former convict found murdered in the grounds of Penderel Lodge, Penderel Parva near Bath, the family estate of Silas Grimpton. "'The dead man has been identified. He was Abel Stokoe, a rough character who formerly made his living as a prizefighter. He was a convicted felon and in fact had been released from prison only three months ago . . . for a number of offences. Occasioning grievous bodily harm; but mostly for house-breaking.'" [*Inspector Morgan of Bath C.I.D.*]
The Adventure of the Shaft of Death

Stone, Inspector of Buckingham C.I.D., heading the investigation into the murder of millionaire Simon Hardcastle. "A stocky, fresh-faced man in a discreet check suit jumped down from the driving seat of the Morris Cowley . . . The strongly-built man came toward us, a welcoming smile on his square-jawed face . . . With his carefully-trimmed moustache and blond hair, turning slightly grey at the temples, he looked like a military man who had retired to the country." [*Parker*]
The Adventure of the Devil's Claw

Stoner, The Rev. George Neville. Rector of Chislington, some twenty miles from the living of Dr. Glyn Campbell, Rector of

Shap in Surrey and Rural Dean of Stapleford. "A hook-nosed, lantern-jawed young man with piercing eyes," Parker observes of a photograph of the man taken before the First World War. Now an ascetic-looking man with a shock of white hair. "He wore a mouse-coloured dressing gown and he stood breathing heavily, looking first at me and then at my companion." [*Parker*]
The Sealed Spire Mystery

Strange, Mr. Justice. Judge who sentenced a group of criminals to ten years in prison at Reading Assizes in 1912 for a £100,000 series of robberies in Berkshire. The robbers, who had broken into a number of mansions in the area, were defiant when the judge sentenced them. John Roberts and Ezekial Walton abused the judge in an enraged manner. The judge referred to the ringleader as "'one of the most dangerous rogues in England.'"
The Adventure of Buffington Old Grange

Strangeways, Dr. Formerly of Leeds, now a country G.P., practising in the remote district of the Gravesend marshes in Kent, where bizarre incidents bring Pons and Parker to investigate. "A robust, bearded figure... dressed in tweeds, with a thick check cap with earflaps and his heavy thigh-boots were liberally splashed with mud. He carried a pair of binoculars in a leather case slung by a strap round his neck and a stout canvas bag at his side had the flap partly open, disclosing plant specimens with ice still clinging to their roots... His broad, strong face was red and burned with wind about the cheekbones and his deepset grey eyes looked at us both with interest... 'I am something of a naturalist and am used to collecting specimens and

bird-watching about the marshes in all weathers. A country G.P. in places like this has few other diversions.'" [*Parker*]
The Adventure of the Crawling Horror

Stringer, Jethro. "The Mad Corinthian of Netherhampton", who featured in an old case of Pons', mentioned by Lyndon Parker *en passant.*
The Adventure of the Six Gold Doubloons

Stuart, Jeremy. The uncle of Miss Elizabeth Stuart of The Old Rectory at Grassington in Surrey. "'Father did not speak much of him. He was the black sheep of the family, I believe... In the classical tradition he emigrated to Australia, I understand.'" [*Elizabeth Stuart*]
The Adventure of the Haunted Rectory

Stuart, Miss Elizabeth. A school teacher from Grassington, near Haslemere in Surrey. "The tall, pale young woman... bore a marked look of suffering on her features. She would have been extremely attractive otherwise, with her tawny yellow hair that fell over her shoulders, her full lips and white, perfect teeth. As it was, she had a drawn expression about the face and a lurking fear in her hazel eyes." [*Parker*]
The Adventure of the Haunted Rectory

Stuart, Mrs. Widow of the Rev. Stuart, Rector of Grassington in Surrey, who had died under mysterious circumstances in his study at The Old Rectory. Mrs. Stuart is extremely nervous and is terrified by sinister events at her home, which brings Pons and Parker to unravel these apparently disparate happenings.
The Adventure of the Haunted Rectory

Stuart, The Rev. Former Rector of Grassington in Surrey, who had died suddenly after seeing something horrific at his study window one evening, "'There was a crash one evening, during the winter-time. Mother ran in, Father was in the study, consulting some old books. He was lying near the bookcase, quite dead by the time Mother got to him, a Bible open at his feet. She swore he had been frightened by something, there was such a look of terror on his face...Our family doctor said it was a heart attack, Mr. Pons. Such an expression was common in angina cases, he said.'" [*Elizabeth Stuart*]
The Adventure of the Haunted Rectory

Sunshine. Obedient little pony which draws a dogcart carrying Pons and Parker to the estate of Hugh Mulvane of Chalcroft Manor in Buckinghamshire, where his uncle has been murdered. An intelligent animal who can find his own way to the stables adjoining the mansion, Mulvane tells Pons.
The Adventure of the Devil's Claw

Swettenham and Fuggle. A well-known estate agents in Highbury, North London, who commissioned Bruce Beresford, the principal of a major photographic studio off the Strand, to photograph The Poplars, a mansion in Highbury, which the owner, Professor Mair, was putting up for sale. But he was murdered in a locked room at his home and Pons realises that Beresford's photographs of the house could be used to trap the cunning murderer.
The Adventure of the Perplexed Photographer

T

Tanner and Tanner. A firm of solicitors in Chalcroft in Buckinghamshire, who hold the will of Simon Hardcastle, a wealthy recluse who lived at nearby Chalcroft Manor who was found dead in the ancient family graveyard on his estate. Pons believes the will holds the key to the old man's murder but the firm's principal, Mr. Tanner, is away on business in Bermuda. But before he can discuss the matter with Tanner on his return the premises are burnt down in a mystery fire. Pons then checks with Somerset House but no will has been deposited there. Nevertheless, Pons aided by Parker finally arrives at the truth.
The Adventure of the Devil's Claw

Tappenden, Solomon. "A little, thin, rat-faced man in a salt-and-pepper suit," in deep conversation with Nicodemus Serafis in the main bar of the Clarendon Court Hotel in Oxhill, Surrey. "'And yet the man with whom he is talking... is one of the most respected Hatton Garden diamond merchants.'" [*Pons*]
The Adventure of the Surrey Sadist

Tebble, Joshua. A farmer from Stavely on the Gravesend marshes, who encounters Pons and Parker when he is out duck-shooting. "A burly, tweeded form lowered the shotgun as we came up. The man smiled affably." [*Parker*] "Nothing like roast duck with your potatoes and green peas." [*Tebble*]
The Adventure of the Crawling Horror

Thornton, Esau. False name given by a murderer and bank robber, who gives a false address in Banstead, Surrey, when registering at the Metropole Hotel in the Strand where he is

eventually unmasked due to the deductive reasoning of Solar Pons.
Death at the Metropole

Thornton, Miss Celia. Mistress of famous portrait painter Aramis Tregorran, who has been arrested for murder after strangling his estranged wife, Sylvia Tregorran, in his studio in Chelsea. Celia Thornton, who lived in St. John's Wood, was an imperious dark-haired woman with a white face and black eyes which flash when she is angry. A brilliant "'experimental chemist whose researches into the nature of crystalline structures has advanced our knowledge so much.'" [*Pons*]
The Adventure of the Singular Sandwich

Three Cardinals. Hostelry in the village of Chalcroft in Buckinghamshire, frequented by Hugh Mulvane, a young college teacher living at Chalcroft Manor nearby, where murder has taken place.
The Adventure of the Devil's Claw

Thwaites, Thaddeus. Pseudonym of a disguised Pons in the sitting room at 7B Praed Street to Parker's annoyance at discovering the apparent stranger there. A "common, vulgar-looking apparition dressed in a loud plaid overcoat, who rose from my comfortable armchair by the fire. He wore an immense, tobacco-stained moustache, his face looked inflamed by drink and his bleary eyes stared at me from beneath matted silver hair." [*Parker*]
The Adventure of the Hound of Hell

Tidmarsh, Vincent. Music master at Chalcroft College in

Buckinghamshire. "A broad-chested, well-made young man with dark curly hair…despite his athletic build the music master had a pallid face which was accentuated by the heavy black moustache he wore." [*Parker*]
The Adventure of the Devil's Claw

Tolliver, George. A distant cousin of the Renfrew family of The Briars, Essex, secret beneficiary of old Silas Renfrew's will. "'He was a strange and eccentric man, though he had become a good friend to me over the years…He and young Adrian Renfrew were great friends as boys, but later Tolliver went to America. He had a bad reputation there, I believe.'" [*Chadburn Bradshaw, estate lawyer*]
The Adventure of the Ipi Idol

Tolpuddle, James. Fifty-seven-year-old butler to Mr. Simon Hardcastle of Chalcroft Manor in Buckinghamshire who discovered the body of his employer lying dead near the old family graveyard on the estate. "A tall, grave-looking man in dark, formal clothes and with grey mutton-chop whiskers in his florid cheeks, came down the steps." [*Parker*]
The Adventure of the Devil's Claw

Tompkins. Well-known grocer of Shoreditch and murderer. "'An end will be put to the activities of Tompkins…once my report is in.'" [*Pons*]
The Adventure of the Surrey Sadist

Toto. [*Note: A bull mastiff belonging to Colonel d'Arcy, which likes to carry his walking stick. "I had been rather puzzled by a low panting noise which had persisted for some minutes, and as I moved to*

offer the Colonel some liquid refreshment, my foot touched something and there was a low growl." [Parker] SJ.]
The Adventure of the Ipi Idol

Travers. Footman employed in the service of Professor Mair, murdered at his mansion in Highbury. He was asked by the murdered man's niece to light some scented candles to take away the acrid aroma of bad coal burning in the grates.
The Adventure of the Perplexed Photographer

Tregorran, Aramis. Society portrait painter accused of murdering his estranged wife Sylvia in his studio in Chelsea. The studio was locked from the inside and the servants had to break the door in. No one else was present in the studio when Mrs. Tregorran was strangled and the case seemed hopeless, but Pons takes it on because Tregorran was an old friend of Parker's. "Never had I seen such a transformation in a man. I had not seen him in the flesh for some years, it was true, but the photographs in newspapers and magazines of the tall, handsome, glossy-haired man had not prepared me for this pale, blanched creature with lacklustre eyes who was escorted into the office by two constables." [*Parker*]
The Adventure of the Singular Sandwich

Tregorran, Mrs. Sylvia. Estranged wife of famous portrait painter Aramis Tregorran who was nevertheless on reasonable terms with her husband and was currently sitting for her portrait in his Chelsea studio, when her husband strangled her. The portrait "...depicted a beautiful, imperious-looking woman with long blonde hair who stared insolently at the viewer from very frank, blue eyes." [*Parker*] "'She was a well-

built and perfectly healthy woman, some thirty-eight years old.'" [*Inspector Jamison*]
The Adventure of the Singular Sandwich

Turner, Jethro. A villager in Stavely, an isolated hamlet on the Gravesend marshes, who was the first to discover the body of Tobias Jessel, a fellow villager notorious for his drunken habits, drowned by falling off a dyke in bitterly cold weather. "'I shall never forget the look on his face, sir,' said the man Turner, inclining his lugubrious countenance toward us." [*Parker*]
The Adventure of the Crawling Horror

Truscott and Sons. A firm of architects practising in the small town of Maldon, near York, who employed Eustace Fernchurch as a young architectural apprentice, later accused of murdering his rival in love, local builder Jabez Bulstrode.
The Adventure of the Hammer of Hate

U

Unnamed Book Dealer searching for rare volumes at a sale in a country Rectory. "This was a giant with red hair and a carefully trimmed moustache. He was about thirty-five years old and very strong and vigorous. But his eyes blinked mildly beneath his thick-lensed spectacles with tortoise-shell frames." [*Parker*]
The Adventure of the Haunted Rectory

Unnamed Housekeeper. Woman who keeps house for George Tolliver of Whitestone Manor, Essex. "A severe-looking woman with shingled hair... no sign of surprise on her pale face. 'You

will find him in his laboratory. It is the large barn at the other side of the house'...And with that she slammed the door." [*Parker*]
The Adventure of the Ipi Idol

V

Vaucher. Swiss police officer who sends a telegram to Pons regarding the missing son of London millionaire Hugo Foy.
The Adventure of the Mad Millionaire

Venner, Gordon. Private secretary to the distinguished film and stage actor, Cedric Carstairs. As a clever modeller and theatrical designer he was once imprisoned for fraud. Now involved in a plot as accomplice to his mistress, Carstairs' wife, Sandra Stillwood, also an actress, to murder Carstairs on stage when he is starring in *Death Comes to Thornfield*, at the Negresco Theatre in London.
The Adventure of the Anguished Actor

Vickers. Former batman and now butler to Colonel John d'Arcy, formerly of West Africa and now the inheritor of his uncle's estate, The Briars, in Essex. "A tall, dark-visaged man in a green baize apron and wearing a batwing collar which stood out in sharp contrast to his sombre clothing. He gave Colonel d'Arcy a stiff bow and was already bending forward to pick up our bags." [*Parker*]
The Adventure of the Ipi Idol

Voss, Karl. "'I expect one call from Bancroft and if it gives me the news for which I have been waiting—that Karl Voss has

been arrested in Holland—then I shall be satisfied.'" [*Pons*]
The Adventure of the Shaft of Death

Voss, Otto. "A tall, strange gentleman, with a heavy beard, dark glasses and expensive-looking clothes... It is beautiful weather, as you can see, sir, but he was all muffled up in an overcoat and scarf," explained Meakins, porter at the Metropole Hotel in the Strand, where Voss had been found lying on his bed in Room 31 strangled. A strong and well-built man of about thirty-five, wearing a heavy tweed suit and speaking with a strong German accent.
Death at the Metropole

W

Walton, Mrs. Elizabeth. Former circus entertainer married to Ezekial Walton, serving ten years in prison for his involvement in a robbery in which £100,000 was never recovered.
The Adventure of Buffington Old Grange

Walton, Ezekial. Hardened criminal sentenced to ten years hard labour for his part in robbing £100,000 worth of property from a mansion known as Buffington Old Grange in Berkshire, described by Mr. Justice Strange at Reading Assizes as "one of the most dangerous rogues in England". A tall man with black hair turning silver and with a dirty whitish scar running down the side of his face. "He wore a heavy knitted jersey such as fishermen wear, dark trousers, and what appeared to be rope-soled sandals." [*Parker*]
The Adventure of Buffington Old Grange

Watling, Roland. A young, dark-haired man, suspected of murdering his aunt, Miss Emily Schneider, to gain her estate, as he is the only heir. But his fiancée, Miss Eunice Chambers, knows that the young London solicitor who had managed his aunt's finances with efficiency, is incapable and comes to Solar Pons in great distress. When Pons and Parker interview Watling in police custody, "He took my companion's hand and pumped it as though he would never let go." [*Parker*]
The Adventure of the Hound of Hell

Westover, Alice. Fiancée of John Hardcastle, under-keeper of the Lion House at London Zoo, who has been accused of criminal activities involving the release of dangerous animals. A slim, fair-haired girl, wearing a smartly tailored suit and a chic hat with a gaily coloured feather. She "had little points of fire dancing on her cheeks…'He is certainly innocent, Mr. Pons,' she said stoutly." [*Parker*]
Murder at the Zoo

Wilson, Jabez. Housing development trickster. "'I have been down to Hoxton ferreting about on the site of a new housing estate. The swindles of Jabez Wilson are about to be put a term to. The mud and debris on the site was somewhat reminiscent of the late war.'" [*Pons*]
[*See also under "Hoxton Builder"*]
Murder at the Zoo

Wilson. Young, dark-haired clerk employed in the office of the Scottish Land Trust in Inverness, who obviously knows nothing about its affairs when Parker questions him, as the

company has been set up by a master criminal to mask a sinister conspiracy.
The Adventure of the Callous Colonel

X

[*Note: There are no characters whose surnames begin with "X" in the whole of Basil Copper's Solar Pons canon.*]

Y

[*Note: There are no characters whose surnames begin with "Y" in the whole of Basil Copper's Solar Pons canon.*]

Z

Zhdnov Twins. Dresdanian midgets, who are circus and music-hall performers, dressed as two children, a boy and a girl, set to guard Miss Helen Helstone, ostensibly their governess, from a band of terrorists intent on assassinating Princess Sonia of Dresdania, who is in hiding in a mansion in Surrey to be to be treated by a Harley Street specialist for a heart condition. "Both are expert at Ju-Jitsu, knife and pistol," Pons observes.
The Adventure of the Frightened Governess

The Sayings of Solar Pons

"AH, THEN, YOU believe in the supernatural, Mr. Pons?"
"On the contrary, Canon, I am inclined to believe the problem is more tangible than that."

The Adventure of the Verger's Thumb

"I have no wish to let such poor ratiocinative gifts as I possess rust in this mellow holiday atmosphere. I must confess I am curious and decided to find out a little more about this oddly assorted couple."

The Adventure of the Verger's Thumb

"You will notice, Parker, that the worst-formed symbols, apart from those scratched out, are all upon the right-hand side. Surely that suggests an obvious explanation."

"But why, Pons?"

"Because of the light, Parker. Whoever wrote this message, sat in the western aisle of the Cathedral to catch the last of the light. The right-hand edge of the paper was in semi-darkness, which was why he had such difficulty. It was obvious the light had almost gone altogether."

The Adventure of the Verger's Thumb

"But I must say all this is a far cry from our peaceful holiday."

"On the contrary, Parker, I am in fine form. I have all the benefits of a holiday together with the mental concentration on a criminal problem which so appeals to my peculiar nature."

The Adventure of the Verger's Thumb

"How could you possibly know that, Pons?"

"Because the road is up there, Parker, and the whole area is a devilish mess. They are using tar and a peculiar mixture of a distinctive reddish sand in their preparation of the road surface. When I see such an amalgam on your own toe-caps it is fairly safe to assume you had been Aldgate way for I know of no other public works currently taking place in the capital using this somewhat original mixture."

The Adventure of the Phantom Face

"You under-estimate your gifts, my dear fellow. I derive a good deal of benefit from your homely summings-up of the little problems that come my way from time to time."

The Adventure of the Phantom Face

"You have been a book-keeper unless I miss my guess . . . Your desk was in front of a window and you sat at right angles to it. I would further infer that you have been employed by the Metropole Hotel for only a short time; say a fortnight at the outside."

Death at the Metropole

"I am sorry, Parker. I sometimes forget that you are not always *au fait* with my cases. I was merely conducting a little experiment in ballistics. Though the characteristics of a bullet striking plaster are different from that of flesh, I fancy my theory will stand up in court. Sufficiently, I trust, to put paid to the unspeakable activities of the abominable Mr. Horace Mortiboys of Epping."

The Adventure of the Callous Colonel

"Oh, yes, the Colonel has a great deal to him. *The Dimensions of Ecstasy* indeed. He is as much at home among the shelves of the library and the higher philosophy as he is at a rough shoot or on one of the crags of his native heath."

The Adventure of the Callous Colonel

"My dear Parker, you are, as I said earlier, a veritable transmitter of light! Here the matter has been staring me in the face, and I need only have taken two physical steps to corroborate my theory. If ever I have been obtuse, it is on this occasion."

The Adventure of the Hammer of Hate

"Motive, my dear fellow. Always consider motive. There were no strong ones in this case."

The Adventure of the Hammer of Hate

"You are extremely gallant this evening, Parker . . . But I fear these sartorial notations are coming between us and the young lady's story."

The Adventure of the Callous Colonel

"It has all the hallmarks of the Colonel's ingenious mind, Parker. The thing is entirely hand-made. The carving, the staining with red varnish, the glass-eyes, the skilful painting of the features, and the heavy spring-mechanism, typical of the skilled toy-maker, bear all the signs of the Colonel's ingenuity. The parcel was post-marked Putney by the bye, so he and his agents are not far away."

The Adventure of the Callous Colonel

"Splendid, Parker... You really are improving all the time. Those are my thoughts exactly and though the conclusion is a trite and obvious one it appears to me that my training is beginning to bear fruit."

The Adventure of the Callous Colonel

"You may tell your master that we are *en route* to Scotland," said Pons crisply. "That will save you a good deal of time and trouble. You may also add—though that is expecting rather too much of human nature—that you are doing your job extremely incompetently. There is an art to observing people without being noticed and you have not yet mastered it."

The Adventure of the Callous Colonel

"There is little to see here, Pons."

"I am inclined to agree with you, my dear Parker. But even a negative result tends to eliminate the possibility of error."

The Adventure of the Baffled Baron

"You fail to see, my dear fellow, because you do not draw the correct conclusions from the data before you."

The Adventure of the Baffled Baron

"There is nothing so boring as London on a winter's day, Parker!"

"I cannot remember having heard you say so for a long time, Pons. As Samuel Johnson once remarked..."

"I am quite aware of what the good doctor said, Parker. You do well to rebuke me but it is extremely chafing to the spirit when the services of a private consulting detective are apparently no longer needed in this great metropolis."

The Adventure of the Horrified Heiress

"I must be the most trying of companions."

"On the contrary, Pons!... Such records of your cases as I have already published have found a vast public which would not agree with your diagnosis."

"Tuppence coloured, Parker... I have always warned you against the somewhat romantic view you take of my little adventures... Always write for the ten per cent of mankind who know what one is talking about."

The Adventure of the Horrified Heiress

"A matter of life and death, Parker. And as you have been such an assiduous chronicler of my little adventures over the past years, I thought you would not care to be left out, despite the inclement hour."

The Adventure of the Frightened Governess

"Patience is a virtue this agency has a great deal of."

The Adventure of Buffington Old Grange

"Are you free to come? You will need your revolver. Though ghosts are impervious to bullets, I fancy Mr. Oldfield's apparitions may prove to be of rather more solid construction."

The Adventure of Buffington Old Grange

"Always return to the original sources, whenever possible, Parker. It saves a deal of time."

The Adventure of Buffington Old Grange

"Always remember, Parker, that what is before one, however outré and extraordinary, must represent the truth. It needs only to be read aright."

The Adventure of the Six Gold Doubloons

"I see you have studied him, Pons."

"Have I not, Parker. Such exotic animals interest me as much as the zoo-keeper absorbed in some rare but savage beast which is put in his charge."

The Adventure of the Mad Millionaire

"In what way may I help you, Pons?"

"By being a catalyst, Parker. You are always that. And by giving me your always valuable support.

The Adventure of the Mad Millionaire

"I am poised on a knife-edge, Parker. I have almost all the threads of this affair in my hands. But my suppositions are circumstantial only. And if I go wrong there may be a dreadful tragedy."

The Adventure of the Mad Millionaire

"You are the supreme catalyst, Parker. You put your objections to the matters under discussion so simply and clearly that

I have no difficulty in eliminating the dross, which facilitates my going to the heart of the matter."

The Adventure of the Mad Millionaire

"Ah, Inspector, you have your methods. I have mine."

The Adventure of the Cursed Curator

"This agency exists to assist those in distress and I would say that you need rest and hot food as a prime requirement. It is a hard journey from Colchester on such an inclement day."

The Adventure of the Hound of Hell

"Do not go on, my dear fellow," said Pons, with a short laugh. "You will cause me to become confused otherwise.

"That day will be marked in my diary in letters of fire, Pons."

"Why, Parker, you are becoming quite poetic in your middle years."

The Adventure of the Hound of Hell

"In my book, Inspector, large sums of money are always sufficient justification, given the temptation and the opportunity."

The Adventure of the Hound of Hell

"Parker and I have our feet firmly on the ground and we are dealing with material facts, not legends, however horrific they may be."

The Adventure of the Hound of Hell

"You speak with the benefit of hindsight, Parker. You are reading far too much into the atmosphere. It is just an ordinary shed in a secluded corner of an overgrown garden but because it has been the scene of a brutal crime that fact colours the surroundings for you. You have too much imagination for a medical man."

The Adventure of the Hound of Hell

"Nothing is so singular as human nature, and I have had long observation of it."

The Adventure of the Hound of Hell

"The Inspector has been looking at the problem of a murderer who walked into that building and never came out. Looked at from another viewpoint, that of the snowfall, it was the problem, in a sense, of a murderer who came out and never went in."

The Adventure of the Hound of Hell

"Don't underestimate yourself, Inspector . . . Ninety-nine police officers out of a hundred would have taken the same line as you. And in ninety-nine cases they would have been right. We have had the good fortune to light upon the hundredth."

The Adventure of the Hound of Hell

"You under-estimate your gifts, my dear fellow. I derive a good deal of benefit from your homely summings-up of the little problems that come my way from time to time."

The Adventure of the Phantom Face

"It is the trivial which often has the greatest significance."

The Adventure of the Phantom Face

"Sometimes, Parker, I think you are a greater droll than even the world takes you for."

The Adventure of the Phantom Face

"Instinct is a major factor in the process of crime detection, my dear Inspector, and you have it in high degree."

The Adventure of the Phantom Face

"I must apologise for these constant interruptions, Miss Hayling, but such sifting and evaluation of points as they arise, together with the comments of my good friend the doctor here, are a valuable factor in refining the ratiocinative processes."

The Adventure of the Callous Colonel

"You have an unfortunate tendency toward repetition, Parker, which would become somewhat wearisome in a person less amiable than you."

The Adventure of the Devil's Claw

"A man whose drawing room is filled with portraits and photographs of his late wife and only child is not concerned with hate and murder, Parker. Such souvenirs are the symbols of love. That was elementary, for a man who had committed a crime would not keep reminders about him.

The Adventure of the Mad Millionaire

"I am not surprised . . . Though it is rather odd that a 2,000-year-old mummy should be frightened by a revolver."

The Adventure of the Cursed Curator

"An odd puzzle for the zoologists, Parker . . . A clawed creature which apparently flies from the trees to settle near Mr. Hardcastle's body. It then scratches up the area all round the body; hops or flaps its way through the graveyard; pauses to dip its claws into water—I have not forgotten your ponds, my dear fellow!—and then simply disappears within the tomb. A remarkable animal; one might almost say mythological."

The Adventure of the Devil's Claw

"Not so, Parker. The springs of sex are mysterious, primitive and atavistic... Human nature is my business."

The Adventure of the Devil's Claw

"Tut, Parker... your romantic disposition is running quite away with you. You have been reading far too much Conan Doyle."

The Adventure of the Devil's Claw

"In my experience old ladies do not wander about their grounds at night in thick snow and in total darkness for the most obvious of reasons."

The Adventure of the Hound of Hell

"The philosophers counsel patience, Parker. In the mind that is once truly disciplined, as the good Marcus Aurelius has it. In a few hours you shall know everything that I myself know about this matter.

The Adventure of the Singular Sandwich

"You must find your work at the Cathedral a great deal different from shoe repairs... That accounts for the calluses on your thumb where you hold the leather as you shape it on your last. They are quite distinctive. When I see in addition that your left shoulder is slightly lower than your right I conclude that you are right-handed and that you have been in the habit of bending over your work in the manner peculiar to cobblers.

Thirty years of that would certainly have its effect on your physique and it is typical of the trade."

The Adventure of the Verger's Thumb

"Could some creature have come out of the ponds on the estate about which Mulvane told us?"

"Perhaps, Parker, perhaps... It is an interesting theory and one all of a part with your colourful imagination. Though rather more Jules Verne than Conan Doyle on this occasion."

The Adventure of the Devil's Claw

"I shall come to it in a moment, Inspector. I find it a mistake to spoil one's dramatic effects by hurrying. There is a touch of the artist in me, and I must be allowed my little histrionic flourishes from time to time."

The Adventure of the Hound of Hell

"It is not so very difficult to deduce, Parker. When I see a meticulous gentleman of sober habit sitting at breakfast unshaven, yet fully dressed but with his tie tied lining outwards and quite awry, the chain of events becomes obvious. Ergo, you were called in the middle of the night, rose hastily, dressed with extreme speed and went out. When you came back it was too late to go to bed. You have not yet shaved but sat down straight away to breakfast. Therefore, you have returned within the hour."

Death at the Metropole

"It is a sad commentary on mankind's foibles, Parker, that different countries cannot learn to live together. There is crime enough, poverty enough and disease enough without nations massacring one another over the finer points of doctrinaire religion or the pink and black shadings on a map."

The Adventure of the Crawling Horror

"Down there, Mr. Pons. I have never seen an old fellow behave in such an odd way."

"I presume you are referring to the retired Willesden plumber with the glass eye who now runs messages for the Metropole Hotel in the Strand."

Death at the Metropole

"There is something almost mystical about a great machine," Pons observed. "And the *Scotsman* is such a locomotive even in an age which has grown *blasé* over steam power."

The Adventure of the Callous Colonel

"You are quite right, Parker. But a wise general makes his dispositions accordingly, taking account of both the weather and the movements of the enemy."

The Adventure of the Callous Colonel

"Your grammar is going to pieces in your agitation, Parker, but I follow your drift. I want you to play out a little comedy in the main office and keep the clerk they employ busy."

The Adventure of the Callous Colonel

"You play your ace well, Bancroft, but I suspected something of the sort. You were a little too reticent on the subject of Rillington's son when you began your narrative."

"As Dr. Parker has so often remarked, Solar, there is no getting around you. I would be grateful if you could take the case.

May I inform Rillington you will be able to stop by this afternoon?"

The Adventure of the Missing Student

"You are not saying a doctor is responsible, Pons?"

"It is possible, Parker. Doctors are not unknown to have performed criminal activities in the long catalogue of man's inhumanity to man."

The Adventure of the Missing Student

"This is a little more helpful, Parker. Careless, to say the least. Coarse brown paper, unusual twine—one of the fingers has been wrapped in an old copy of *The Lancet*."

The Adventure of the Missing Student

"I am glad you have been frank, Mr. Rillington. But you may set your mind at rest. There has obviously been a mistake. The man who kidnapped young Rillington is an amateur. He got the wrong Silas Rillington. Unless I miss my guess, we want Silas Rillington, the millionaire copper-king."

The Adventure of the Missing Student

"An excellent idea, Pons. I have some chocolate here in my pocket. And I will just slip down to the buffet for some beer."

"I can see that my training is bearing fruit. You are becoming quite the seasoned campaigner."

The Adventure of the Missing Student

Solar Pons Plot & Dialogue Notes

AMONGST BASIL COPPER'S papers was an envelope marked "Plot Notes & Dialogue Notes" containing numerous scraps of thin paper featuring several surprisingly compact story outlines and some prospective dialogue exchanges for his Solar Pons novellas.

Much of this material, dating from between March 29th, 1977 and December 24th, 1978, was used—or at least revised—for his existing Pons Canon, after which he would cross it through with a pen to show that he was finished with it. A number of examples of these pages, many typed on a manual typewriter in block capitals, appear over the following pages.

However, much more interestingly, the envelope also included a few brief but tantalising jottings of ideas for stories that were planned for future volumes but never written.

In an undated notation headed "The Dossier of Solar Pons", Basil mentions:

THE ADVENTURE OF THE AMIABLE APIARIST.
Vicious bees trained to kill by scent . . .

The remainder of the sheet of paper is taken up with notes for *The Solar Pons Companion*, which he was apparently already working on around the same time.

On May 23rd, 1978 Basil had written to James Turner: "I've already, this morning, worked out a lost love for Pons. I've given her the name of Lady Georgina Peel. How does that grab you? She would be rather like Diana Rigg in *The Avengers*."

The note reads:

> LADY GEORGINA PEEL. "THE WOMAN".
> IN LATER ADVENTURE ON SCANDAL IN BOHEMIA LINES . . .

From this it was obvious that the author was planning to give Pons his very own female adversary along the lines of Conan Doyle's Irene Adler.

In an enigmatic note typed on July 27th that same year, Basil wrote:

> End of novel or short story.
> He had had too much Cinzano . . . almost half a bottle.
> There was a gramophone playing somewhere, sunlight sparkled on the water and it was always summer.

This may not even have been intended for a Pons story, although it was in the same envelope as the other notes and on a single sheet of the same writing paper.

In October 1978, Basil revealed in a letter to James Turner that he was "Thinking about doing a final story for this collection set against a railway background, which could be fun". On the 10th of that month, Basil wrote a pithy one-line idea for a story in the proposed sixth volume of Pons stories:

RAILWAY THRILLER. STATION HAUNTED.

Finally, there were various proposed book titles scattered amongst the new plot ideas, including *Secret Cases of Solar Pons*, *The New Adventures of Solar Pons*, *The Longer Adventures of Solar Pons*, *Six Problems for Solar Pons* and *In Re: Solar Pons*.

This material gives us a rare insight into the thought process behind the creation of Basil's Pons stories and makes us wish all the more he had completed the six extended volumes that he had initially planned to write for Arkham House.

—Stephen Jones

(2)

ADVENTURE OF THE CRAWLING HORROR. Plot.

GHASTLY PHOSPHORESCENT FIGURE CRAWLING FROM MARSH TO HAUNT SILAS GRIMSTONE AND HIS NEICE SYLVIA. COUSIN MURDERED IN MARSH BY GRIMSTONE FOR HIS FORTUNE? ESTATE THEN PASSED TO HIM AND THE NEICE. SOMEONE EITHER SUSPECTED OR KNEW THIS AND MASQUERADING AS PHANTOM TO MAKE HIS CONFESS? DEAD MAN'S SON? TWIST FROM NORMAL. IN END IT IS PONS' CLIENT WHO MEETS HIS DEATH IN THE MARSH TRYING TO KILL THE SON OF THE RELATIVE... SON HAS BEEN ABROAD AND COME HOME NOW. LIVING INCOGNITO IN NEIGHBOURHOOD IN MARSHES NEAR GRAVESEND.

'THE ADVENTURE OF THE CRAWLING HORROR' #2

3

PONS AND PARKER PRESENT WHEN HORRIFIC FIGURE WITH BLUE FIRE APPEARS ACROSS THE MARSH AT NIGHT: GRIMSTONE ALMOST COLLAPSES. PONS AND PARKER INVESTIGATE ALONE AT NIGHT AND FIND TRACES IN THE MARSHY GROUND. PONS LOOKS WITH HIS FLASH AND GIVES A GRIM SMILE: SEVERAL SUSPECTS LIVING IN ISOLATED AREAS. RED HERRINGS, OF COURSE. THOUGH PONS/VISITS ONE HOUSE WITH MAN AWAY. THIS IS NEPHEW RESPONSIBLE.

AT INTERVIEW GRIMSTONE SAYS, "GOODNESS ME, IS THAT THE TIME. I MUST BE AT CHARING CROSS EARLY IN THE MORNING. OUR LOCAL CARRIER HAD TO COME TO LONDON TODAY, SO I HAVE COME UP WITH HIM TO SAVE EXPENSE."

"I THOUGHT YOU SAID YOU CAME BY TRAIN " SAYS PONS. MISER GIVES HIMSELF AWAY.

HAD TO BE DUSK BECAUSE OF PHOSPHORESENCE. HAD TO BE ALONE BECAUSE HE WANTED TO DRIVE HIM MAD OR MAKE HIM CONFESS TO THE MURDER. HAD TO HAVE HUT OR SOMEWHERE HE COULD MAKE UP: WATER TOO TO GET MUD AND MUCK OFF HIS CLOTHING. COULD BE NATURALIST WHO HAUNTED MARSH. PONS CHECKS IN VILLAGE ON FAMILY HISTORY: HEARS THAT BROTHER DISAPPEARED YEARS AGO: GRIMSTONE WAS GIVEN LETTERS OF ADMINISTRATION: BROTHER WAS PARTNER? KILLED HIM FOR HOUSE AND FIRM. SON HAD COME BACK. DID NOT INTEND NIECE TO SEE APPARITION, ONLY GRIMSTONE: SON GROWN UP NOW AND CAME FROM ABROAD ONLY YEAR EARLIER: TOOK TIME TO PLAN HIS REVENGE. PONS LETS HIM GO. PONS REALISES PHANTOM MUST KEEP TO MARSH.

OLD TOBIAS JESSEL, DRUNKARD, SEES PHANTOM OF MARSH. PONS FINDS HIM IN BAR AND THEY TALK ABOUT IT. PONS GIVES HIM MONEY. HE SPENDS IT ON DRINK: LATER FOUND DROWNED IN MARSH. OLD GRIMSTONE APPALLED AND THINKS HE HAS BE

'The Adventure of the Crawling Horror' #3

Grimstone's neice comes out in end and says it is true he committed murder.

MURDERED. SO DOES PARKER. BUT HE HAS MERELY DROWNED IN MARSH WHILE DRUNK, AS DR STRANGEWAYS PROVES. STRANGEWAYS SUSPECT BY PONS. ALWAYS ABOUT MARSHES. PONS AND PARKER CHASE PHANTOM IN ONE SCENE AND COME ON DOCTOR WITH HIS GLASSES ON MARSH. SUSPICION TOWARD HIM. AWAY FROM PLEASANT YOUNG MAN MET AT HOTEL BAR...

SECTION 4. EVENING AT INN. MEET YOUNG VISITOR (FROM CANADA): OLD DRUNK: TELLS PONS STORY: LATTER GIVES HIM MONEY. FOUND DEAD ON MARSH NEXT DAY. OUT ON MARSH IN MORNING: FIND DOCTOR'S HIDE: ALSO ANOTHER SUSPECT ACTING SUSPICIOUSLY. "PHANTOM" HAS PHOSPHORUS ON ONE SIDE ONLY: BY TURNING ROUND AND STANDING STILL HE DISAPPEARS. PONS PUZZLED: SEEMS SUPERNATURAL. PONS AND PARKER SEE PHANTOM, SHOOT AT IT. PONS FINDS BLOOD. DOCTOR HAS BANDAGED WRIST: SAYS HE CUT HIMSELF OPERATING ON PATIENT. MEET SYLVIA GRIMSTONE COLLECTING FLOWERS: TELLS PONS ABOUT BROTHER DISAPPEARING... WENT ABROAD. HAPPENED 15 YEARS EARLIER... FIGURE HAS OLD-FASHIONED CLOTHING: YOUNG GRIMSTONE HAS ONE OF HIS FATHER'S OLD SUITS...

NEXT STORIES: LONDON: JAMISON: BANCROFT: SUPT HEATHFIELD: CHARACTER READING FROM CLIENTS ETC...MORE DETAIL OF 17B...

KNIGHT PRETENDS A LIMP AND ASKS STRANGEWAYS TO TREAT HIM FOR A SPRAIN TO DIVERT SUSPICION. HE BANKED ON THE DOCTOR, IN A CROWDED BAR, NOT BEING INTERESTED IN ANYTHING SO TRIVIAL. HE WAS RIGHT. SUSPICION PUT ON STRANGEWAYS BY PONS LOWERING HIS VOICE WHEN HE CAME IN ETC. ASKED JESSEL ABOUT PHANTOM. FOUND IT WAS DOWN BELOW BANK AND ON A WINDY NIGHT WHICH MEANT "APPARITION" DID NOT HEAR FOOTSTEPS ON ROAD ABOVE. PONS DEMONSTRATES ON MARSH, TO PARKER'S

'THE ADVENTURE OF THE CRAWLING HORROR' #4

THE SECRET FILES OF SOLAR PONS. 1

Pons 2.

THE ADVENTURE OF THE

CRAWLING HORROR

*1-

13/8/77.

"THERE ARE SOME things, my dear, Parker, into which it is better not to inquire too closely. They are too deep for words".

"Eigh, Pons?"

It was a bitterly cold January day; still, with a touch of ice in the air. I had finished my rounds earlyxxxx it was just dusk and I was reading the newspaper in front of a glowing fire in our quarters at 7B Praed Street whilexmyxfriendxSolarxPonsxxx awaiting tea, while my friend Solar Pons busied himself with a gazeteer at a small table near the window. He turned his lean, feral face towards me and smiled faintly.

"I see from the headlines there that you had been reading xxxx of the Bulgar atrocities. From the expression on your face I surmise that the massacres in that quarter have moved you deeply".

"Indeed, Pons", I rejoined. "It recalled to my mind my own experiences in the field".

Solar Pons nodded and pushed back his chair from the table.

16/5/77.

'The Adventure of the Anguished Actor' #1

WIFE HAS 15 MINUTE BREAK OFF STAGE. SECRETARY'S HOBBY IS MODELLING. SEES HIS SISTER..

PONS 3. ADVENTURE OF THE AGONISED ACTOR.

ELIJAH HARDCASTLE, FAMOUS FILM AND STAGE ACTOR. RECEIVING DEATH THREATS. SMALL FIGUR OF HIMSELF IN COSTUME, KEEP ARRIVING BY POST. NO MESSAGES: IN EACH CASE HE IS A CORPSE I.E. LYING DEAD WITH DAGGER OR SWORD OR SOMETHING OF THAT NATURE. CLEVER MODELS. REVENGE: LOVED GIRL AND JILTED HER. FELLOW ACTOR? OLD DRESSER? LOTS OF SUSPECTS. IN LIVERPOOL ACTOR NEXT TO HIM KILLED BY ARROW DISCHARGED FROM STAGE BOX... SHORT ADVENTURE THIS TIME. AIMED AT HIM. FINAL FIGURE IN PARCEL THAT ARRIVED PREVIOUS DAY SHOWS ACTOR IN NEXT ROLE. KEEPS METAL BOW, WHICH FOLDS UP, IN VIOLIN CASE† MAN WITH CASE SEEN AROUND THEATRE BUT HE MINGLES WITH THEATRE MUSICIANS: PONS SUDDENLY NOTICES THERE ARE 16 PEOPLE IN THEATRE ORCHESTRA INSTEAD OF 15; LONDON THREATRE FINALE. AT END ~~XXXXXX~~ PONS MAKES HIS REMARK ABOUT GOING TO SEE VALENTINO...AT CINEMA..

MAN'S WIFE: JEALOUS AT ALL HIS CONQUESTS. PONS SEES CONTEMPT ON HER FACE. ALSO ACTRESS, DRESSED AS BOY...? CONSPIRING WITH HER OWN LOVER, SO THAT SHE CAN MARRY HIM? LOVER ACTS SUSPICIOUSLY, SO DIVERTING ATTENTION??? PONS SEES THROUG THIS. WOMAN HAS ONLY LIMITED TIME ON FIRST NIGHT AS HARDCASTLE ALWAYS RINGS HER WHEN HE IS AWAY...

PONS SPEAKS UTTER NONSENSE AT ONE POINT TO PUT SECRETARY AND WIFE OFF THEIR GUARD. ARRESTS SOMEONE BEFORE SHOW. THEN REAPPEARS IN DISGUISE IN THEATRE AND PREVENTS TRAGEDY. TACKLES HARDCASTLE AND BRINGS HIM DOWN, ARROW GOES INTO SCENERY. MURDERER ESCAPES BUT PONS SAYS IT DOES NOT MATTER. ARRESTS HARD-BREATHING

Mrs H.

'THE ADVENTURE OF THE ANGUISHED ACTOR' #2

2

THIS IS WHY PONS SPEAKS OF OUTSIDE MENACE ALL TIME, TO PUT WIFE AND SECRETARY OFF THEIR GUARD... MURDER HAD TO BE ON STAGE WHERE THERE WERE HUNDREDS OF SUSPECTS, BOTH IN AUDIENCE BEHIND SCENES ETC. PONS AS OLD MAN WITH BEARD PREVENTS TRAGEDY. AT END SLIM MAN WITH VIOLIN CASE ABOUT TO PASS; PONS TRIPS HIM AND PULLS OF RUBBER MASK TO DISCLOSE SANDRA STILLWOOD... ESTABLISH THAT ABRAHAMS IS GOOD MODEL MAKER?.

PONS [illegible] AS WELL KNOWN DESIGNER?

'The Adventure of the Ignored Idols' #1

PONS PLOT 5.

MENTMORE MUSEUM.

FORGER AND THIEF, CHARLES BRINSLEY LAFONTAINE, WITH WHOM PONS HAS ALREADY CROSSED SWORDS, HAS WARNED THE MUSEUM THAT HE MEANS TO STEAL THEIR TREASURES, THE BAKU IDOLS, A SET OF GOLD EFFIGIES WORTH ABOUT £30,000. HE WARNS MUSEUM WITHOUT GIVING HIS NAME IN COPPER * PLATE WRITING. BUT HE IS REALLY AFTER SOMETHING ELSE, MUCH MORE VALUABLE AND TRYING TO DISTRACT ATTENTION. NO-ONE KNOWS HIS REAL NAME AND HIS FACE IS NOT KNOWN EITHER, AS HE IS A MASTER OF DISGUISE. ESCAPED PONS BEFORE AND HE ESCAPES THIS TIME, THOUGH PONS FOILS HIS EFFORT: DISGUISED AS MUSEUM ATTENDANT AT ONE STAGE, PONS HITS HIM WITH CANE AND PARKER PULLS FALSE BEARD OFF BUT HE ESCAPES AND TRIES AGAIN: GUARDS DOUBLED AND LOT OF STRANGERS AT MUSEUM WHICH MAKES THINGS DOUBLY DIFFICULT. LOT OF RED HERRINGS, WITH VISITORS TO MUSEUM BEHAVING IN ECCENTRIC MANNER: PARKER RUSHES TO WRONG CONCLUSIONS OF COURSE... MUSEUM DIRECTOR COLONEL FRANCIS LODER. SUPERINTENDENT STANLEY HEATHFIELD IN CHARGE FOR SCOTLAND YARD: JAMISON NOT SEEN ON THIS OCCASION.

PARKER READS IN PAPER THAT COUNT FERZETTI IS IN LONDON AND LEAVES ON MONDAY MORNING PONS GOES MAD: TELLS PARKER THAT ATTEMPT WILL BE MADE TO STEAL PORCELAIN ON SUNDAY NIGHT. COUNT FERZETTI, IS WORLD'S GREATEST XXXXXXXX PRIVATE COLLECTOR OF PORCELAIN. THAT NIGHT KEEP WATCH, HEATHFIELD ON BAKU IDOLS, PONS AND PARKER ON CERAMICS. FIRE BREAKS OUT IN MUSEUM.

'The Adventure of the Ignored Idols' #2

DESPITE PONS' EFFORTS PORCELAIN IS STOLEN. PONS IS DISGUISED AS MUSEUM ATTENDANT AND STRUGGLES WITH LAFONTAINE. PARKER MISTAKES PONS FOR THE THIEF AND ATTACKS HIM, ALLOWING OTHER TO GET AWAY. EARLY IN MORNING, AT SIX A.M. GO TO COUNT AT HIS HOTEL: PONS CHALLENGES HIM. SAYS, YES HE IS BUYING PORCELAIN BUT DOESN'T KNOW WHERE IT COMES FROM. PONS SEES LEATHER CASE ON TABLE. COUNT SAYS YES, THAT IS IT, WHEN PONS CHALLENGES HIM . PONS MAKES A BARGAIN: HE WILL SAY NOTHING OF SOURCE IF HE RETURNS IT COUNT AGREES, REGRETFULLY, ESPECIALLY WHEN PONS TELLS HIM COLONEL SANDERS MIGHT HAVE DIED HAD THEY NOT DISCOVERED HIM IN THE STORE ROOM. SANDERS IS AN OLD FRIEND. PONS SAYS WHAT WILL HE DO ABOUT HIS CHEQUE: FERZETTI ADDS THAT HE WILL TEAR IT UP. PONS REALISES THIEF IS STILL IN ROOM. SEES SHOES UNDER CURTAIN AND YOUNG MAN, STRUGGLE IS OVERPOWERED. PARKER ATTEMPTS TO PULL OFF HIS MOUSTACHE BUT THERE IS HOWL OF PAIN. YOUNG MAN IS FROM GENUINE DEALERS, HIRED BY LAFONTAINE. HE WAS TO HAVE SENT THE CHEQUE TO A POSTE RESTANTE IN GENEVA. PONS SAYS IT WOULD BE USELESS TO GO THERE. LATER, AFTER STORY HAS APPEARED IN PAPERS, PONS GETS MESSAGE IN COPPER PLATE WRITING. WE SHALL MEET AGAIN...

'THE ADVENTURE OF THE HORRIFIED HEIRESS' #1

Pons 6

PONS 6. EDMUND ROSEACRE, BRUTE TRYING TO GET HIS NIECE'S ESTATE.

OR HAS ALREADY SPENT IT WITH MARCUS THE LAWYER'S HELP AND IS TRYING TO PREVENT HER FROM KNOWING IT. MURDERS LAWYER? OR TRIES TO MURDER HER?

ROSEACRE ASKS MARCUS TO HOUSE AND MURDERS HIM. HAS FOUND ANOTHER MAN WHO IS EXACT DOUBLE. CRIMINAL WHO IS EXPERT FORGE . OR TWIN BROTHER? HE TAKES LAWYER'S PLACE. PONS FIND HE HAS CLOSEI

'THE ADVENTURE OF THE HORRIFIED HEIRESS' #2

HIS OFFICE AND DISMISSED HIS STAFF: RETIRED AT 50. BUT HE AND ROSEACRE WERE DIVIDING ESTATE BETWEEN THEM. ROSEACRE KNEW GAME WOULD BE UP WHEN GIRL REACHED HER 21ST BIRTHDAY. INVITED FAKE MARCUS TO HOUSE.

CAME TO HIS BEDSIDE IN NIGHT AND TRIED TO PUT ROPE ROUND HIS NECK. CRASHED THROUGH WINDOW. GIRL WOKE UP AT TERRIBLE CRY. SAW STRANGLED FACE OF LAWYER AT WINDOW.

ROSEACRE SAYS SHE MUST HAVE HAD NIGHTMARE. MARCUS HAD LEFT HOUSE. THEN FOUND NEWSPAPER LAST NIGHT WHICH SAID MARCUS HAD BEEN FOUND HANGED IN HIS LONDON LODGINGS. ROSEACRE HAD TRANSPORTED HIM THERE. BLAMED ALL DISPERSAL OF ESTATE ON HIM. BUT PONS EXAMINES HOUSE, FINDS WINDOW BROKEN: FINDS ABOUT OFFICE BEING CLOSED ETC. THEN PLANS A DENOUEMENT FOR ROSEACRE WHICH RESULTS IN HIS DEATH. THEY FIND ORIGINAL LAWYER'S BODY BURIED IN GROUNDS. GIRL'S DOG NOT ALLOWED IN GARDEN. SCRATCHES ROSEBEDS: DOG IS POISONED LATER AND UNCLE SAYS SHE MUST NOT HAVE ANOTHER. PONS PIECES ALL THIS TOGETHER LATER. THEN FINDS AT END GIRL HAS ONLY FEW THOUSAND POUNDS LEFT OF OVER £40,000. SAYS SHE DOES NOT CARE FOR THE MONEY BUT IS NOW FREE TO LIVE HER OWN LIFE WITH MAN OF HER CHOICE. WILL BE ABLE TO SELL HOUSE AS WELL SO SHE WILL NOT BE SO BADLY OFF...

MARCUS DID NOT OPEN ANOTHER OFFICE BECAUSE HE WAS NOT QUALIFIED AS A LAWYER AND WOULD SOON HAVE BEEN EXPOSED.

PEOPLE IN VILLAGE SAY MARCUS WAS OFTEN AT HOUSE. CAME AT NIGHT WHEN YOUNG GIRL WAS ASLEEP.

FAKE LAWYER WAS DRAWING ON ESTATE WITH FORGED SIGNATURE...

ROSEACRE HAS TO ATTEND INQUEST ON FAKE MARCUS: WHILE HE IS AWAY PONS HAS GARDEN DUG UP, FIND BODY. CONFRONTS

'The Adventure of the Horrified Heiress' #3

MURDERER ON HIS RETURN, AFTER VIGIL IN LONELY HOUSE. PARKER HAS HIS REVOLVER. BIZARRE AND HORRIFIC FINAL SCENE. ROSEACRE CONFESSES AFTER PONS TELLS HIM THAT JAMISON HAD BEEN TO BANK AND FOUND MOST OF MONEY GONE. ROSEACRE HAD RANSACKED THE FAKE MARCUS' QUARTERS AND REMOVED ALL HIS PAPERS OR BURNED THEM IN FIREPLACE. PONS AT ONCE REALISES SIGNIFICANCE OF THAT AS WELL. PARKER COVERS ROSEACRE WITH REVOLVER BUT HE RUSHES OUT OF ROOM: BREAK OPEN DOOR OF STUDY AND FIND HIM LYING POISONED.

'THE ADVENTURE OF THE HAUNTED RECTORY' #1

THE SECRET FILES OF SOLAR PONS.

29/3/77.

RECTOR OF SMALL VILLAGE NEAR HASLEMERE, DIED MYSTERIOUSLY IN HIS STUDY. WHILE LOOKING UP SOMETHING? TWO YEARS BEFORE STORY OPENS: FRIGHTENED PEOPLE OFF... MISS STUART CONSULTS PONS: LIVE IN HOUSE NEAR CHURCHYARD. TERRIBLE THINGS HAPPENING. THINGS DISTURBED IN STUDY. PONS REALISES SOMEONE IS TRYING TO SCARE THEM OFF. OR FIND SOMETHING IN HOUSE. ROBBERY OR PROCEEDS: CHURCH PLATE HIDDEN? MAN WENT TO PRISON FOR TWO YEARS. OUT AGAIN NOW...

FATHER STANDING NEAR LIBRARY WINDOW WHEN MAN HE THOUGHT DEAD APPEARS? RECTOR'S EVIL BROTHER: BLACK SHEEP OF FAMILY. STOLE HAUL AND HID IT IN VAULT IN CHURCH. PUT CLUE IN OLD BIBLE OR PRAYER BOOK, IN CASE ANYTHING HAPPENED TO HIM. BOTH SENT TO PRISON. HE DIED IN PRISON. CONFIDED CLUE TO ACCOMPLICE: HE WAS RELEASED AFTER TWO YEARS AND CAME BACK. GIRL SAW EVIL FACE AT WINDOW..

HARUM SCARUM, BLACK SHEEP BROTHER, IMPRISONED FOR THEFT; BELIVED TO BE IN AUSTRALIA: ONCE LIVED WITH RECTOR XXXX AT TIME WHEN THERE WERE SERIES OF BURGLARIES IN NEIGHBOURHOOD. PRESENT RECTOR MUST BE SINISTER AND MYSTERIOUS. BROTHER HAD BEEN ENGAGING IN LARGE-SCALE THEFTS: LEFT LOOT UNDER MEMORIAL OF CHILDREN IN CHURCH. LEFT CLUES IN BIBLE IN STUDY IN FORM OF CHURCH VERSES: STARTING WITH LEVITICUS 4 ETC. GOT IDEA FROM MOONFLEET. SAYS PONS, LAUGHINGLY, MAY I COMMEND THE WORKS OF J. MEADE FAULKNER TO YOU, PARKER. MOONFLEET IS ADMIRABLE". HAS SEEN CONNECTION. THEN BROTHER IMPRISONED. ESCAPES AND COMES BACK FOR LOOT. SHOCK WHEN RECTOR SEES HIM AT WINDOW: DIES OF HEART ATTACK. BROTHER RECAPTURED AND DIES IN PRISON BUT NOT BEFORE CONFIDING SECRET

IN FELLOW

'THE ADVENTURE OF THE HAUNTED RECTORY' #2

2

PRISONER. HE IS RELEASED AND COMES BACK TO HOUSE AND TRIES TO FIND BIBLE. MAN HAS ONLY TOLD HIM IT IS IN BIBLE. FINDS IT XXXX BUT DROPS IT WHEN GIRL SCREAMS. MISS STUART PICKS UP SLIPS OF PAPER AND PUTS THEM BACK IN BIBLE: OR WRONG ONE? PONS RINGS HOME OFFICE, AFTER ASKING GIRL ABOUT RELATIVES: GIRL MENTIONS XXXXXXX FATHER'S BROTHER: PONS GETS STORY ABOUT MAN DYING IN PRISON. BREAKS CODE, ENTERS CHURCH AND GOES INTO VAULT. FAMOUS CRESSWELL SILVER, BARON CRESSWELL. PONS RECOGNISES CREST: WORTH FORTUNE. REMOVES STUFF AND THEY BAIT TRAP. PUT IN ADVERTISEMENT ABOUT RECTORY LIBRARY ABOUT TO BE DISPOSED OF. VARIOUS PEOPLE CALL? ONE OF LOCAL NEIGHBOURS DISGUISED. SNARLING ATTACK AS PONS AND PARKER CAPTURE HIM AT NIGHT IN VAULT. RECTOR MUST ALSO BE SUSPICIOUS... PONS SUSPICIOUS BECAUSE NO-ONE SAW BEARDED MAN? [illegible]

'THE ADVENTURE OF THE SINGULAR SANDWICH' #1

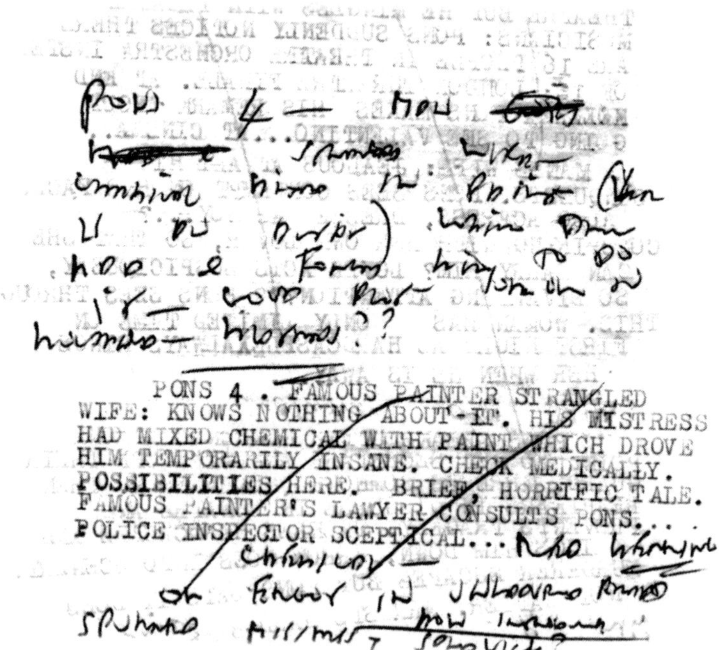
PONS 4. FAMOUS PAINTER STRANGLED WIFE: KNOWS NOTHING ABOUT IT. HIS MISTRESS HAD MIXED CHEMICAL WITH PAINT WHICH DROVE HIM TEMPORARILY INSANE. CHECK MEDICALLY. POSSIBILITIES HERE. BRIEF, HORRIFIC TALE. FAMOUS PAINTER'S LAWYER CONSULTS PONS... POLICE INSPECTOR SCEPTICAL...

'The Adventure of the Singular Sandwich' #2

PRIVATE STAIRCASE AT SIDE. MISTRESS SLIPPED UP: FOUND FOOD ON TRAY OUTSIDE AS USUAL, SUBSTITUTED SANDWICH. WIFE CAME UP TO SEE HIM, WAS STRANGLED WHEN HE WENT INTO FIT AN HOUR LATER... OR ACCOMPLICE IN HOUSE. MISTRESS JILTED:..

KEY NOT IN LOCK OUTSIDE, BECAUSE MISTRESS HAD LOCKED IT. DOOR BROKEN IN. SHE WAS HIDING IN HOUSE? OR CAME BACK IN EVENING WITH OWN KEY: PUT DOOR KEY BACK IN INSIDE. PONS THEN REALISES THIRD PERSON HAS HAD A HAND IN THE AFFAIR.

ASKS JAMISON: HAD NOT LOOKED FOR KEY. THEN FINDS IT BACK IN LOCK.

"I DID NOT NOTICE THAT, MR PONS". "THERE IS ONLY ONE CONCLUSION TO BE DRAWN, JAMISON".

PONS NOTICED SEVERAL THINGS: KEY, WHICH WAS SIGNIFICANT. TREGORRAN HAD BEHAVED LIKE A MADMAN, AND REMEMBERED NOTHING: WHICH INDICATED A DRUG. THE METHOD? SANDWICH AND BEER. LATER INDICATED BY MRS MANDEVILLE THAT SHE HAD SENT UP STEW OR SHEPHERD'S PIE. PONS FINDS REMAINS OF MEAL IN STONE UMBRELLA STAND IN LOBBY OF STUDIO. SHE MUST COME BACK AND CLEAR THEM OUT OR REMOVE SANDWICH? KEEPS WATCH. HAS PORTION OF SANDWICH ANALYSED. TWO MISTRESSES MIGHT HAVE BEEN INVOLVED. ONE WAS JEALOUS OF HIM (RED HERRING: SUSPECTED SOMEONE ELSE BUT DID NOT WANT HIM INJURED IN ANY WAY). LADY CYNTHIA HARRISON RESPONSIBLE. CLEAR WIFE AND REVENGE ON TREGORRAN AT SAME TIME.

WOMAN NOT AT HOME? HUSBAND UNDER SUSPICION? OR NO-ONE. HOPELESS CASE.

PONS HAS ALREADY ABSTRACTED LITTLE PIECE OF SANDWICH. DISCOUNTED BEER AS BEING EASILY TRACEABLE: THEN REMAINS OF MEAL DISAPPEAR. FIND SOUP ETC. IN STONE UMBRELLA JAR TO PARKER'S PUZZLEMENT. SENDS MESSAGE TO W

'THE ADVENTURE OF THE SINGULAR SANDWICH' #3

@ 4

WOMAN AND DRAWS HER TO 7B PRAED STREET. HER CONFESSION IS OVERHEARD BY JAMISON AND MECKER CONCEALED IN A CUPBOARD."I AM AFRAID I COULD NOT LET YOU INTO THE SECRET, MY DEAR FELLOW. YOUR FEELINGS ARE SO HONESTLY TRANSPARENT THAT YOU COULD NOT HAVE KEPT UP THE MASQUERADE..." REVENGE THE MOTIVE...

LET US HOPE IT WILL HAVE TAUGHT MR TREGORRAN A MUCH-NEEDED LESSON... BETWEEN THE TWO OF THEM HE WAS BOUND TO COME TO DESTRUCTION SOONER OR LATER."

EVIDENCE OF A THIRD HAND IN IT FROM THE BEGINNING: DISCOUNTED THE SERVANTS. WHEN I LEARNED THAT TREGORRAN'S MISTRESS WAS XXEHEMIX AN EXPERIMENTAL CHEMIST BY PROFESSION, I FELT CERTAIN THAT THE ANSWER LAY IN THAT DIRECTION. SHE COULD NOT BE CERTAIN OF MURDER BUT AT ANY EVENT SHE SAW IT, IN HER JEALOUS POSSESSIVENESS, AS AN ADEQUATE REVENGE NOT ONLY ON HER LOVER BUT ON THE WIFE WHO HAD FOR SO LONG STOOD BETWEEN HER AND THE HUSBAND.

PONS CALLS AT HER HOUSE AND TAKES A PURSE WITH HER INITIALS: SAYS SHE HAS DROPPED IT IN THE STUDIO. SHE SAYS SHE LEFT IT THERE ON ANOTHER OCCASION, BUT BECOMES FLUSTERED AND OFF BALANCE.

BEER BOTTLE WAS OF SPECIAL LAGER WITH SEALED CAP: DID NOT THINK CELIA THORNTON WOULD HAVE TAMPERED WITH THAT BUT THEN DIRECTED HIS ATTENTION TO THE SANDWICHES.

"I FIND YOUR QUESTIONS OFFENSIVE, YOUR IMPLICATIONS ODIOUS AND YOUR CONCLUSIONS ENTIRELY ERRONEOUS."

"INDEED", SAID PONS, WITH A TWINKLE IN HIS EYE.

'The Adventure of the Singular Sandwich' #4

TREGORRAN'S MISTRESS A CHEMIST. "She did not know he would murder, Parker. But she meant to do him grave mischief".
HOW LONG AFTER EATING THE SANDWICH WOULD HE HAVE TAKEN TO GO MAD?

ergot, n., a disease of grasses (esp. rye) and sedges due to Claviceps purpurea: a seed so diseased. - n. ergosterol, an unsaturated sterol got from ergot. - v.t. ergotise, ize, to affect with ergot or with ergotism. - n. ergotism, poisoning caused by eating bread made of rye diseased with ergot. (Fr.)

lysergic acid, a substance, $C_{16}H_{16}O_2N_2$, got from ergot, causing (in the form of lysergic acid diethylamide) a schizophrenic condition.

'THE ADVENTURE OF THE VERGER'S THUMB' #1

THE EXPLOITS OF SOLAR PONS.

No 1. The Adventure of the Verger's Thumb

PONS AND PARKER ON HOLIDAY IN NORWICH FOR FORTNIGHT. IN CATHEDRAL GO INTO CRYPT, SEE COUPLE QUARRELLING: LEAVE OBJECT ON GROUND. TURNS OUT TO BE CONTAINER WITH PAPER IN WITH CODE? RED HERRING: OR PART OF MAIN PLOT. THEN VERGER OF CATHEDRAL COMES TO PONS. HE HAD INJURED HIS THUMB ON CURIOUS CARVING IN ANOTHER PART OF THE CATHEDRAL. DEAN OF NORWICH ENLISTS PONS HELP IN MYSTERY: STRANGE PEOPLE MEETIN IN CATHEDRAL... USING IT FOR CODED MESSAGES AND PASSING THINGS? OR PROCEEDS OF ROBBERY? OR MAN ESCAPED FROM PRISON?

~~PONS EXPLAINS ABOUT MIGG'S CALLOUSES ON THUMBS, SLIGHTLY HUNCHED SHOULDER FROM HIM BEING BOWED OVER HIS LAST ETC.~~

OR ESCAPED CONVICT ALREADY BEING HIDDEN IN CATHEDRAL? ANOTHER MAN WITH HIM. BOTH EATING ON BENCH IN DUSK. DURING DAY MINGLING WITH TOURISTS ETC. PERHAPS ROBED? OR DISGUISED IN SOME WAY. AT NIGHT HIDDEN IN A COFFIN WITH AIR-HOLES IN IN CRYPT. MAN HIDDEN SAW VERGER GOING TO PICK UP MESSAGE: INSERTED KNIFE INSIDE GARGOYLE'S HEAD AND PRICKED VERGER'S THUMB: HE DROPPED MESSAGE AND TOOK OFF. GOOD-LOOKING MAN AND WOMAN HAVE ENGINEERED ESCAPE: SHARING MONEY. CONVICT HID MONEY IN CRYPT WHEN REBUILDING WORK WAS GOING ON. MESSAGES WERE SOMETIMES LEFT FOR TWO REASONS: CONVICTS GIVING INSTRUCTIONS ABOUT HIDDEN MONEY: PEOPLE AT HOTEL GIVING INSTRUCTIONS ABOUT PLANS FOR ESCAPE.

CONFESSIONAL HAS GARGOYLE IN IT...
PONS FINDS BREATHING HOLES IN LID OF

COFFIN, DONE WITH WORKMAN'S DRILL

'The Adventure of the Verger's Thumb' #2

ROBBERY AND KILLING: MEN IN CATHEDRAL TALKING OF ROBBERY, OF COURSE. CONVICT SAYS HE WOULD KILL KOCH IF HE BETRAYED THEM. MANY PEOPLE IN CATHEDRAL. MAN WHO COLLECTED MESSAGE FROM BOWL ~~XXXXXXXX~~ LEFT ANOTHER IN CRYPT. SEE KOCH AND GIRL AGAIN. SAYS THEY WILL BE READY THAT NIGHT.. MAKE SURE THESE FACTS FIT. PONS AND PARKER HIDE: MEN PICK UP MESSAGE IN BOWL IN MONTRESOR CHAPEL, LEAVE ANOTHER MESSAGE IN SAME CONTAINER IN CRYPT STATUE: KOCH AND GIRL PICK IT UP. PONS AND PARKER SEE THEM AT DINNER AT HOTEL. THEY LEAVE AND GO DOWN TO CABIN CRUISER: PONS ALREADY HAS ITS NAME. MOORHEN? DROPS ON CABIN TOP FROM LOW BRIDGE: HEATHFIELD'S MEN WAITING . BIGGER MAN KNOCKED OVERBOARD AND OTHERS GIVE UP. TWO AUSTRIANS WHO WERE INTERNATIONAL THIEVES, MASTER-MINDED COUP. HOW DO PEOPLE GET INTO CATHEDRAL AFTER DARK: KOCH AND GIRL HAVE BRIBED ONE OF WORKMEN TO LEAVE SMALL SIDE DOOR OPEN... SIDE CHAPEL WAS RANSACKED BECAUSE MEN ARE SO DUMB THEY CAN'T REMEMBER, WITH RENOVATIONS, WHICH ONE THEY HID IT IN: BENEATH ALTAR. THEY DRESS IN CHORISTER'S ROBES DURING DAY OR SIT AS WORSHIPPERSS AT NIGHT SLEEP IN CRYPT... MAN WAS COMING OUT FOR DROP WHEN CANON SAW HIM...

'THE ADVENTURE OF THE VERGER'S THUMB' #3

MISSING LINES

3

The bright June day continued, the engine joyfully shovelled black smoke over its shoulder as it vibrated its way over the flat countryside amid the noise and bustle of Norwich Thorpe Station, bedecked with coloured posters featuring Broadland yachts apparently sailing across the rich fields and shouting the attractions of Yarmouth as a seaside resort.

"Did I not say it was agreeable, Pons?"

"Indeed, Parker," said Solar Pons drily, skilfully dodging aside to avoid a covey of small boys carrying fishing rods.

We had nothing except light hand luggage so after surrendering our tickets we walked out into the brightness of the station concourse, avoiding the taxi-rank and instead crossing the road to walk by the broad, brown waters of the Yare, where tall-masted sailing boats bobbed alongside the quay at Norwich Yacht Station.

Across the bridge, we let the flow of pedestrians take us into the heart ~~of the city where the great spire of Norwich Cathedral floated like some huge~~ ship at anchor, and reported ourselves at the Royal George Hotel, where we were expected. A shocked attendant took our luggage and whisked it immediately to our comfortable rooms. When we had again descended, Pons consulted the huge grandfather clock in the hall.

"It is still only a quarter-past twelve, Parker. What say you to another short promenade before lunch?"

We slipped out of a side entrance; it was market-day apparently and a rich display of stalls, selling a fantastic variety of goods stretched as far as the eye could reach across a vast square near the Cathedral, the reds, golds and greens of their canvas roofs making a colourful, mediaeval pattern that was eye-aching in the bright summer sun.

Solar Pons looked at the rich life about him, his keen eyes taking in the details of the individual faces, a thin plume of smoke from his pipe rising into the summer air.

After a short while wandering about in this manner we turned our steps back in the direction of the Cathedral, pausing in the Close to examine the moving memorial to Nurse Edith Cavell and then crossing the road to traverse

'The Adventure of the Verger's Thumb' #4

36

the writing room of the hotel in the afternoon and when he joined me for tea had been a little more communicative.

We had walked by the riverside for a little while and now, as we made our way toward the towering pile of the cathedral, he became almost expansive.

"Let us just put out thoughts in order, Parker. Give me the benefit of your observations on this little problem".

21/11/77.

I fingered the fly-tying device in my pocket thoughtfully.

"I am betinning to see some light, Pons, But I cannot see how you have arrived at your conclusions. You think the two rough men in the cathedral might be the two escaped convicts, Pons?"

Solar Pons blew out a lazy trail of blue smoke over his shoulder. "That was elementary, Parker".

"But why the Cathedral, Pons? So public..."

Solar Pons smiled.

"Exactly, my dear fellow. A great public building is the perfect place of concealment. Hidden amongst the crowd, as it were

'The Adventure of the Death at the Metropole' #1

PONS 3. MURDER AT METROPOLE.

METROPOLE HOTEL MURDER.

MAN CAME TO HOTEL WITH STOLEN MONEY? DISGUISED. NOT SAME MAN KILLED? MAN CAME TO GET HIM FOR HIS SHARE: MAN IN ROOM KILLED HIM AND CHANGED IDENTITIES. BAG MISSING. NO-ONE KNEW HOW HE COULD GET IN AND OUT. MANAGER TELLS WEIRD STORY BUT IT IS THE TRUTH. JAMISON ARRESTS HIM, OF COURSE. WRONG MAN.

VOSS HAD POWERFUL VOICE BUT WITH HEAVY ACCENT. DID NOT SPEAK MUCH BECAUSE HE DID NOT WISH TO GIVE HIMSELF AWAY. PONS REALISES MEAKINS COULD NOT HAVE KNOWN WHETHER HE SPOKE GOOD ENGLISH OR NOT FROM BRIEF COMMUNICATION HE HAD WITH HIM. INTERVIEWS RECEPTIONIST AS WELL. FAKE VOSS MURDERS REAL GERMAN WHEN HE COMES FOR MONEY. THAT WAY STAGED PERFECT CRIME. HAD ALREADY UNOBTRUSIVELY REGISTERED UNDER ANOTHER NAME AND PERSONA IN HOTEL EARLIER THAT DAY. REALISED HIS ENEMIES WOULD KILL HIM AND LAID A FALSE, VERY DISTINCTIVE TRAIL. ADVENTURE OF THE DOUBLE GUEST OR SOMETHING LIKE THAT. LEAVES LOTS OF FAKE CLUES AND BIZARRE RED HERRINGS: WEIRD THINGS ABOUT TO PUT JAMISON ON COMPLETELY WRONG SCENT. STRANGE THINGS TO CLERK AS WELL. PONS CHUCKLES AS HE SEES JAMISON'S FOOLISHNESS. GOES DOW REGISTER AND SEES MARKED SIMILARITY BETWEE TWO SETS OF WRITING AND ARRESTS GUEST LEAVING UNDER YET ANOTHER PERSONA. GOOD POSSIBILITIES HERE.

JAMISON AND PARKER BAFFLED OF COURSE BUT PONS IMMEDIATELY GRASPED MAN IS LAYING A FALSE TRAIL: THEREFORE, HE IS NOT THE ONE WHO IS MURDERED.

DOOR NOT FORCED: PONS REALISES MUST HAVE BEEN OPENED WITH KEY. PASS KEY IS AT DESK. THEREFORE SOMEONE IN HOTEL MUST HAVE BORROWED IT TO GET IN BECAUSE VOSS' KEY IS ON TABLE. NIGHT RECEPTIONIST WAS AWAY FROM DESK FOR HALF AN HOUR IN AMOROUS DALLIANCE? KEY TAK

'The Adventure of the Death at the Metropole' #2

2

TAKEN IN THAT TIME AND REPLACED. MAN WHO WAS TRYING TO KILL FAKE VOSS (I.E. VOSS HIMSELF) TRIED TO SURPRISE HIM BUT PARTNER WAS WAITING FOR HIM AND STRANGLED HIM. PUT KEY BACK ON BOARD WHEN HE WENT DOWNSTAIRS AND R SUMED PERSONA OF OTHER GUEST, ARTHUR BROWN OF CAMBRIDGE. BAG FULL OF DEUTSCHMARKS

GERMAN NEWSPAPER CUTTINGS IN DRAWER IN BEDROOM WHICH FAKE VOSS HAD OVERLOOKED: JAMISON THOUGHT THEM OF NO IMPORTANCE. PONS' GERMAN JUST GOOD ENOUGH TO SEE THEY ARE TO DO WITH BANK ROBBERY: TWO MEN INVOLVED, WHO HAD SPLIT UP AND BELIEVED TO HAVE LEFT COUNTRY PERHAPS FOR HOLLAND. ROBBERY IN HAMBURG. PONS IMMEDIATELY SEES THE SIGNIFICANCE. FINDS CABBY OUTSIDE HOTEL WHO HAD TAKEN CLEAN-SHAVEN MAN FROM METROPOLE TO THEATRICAL COSTUMIERS IN JERMYN STREET. PONS AND PARKER GO THERE: PARKER WAITS OUTSIDE AND SEES PONS AND ASSISTANT IN CONVERSATION: FINAL LINK NEEDED. GETS DESCRIPTION OF CLEAN-SHAVEN MAN WHICH MATCHES OTHER GUEST. WHY DID HE NOT LEAVE HOTEL IMMEDIATELY? FLAW HERE WHICH MUST BE EXPLAINED. GOING TO CHANGE MARKS IN LONDON FOR ENGLISH MONEY, OF COURSE.

FAKE GUEST HAS STICKING PLASTER ON HIS FINGER.

PONS 4 MENTION VARIOUS OTHER BIZARRE CASES PONS HAS HANDLED. MAN WOULD NOT HAVE WORN DARK GLASSES IN BED. FAKE VOSS HAD STRANGLED HIM IN HIS CLOTHES: THEN DRESSED HIM IN PYJAMAS ETC. BUT DARK GLASSES THERE TO MATCH UP WITH PERSONA HE HAD ALREADY CREAT D.

TWO GERMAN NEWSPAPERS: HEAVY VALISE: NEWS OF ROBB RY AND DISGUISE SOON PUT HIM ON RIGHT TRACK.

VOSS WAS AN EXPORT OFFICIAL, WHICH WOULD MEAN HE COULD BRING THINGS THROUGH CUSTOMS. FAKE VOSS DOUBLE-CROSSED H

'THE ADVENTURE OF THE DEATH AT THE METROPOLE' #3

HIM AFTER THEY LANDED IN ENGLAND.

Lady Georgina Peel

"The Woman"

LADY GEORGINA PEEL. "THE WOMAN".
IN LATER ADVENTURE ON SCANDAL IN BOHEMIA LINES...

METROPOLE. FAKE VOSS WAITED FOR REAL VOSS AND KILLED HIM: LEFT DOOR UNLOCKED AND THEN LOCKED IT WITH HIS ROOM KEY. HAD ALREADY TRANSFERRED CONTENTS OF VALISE (I.E. STOLEN MONEY) TO HIS ROOM WHICH HE HAD BOOKED IN THE NAME OF ESAU THORNTON. UNDRESSED BODY AND PUT ON PYJAMAS, DRESSING GOWN AND PYJAMAS HE HAD HIMSELF WORN. HAD TO STAY IN HOTEL BECAUSE HE WAS CHANGING MONEY INTO ENGLISH CURRENCY IN SOHO."ONLY HALF A MILE FROM SOHO", SAYS PONS. WENT DOWNSTAIRS AS THORNTON, OSTENSIBLY TO PUT HIS KEY IN RACK: NO-ONE THERE SO TOOK PASS KEY TO VOSS' ROOM. MADE SURE HE HAD BEEN SEEN TO CHECK INTO HOTEL BY REAL VOSS. WENT BACK UP WITH PASS*KEY. LEFT HIS OWN ROOM KEY, ON TABLE, LOCKED DOOR WITH PASS KEY AND TOOK IT BACK DOWNSTAIRS AND RETURNED IT TO RACK UNSEEN. THEN WENT TO HIS OWN ROOM AS THORNTON..

Ends "One of Mrs Johnson's excellent suppers"

Johnson

"It has been a lesson to me, Mr Pons!"

'The Adventure of the Death at the Metropole' #4

RE-TOOL END OF DEATH AT THE METROPOLE.

PONS FOUND TRACES OF HEAVY SHOES XXXXXX [illegible] NEAR DOOR: STRANGLED HIM WHEN HE CAME IN AND DRAGGED HIM OVER TO BED... HEEL MARKS QUITE CLEARLY INDENTED.

2 NEWSPAPERS WERE THREE WEEKS OLD BUT WERE CAREFULLY PRESERVED. THEREFORE SOMETHI[NG] IN THEM OF SIGNIFICANCE. TWO ITEMS ONLY BOTH CONNECTED WITH THE BANK ROBBERY.

3 PASSPORT WAS THAT OF VOSS: NO MISTAKING THE FACE. QUESTION THEREFORE THAT CAME AT ONCE TO MIND WAS THE MAN WHO ARRIVED AT HOTEL VOSS OR NOT. CIRCUMSTANCES LED ME TO CONCLUDE THAT HE WAS SOMEONE DISGUISED AS VOSS. BUT WHAT WAS POINT? TO POINT POLICE IN DIRECTION OF SOMEONE FROM HAMBURG? VOSS WAS NOT IN HOTEL: BETTER TO HAVE HIM ALREADY REGISTERED AS GUEST.

4 PASSPORT WAS GENUINE, THEREFORE VOSS WAS GENUINE. BUT FIRST MAN WAS NOT.

5 I COMMENDED HIS PROFESSION TO YOU, PARKER. EXPORT OFFICIAL. IT IMMEDIATELY SUGGESTED THAT THEY MIGHT SIMPLY HAVE BROUGHT THE LUGGAGE THROUGH.

DIDNT' SPEAK MUCH TO RECEPTIONIST: THEREFORE, VOICE DISGUISED.

CHECK DEUTSCHMARK EQUIVELANE OF THE STERLING: 100,000 POUNDS.

'THE ADVENTURE OF THE CALLOUS COLONEL' #1

PLOT OF PONS NO. 4. VOL 4.

PONS' ANTAGONIST IS COLONEL ALISTAIR MCDONALD OF INVERNESS, "THE THIRD MOST DANGEROUS MAN IN EUROPE". CRACK SHOT, BIG-GAME HUNTER, PHILOSOPHER, AUTHOR OF "THE DIMENSIONS OF ECSTASY (1923) AS HIS ENTRY IN WHO'S WHO PUTS IT. TRIES TO KILL PONS BY SENDING HIM AN IDOL WITH A POISONED NEEDLE. AN INGENIOUS TOY-MAKER, WHICH GIVES SCOPE FOR SOME GOOD SCENES. PONS HAS ALREADY BEEN ENGAGED BY MISS JENNIFER HAYLING OF WORTLEY HALL, NORFOLK AND INVERNESS. COLONEL HAS BEEN PRESSING HER TO SELL HER SCOTTISH HOME, LEFT HER BY HER PARENTS, AND ABOUT 300 ACRES OF LAND. SERVANTS TERRORISED. ONE PARTICULARLY NASTY BRUTE, AGENT OF MCDONALD, WITH FLAMING RED BEARD. GETS HIS COME UPPANCE FROM PONS AND LATER FOUND WITH NECK BROKEN AT FOOT OF CRAG. MCDONALD DISPOSED OF HIM WHEN HE FEARED PONS WAS GETTING TOO CLOSE TO TRUTH. STORY ENDS WITH GREAT STALK IN MISTY HIGHLANDS WITH COL HIMSELF FALLING TO HIS DEATH IN RAVINE. CLIFF-HANGER, LITERALLY. HIS SPECIAL RIFLE IS USELESS. OIL BEARING SHALE BENEATH MISS HAYLING'S LAND? MCDONALD HAS FLOATED A HUGE CONSORTIUM FOR OIL WITH THOUSANDS OF PEOPLE RUSHING TO BUY SHARES. MCDONALD NEEDS HER LAND BECAUSE OF A FAVOURABLE GEOLOGICAL SURVEY ON THE SITE. BECAUSE OF MOUNTAIN, GRANITE OUTCROPS AND LIE OF LAND, SOFT EARTH THERE IS THE ONLY WAY TO GET DOWN TO IT AND START DRILLING. HAD OFFERED HER £30,000 WHICH MAKES PONS SUSPICIOUS. ACCIDENTS TO SERVANTS WHICH MAKES GIRL DETERMINED TO FIGHT. MAN WITH RED HAIR LET SOMETHING DROP ABOUT "THE COLONEL" AND OTHER MAN WITH HIM (LAWYER) CHECKED HIM STRAIGHT AWAY. THEN SAW MCDONALD WITH MAN. LATER HE IS KILLED BECAUSE OF HIS INDISCRETIONS. AT END OF STORY PONS SAYS WITH REMARKABLE PRESCIENCE "WHO KNOWS, PARKER, THERE MAY WELL BE OIL BENEATH SCOTTISH SOIL AND SCOTTISH SEAS.

'THE ADVENTURE OF THE CALLOUS COLONEL' #2

WHETHER IT WILL COME IN OUR TIME IS ANOTHER MATTER. WE SHALL HAVE TO WAIT AND SEE".

AND HE PUFFED CONTENTEDLY AT HIS PIPE...

PONS CONSULTS MAP WHICH MAKES MATTER CLEAR: HER 300 ACRES IS SURROUNDED BY COLONEL'S LAND AT THAT POINT BUT IT IS MOUNTAINOUS AND WOULD BE RUINOUSLY EXPENSIVE TO DRILL ON TOP OF MOUNTAIN. BEN MORAG (MOUNTAIN)... CONSULTS COMPANY RECORDS AND ALSO LOCAL ESTATE AGENTS FOR REPORTS ON SHALE OIL?

SAYS PONS, "IT IS OBVIOUSLY THE LAND HE IS AFTER. THE HOUSE WOULD BE OF NO USE TO HIM AT ALL." SOON SAW ANY ONE OF A HUNDRED PROPERTIES SCATTERED ABOUT THE HIGHLANDS WOULD HAVE SERVED HIM AS WELL. PONS AND PARKER SNEAK UP TO MCDONALD'S MANSION ONE NIGHT AND SEE CONFERENCE OF VILLAINS TAKING LACE. DOGS LET LOOSE AND THEY HAVE TO TAKE TO THEIR HEELS. STEP IN ICY STREAM. BACK TO MISS HAYLING'S HOUSE FOR HOT BATH AND WHISKY. "NASTY BRUTES", SAYS PARKER. OF COURSE, COLONEL IS NOT SERIOUS ABOUT OIL, WHICH IS OF NO USE SUPPOSEDLY: ONLY FLOATING A FAKE COMPANY...

[illegible]

GET MAP. PONS AND PARKER WALK ON HILL.

CORONER'S COURT DID NOT INVESTIGATE VERY FULLY. (CHECK ON SCOTTISH PRACTICE). TRAP STILL IN STREAM. PONS GOES DOWN TO INVESTIGA FINDS NEXT DAY THAT REMAINS OF TRAP HAVE BEEN BURNED BY LOCAL FARMER. SHAFTS HAD BEEN SAWN THROUGH, OF COURSE.

PHILOSOPHICAL QUOTATION

WORK?

PONS VISITS GEOLOGIST WHO IS GENUINE CONFIRMS PRESENCE OF SHALE OIL UNDER LAND AND GIVES PONS COPY OF HIS REPORT...

ONLY PLACE ~~WORK~~ IN THAT PART OF SCOTLAND WHICH HAS OIL, THOUGH NO COMMERCIA

[illegible]

'THE ADVENTURE OF THE CALLOUS COLONEL' #3

PONS FINDS PROSPECTUSES AND BROCHURES. GIRL IS HOLDING THINGS UP. WHEN THEY FAIL TO DRIVE THEM OUT, HAVE TO GET RID OF HER.

COLONEL CHALLENGES PONS TO A DUEL WITH RIFLES: PONS ACCEPTS AS THERE IS MIST. KNEW IT WOULD BE IMPOSSIBLE AND ASSUMES HE WILL ATTEMPT TO MURDER HIM. PUTS UP A DUMMY WHICH THE COLONEL SHOOTS AT. PONS SHOOTS AND WOUNDS HIM IN A CHILLING FINALE AND EVENTUALLY HE FALLS TO HIS DEATH IN THE RAVINE.

PONS FINDS SHALE OIL REPORT. PARKER ASKS WHAT IS POINT. PONS SAYS IT IS SWINDLE AND PEOPLE WILL ANSWER BROCHURES IN THOUSANDS. IN FINALE MCDONALD COMES TO HOTEL AND CHALLENGES PONS TO DUEL. IT IS MADNESS, PONS/, SAYS PARKER. BUT PONS ACCEPTS NEVERTHELESS. TWO SPORTING RIFLES. AT GLEN CORRIE. "MEET ON TOP OF BIG ROCK", SMILES COLONEL. PONS SMILES ENIGMATICALLY. WHEN THEY GET THERE HAS PACK WITH HIM. SEARCHES TERRAIN WITH BINOCULARS, BEHIND ROCKS. PUT UP DUMMY. IT IS IMMEDIATELY SHOT WITH TELESCOPIC SIGHTED RIFLE. PONS SMILES. COLONEL COMES OUT AND PONS WOUNDS HIM IN [illegible]. MIST COMES DOWN. "HIS RIFLE IS USELESS NOW," SAYS PONS. STALKING MATCH ON CRAG. MCDONALD SLIPS TO DEATH IN RAVINE DESPITE PONS' EFFORTS TO SAVE HIM. "NO TROUBLE FROM POLICE SAYS, PONS. WE MUST REPORT THIS TO POLICE AT INVERNESS. TAUT, TERSE NARRATIVE WITH MORE ON CONFLICT THAN ON DETECTION...

START NEXT ONE. OF ALL THE CASES MY FRIEND SOLAR PONS WAS INVOLVED IN, NONE MORE SOMBRE AND BIZARRE THAN THAT OF...

FERGUSON SPRAWLING ON GROUND AFTER SINGLE STICK FIGHT WITH PONS. MCDONALD STEPS OUT OF SHADOWS. "CONGRATULATIONS, MR PONS. YOU HAVE NOT LOST YOUR DEXTERITY, I SEE". PONS BOWED. "NEITHER YOU YOUR INGENUITY, I SEE. SPRING CATCHES OPERATING SURPRISES WERE ALWAYS YOUR SPECIALITY, WERE THEY NOT". MCDONALD'S SMILE FADED.

'The Adventure of the Callous Colonel' #4

"I FANCY WE SHOULD HAVE FOUND THE SHAFTS HALF SAWN THROUGH".

"I HAVE NO DOUBT THE SHAFTS OF THE DOG-CART WERE PARTLY SAWN THROUGH, CAUSING THE DEATHS OF THOSE TWO UNFORTUNATE PEOPLE. YOU EMPLOYED MERGUSON, AN INDISCREET BRUTE AND BULLY, INTENDING TO MAKE HIM THE SCAPEGOAT. WHEN HIS USEFULNESS HAD EXPIRED YOU HAD HIM MURDERED BY STAGING AN ACCIDENT ON THAT CONVENIENT CLIFF".

COLONEL MCDONALD HAD STOOD STOCKSTILL, HIS ONLY MOVEMENT BEING THE INSISTENT TAPPING OF HIS DOG-WHIP ON THE TOP OF HIS HIGHLY-POLISHED RIDING BOOT. NOW A NERVE TWITCHED IN HIS CHEEK. THAT AND HIS BLAZING EYES WERE THE ONLY INDICATIONS OF THE ANGER WITHIN.

"STRONG WORDS, MR PONS", HE SAID IN THAT UNCANNILY SOFT VOICE. "STRONG WORDS. AND ONES YOU ARE GOING TO FIND DIFFICULT TO PROVE

"I AM NOT TRYING TO PROVE THEM", SAID PONS WITH A FAINT SMILE. "I AM MERELY SPEAKING MY THOUGHTS ALOUD".

COLONEL APPEALS TO PONS' SPORTING INSTINCTS...

"WHAT DID YOU PUT IN THE ~~LETTER~~ Telegram, PONS?"

"I APPEALED TO HIS VANITY, PARKER. I KNEW HE COULD NOT RESIST".

ROCK KNOWN AS THE SENTINEL.

SOLAR PONS LAUGHED. "GOOD HEAVENS, I HAVE NO INTENTION OF PLAYING INTO HIS HANDS, PARKER. I HAVE COME WELL PREPARED".

HE TAPPED THE RUCKSACK HE CARRIED.

GETS WEATHER FORECAST BEFORE HE GOES OUT.

OILSKIN TOBACCO POUCH WITH FERGUSON'S INITIALS.

THIS MATTER MUST BE SETTLED BETWEEN US. YOUR TERMS OR MINE. PONS.

'THE ADVENTURE OF THE CURSED CURATOR' #1

No. 5. VOL 4 . SOLAR PONS. 10/10/78.

THE ADVENTURE OF THE CURSED CURATOR
AMBULANT MUMMY?

Biggs. MEMBER OF THE CORONEL CLUB BECAUSE HE IS WEARING THE DISTINCTIVE TIE OF THAT ESOTERIC ORGANISATION. BACHELOR, BECAUSE THOUGH WELL DRESSED HE IS, IF HE WILL FORGIVE ME SAYING SO, UNTIDY AND HIS COLLAR, THOUGH SPOTLESS IS HEAVILY CRUMPLED AND HIS SHOES NEED CLEANING. I COULD NOT IMAGINE ANY CONSCIENTIOUS WIFE LETTING A MAN SO IMPORTANT AS THE CURATOR OF A MAJOR MUSEUM OUT WITH HIS COLLAR AND SHOES IN THAT STATE".

"Again correct, Mr Pons", said Biggs, with a rueful glance at his shoes.

"And the cinema Pons".

"When Mr Biggs took out his handkerchief just now, a n umber of ticket stubs fell unnoticed to the carpet. There are more than a dozen of them and I notice they are for The Everyman, the Cameo, the Astor and the Rialto. The colour of the tickets tells me that they were issued this year. It is only the beginning of April, which means that Mr Biggs must go at least once a week".

"Correct again, Mr Pons". Re-tool.

"Bach?"

"He has no less than three publications devoted to Bach on the chair yonder. They all bear a newsagent's scribble wit his name.

Biggs almost laughed at this point.

"You are right. I always like to read something on the Tube".

"Those issues are for February, March and April of thks year. Therefo e, I deduce you have be n away on a long trip. When I see a newish guide to Alexandria there, again with your initials on the cover, much

'The Adventure of the Cursed Curator' #2

2

stained and thumbed and I see the remnants of ~~a tan~~ Parker's high complexion-- it requires no very great deductive feat to infer that you have recently returned from a trip to Egypt, possibly for the Museum."

"It is still remarkable, Mr Pons", said Biggs enthusiastically.

He resumed his seat with a clouded brow.

"However, it may have been my Egyptian trip which has precipitated my present troubles".

Went to the cinema twelve times in first six weeks of the year. i.e. twice a week.

Some good cinemas near the museum.

SERVANT PUT DOPE IN BOOL FOR SHIPMENT. LONDON AGENT TRYING TO STEAL THEM: THEY GO ASTRAY SOME WAY? SAME MAN WHO WAS ONLY DISGUISED AS NATIVE. AGENTS TRY TO FRIGHTEN BIGGS WITH HORRIFIC THINGS IN MUSEUM. PROMISING BUILD-UP HERE...

OTHER DOPE SMUGGLERS KNEW THE STUFF WAS BEING SHIPPED TO ENGLAND. INFILTRATED SITE AND USED BREAKAGES AND PORTERS' DISPUTE TO OPEN WINE JARS, WHICH THEY THOUGHT CONTAINED THE DRUGS, WHICH THEY WANTED TO STEAL. ONE OF THEIR NUMBER KILLED.

USE HOWARD CARTER'S BOOK ON THE TOMB OF TUTANKHAMUN FOR BACKGROUND MATERIAL AND DETAIL.

TREASURE IN CRATES AND ACHMED, THE POLICE OFFICER THERE TO GUARD IT. BUT

'The Adventure of the Cursed Curator' #3

3

CRATES WITH VALUELESS OBJECTS HAD BEEN TAMPERED WITH: PONS SAW AT ONCE THAT SOMETHING INSIDE THE SEALED JARS WAS INVOLVED DRUGS OR JEWELLERY: OR BOTH. CRATE HAD BEEN MARKED WITH RED PAINT DELIBERATELY. STUFF PUT IN JARS ON SITE BY WORKMAN: ATTEMPT MADE TO OBTAIN THEM ON SITE BY RIVAL GANG AND THE INTRUDER KILLED. MASTER MIND BEHIND IT TRAVELLED ON SAME SHIP: DISGUISED AS MUMMY? FIRST KILLED ACHMED: PUSHING HIM UNDER A BUS.

"RUN OVER A BUS!" OH, COME NOW, MR BIGGS, YOU CANNOT POSSIBLY CONCEIVE THAT TO BE AN ACCIDENT?"

"I REPORTED IT TO THE POLICE AND INSPECTOR JAMISON WAS OF THE SAME OPINION, MR PONS".

PONS STARED AT ME IN SILENCE.

ONE OF GUARDS DRESSED UP AS MUMMY TO ACT AS DECOY: PONS "UNMASKS" HIM. THEN EGYPTIAN GOES INTO OFFICE TO TRY AND UNDO JARS. HE IS VISITOR TO MUSEUM? HIDDEN IN MUSEUM. OR LONDON AGENT FOR DRUGS...

"MIDDLE EAST ONE OF THE BIGGEST AREAS OF THE WORLD FOR DRUG-SMUGGLING, PARKER".

GO TO MUSEUM AND MEET CHARACTERS: PONS BAITS TRAP, THEY WAIT IN EGYPTIAN ROOM AT NIGHT AND TERRIBLE FIGHT BREAKS OUT BETWEEN SECURITY GUARD AND "MR BIG". PONS FIRST INTERVIEWS GUARDS AND THEN SELECTS ONE HE SUSPECTS THROUGH A RATIOCINATIVE FEAT. LATER DRAPS HIM SIMPLY AND DARINGLY.

PONS SAYS THEY HAVE NO TIME TO LOSE.

'The Adventure of the Cursed Curator' #4

RED HERRINGS: WEIRD PEOPLE ON MUSEUM STAFF WHO MUST ACT SUSPICIOUSLY: ENORMOUS GUARD WHOM PARKER SUSPECTS IMMEDIATELY. PONS IMMEDIATELY SEES OTHER MAN, THOUGH SMALLER, IS YOUNGER AND FITTER AND WEARS RUBBER-SOLED SHOES. EGYPTIAN DETECTIVE IN WITH THIEVES: THAT'S WHY HE WAS PUSHED UNDER BUS. MAN ALREADY KILLED AT DIGGINGS... DETECTIVE HAD BEEN KILLED IN CAIRO: PONS CABLES TO POLICE THERE. HE HAD IDENTITY CARD STOLEN FROM DEAD MAN. BIGGS ONLY MET HIM SEVERAL DAYS OUT AFTER HE HAD BEEN TIPPED OVERBOARD. OR EGYPTIAN POLICE CABLE BACK THEIR DETECTIGE FOUND IN NILE... THIEVES TRIED CURATOR'S OFFICE BUT STUFF NOT THERE. RED-MARKED CRATE IN ANNEXE STRONG-ROOM...

PARKER IS ABOUT TO GIVE THE GAME AWAY WHEN PONS TREADS ON HIS FOOT.
EXPLAIN WHY PONS WAS RIGHT ABOUT DETECTIVE FROM CAIRO BUT LATER FOUND THE MAN KILLED UNDER THE BUS WAS A SUBSTITUTE. TWO GROUPS OF PEOPLE INVOLVED. MAN CALLED NAHAS PASHA WHO VISITS MUSEUM AS SCHOLAR?

DOPE SMUGGLERS SEIZED OPPORTUNITY OF HIDING SHIPMENT IN POTS: ON SITE IN VALLEY OF KINGS: BEFORE THEY COULD MOVE IT STUFF HAD BEEN GIVEN TO LONDON MUSEUM. DECIDED TO DISTRIBUTE IT IN LONDON: RIVAL GANG TRIED TO BREAK INTO CRATE BUT WAS KILLED. THEIR MAN ON BOARD SHIP FIRST KILLED CAIRO DETECTIVE BY TIPPING HIM OVERBOARD, THEN ASSUMING HIS IDENTITY. CRATE HAD BEEN MARKED BY RED PAINT: FEINT MADE FOR MUSEUM VALUABLES WHILE THEY WILL STRIKE AT POTTERY. TRIED TO KILL BIGGS SO THAT THEY COULD GET HIS KEYS AND OPEN LOCKED STRONG ROOM....

PONS CALLS FOR EMPLOYMENT RECORD OF MUSEUM STAFF: MORTICOTT HAD BEEN THERE FOR 15 YRS. ONLY ONE OTHER MAN STRONG ENOUGH TO LIFT THE VASE. PRENDERGAST HAD ONLY BEEN THERE A FEW WEEKS. OBVIOUS, SAYS PONS.

'THE ADVENTURE OF THE CURSED CURATOR' #5

PONS MUSEUM INVESTIGATIONS.

CLEAR UP AND MAKE PLAIN

1 ACHMED COOL RASCAL: THOUGH FAKE REPORTED TO SCOTLAND YARD AS NORMAL IN HIS ASSUMED PERSONA, TO PUT CAIRO POLICE OFF TRACK

2 MENTION AGAIN BIG MAN MAKING MASK APPEARANCES TO SPREAD ALARM AND CONFUSION.

3 BUSINESS WAS PUT ON AS A FEINT TO MAKE MUSEUM STAFF PUT STRONGER GUARD ON CAIRO TREASURES: OPPOSITE WAS TRUTH, IN FACT.

4 WEIRD GOINGS ON WERE NOT INITIALLY REPORTED TO SCOTLAND: JAMISON MUST BE AWARE OF THIS AND MENTION IT GRUMBLINGLY.

WHY WAS IT ASSUMED THEY WERE AFTER THE TREASURE.

PONS SAYS TREASURES WOULD HAVE BEEN STOLEN EVEN BEFORE THEY LEFT EGYPT.

'THE ADVENTURE OF THE CURSED CURATOR' #6

NL - Dulap

Museum Plot.

Said Pons, "To me the whole idea of the treasure of the Valley of the Kings was a non-starter. It was far too celebrated for such a coup and no-one in the world could handle such treasure. ~~From the~~ So I concentrated on the sealed jars. Inspector Achmed was the key man here and when Scotland Yard was informed that the real Inspector had been murdered in Cairo and had never left the city it became clear that the jars were the real objective. But the plan went awry with the murder of the fake Achmed. ~~who was obviously the key man. Three of~~ Kroll's men panicked. That ~~trick~~ attempt on Mr Biggs' life was actually inimical to their plan and crude in the extreme. Though if Mr Biggs had been killed and Prendergast had seized the keys I have no doubt they would have had the consignment of drugs and would have been out of the museum within half an hour.

"As members of the staff, recruited at short notice, due to the Museum's expanding activities, they were excellently placed to aid ~~the bogus Inspector~~ Achmed, who was obviously the guiding force behind the ~~xxxxx~~ team, and the professional safe-man they had to employ in the end. The mummy-mask was merely a device to spread alarm and despondency among the genuine staff members and act as a cover for the real attempt to recover the drugs.

"These activities, of course, ~~was with~~ were designed with the whole object of the Museum putting ~~axxxxxxx~~ an already stronger guard on the Cairo treasures and therefore to further deplete its thin staff while the actual plan, ~~as~~ we have seen, was in fact the opposite. Prendergast and Scott, ~~of course,~~ would have been able to let people into the Museum by a side door after hours and I have no doubt they would have succeeded in their objective had not the ill-advised attempt been made on the Curator's life".

Inspector Jamison was looking a little pink about the neck and cheeks.

"If you had reported these strange manifestations to me in the first place", Mr Biggs", he rumbled, "Scotland Yard might have put paid to the whole matter without bothering Mr Pons".

"Might is a big word, Inspector", said Pons with a twinkle in his eye.

'THE ADVENTURE OF THE CURSED CURATOR' #7

Nr - Pons

308

"I therefore selected the two newest men, ... and ...., as being prime suspects, knowing also that more than one night-guard would have been involved in the mummy deception. It would have been highly risky otherwise for the man in the next section could easily come across him before he had time to change back into his uniform. In the event this supposition turned out to be correct".

"But what about the man with the acetylene-torch, Pons?"

My companion shook his head.

"A mere tool. Parker. Oh, someone cool of brain and a professional expert at his job. Kroll's people were getting worried and were evidently under pressure from the Baron. The murder of Kroll's man, pushed under a bus by a member of the group seeking the drugs, was undoubtedly the catalyst. They resorted to crude methods. The only way to get access to their cargo was by eliminating the Curator and stealing the keys to the strong-room. This they attempted and it was only by a miracle that Mr Biggs escaped that murderous attack. Wisely he came immediately to me, with the conclusion we have seen." I expected some sort of diversion but was almost taken off guard by the boldness of the methods used".

He turned back to the little man.

"Tell me, Mr Biggs. One thing still puzzles me and may have a profound bearing on your experiences. Did your friend Nazreel Pasha know Achmed personally? The answer might be of vital importance".

Biggs turned red and shifted his feet on the carpet.

"I see your drift, Mr Pons. So far as I know Nazreel Pasha did not have any personal contact. He recommended Achmed to me one day in Cairo and he turned up at my hotel the following day".

"I see".

Solar Pons got up from his chair and stood smoking thoughtfully for a moment or two.

"By which time the unfortunate Chief Inspector was already floating in the Nile. Nevertheless, it is a point which needs clearing up. High-ranking Museum officials in places like Egypt are not averse to making fortunes on the side from drug-running, if Mr Biggs will forgive the suggestion. A discreet word with the Cairo police authorities should take care of that, Jamison".

'The Adventure of the Cursed Curator' #8

Mr Fowlers

309

Jamison stuck out his jaw pugnaciously.

"I take your drift, Mr Pons. I will do the necessary. I have learned a great deal here tonight".

"Life is a university, Inspector", said Solar Pons quietly. "We can all learn a great deal by using our eyes and ears as we progress from day to day".

He looked at me inquisitively.

"Now, if you have no further questions, Parker..."

"None, Pons", said I, getting to my feet.

My companion smiled reflectively.

"I would give a great deal to see the Baron's face tonight".

He held out his hand to Biggs and the Inspector in turn.

"And now, Parker, it is almost one in the morning. I would not like to incur Mrs Johnson's displeasure by keeping you out so late".

-.-

Finished 5.51 p.m. Friday.
December 24th, 1978.

THE ADVENTURE OF THE NORTHLEACH STOCKS

-- see picture. Corpse of man clad in outlandish costume found dead in stocks one mid-summer morning. At first taken for a masquerader. Pons, vacationing in neighborhood, called in. Cf. Aleister Crowley's Satan-worship. Pons deduces man has been at Black Mass celebration somewhere in neighborhood. Gloucestershire in Cotswolds. Northleach is in vicinity of Avebury and Marlborough, between which are the dolmen called the Devil's Den and numerous Grey Wethers or sarsen stones. On Windmill Hill, also nearby, 1¼ M. to No. of Beckenhampton is neolithic camp with 3 concentric ditches broken by causeways. ... Avebury Circle, greatest megalithic monument in world. Within vallum, 1480 yds. in circuit, is large fosse, on edge of which stands ring of upright stones, of which 9 remain. In central space 2 double concentric circles, once consisting of about 600 stones, of which only 6 now erect, unhewn stones older than Stonehenge. Largest weighs over 60 tons. ADV. OF AVEBURY SACRIFICE? See Baedeker's ENGLAND pages 101-2. Avebury across Salisbury Plain from Marloborough by bus? Possible. Pons cd. be visiting in Marlbosough. Avebury 6 m. north of Marlborough. ADV. OF THE SARSEN STONES? See page 139 Blue Guide to England.

OUNTRY LIFE—JANUARY 18, 1962 101

W. R. Bawden

VILLAGE STOCKS AND PILLORY: NORTHLEACH, GLOUCESTERSHIRE

The Adventure of the Northleach Stocks

IN JUNE 1978, Arkham House editor James Turner sent Basil Copper a copy of two documents he found amongst August Derleth's Solar Pons papers, relating to a Pontine adventure that the author never lived to write.

"It's fascinating to see how he went about this," Turner wrote, "clipping a photograph from *Country Life* and then plotting a story around it." He told Basil: "If you ever wish to employ this Satan Worship idea in the new Pontine series you are more than welcome to it, but I include this material mainly to show you how August went about his creative work."

Basil acknowledged: "The August material you kindly copied is fascinating and would be an excellent idea for a further Pons adventure . . . I'll file the stocks idea for future use in Vol. 5 . . . There's no reason why we shouldn't keep this series going indefinitely, so long as Pinnacle continue to play ball."

Basil did get around to jotting down a few notes and filing them in his envelope of "Plot Notes & Dialogue Notes":

> Pons. One story of Suffolk with death in the stocks.
> One in which Pons is reputedly dead.

"My death has been greatly exaggerated, Parker."

Unfortunately, with the eventual collapse of the Pinnacle Books deal, nothing ever came of the idea.

—Stephen Jones

PAINTING PONS: ARTIST BEN STAHL

BEN STAHL WAS born in Chicago, Illinois, on September 7, 1910. A self-taught artist, he won a scholarship to the prestigious Art Institute of Chicago when he was only twelve, and four years later his work was displayed in the Art Institute's International Watercolour Show.

Stahl worked as a commercial artist for many years. His art ranged from painting the poster design for the movie *Ben-Hur* (1959), illustrating such books as *The Innkeeper's Wife* by A.J. Cronin, a limited edition of *Madame Bovary* and the 25th Anniversary edition of *Gone with the Wind*, to appearing in numerous magazines—including *Women's Home Companion*, *Cosmopolitan*, *Esquire*, *Picture Post* and, from 1933 onwards, more than 750 issues of *The Saturday Evening Post*.

Among his many book cover designs—which included Charles L. Grant's early horror novels *The Hour of the Oxrun Dead* (1977) and *The Sound of Midnight* (1978)—were the covers for Pinnacle Books' entire *Solar Pons* series. Beginning in 1974 with the first volume, *The Adventures of Solar Pons*, Stahl painted the covers of all seven paperbacks by August Derleth, culminating in *Mr. Fairlie's Final Journey*, before continuing with the four Pons books written by Basil Copper.

His clean, angular lines and subtle hues gave the covers a timeless quality, while also no doubt appealing to a more contemporary readership.

"I want my paintings to excite the senses," the artist explained. "I was never one for fine detail. I always try to get to the guts of a painting—to line and form. To me, Art is a search for vital arrangements of line and form that trigger an emotional response."

Stahl worked as a teacher at the Art Institute of Chicago, the American Academy of Art and the Art Students League of New York, amongst other institutions, and he was a recipient of more than fifty national awards, including the Saltus Gold Medal of the National Academy of Design in 1952.

As an author, he wrote and illustrated the novel *Blackbeard's Ghost*, which was made into a movie by Walt Disney Productions in 1968 starring Peter Ustinov, while a sequel entitled *The Secret of the Red Skull* was illustrated by his eldest son.

On April 26, 1968, thieves broke in to Stahl's Museum of the Cross in his hometown of Sarasota, Florida, and carefully stole the complete set of fifteen six-feet by nine-feet paintings depicting scenes of the crucifixion of Jesus Christ, fourteen of which had been done for a special 1954 edition of the *Bible* published by the Catholic Press. Neither the thieves nor the paintings were ever found.

The artist died of cancer on October 19, 1987, in Sarasota's Memorial Hospital. He was 77 years old. His friend and colleague, the great American artist Norman Rockwell, once said: "We are but illustrators, but Ben Stahl is among the masters".

—Stephen Jones

The Dossier of Solar Pons (Pinnacle Books, January 1979)

The Further Adventures of Solar Pons (Pinnacle Books, August 1979)

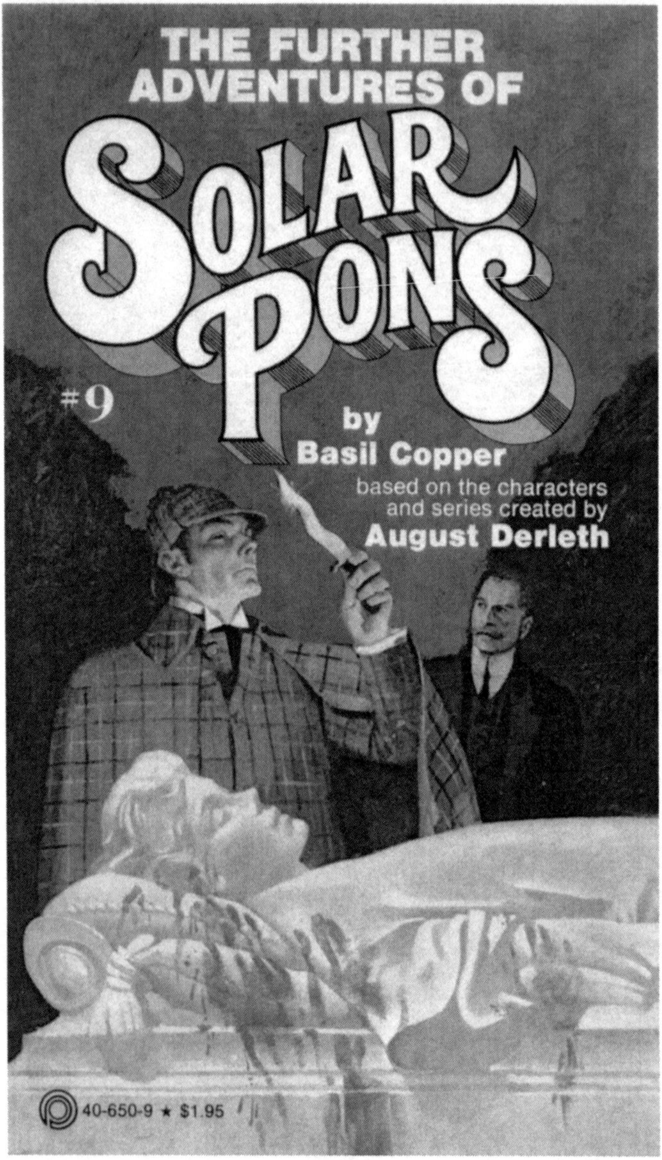

The Secret Files of Solar Pons (Pinnacle Books, October 1979)

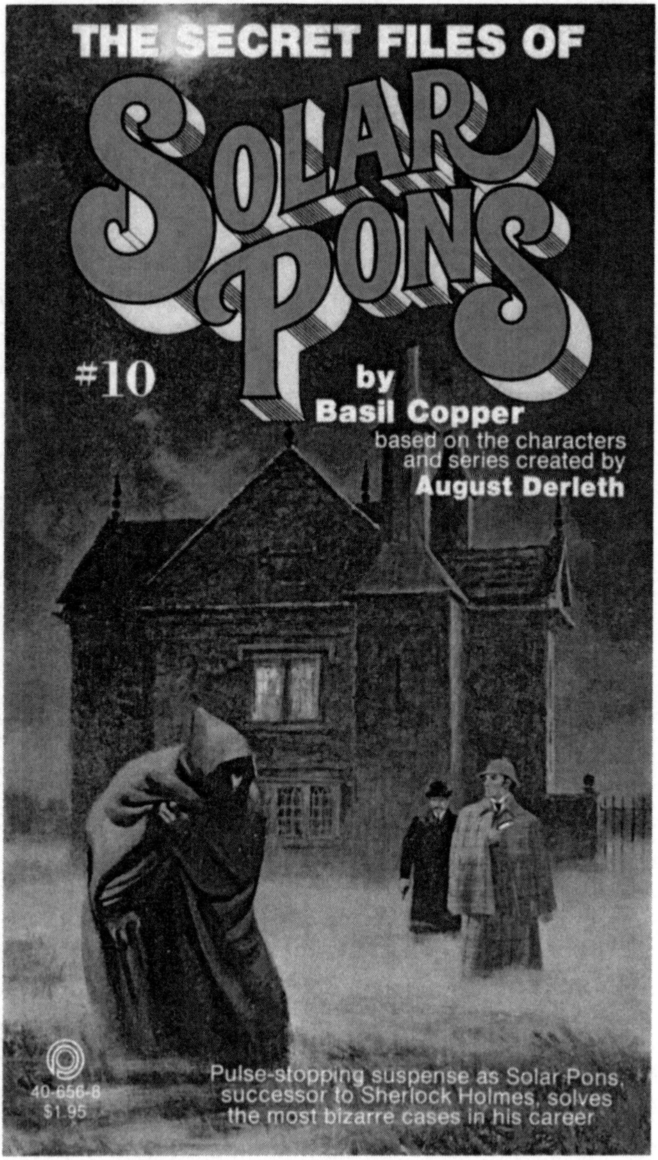

The Uncollected Cases of Solar Pons (Pinnacle Books, January 1980)

The Adventure of the Defeated Doctor

In May 1977, James Turner—the then-editor at Arkham House—suggested in a letter to Basil Copper that he might want to consider changing the name of the unseen chief villain in 'The Adventure of the Baffled Baron' from "Baron Ennesfred Kroll" to "the Doctor", in keeping with August Derleth's affectionate pastiche of Sax Rohmer's insidious Dr. Fu Manchu. Basil agreed to subtly change the dénouement, *as well as coming up with the necessary title change (which had not occurred to Turner), and this was how the following story appeared in* Solar Pons #9: The Further Adventures of Solar Pons *(1979) for its one and only previous appearance. The author's original version finally saw print under its preferred title in 2005 in* Solar Pons: The Final Cases. SJ.

1

"AH PARKER, I see that our old friend Jamison is in difficulties again."

"You have the advantage of me, Pons."

"Naturally. You do not command a very good view of the window from your position at the breakfast table. And the casements opposite are making an excellent reflector for the sunshine, which penetrates even into the interior of the police car."

It was a beautiful morning in early June and my friend Solar Pons was standing smoking a reflective after-breakfast pipe at the window of our sitting room at 7B Praed Street.

I remained sitting at the table and spread some more marmalade on my second slice of toast.

"He is exploiting your talents, Pons."

"Possibly, Parker, possibly. Though it would not do to underestimate the doggedness of Inspector Jamison. Obtuse he may be occasionally; and plodding certainly; but method and devotion of duty usually get him to his destination in the end."

"You are being unusually generous this morning, Pons."

"Am I not, Parker?"

Solar Pons smiled amiably.

"But then it is such a superb morning and London has been extremely dull of late. Jamison's arrival may mean action and opportunity. I have been chafing at the bit this last week and our somewhat heavy-footed colleague may unlock the gates for us. You have no objection, I take it?"

"I, Pons? Most certainly not. I am taking a sabbatical today in any case."

"Excellent, Parker. You are usually on your rounds by this time. Ah, here is Mrs. Johnson at the door now."

The beaming, well-scrubbed face of our excellent landlady had indeed appeared round the panel and at Pons' crisp summons to enter she ushered in the worried-looking figure of

Inspector Jamison. Pons had already thrown off his old grey dressing-gown and donned his jacket and now he strode forward, his face alert and quite transfigured from its languid expression of a few minutes earlier.

"Welcome, Jamison. Will you not have some coffee?"

"Thank you, Mr. Pons. It has been a week and a half I can tell you."

The Scotland Yard man sank into an armchair indicated by Pons and mopped his brow with a polka-dot handkerchief. His sallow face was beaded with perspiration and his complexion looked grey.

"You need a holiday, Inspector," I suggested.

Jamison gave a wry smile as he put his handkerchief back in his pocket.

"You will have your little joke, doctor."

Mrs. Johnson had withdrawn to her own quarters and Pons passed the big cup of black coffee over to Jamison who seized it as though he had not taken nourishment for a fortnight.

"Trouble?"

Inspector Jamison nodded, a gloomy expression on his face.

"Difficulties, Mr. Pons. I should be glad of a little help."

"This agency exists to assist the forces of law and order, Jamison. Pray be more specific."

Solar Pons drew up a chair to the table opposite the Inspector and tented his fingers before him, while his deep-set eyes searched our visitor's face.

"It is a crime of capital dimensions; it has happened within the past twenty-four hours; and there is great pressure on you from above."

Jamison's face turned a mottled colour.

"How did you know that, Mr. Pons?" he snapped.

Solar Pons smiled.

"It is obvious, Jamison. You would not seek my advice unless it were important. Similarly, the same set of criteria apply if you are stuck in your investigations. I estimate it would take you no more than twenty-four hours to conclude that the matter is beyond you. So with pressure on you from above—perhaps from Superintendent Heathfield or even the Commissioner himself—you come to me."

There were dull red patches burning on Jamison's cheeks now.

"You have an unfortunate way of putting it, Mr. Pons," he mumbled. "But basically you are correct."

Solar Pons leaned back in his chair, a thin smile on his face.

"What is the problem?"

Jamison put down his coffee cup on the table with a thin clink in the silence.

"Romane Schneider is dead, Mr. Pons."

Pons looked at Jamison in silence, his brows drawn, while my own astonishment must have shown on my face.

"The sculptor, Inspector? The one who has the International Exhibition on in London at the present time?"

"One and the same, Dr. Parker. Though I know little of such matters he is described as the greatest sculptor this country has ever produced."

Solar Pons' eyes were sparkling and he looked at our visitor piercingly from beneath the lids.

"How did he die, Jamison?"

"Murdered, Mr. Pons. In his own studio in Hampstead. Done to death with one of the mallets he used for his sculpture work."

There was something so evocative in Jamison's hushed tones

as he came to the last sentence that an involuntary shudder passed through me.

"When was this?" asked Solar Pons, opening his eyes.

"The early hours of this morning, Mr. Pons. It will be in all tomorrow's editions.

He paused and looked uncomfortable.

"It was a sore point with me, Mr. Pons. I will be quite frank. It took me only a few hours to see that the matter presented certain difficulties."

"Which has brought you here at breakfast-time?"

"Exactly."

Jamison took out his handkerchief again and mopped the nape of his neck with it.

"I have seldom seen a more pointless sort of crime, Mr. Pons. There was no robbery as far as we can make out; no one had a motive; and the studio had not been broken into."

Solar Pons shook his head, a reproving expression on his face.

"Come, Jamison. How many times have I told you? No visible motive. There is always a motive for every crime, however pointless it may appear to the casual bystander."

"You are undoubtedly right, Mr. Pons. But I have seldom been faced with such difficulties. Could you spare the time to step around?"

"Certainly. But first I should like to know a little more about the details. We have time for that, I should imagine?"

"Certainly, Mr. Pons," said Jamison gloomily. "Whoever murdered Romane Schneider will be miles away by now."

Pons held up his finger reprovingly.

"We do not know that, Inspector. And it is useless to speculate without sufficient data."

He looked across at me with satisfaction.

"And as the crime was committed only a few hours ago it means that the trail is fresh."

"You may well be right, Mr. Pons," Jamison went on lugubriously.

"Come, Jamison," said Pons cheerfully. "I have never seen you so down. Pray favour us with some facts."

Jamison put his handkerchief away for the second time and frowned at me before turning his attention to my companion.

"A patrolling constable found the body of Mr. Schneider at three o'clock this morning, Mr. Pons. He saw the light from the skylight. Mr. Schneider lives in a big house in the Vale of Health, which is just off Hampstead High Street."

"Yes, yes, Jamison," said Pons irritably. "I am tolerably familiar with the area. Get to the facts and leave the guidebook details to friend Parker here when he comes to write up the case."

He smiled wryly, ignoring Jamison's frown of discomfiture.

"Very well, Mr. Pons," he continued in a weary voice. "P.C. Daniels would not normally have bothered about a solitary light at that time of the morning except that he knows the area; knows the house; and also knows that Mr. Schneider rarely works by artificial light; and never after ten o'clock in the evening. He is a man of very fixed personal habits. Or was."

"I see."

Solar Pons' eyes were very steady and piercing as he stared at the Inspector.

"So he decided to investigate the light, Mr. Pons. He did not want to arouse the house, which was in darkness. It is a Georgian building and he walked to the back, through the extensive garden to where the studio stands. It is a detached building of some size. It has a garage and store-rooms at the bottom and a timber staircase and balcony which give access to the studio on the first floor."

"I think I know the house, Pons," I put in. "Cheneys, is it not?"

Inspector Jamison nodded.

"Correct, Dr. Parker. You have an excellent memory."

"It is improving, Jamison," said Pons. "I give you that. You were saying?"

"P.C. Daniels walked up the stairs, Mr. Pons, and knocked. He received no reply. The door was locked so he went round the verandah. There were thick curtains over the windows on the far side. What he saw through a chink in the coverings brought him back to the front where he broke the glass-panelled door in to gain admission. What he found inside made him so sick that he had to come out again for air."

"Heavens!" I exclaimed. "Shocking, was it?"

Jamison nodded.

"Horrible, doctor. Mr. Schneider had been badly battered about the head with one of his own mallets as though by a maniac. So ferocious was the attack that there was blood all over the room; on the base of a statue on which he had been working; and the handle of the mallet itself, though of thick wood, had been clean snapped off. There were no fingerprints, as the murderer had worn gloves."

Solar Pons leaned forward in his chair, thin plumes of smoke from his pipe ascending to the sitting-room ceiling in the still June air.

"You intrigue me, Jamison. I take it the body is still in situ?"

Jamison nodded.

"Nothing has been disturbed, Mr. Pons. Our own people have been there, of course, but we have used extreme care."

Solar Pons rubbed his thin hands together

"Excellent, Jamison. To what conclusion did your constable come?"

"He very wisely telephoned his own station, Mr. Pons, and the C.I.D. were soon out there under a very experienced man named Mooney. He got on to the Yard within the hour, not only because Schneider was such a famous man but because of the extraordinary circumstances."

"Pray tell me about them."

Jamison shrugged.

"I hardly know where to begin, Mr. Pons. We did not arouse the household at that time of the morning and carried out our preliminary investigations as quietly as possible. Our police doctor confirmed that Schneider died earlier that evening, of shock and haemorrhage when the skull was crushed with the first blow. The door of the studio was locked and there was no key; we found no signs on the staircase or door that would indicate forcible entry. The skylight is more than twenty feet from the floor and was locked. Moreover, there are no other entrances and exits and the only key to the door known to be in existence was in the dead man's waistcoat pocket."

"You intrigue me, Jamison."

"I am glad you are able to feel so light-hearted about it, Mr. Pons. This, on top of all my other current cases, beats everything."

"If you did not rouse the household, how did you know that Schneider had the only key?"

Inspector Jamison looked smug.

"For the very good reason, Mr. Pons, that we kept details of the house in a book at the local police station. It is standard routine where there is much valuable property on a particular premises. Mr. Schneider asked our local people to keep an eye on the house and studio, and he always notifies them when he goes on holiday. They asked for a spare key but though he supplied them with one for the house he refused in the case of the studio, emphasising that he had the only one, which was never off his person."

"I see. What about the floor of the studio, Jamison?"

"We thought about that. Heavy tongued and grooved pine throughout, highly polished; with a platform for sitters up at one end."

"Hmm."

Solar Pons rubbed his chin thoughtfully.

"And the garage and store-rooms underneath?"

"Nothing, Mr. Pons. I looked through the garage window with a torch soon after I arrived on the scene but it has a solid cement ceiling. So far as I can make out, the storehouses are crammed from floor to ceiling with crates and packing cases."

"So you have not yet appraised the household of Mr. Schneider's death?"

"That is correct, Mr. Pons. But my colleague, Inspector Buckfast, intended to do so. At a reasonable hour, of course, when the occupants were up and about. Mr. Schneider was a bachelor and had only a secretary and housekeeper living on the premises."

Jamison glanced at his watch.

"He would have done so by now at any rate. And we may well learn more from them. Schneider had enemies, I should imagine."

Pons' face bore the alert and keen look that I had observed so often.

"Ah! Whom, for example?"

The Inspector shook his head.

"Every man in the artistic world and especially a pre-eminent man like Mr. Schneider had them, Mr. Pons. Ranging from the critics to fellow artists."

Jamison had a self-satisfied expression on his features as he sat facing Pons and I could see my companion had a small crease of humour at each corner of his mouth.

"I am much obliged to you for the lecture, Inspector. I had no idea that you were so well-informed in such matters. But you no doubt discovered something in his studio to give you that impression?"

Inspector Jamison looked uncomfortable.

"Well, that is so, Mr. Pons. I took the opportunity of perusing the brochure of Mr. Schneider's current Exhibition while I was there. It had fully documented notes on his career."

Solar Pons smiled.

"You have been most frank, Jamison. It does you credit."

He looked across at me.

"Well, Parker, as it is your day off and you have nothing better to do, perhaps you would care to step around with me? It is not often that Inspector Jamison is at such a dead end and I am feeling unusually public-spirited on such a beautiful morning."

2

A short drive through relatively traffic-free streets brought us to the scene of the tragedy. We turned off Hampstead High Street and drove uphill for a short distance through the Vale of Health. The entrance to Cheneys was in a small lane and the house itself, trim and sparkling with white paint and yellow front door, looked prosperous and cheerful across the soft arc of the green.

Jamison ordered the driver to stop a little distance away and we walked in the welcome shade of leafy trees up to a driveway which led down the side of the house. There was another police car parked nearby and a thin, sandy-haired man in a dark brown suit, with a worried expression on his face, came hurrying down toward us as soon as we were seen.

"This business gets stranger every minute, Inspector," he said curtly.

His faded blue eyes looked curiously at us.

"This is Mr. Solar Pons and his colleague, Dr. Lyndon Parker," said Jamison by way of introduction. "My associate, Inspector Buckfast."

"Delighted to meet you both, gentlemen."

Buckfast's expression was cordial and friendly but the worried look remained. He fell into step with us as we walked along the side of the house, ignoring the salute of the constable stationed in the driveway.

"Something wrong?" queried Jamison.

The other man scratched his head.

"I went to the house about an hour ago. Apparently Schneider rented it to some people called Gantley six months ago. They have no connection with him. They have the use of the building below the studio but Schneider naturally retained the latter for himself. From what I gather Schneider suffered some financial reverses and decided to let. He himself now rents a smaller house on the other side of the Heath."

Jamison raised his eyebrows.

"That puts a different complexion on the matter. Have the Gantleys anything to tell us?"

Buckfast shook his head.

"They see Schneider come and go from time to time, of course. They were most helpful but they neither saw nor heard anything last night. I have not told them of the tragedy, of course. They think there has been a burglary."

Inspector Jamison nodded his head in satisfaction.

"I should like a look at the rest of the studio block, nevertheless."

"There is no difficulty about that. I have the keys."

Jamison turned to us.

"Which would you like to see first, Mr. Pons?"

"Oh, the studio, of course. The garage can come later, though I fancy it will tell us little if you have already examined it."

The studio block itself was a handsome, timbered structure, built of stone in rustic style for the lower portion and with mock Tudor beams in the upper. Jamison led the way up the wide teak staircase, pointing out the massive doors to the garage and store-rooms as we ascended. After a short distance the staircase turned at right-angles, terminating in a covered landing with glass windows.

A constable was on guard at the carved oak door and we went through into a large lobby which contained some coats and hats, together with dusty smocks hanging on pegs; a heavy door-mat; and some canes and walking sticks in a rack. There was a large, gilt-framed mirror, full-length, hanging on the far wall.

Jamison pushed open the inner door and we were soon able fully to realise the horror of the situation which had confronted P.C. Daniels in the small hours of the night.

The studio was a high, long room with white walls and oak beams set diagonally. It was lit from a vast circular skylight about twenty-five feet overhead and there were several hanging lamps of antique pattern but wired for electricity, suspended from the ceiling. The floor was made of heavy pine planking, as Jamison had said, and was evidently buttressed from the store-rooms below to take the enormous weight of the masses of sculpture set about on metal plates and in various stages of completion.

There was a large platform up at one end of the room, approached by shallow steps, and with a polished hand-rail round it. There was an easel on the platform and a drawing board with a hanging lamp above it. There was also a camera on a tripod but my eyes passed over all this at a glance.

Everyone who entered had riveted their gaze on the thing that was sprawled before a piece of white marble sculpture in front of the platform and just a few feet away. The beauty of the statue was in such marked contrast to the awful, bloodied creature lying in an agonised posture beneath it that I think we were all momentarily struck dumb. Even Pons' iron nerve was visibly shaken.

"Venus Aphrodite," he murmured. "This would have been an exquisite piece of work had its creator lived."

Inspector Jamison cleared his throat.

"I don't know about that, Mr. Pons," he murmured. "But she is certainly a beautiful lady."

I caught the faint glimpse of a smile in the mocking glance Pons turned on me at the Inspector's *gaucherie*; that and the marvellous expression on the face of the naked goddess rising from the astonishingly sculptured spray had lightened the moment and I stepped forward briskly as Pons said, "Your department, Parker, I think."

I was already on my knees by the remains of Romane

Schneider. He lay with his knees drawn up, his arms outstretched. The fury of the attack had been so great that the whole of the front of the skull had been caved in; death must have been instantaneous. Blood was thickly encrusted in the hair and face and was running from the ears, eyes, mouth and nose.

Great gouts of blood were splashed for yards about the floor and up the base of the statue and the heavy mallet with the broken handle which lay upon the planking was smeared with blood and brains.

I had difficulty in finding a suitable spot in which to kneel with safety but rapidly concluded my examination.

"I agree entirely with the police surgeon's conclusion, Pons," I said. "I can find nothing further."

I rose and dusted my trousers. Pons had already produced the powerful pocket lens, which he habitually carried, and was making a minute examination of the statue, the floor and the immediate area of the body. Jamison and Buckfast stood, a thoughtful group, at the edge of the platform and watched in silence.

Pons straightened up with a grunt.

"The murderer was a man over six feet tall; of enormous strength; but at the same time able to walk as quietly as a cat. The death of Schneider was obviously a matter of great urgency and carried out with technical precision. The motive, when it can be discovered, was so important that it was necessary to eliminate Schneider as rapidly as possible."

I glanced at the two detective officers who were standing open-mouthed upon the platform.

"Come, Pons," I protested. "That the murderer was a man of enormous strength, is fairly obvious. But how do you arrive at your other conclusions?"

"It is surely elementary, Parker," said Solar Pons quietly. "From a careful examination of the body I estimate that Schneider was a man of some five feet eleven inches, perhaps six feet. The single shattering blow that snuffed his life struck him squarely on the crown of the head, carried on into the brain pan and caved in the front of the skull at the same time. To do that the man of normal height, were he tremendously strong, would have to stand upon a box or some form of support. No, Parker, the man who took Schneider's life would need to be at least six feet four inches in height to inflict such a blow. What say you, Jamison?"

The Inspector scratched his head.

"You are certainly correct, Mr. Pons, now that you have pointed it out. We have established Mr. Schneider's height as being five feet eleven."

Solar Pons gave me a thin smile as he turned back to look at the statue of Aphrodite.

"Very well, Pons. But the cat-like qualities?"

"The murderer came from the direction of the door, Parker. To do that he would have to walk a long way. It was obvious that Schneider was at work upon the statue, with his back to the door. Therefore, it was not until his attacker reached him that he became aware of his presence. Will you stand over here, Parker? There, that is correct. Your shadow, as you will notice, is now thrown across the base of the statue. Schneider whirled to receive the mallet blow upon the crown and front of the head. He died instantly."

"That is undoubtedly right, Mr. Pons," said Inspector Buckfast quietly. "But how did his attacker escape?"

"We have yet to establish that, Inspector. But it is obvious that he walked back toward the door. And equally obvious that he dried his shoes at a point here. There was a light rain last night."

Pons walked rapidly to a spot below the railed platform where the two police officers stood and examined the planking minutely with his lens.

"Here, you see, he has wiped his shoes upon the planks. When they were sufficiently dry to leave no marks, he then left. Let us just see . . ."

Pons moved from board to board, his movements intent and bird-like, his ascetic face alight with concentration. Impressed despite themselves, Jamison and Buckfast remained silent.

"There is a little dust but not enough," said Pons presently, rising from his bent posture. "The traces become illegible halfway between the door and the platform."

He glanced upward at the skylight far above our heads.

"It is possible that he was lowered by a rope from above, though unlikely. We shall want that skylight carefully examined, Jamison."

"We have already done so, Mr. Pons."

"I am aware of that. But the operative word is carefully. I suggest it was done cursorily in the early hours of this morning. Incidentally, why was not P.C. Daniels aware that Schneider had let his house and moved?"

"I have already asked him that, Mr. Pons. He is on nights and would not have been aware of any such move. He usually saw Schneider at the studio or thereabouts. Daniels was sometimes in the habit of trying the studio door in the small hours on his beat."

"Hmm."

Pons stood frowning, tugging at the lobe of his right ear as was his habit in moments of great concentration.

"You have not yet told us why the act was so important, Pons, and how you arrived at the conclusion that Schneider had to be eliminated as soon as possible."

Solar Pons turned his piercing glance upon me.

"Tut, Parker, it is self-evident. Learn to use your own ratiocinative faculties. The blow proves that. One colossal, shattering stroke that extinguished life in a second. Schneider had to be killed as quickly as possible. That stands out clearly. The murderer obviously seized the nearest tool to hand; the mallet undoubtedly came from this table here, halfway between the door and the statue."

"You are right, Pons, as always," I muttered.

Solar Pons smiled thinly.

"Right on this occasion, Parker. I am not always so, as I would be the first to admit."

"But could it not have been jealousy or some mad rage, Pons?"

My friend shook his head.

"A jealous rival you mean? A feud in the artistic world? It is barely possible. A person in a mad rage would have gone on battering at the body long after life was extinct. But this was one devastating blow. One would say a clean blow if it had not left such an abattoir-like aftermath."

He looked round with distaste, turning his gaze up to the two silent men in front of us.

"You are right in one thing, Jamison. This is a case which presents a number of baffling aspects. We will just look at the store-rooms below before questioning the occupants of the house."

3

"There is little to see here, Pons."

"I am inclined to agree with you, my dear Parker. But even a negative result tends to eliminate the possibility of error."

We stood in the garage below the studio, Inspector Jamison gloomily behind us. Inspector Buckfast had excused himself and gone back to Cheneys to warn the occupants of our impending arrival.

As Jamison had already told us, the roof of the garage was made of metal girders and cement and there was obviously no way into the studio from the ground. As I moved aimlessly about the floor, noting the Rolls-Royce Silver Ghost and the other opulent touring car in the interior, my mind was overcome by the obvious difficulties in reconciling the facts of Romane Schneider's death. There was no way into the studio; there was no reason to believe there had ever been a second key to the front door; and Pons had already ascertained that the door in question had not been tampered with.

Even as the thought crossed my mind there was a shadow at the garage entrance and a plain-clothes man reported to Inspector Jamison, "The skylight has obviously not been opened for several years, sir. It is secured with heavy bolts from the inside and when we tried to open it, we found the framing screwed down."

Inspector Jamison thanked his subordinate and turned to Pons, his lugubrious features even more grave.

"It just gets more difficult, Mr. Pons."

"On the contrary, light is beginning to show, Jamison. By blocking it out we must eventually arrive at one compact beam which will illuminate the truth for us."

Jamison frowned at me.

"Very picturesquely put, Mr. Pons. Let us just hope you are right."

He led the way through a connecting door in the wall of the garage to a large storage area on the right. This was divided into brick bays and the place was, as Jamison had already told us, jammed from floor to ceiling with crates and boxes. Pons looked keenly about him in the shadowy light. It was difficult to see the thick pine boarding but it was evident that the ceiling was solid and heavy. Moreover, the crates in the bays extended to within an inch or so of the woodwork overhead.

"Just as I told you, Mr. Pons," said the Inspector.

"What is in these boxes, Inspector?"

"I understand from Buckfast that Colonel Gantley, the gentleman who has leased Cheneys, is an antique dealer and importer of curios. Some of the stuff is very valuable, according to Buckfast; while other material is oriental workmanship of no very great value imported into the country for the Colonel's business. He has a shop in Hampstead High Street, which was why he wanted to move nearer his premises."

"Just so," said Pons languidly, looking through half-closed eyes at the legends stencilled on the wooden boxes immediately in front of us.

"The gentleman certainly seems to have very extensive sources, Parker. Hong Kong, Manila, Singapore, Peking and Hangkow are just a few of the names I see before me."

He stepped round a bundle of straw and looked sharply at a small porcelain Buddha which had been unpacked on a rough wooden bench.

"Rather charming work, wouldn't you say so, Parker?"

"Excellent, Pons," I agreed.

Indeed, the workmanship was first-rate and I was surprised to see that the label bore a price of only seven guineas.

"It is astonishingly cheap, Pons."

"Is it not, Parker. But then labour is plentiful in the East, as you are no doubt aware."

"I should not mind that on the mantel at 7B, Pons."

"As you say, Parker, a nice piece. No doubt you may make the Colonel an offer for it when we see him in a moment."

Pons moved away and as he did so his shoes made a harsh, gritty noise on the cement floor of the store-room. Jamison had already turned back to the open air as the thin form of a man came hurrying down the garden toward us, visible through the half-open door. To my astonishment Pons was on his knees, scraping with his fingernails at some white substance on the cement.

My amazement was increased when I saw him tentatively taste it with the extreme tip of his tongue. He put his hand back in his pocket, turned to me and then we were walking up the garden to meet the hurrying figure, before I had time to make any comment on this strange behaviour.

Colonel Gantley turned out to be a tall, fussy-looking man in his early sixties with whitening hair and a frayed silver moustache. He had deep furrows at the corners of his mouth that made his yellow face look like something out of one of those plays set on tropical islands which were becoming the vogue in the West End. He wore a lightweight drill suit with military-style buttons and his brown eyes twinkled benevolently from behind silver-rimmed spectacles.

"A disturbing business, gentlemen," he said briskly, as Jamison introduced us. "I hope that nothing has been stolen from my premises."

"They were all secure, sir," said the Inspector. "And thank you for letting us look around."

"Always anxious to assist the police," said the Colonel, clasping my companion by the hand. "Mr. Solar Pons. It is a pleasure, my dear sir. But you are surely not interested in this trifling affair of my neighbour's burglary?"

Pons gave a dry laugh.

"Not at all, Colonel. I am assisting the police in another matter and, needing to consult Inspector Jamison, was told I could find him here."

"I see. Well, I am at your disposal, gentlemen, but I do not think I shall be of much help."

"One never knows," said Jamison mildly. "You heard nothing at all during the night, I understand?"

"Nothing, Inspector. But then I am a very heavy sleeper and my room is at the side of the house. Of course, anyone could have approached the studio by way of the drive. The gates are never locked. Mr. Schneider sometimes leaves at a late hour. I hear his car during the night on occasion."

"Indeed," said Pons casually.

We were strolling back down the garden now in the bright sunlight, the faint hum of the traffic coming from the main road which passed through the Vale of Health.

"You have not contacted Mr. Schneider, then?" said Colonel Gantley.

Inspector Jamison shook his head.

"We have rung his house, of course. But I understand from his secretary that Mr. Schneider is away at present."

"I see. Well, I hope you catch your man. Now, if there is nothing further, I must get back to my business."

"By all means, Colonel. I am sorry to have taken your time."

We shook hands with the Colonel and watched as he strode back down the driveway to where his car was parked in the side road. A few moments later its engine faded into the general traffic noise.

"So much for that, Pons," I observed.

Solar Pons had been silent, idly drawing patterns in the dust at his feet with the toe of his shoe.

"As you say, Parker."

Jamison frowned, screwing up his eyes against the strong light.

"What next, Mr. Pons?"

"I really think a call at Mr. Schneider's private residence is indicated, Jamison."

"Just as you say, Mr. Pons."

Schneider's new address proved to be a narrow-chested three-storey house of mellow red brick, just off the bustle of Hampstead High Street. The brass fittings of the red front door sparkled in the sunlight and in the small front garden I recognised a granite phoenix created by Schneider, which had once been exhibited at the Paris Exposition.

The door was opened for us by Inspector Buckfast, who had preceded his colleague. He jerked his thumb back over his shoulder.

"I have just told his secretary, Godfrey Horrabin. He has taken it badly. The housekeeper, Mrs. Biggins, is resting in her room."

Jamison nodded without speaking and a moment later Buckfast led the way down a thickly carpeted corridor to a well-appointed study where the secretary was waiting.

Godfrey Horrabin turned out to be a dark-haired man of about thirty, with an ashen-white face and full lips from which the colour had now fled. He rose from his employer's desk as we entered and I then realised he was of an enormous height, well over six feet tall. I shot a significant glance at Pons but he appeared to be occupied in looking about him at the contents of the study as Buckfast introduced us.

"I am sorry, gentlemen, but this has been a dreadful shock. A dreadful shock."

Horrabin slumped back into his chair and passed a handkerchief over his face. Pons sat down opposite him at the other side of the desk and looked at him sympathetically.

"I quite understand, Mr. Horrabin. These things tend to fell one at the time. You'll forgive me, Jamison, for asking the questions."

"Go ahead, Mr. Pons."

Jamison and I sat down in padded leather chairs which were set near the desk and I looked round curiously as Horrabin fought to control his feelings.

"You have been with Mr. Schneider how long?"

"For the past five years, Mr. Pons."

"So that you know him and his habits fairly well?"

"As well as anyone could, I should imagine."

The secretary replaced the handkerchief in the breast pocket of his blue jacket and appeared more composed.

"Was he a tempestuous man? One who would have made many enemies in the course of his career?"

The secretary gave a faint smile which momentarily lightened his features.

"Like most artists he was extremely temperamental. He had been involved in some tremendous arguments and on occasion in actual physical violence."

Pons' eyes were fixed on the secretary's face. He tented his fingers before him and leaned back in his chair, his whole figure expressing dynamic energy.

"Tell me about it, Mr. Horrabin."

The secretary shrugged.

"It is a well-known story, Mr. Pons. A famous rivalry between two sculptors. I have known them take each other's mallets and actually demolish portions of each other's work with which they were offended."

"Indeed."

Solar Pons' eyes were sparkling now.

"You are referring to Sir Hercules Kronfeld, I take it?"

Horrabin looked surprised.

"You knew about it, Mr. Pons?"

My friend chuckled.

"One could hardly avoid it. I would not say that the world of sculpture is one with which I am entirely *au fait*. But I do read the newspapers assiduously and I do seem to remember an item about two years ago when the couple were engaged in a *fracas* at the Paris Salon."

"You are perfectly right, Mr. Pons. They were once good friends but their rivalry developed to such an extent that one could say that only hatred kept them together."

"An extremely apt summing-up," said Solar Pons. "And one that might well apply to many marriages. Eh, Parker?"

"No doubt you are right, Pons."

Solar Pons cupped his lean fingers round his right knee and rocked to and fro as he regarded the secretary keenly.

"You have opened up a fruitful field for investigation, Mr. Horrabin. Are there any other people to whom you would particularly wish to draw my attention?"

The secretary shook his head.

"I cannot think of any, Mr. Pons. There were a number of rows, of course. Various critics and journalists displeased Mr. Schneider from time to time. But the feud with Sir Hercules is the one which stands out."

Pons nodded, tugging at the lobe of his right ear.

"Is Sir Hercules in London, do you know?"

"I believe so, Mr. Pons. He actually telephoned Mr. Schneider a few days ago. He lives in Chelsea. I will get you the address."

"Thank you, Mr. Horrabin. And now, if you will excuse us, I would just like to look around this study for half an hour or so."

"Certainly, Mr. Pons. You have only to press that button there if you require my services. It is connected directly with my quarters."

He pointed to a brass bell-push set into the surface of the desk and quitted the room. Solar Pons sat quietly for a moment, before searching in his pocket for his pipe. He turned to the Inspector as he lit it.

"What do you make of that, Jamison?"

The Inspector wrinkled his brow. The three of us were alone in the room now, Inspector Buckfast having left us at the door. I could see him through the window, painstakingly quartering the garden outside, scrutinising every inch of pathway and turf.

"You mean his size, Mr. Pons?"

Jamison's face lightened for the first time since he had requested Pons' help.

"Well, he is certainly big enough, Mr. Pons. He fits the bill."

"I did not say he did it, Inspector. But it is a possibility which we must not overlook. It is motive which interests me at the moment. And after all, London is full of men who are more than six feet tall. It is the ones who have been in contact with Mr. Schneider who interest us. What say you, Parker?"

"Just what I was thinking, Pons."

Solar Pons smiled faintly.

"You are ever the receptive listener, Parker. That is an invaluable quality and one consistently underrated by the world."

"You are too good today, Pons."

"It is the weather, Parker. I find the combination of such a day and a case of this complexity irresistible."

Inspector Jamison threw up his hands and looked at me helplessly but Pons was already on his feet, his smile intensified, as he went rapidly back and forth across the shelves of the dead man's study.

We waited silently as he continued with his examination. He paused in front of a row of letter files and lifted one out. He put it down with a grunt and started to go through the contents. Soon he had three open on the desk before him. He threw a bundle of envelopes over to me.

"What do you make of those, Parker?"

I scanned the contents with rising agitation, passing them to Jamison before I had finished.

"Why, these are love-letters, Pons!" I said with indignation. "And not to put too fine a point on it, the man sounds an unmitigated swine!"

"Does he not, Parker," said Solar Pons with a dry chuckle. "Letters from a wide variety of different women, most of them with a grudge. And significantly, the studio has been used as a rendezvous, it seems clear."

"A deplorable business, Pons."

Solar Pons pulled at the lobe of his left ear and regarded me thoughtfully.

"You take an altogether too moralistic view of the world, Parker, if you do not mind me saying so. An artist of Mr. Schneider's calibre and one barely into his fifties would be bound to attract the attention of women. A famous name is like a magnet to a certain type of feminine personality."

"For a bachelor you seem to know quite a bit about it, Mr. Pons," put in Jamison sourly.

Creases of amusement appeared at the corners of Solar Pons' mouth.

"A touch, a distinct touch, Jamison," he murmured. "But as Dr. Johnson once said, a man does not have to be a carpenter to criticise a table. These letters raise a number of interesting possibilities."

I stared at Pons as he went on sifting through the correspondence in the files on the desk before him.

"Surely, Pons," I began. "You do not mean to say a woman committed this crime?"

Solar Pons shook his head.

"I hardly think so, Parker. It is not a woman's type of crime. The female mind is far more subtle, which is why we have so many lady poisoners in the annals of murder. And I hardly think a woman would have had the strength to strike Schneider in that fashion. She would have had to have been an Amazon indeed. And as I have already indicated, there would have been a multiplicity of blows in the case of a jealous rage. Even Inspector Jamison here referred to a battering when he consulted me. Yet we have one blow only."

"That was an error on my part, Mr. Pons," Jamison put in.

"It is still difficult for me to believe such damage could be inflicted on the human frame with a single stroke."

Solar Pons put the files back on the shelves and sat down at the desk.

"Nevertheless, these letters are of considerable interest."

Light broke in.

"You mean a jealous husband might have killed his wife's lover, Pons!"

"It is not outside the bounds of possibility, Parker. I have not yet made up my mind. But now, if you are ready, Inspector, we shall see what Sir Hercules Kronfeld has to say for himself."

4

Our destination was one of those tall, elegant and extremely expensive houses in Cheyne Walk, which command a magnificent view of the Thames frontage and Chelsea Bridge from the topmost windows. Our driver pulled in from the traffic stream and we walked up the leafy crescent to a large house in the middle which, to gather from the white trellis-work sparkling in the sunshine, boasted an extensive roof-garden.

"Sir Hercules appears to live in some style, Pons," I observed.

"Does he not, Parker. It would seem that his star is in the ascendant whereas, if Colonel Gantley's information be correct, Mr. Schneider's was waning. If not from an artistic, certainly from a financial point of view."

"It is often the case, Pons, in the world of the arts."

"You astonish me with your knowledge of such matters, Parker," said Solar Pons gravely.

His ring at the front door bell brought a trim little maid in her early twenties, an appealing sight with her lace collar and cuffs and bobbed dark hair; and we were speedily shown through an elegant suite of rooms to Sir Hercules' studio. This was a spacious room on the second floor with a huge skylight and large oval window to admit the north light.

Sir Hercules himself was a gigantic figure with a beard heavily flecked with grey. Contrary to my expectations he was elegantly dressed in a light grey suit and blue bow-tie and his fresh complexion and careful grooming completely belied the conventional picture of the artist. He was leaning carelessly against a winged female nude, evidently one of his own works, while he carried on a murmured conversation with an elegant young man with patent leather hair and a soulful expression.

As we were announced he excused himself to his companion and came striding down the room toward us. So massive was he that the studio seemed to tremble as he advanced. Solar Pons' eyes had a mild twinkle as he gazed at the Inspector. Sir Hercules Kronfeld was close to us now, looking from one to the other with an inquiring expression on his face. He gave a wry chuckle.

"My accountant."

He jerked his thumb in the direction of the figure by the statue. "All the same these young fellows nowadays. They seem to think we're in this for art's sake."

He chuckled again and pumped Inspector Jamison's hand.

"Pleased to meet you, Inspector, though I don't know why I should be so honoured."

"I am sorry for the intrusion, Sir Hercules. This is Mr. Solar Pons and Dr. Lyndon Parker."

The deep brown eyes swivelled and studied us closely.

"It is always interesting for a master in one field to meet a *maître* in another, Mr. Pons."

"You are too good, Sir Hercules."

"We will not keep you a moment, sir," Inspector Jamison broke in without further preamble. "We have come in the matter of Romane Schneider."

Sir Hercules Kronfeld looked at the Inspector in silence for a moment. His manner was distinctly cooler and little flecks of anger were dancing in his eyes.

"I do not care to hear anything of that unmitigated charlatan, Inspector, and I will thank you not to mention that man's name within the walls of my house."

Jamison reddened but pressed on stolidly.

"I'm afraid we're going to have to mention it, Sir Hercules. This is a Scotland Yard matter."

"Oh."

There was intense curiosity on the sculptor's face.

"What has he been up to now? I should be glad to hear you are on the point of arresting him, but that is too much to hope for."

"You did not like him, then, Sir Hercules?"

"I? I detest him."

"You need do so no longer," interrupted Solar Pons quietly. "He has been murdered in the most brutal and horrifying manner."

A remarkable change had come over Sir Hercules. Pons' words seemed visibly to deflate him. He staggered. His face went white and he moved over toward a wooden stand supporting one of his sculptures, bracing himself with a thick, fleshy hand. His lips moved once or twice but he was unable to articulate the words.

"It seems to be a shock to you," went on Solar Pons calmly. "I have often observed that the removal of an object of hatred may be as traumatic as that of a loved one."

Sir Hercules had recovered himself by now. He cleared his throat harshly.

"Forgive me, gentlemen," he murmured. "It was a shock, I must admit. I hardly know what to say."

"You are unable to help us, then, in the matter of Mr. Schneider's death?" muttered Jamison.

Sir Hercules fixed him with a stern glance.

"I? How on earth could I help? I have not even seen him for three months."

"A pity," the Inspector went on. "I had hoped you might have thrown some light on the matter."

"You must disabuse yourself of that, Inspector. Like me, Schneider had many enemies. It is inevitable in the art world, I am afraid. How did he die?"

"Struck on the head with tremendous force with one of his own mallets. His skull was completely shattered and he must have expired instantaneously."

Sir Hercules Kronfeld drew in his breath with a shuddering sigh.

"Horrible, Inspector. Just horrible. I did not think I could feel so drained."

"I am sorry to be the first to bring you the news. Have you anyone in mind who might have done this dreadful thing?"

Sir Hercules, obviously moved, now had his back turned but faced us again. His lips were trembling and his features were still bleached of all colour.

"No one, Inspector. He had no specific enemies that I know of."

He gave a short, cynical laugh.

"Except myself."

"Pray do not punish yourself, Sir Hercules," said Pons quietly.

The sculptor shot him a shrewd glance.

"You are a remarkable man, Mr. Pons. I can see that the true situation has not escaped you."

Pons smiled wryly.

"We have many examples in the arts. Gilbert and Sullivan in more recent times, of course."

Inspector Jamison had watched this exchange with obvious bewilderment.

"I do not see how this helps us, Mr. Pons," he said heavily.

"Of course not, Inspector," said Solar Pons. "We must be going. We can do no good here and I am sure Sir Hercules has much to occupy him."

He rested his hand lightly on the sculptor's shoulder as he passed. Sir Hercules recollected himself with an effort.

"Good day, gentlemen. You will forgive me for not showing you out."

We were silent as we walked back through the house, preceded by the same parlour-maid who had let us in.

"Well, Mr. Pons," said Inspector Jamison as we regained the street. "A giant of a man. One with strength enough and opportunity enough to commit such a crime. I shall have him carefully watched."

Solar Pons raised his eyebrows.

"Take my advice, Jamison, and direct your attention elsewhere," he advised.

Jamison frowned.

"Come, Mr. Pons," he said. "You are not omniscient. We

know Sir Hercules and the dead man were bitter enemies. There is reason enough for the committing of such a crime, surely . . . "

"You have still to explain how Sir Hercules got in and out of that studio like a puff of smoke, Jamison. It really will not do."

Jamison's face assumed a stubborn aspect which I knew of old.

"Nevertheless, Mr. Pons, you must allow me to pursue this affair in my own way."

"Certainly, Inspector. That is your prerogative. I think we have done all we can for the moment, Parker. Allow us to bid you good day, Jamison."

5

"What do you make of it, Parker?"

We were seated in our comfortable sitting-room at 7B Praed Street. Pons had been silent for the last hour, after the tea-things had been cleared away, and the upper air of the room was blue with pipe-smoke.

"You already know my feelings, Pons. It is baffling indeed."

"Nevertheless, I should like to have the benefit of your observations in the matter."

I put down my newspaper and regarded my companion sceptically but there was nothing but concerned interest in his face. Beams of evening sunlight, striking through the windows that overlooked Praed Street, made a scarlet mask of his face as he waited for my reply.

"We have no motive, Pons."

"Exactly."

"We have a studio which was locked and to and from which no one apparently came or went."

"The salient points have not escaped you, my dear fellow."

"The murderer, according to your conclusions, must have been over six feet tall."

"Agreed."

"His greatest enemy, Sir Hercules, fits that physical description."

"So do a great many men."

"His secretary, Godfrey Horrabin, for example, Pons?"

Solar Pons gave a dry chuckle and looked at me mockingly.

"You now have two suspects, Parker. I suggest we may find a third—or even a fourth—before this case is over."

He rose, stretched himself and walked casually across toward the window.

"Are you free to accompany me this evening?"

"Certainly, Pons."

Pons came back from the window and sat down again.

"It is a pity it does not get dark until almost after ten o'clock at this time of the year. It would be better to go there after dark. It would not do to let Colonel Gantley see us in his garden at night. He might suspect us of being burglars."

"What on earth are you talking about, Pons?"

"Nothing, Parker. It is just that I have a mind to look at that studio again. I fancy Jamison will not have the body removed until after dark. Discretion is one of the virtues of the British police, after all."

"But how will we get in, Pons?"

"I took an impression of the key when we were at the studio this morning, Parker. I have had it made up this afternoon."

I stared at Pons in astonishment.

"I fail to see . . . "

"You fail to see, my dear fellow, because you do not draw the correct conclusions from the data before you. You remember the letters we found in Schneider's study?"

"It will be a long time before I forget them, Pons."

"Exactly. Yet those letters told you nothing?"

"That the sculptor was a cad and an unscrupulous cheat where women were concerned."

"Tut, Parker. We are not concerned with moral strictures. Murder has been done."

"I realise that, Pons."

"The studio was a quiet, discreet place. Schneider was not known to use it at night. He sculptured female nudes there. And he would not give the key to his local police-station."

I stared at my companion for a long moment.

"I see your reasoning, Pons, but I cannot quite grasp the conclusion."

Solar Pons made an irritated clicking noise with his tongue.

"I am bluntly suggesting that Schneider, a successful and well-known sculptor, was quite patently a secret womaniser on an heroic scale. What more likely rendezvous for his amorous intrigues than the studio?"

"I follow that, Pons, but where does that lead us?"

Solar Pons' face expressed sorrowful resignation.

"The studio is altogether too open and simple, like the face of an ingenuous man. There has to be something else beneath it. What more likely a secret entrance so that his lady friends could come and go without being suspected? And also that they be kept from seeing one another if one ever came to the front door? Or their husbands. Do I make myself clear?"

I gulped.

"Good heavens, Pons. It is crystal clear, now that you put it like that. The skylight, perhaps..."

Solar Pons laughed. It was not an unkind laugh but it cut nevertheless.

"We must look to the ground, not skywards, Parker. Though it seems unlikely from the solid construction of the studio, there must be a way in from below."

"Ah, the garage?"

Pons shook his head.

"The ceiling was of solid cement. Most likely the store-room."

I smiled.

"You mean that Schneider's style was cramped by his letting Cheneys to Colonel Gantley? Necessity compelled him to do so. Perhaps he hoped to continue his liaisons but the stacking of the crates for the Colonel's business prevented the use of the secret entrance?"

"It may well be," said Pons airily. "There are a number of intriguing possibilities. Linked, I have no doubt, with the extortionately high rent charged by Schneider for his house."

"I do not follow you, Pons."

"It would not be the first time, Parker. Nevertheless, while going through Schneider's papers today I found some interesting documents, obviously over-looked by Jamison and his colleagues. The late Romane Schneider was charging the Colonel £100 a week for the use of Cheneys."

I stared at my companion in stupefaction.

"You cannot mean it, Pons?"

"The figures are there, in black and white, Parker. Intriguing, is it not? However, I suggest we set off. A walk in this agreeable weather will not come amiss. It should be dark by the time we arrive."

A few minutes later, having appraised Mrs. Johnson of our

departure, we were walking through the streets of London in the pleasant warmth of a perfect summer evening. It was cool in the shadows of the buildings after the intense heat of the day and my spirits rose as we walked up Gloucester Road in the direction of Hampstead. Traffic was light at this time of the evening and there was a good sprinkling of cyclists so that dust, the plague of the London summer, was at a minimum.

Solar Pons strode out at a great pace, discoursing on a wide variety of topics and I listened with interest, interpolating a question or a monosyllabic remark from time to time. So absorbed were we that I hardly noticed the closing in of dusk but the lamps had just been lit when we at last turned into Hampstead High Street and on to the Vale of Health.

To my surprise Pons stepped aside and led me to a public house, where a few chairs and benches were set outside on the green turf. It was a cool and pleasant spot while we waited for the last of the light to die from the sky. There were but a few bars of blood red lingering in the west and the hill was a lime-yellow glow of gaslights before Pons rose from his seat and started off across the turf.

I was at his heels as he circled round, keeping a sharp eye on Cheneys in its quiet cul-de-sac. There were lights in the upper rooms of the house but so far as I could make out, the studio building at the rear was in darkness.

"Is this likely to be dangerous, Pons?" I asked, as we gained the road at the far side of the green and continued our walk onwards.

"Most decidedly, Parker, if my calculations be correct," said Pons.

"The police appear to have withdrawn and conditions are ideal."

"For what, Pons?"

"For our purpose, my dear fellow."

"Perhaps I should have brought my revolver?"

"I had not overlooked it, Parker. Thinking that you might need it I took the liberty of bringing it along."

And Solar Pons produced the weapon from the inside of his jacket pocket with a thin smile.

"Really, Pons!" I protested, thrusting it into my pocket. "I sometimes think you must be clairvoyant."

"Hardly, Parker. Merely thoughtful, but I do sympathise with your feelings."

We had turned again now and I was aware of a gigantic figure silhouetted against the gas-lamps in front of us.

"Good evening, Mr. Pons. Thought I might find you here, sir."

The police constable touched the peak of his helmet and came to a stop in front of us. So huge was he that he towered over Solar Pons, despite his own not inconsiderable height.

"Ah, P.C. Daniels, is it not? The man who found the body?"

"Nasty business, Mr. Pons. I understood from Inspector Jamison that you had been consulted. I have not seen you, sir, since that murderous affair in Paddington. Right on your own doorstep."

"Ah, the anarchists," said Pons, his keen eyes searching the giant's face. "I have not forgotten your services on that occasion. And in any event your remarkable physique makes you a difficult man to forget."

The constable laughed shortly. He was a man of about thirty with a heavy black moustache which stood out like a great bar of shadow on his alert, intelligent face.

"I must admit there are not many things I fear on night

beat, Mr. Pons, but that business of Mr. Schneider gave me a nasty turn."

"I can well imagine, constable. Tell me, has the body yet been removed?"

"Not twenty minutes since, Mr. Pons. You have just missed Inspector Jamison. Did you wish to gain entry to the studio, sir? The Inspector has the only key."

"It is no matter, Daniels. I was merely mulling over some problems in my mind. By the bye, I have not yet seen anything of the murder in the early editions this afternoon?"

The constable shook his head.

"It is being handled very discreetly, Mr. Pons. Inspector Jamison has not made any announcement as yet, though I have no doubt the newspapers will have got hold of it by this time tomorrow."

"No doubt. Well, I must not keep you, Daniels. Goodnight to you."

"Goodnight, sir."

The constable touched the brim of his helmet again and moved off in the dusk, like an amiable but potentially dangerous bear. I looked after him thoughtfully, conscious of Pons' eyes on me.

"Formidable is he not, Parker?"

"Yes, Pons. Gracious, you surely do not suspect him of the crime?"

"It has been done before, Parker. Notably in a work by G.K. Chesterton. But I do not think that nature is imitating art in this case. I am merely pointing out that we begin to have a plethora of huge men in this case. Daniels is the third. Perhaps we may have more luck with the fourth."

"I am becoming more and more confused, Pons," I said. "One would have thought the singularity of the crime in the locked studio, let alone the height of the murderer, would have simplified matters. Instead, we have a multiplicity of suspects."

Pons chuckled drily.

"Have we not, Parker. But I think light is about to break."

6

And he said nothing more until we had skirted the bright windows of Cheneys and were standing within the deep shadow of the back garden. We cautiously crossed the lawn and once again came out on the paved concourse fronting the garage and storeroom block below the studio. The moon was shining brightly and reflected a metallic sheen from the great domed skylight of the studio.

"I would give a great deal to have been at that skylight when Schneider was attacked, Pons," I whispered.

Solar Pons nodded.

"Each to his own last, my dear fellow. You would have robbed me of a most fascinating problem had you done so."

He put his hand on my arm and drew me over toward the garage door. To my surprise he produced a metal instrument from his pocket and bent over the padlock. A minute or two passed and then there was a faint click. Pons turned to me.

"Now, inside with you, Parker, and be quiet about it."

I slipped through the door and waited until he had softly closed it behind us, leaving the padlock hanging from the hasp outside.

"I thought we were going into the studio, Pons," I whispered.

"Later, Parker. You forget the crates in here. It would not do to wreck the Colonel's precious imports."

I nodded, following close behind as Pons tip-toed through

the garage, past the bulky forms of the two automobiles it contained. As we had seen that morning, there was a connecting door to the store-room, which was unlocked. Solar Pons led the way to the far wall and gazed up through the gloom at the piled boxes which climbed toward the ceiling.

"This will be a difficult job, Pons."

My companion shook his head.

"I think not, Parker, if my suppositions be correct. Just place that large box at the foot here, will you."

I helped him slide the crate over. Solar Pons fingered the lobe of his left ear and looked at me reflectively in the gloom.

"Just as I thought, my dear fellow. A natural staircase."

I soon saw what he meant, for he simply marched up the slope of heavy boxes, which were arranged in tiers, rather like steps. I followed and joined him on the topmost crate.

"What now, Pons?"

"Nothing could be simpler, Parker."

So saying he pulled at the large boxes in front of him, which stretched from the crates to the ceiling. I gasped, for the enormous pile, at least ten feet high, came away with the utmost ease, Pons holding the lowest between the tips of his fingers. He chuckled at my expression.

"As I suspected. Mere cardboard, Parker, glued together. You will see that there is nothing between the crates on which we are standing and the floor yonder. Just help me with these other piles."

In a few minutes we had removed all four piles of boxes, and placed them lower down. We now had a clear space from floor to ceiling, revealing a large expanse of concrete at the rear of the wooden crates. Pons glanced keenly at the slatted wooden ceiling revealed.

"We can learn nothing further here, Parker. The answer must lie in the studio above. Come."

Gaining the outside and first making sure that there was no one else in the garden, Pons crept quietly up the staircase to the studio. I followed quickly, just in time to see the lean form of my friend glide through the door, which he had swiftly opened with the duplicate key. I moved toward the light switch but Pons instantly stopped me.

"I think not, Parker. It is annoying, I know, and will make the task doubly tedious but we must work without the benefit of the main light."

He moved over cautiously through the studio into which silvery moonlight was filtering from the skylight above. The body of the unfortunate sculptor had been removed, as P.C. Daniels had told us, but the tarpaulin which covered the spot where he had lain and the gouts of blood upon the statue of Venus Aphrodite were a vivid reminder of the brooding horror of that moment when we had first entered the chamber of death.

Pons had a small torch out now and was moving cautiously across the planking of the floor. To my surprise he ignored the main studio and went up the shallow staircase to the platform where the easel stood. Pons remained musing for a moment, his right hand stroking his chin, while the beam from his torch played quickly up and down the flooring.

"Why do you feel any entrance must be here, Pons?" I whispered.

"Simply because there is no other place, Parker," said Solar Pons. "The crates below are solid, except for those we have just removed. The corner of the cleared area corresponds to this platform here. Besides, the buttressed sections below would not allow it."

"I saw no buttresses, Pons."

"Because you were not looking for them, my dear fellow. There were several steel beams, against which boxes and crates had been stacked for the purposes of Colonel Gantley's antique business. We must not forget the enormous weight of these sculptures."

"But I cannot possibly see how there could be an entrance, Pons. As we have just noted the ceiling below here is solid."

Solar Pons turned to me. In the dim light of the torch his eyes were twinkling.

"I have already pointed out, Parker, there must be an entrance. Otherwise, Romane Schneider would still be alive. You really must learn to eliminate all inessentials."

He turned from me and gave an experimental tug on the cord by which the overhead light was suspended. Satisfied, he moved over to the polished wooden railing that surrounded the platform and examined it carefully. When he had concluded his scrutiny he turned to the camera and tripod. He next went over the floor, section by section. All this took more than twenty minutes and I must confess my heart sank as the time passed without his discovering anything out of the ordinary.

He straightened up eventually and dusted the knees of his trousers. I was surprised to see an expression of alert excitement on his features.

"This does not bode well, Pons?"

"On the contrary, it tells me everything, Parker."

He moved over to the heavy wooden easel which stood in one corner. There was no canvas on it and I would not have given it a second glance. But as Pons grasped it he gave an exclamation of satisfaction.

"As I suspected, Parker. The whole thing is fastened to the floor."

"To the floor, Pons?"

"Yes, Parker. If I am not much mistaken it is used as a lever. Just hold the torch will you and stand close by me."

I took the flashlight from him and steadied it up on the wooden structure. Pons bent to it with a grunt. His hands moved about, seeking a purchase, and then he had thrown his whole weight against it as though it were a point-lever in a railway signal cabin.

"There is a counter-weight, evidently," he said thoughtfully as there came a perceptible rumble. I was so startled that I almost dropped the torch when a black hole suddenly appeared in the flooring of the platform, growing longer until it reached almost to my feet.

"Brilliantly ingenious," said Solar Pons, taking the torch from me and casting its beam down the stairwell.

"As you will see the boarding was not tongue and groove up here, but fitted flush. It was the only possible explanation to the mystery."

I now saw that the heavy pine planks of the floor had separated to form steps; they were held from beneath by flat pieces of metal screwed to them and which from below I had taken as strengthening bands for the ceiling. The whole thing resembled nothing so much as a gigantic piece of trellis-work.

"But why all this elaboration, Pons?"

"Supposing some of Mr. Schneider's lady-friends were illustrious names, who could not afford a scandal, Parker. What simpler than the pretence of renting a garage in this quiet spot. The lady could simply drive her car in, lock the door behind her and ascend to the studio from the interior of the store-room and no one the wiser."

I gazed at Pons in mute admiration.

"You are undoubtedly right. You knew this all the time, Pons!"

Solar Pons slowly shook his head.

"I knew there had to be an entrance. The motive for it did not cross my mind until we found those letters in Schneider's study."

He put his hand on my arm, his head on one side.

"Have your revolver ready, friend Parker. Something is moving in the garage below. I fancy I have just heard the outer door softly close. Take no chances but if you have to shoot try to wound rather than kill. I will just get to the light-switch yonder."

He moved silently away, extinguishing the torch. I had the revolver in my hand when the staircase trembled to a furious tread and a gigantic shadow rushed toward me in the bleached moonlight.

7

There was a savage cry which made my nerves jump but my hand was steady enough as I levelled the revolver. The huge figure reached the top of the stairs and turned toward me with incredible speed, the heavy mass of timber held threateningly over its head.

"For heaven's sake, man!"

Pons' voice, crisp and incisive, rang out as there came the click of the light-switch and the studio was bathed in incandescence. I stood as though paralysed but I came to myself at Pons' cry.

"Fire for your life, Parker!"

The vast man with the yellow face distorted with hatred was almost on me when I squeezed the trigger. He grunted and turned aside, scarlet spreading on his shoulder. I jumped back to the edge of the platform as he fell with a crash, the heavy billet of wood flying from his hands. Pons was beside me in a flash, pinning the fallen giant.

"Help me with this rope, Parker. A flesh wound only, I fancy, but he will be formidable indeed when he recovers from the shock."

I swiftly helped him to pinion our prisoner's hands and when we had secured him, I urged him up with the revolver. The heavy yellow face was sullen, the eyes burning viciously with pain and anger.

"Take no chances, Parker," said Pons coolly. "If he tries anything further shoot him in the leg."

The Chinese, who was dressed in blue chauffeur's livery, with white gloves, turned to Pons.

"I no understand."

"I think you understand well enough," said Pons equably.

He helped the groaning man into an armchair which stood just below the platform. He crossed over to me to take the revolver.

"Now, Parker. Your department, I think."

He covered the Chinese while I made a rapid examination and roughly bandaged the wound with my handkerchief. I pressed it back and bound it with an old trunk strap I found in the corner of the room.

"A flesh wound only, Pons. It has gone right through."

Pons smiled slightly.

"You have been fortunate, my friend. Dr. Parker here is an excellent shot. Though I fear you have been spared merely to provide work for the hangman."

The chauffeur shook his head stubbornly.

"I no understand. I see light. Think burglars."

Solar Pons' smile widened.

"I think not. It really will not do. This man is undoubtedly the murderer of Romane Schneider, Parker. Though obviously the tool of others."

"I do not understand, Pons."

"You will in due course, Parker. We are nearly at the end of the road. But here, for a start, is the big man we were looking for."

"He is certainly that, Pons."

"Is he not?"

Solar Pons had a mocking smile on his face.

"We will just have a few words with his employer."

"His employer, Pons?"

"Certainly. Colonel Gantley."

I stared at Pons in puzzlement.

"Come, Parker. It does not take very much reasoning. This is Colonel Gantley's chauffeur and general factotum or I will give up my title to whatever reputation my modest talents have earned me."

"But what has Colonel Gantley to do with this, Pons?"

"Everything, Parker. He pays £100 a week for Cheneys, as a start. And by the time we have crossed the strip of lawn which separates this studio from the house, I shall no doubt have thought up a few more questions for him."

He prodded the bound giant to his feet. With me following behind we descended the outer stairs of the studio and picked our way through the garden to where the lights of the Colonel's house burned dimly before us.

A dark-clad servant answered Pons' insistent ringing at the bell and stared in disbelief at the bloodstained form of the groaning chauffeur.

"Kindly announce us to your master," commanded Solar Pons.

As the man still stood there Pons pushed him aside unceremoniously.

"On second thoughts we will announce ourselves. Where is the Colonel?"

"In the drawing room, sir," the man stammered.

But our dramatic entrance had already been heard and before we were halfway across the luxuriously appointed hallway with its hanging brass lantern, a mahogany door on the far side opened and Colonel Gantley came out, his hair shining silver in the lamplight.

"What is the meaning of this outrageous violation of privacy, sir?"

"It means, Colonel Gantley, that your little charade is over. Unless you wish the entire household to hear, I advise that we adjourn somewhere private to talk."

The Colonel's face was suffused with rage as he took in the state of the chauffeur.

"Chang! What have you been up to?"

Then a shock passed across his face. It was cleverly done but I could have sworn he was acting.

"Why, it's Mr. Pons, is it not? We met this morning."

"You would have a short memory indeed, Colonel, if you had forgotten already."

The Colonel was leading the way into the drawing room. A tall, dark man who was sitting near the fireplace with a glass of brandy in his hand made as though to jump to his feet but the Colonel signalled to him with a lowering of the eyelids and he relaxed on to the divan again.

"This is my associate, Mr. Belding."

Solar Pons inclined his head curtly and turned back to our reluctant host.

"You will be pleased to hear that we have found the man responsible for the death of Romane Schneider, colonel. Your chauffeur here."

Colonel Gantley gasped and took a step toward the big Chinese, who stood with impassive, if pain-wracked, features.

"Romane Schneider? Murdered? How terrible!"

"I said nothing about a murder, Colonel," said Pons blandly. "Though I see you know all about it. Remarkable in view of the fact that we mentioned only a burglary."

The Colonel's face went ashen and he made a choking noise. The man by the fireplace leapt up but I already had my revolver out.

"I think not," said Solar Pons gently. "Dr. Parker here is a crack shot and we have already had enough violence for one evening. If you have a weapon in your inside pocket there, Mr. Belding, I sincerely advise you to drop it."

Colonel Gantley's forehead was beaded with sweat and he seemed to sag suddenly.

"Do as Mr. Pons says," he advised his colleague.

"Pray collect it, Parker. I will look after these two. Now, Colonel Gantley, I urge you to make a clean breast of things. You are already an accessory to murder and the other charges I will proffer should assure you at least twenty years in prison. It is in your interest to co-operate."

I took the heavy calibre pistol from the dark-haired man and motioned him over to join Gantley and the Chinese on a divan at the other side of the fireplace. Gantley sank into the cushions and passed a handkerchief over his face.

"I see it is useless to dissemble, Mr. Pons. Just what exactly do you know?"

"That is better, Colonel Gantley," said Solar Pons crisply. "When there is truth between us, we may progress. If you assist the authorities in this matter, they may be inclined toward leniency. Otherwise, I can promise nothing."

A groan trickled out from beneath Gantley's tight-pressed fingers.

"You are right, Mr. Pons. I did know about Schneider's murder. But I want you to believe I had nothing to do with it; it was not ordered by me and I was appalled and horrified when I learned what Chang had done."

Solar Pons' expression was grim and stern as he looked down at the abject figure of the Colonel.

"I am inclined to believe you. And it may be that you have been more of a dupe than anything else, though there is little excuse for you. You have been engaged in a foul and inhuman trade and must take the consequences."

"I do not understand you, Pons," I began, when my friend silenced me with a gesture.

"You must realise, Colonel Gantley," he went on, "I can promise nothing, though my recommendation to the police authorities might carry some weight if I were able to present them with a watertight case."

We were interrupted at that moment by a loud rapping at the door.

"Are you all right, Colonel? Do you wish me to call the police, sir?"

"Certainly not!"

The Colonel's voice was a strangled squawk and Solar Pons gave me a thin smile as the Colonel hurried over toward the door. I noticed that Pons remained close behind him while I kept my pistol trained upon the second man before me. There was a muffled colloquy at the door and then Gantley was back.

"I will tell you everything. I hardly know where to begin, Mr. Pons."

"Let me tell you what I have learned, Colonel. Then you can fill in the missing pieces."

"Very well, sir."

Solar Pons went over to stand at a point midway between the two men. He made a subtle gesture to me with the thin fingers of his left hand and so I continued to cover the dark man, Belding. The chauffeur, Chang, sat silent and impassive, nursing his wound, his face white despite his yellow pigmentation. His eyes burned vindictively into mine.

Solar Pons faced me in a contemplative mood and began to speak to me as though we were alone at 7B Praed Street.

"There were two baffling mysteries about this case, Parker. The murder of Romane Schneider in a sealed room and the lack of motive. You now know how the murderer gained access."

"But I still do not know why, Pons."

"Precisely, Parker. I shall proceed to tell you if I am allowed freedom from interruption. The puzzle in the sealed room was the method of entry and exit. There had to be one because the murderer could not just vanish into thin air. He had also to be a huge man, as I had already demonstrated, because Romane Schneider was about six feet tall and had been hit squarely upon the crown of the head with shattering force. As the skylight, the obviously solid walls and the main door were ruled out for the reasons we have already discussed, there remained only the flooring.

"I had already noticed from the building below that it would have been impossible for anyone to have gained entry from the garage as it had a solid cement ceiling. That left only the storeroom and a number of interesting possibilities emerged. There were various buttresses and pillars which, to my mind, ruled out a staircase in that portion of the building. It had to be a staircase or ladder because of the height of the studio from the ground. There was only one possible place and I immediately saw that it corresponded with the position of the raised platform in the studio above."

Solar Pons paused and looked at the crushed form of Colonel Gantley with glittering eyes. The man Belding held himself coiled tightly like a spring but I held the revolver ready and the expression on my face evidently deterred him.

"You may recall that I paid particular attention to the studio flooring, Parker. And that I found traces of the murderer which petered out near the foot of the shallow stairs leading to the platform. That merely reinforced my suspicions and I soon saw that though the floor was apparently solid, there were faint cracks between the pine planking at various points, instead of the tongue and groove joints which obtained elsewhere. I was convinced that an entrance would be found there and so it proved. We then had the problem of why the staircase existed and who had used it.

"I had only to see Godfrey Horrabin and Sir Hercules Kronfeld to eliminate them from my inquiries. Though both physically fitted the requirements it was obvious, from the frank and open way in which he answered my questions and my reading of his character, that Horrabin would not have destroyed his own livelihood as the dead man's secretary. Similarly, Kronfeld was genuinely moved at his old enemy's death; as I observed, there was a similar love-hate relationship between Gilbert and Sullivan. Sir Hercules had been a personal friend until the two men quarrelled; in my opinion the feud between the two men, real or supposed, added salt to life for both.

"Two vital pieces of information emerged from my examination of Schneider's study, both of which had been overlooked by Jamison. Or rather, no proper conclusions had been drawn from them. The existence of the staircase which led only to the store-room and garage was far more plausible when it became clear that the dead sculptor was a notorious womaniser. Discretion was assured when a woman had only to drive her car into the garage, using a key supplied by Schneider, and gain access to the studio secretly and privately by using the stair-case.

"Though we have not had time to find it, there is obviously a button or some mechanism down below which operates the thing from the store-room. The motive for the crime was supplied by my finding among Schneider's papers that Colonel Gantley here was paying the incredible sum of £100 a week for the privilege of renting Cheneys. It would have to be a profitable antique business indeed which could support such an outlay."

Colonel Gantley gave another groan and turned a haggard face toward Pons.

"Shall I tell you why Colonel Gantley paid Schneider £100 a week, Parker?"

I nodded.

"Because so much money was being made by the Colonel and his associates that money was no object. There were certain pressures on them and they had to get a respectable address with storage facilities immediately."

Colonel Gantley spoke.

"The police had just raided our headquarters in Limehouse, Mr. Pons. I had instructions from above to evacuate all our supplies from Deptford. I brought them here just in time."

Solar Pons started tamping tobacco into the bowl of his pipe.

"I suspected something of the sort. I remembered the newspaper reports a short while ago. And my suspicions became aroused when I saw the crates which had come from such places as Hong Kong and other cities in the Far East."

"I wish I knew what you were talking about, Pons," I protested.

"Tut, Parker, it was a simple deduction," said Solar Pons, lighting his pipe. "Following the murder some of the crates had been hastily moved and part of the contents spilled. You may remember I tasted some white powder which was on the floor. As a doctor, Parker, the implications should have been obvious."

"Drugs, Pons!"

"Of course, my dear fellow. Cocaine and opium, mainly, I should imagine. Hong Kong is one of the great clearing houses for the trade in the Far East. Furthermore, all the crates we saw were marked with red stars. I felt certain in my mind that these would be sure to contain genuine antiques or souvenirs. Colonel Gantley here was only a tool, part of a large ring. I have a shrewd suspicion who was at the centre of the web."

"I beg of you, Mr. Pons," said Gantley, in a shaking voice. He looked quickly at Belding, bit his lip and turned away again.

"But what has all this to do with the murder, Pons?"

"Everything, Parker. Let us just reconstruct the matter. Romane Schneider was in financial difficulties, we already know. He decided to let his house and rent a less expensive one. He was naturally delighted when Colonel Gantley turned up at the estate agents and made his extravagant offer. But may we not conjecture that after some weeks of tenancy, his curiosity got the better of him? Why was an antique dealer like Colonel Gantley, a man with a relatively modest income, so keen to pay £100 a week?

"Why did he store so many things from the Far East inside the rooms below the studio? And why did he employ Chinese almost exclusively among his outside staff? That was so, was it not, Colonel Gantley?"

"You are guessing, Mr. Pons, I imagine. But you are right, yes. A number of Chinese have been here. I have told my superiors about it, but these men are experts at the trade. Mr. Belding was their supervisor."

"You fool!"

Belding had sprung up with a white face before I could stop him and struck the Colonel in the mouth. I caught the dark man across the skull with the barrel of my pistol and he dropped noiselessly on to the divan.

"Well done, Parker," said Pons drily. "I see that your reflexes have lost nothing of their hair-trigger reaction. You had best examine him. I do not think we need fear trouble from Colonel Gantley."

I gave the dark man a cursory examination while Pons took the pistol and covered the chauffeur.

"He will be out for half an hour, Pons," I said.

"Excellent. That should be time enough. Where was I? Ah, yes, Romane Schneider's fatal curiosity. As the months went by the movements and actions of his intriguing neighbours aroused his suspicions. Two nights ago he stayed in his studio after dark, keeping all the lights off.

"When he judged it was safe, he let down the staircase. I submit he had already looked through the store-room window and noted that there were no crates in the area beneath. He crept down in the dark and made a thorough examination. What he discovered we shall never know. But the contents of the warehouse were so vitally important that the intruder could not be allowed to live. Or that was the reasoning of this man here."

Pons looked thoughtfully at the sullen Chinese.

"I fancy we shall hear nothing from his own lips. He is certainly inscrutable enough for that, though there is enough circumstantial evidence to ensure him the hangman's rope. Schneider was in the store-room when he heard a sound. It might have been the Colonel's car returning. At any rate Schneider, thoroughly frightened, ran back up the staircase and regained the studio.

"He dared not return the staircase to its original position because of the noise. He decided on boldness. He put on the light in his studio as though he had just come in and started work on one of his sculptures. Unfortunately for him the Chinese must have seen the light shining down through the staircase and went to investigate. He saw at once how things were and being a man of action took the decision into his own hands to eliminate Schneider.

"He crept quietly up the staircase—perhaps under cover of the car engine he had left running below—and struck Schneider down from behind with his own mallet. He then retreated to the ground floor and informed the Colonel of his action."

"Brilliant, Pons." I said.

"It is a reconstruction only, Parker," returned Solar Pons. "We shall need the Colonel's verification."

"It is correct in every detail, Mr. Pons," said Colonel Gantley, looking at my companion with something like awe. He had a handkerchief to his face and staunched the blood from his cut lip.

"Of course, my horror at the crime can be imagined, but it was all too late. We made a thorough search of the store-room and found a small lever at floor level which operates the staircase from below. After I had made an examination of the studio and made sure there was nothing incriminating left behind, we put the stairs back, left the lights on and piled up crates and boxes to ceiling level. We spent another hour in removing the remaining drugs to the cellar of this house."

"You did admirably well under the circumstances," said Solar Pons ironically. "I am sure you will correct any details in which I have gone wrong."

Colonel Gantley shook his head.

"I have only myself to blame, Mr. Pons. Easy money was my downfall, as it has been for so many others. I had been cashiered from the Indian Army. I returned to the old country but nothing I touched prospered. I started an antique business but that was foundering. I was desperate for ready money when I met Belding in a public-house one evening about a year ago.

"He told me of a way I could make money and I slowly became enmeshed. My business, which had legitimate contacts in the East, was useful, you see, and the men behind the trade found I provided a respectable façade. There is no excuse for me, I know; I have helped to ruin countless lives—and now this."

"There is one way you can redeem yourself," said Solar Pons, a stern look upon his features. "The names and addresses of every contact and as many men as possible higher up in the organisation."

Gantley shook his head.

"Belding was my only major contact. And the Chinese we employed. I will give what help I can."

"Be sure that you do."

Solar Pons stood deep in thought for a moment, pulling gently at the lobe of his left ear, while a thin column of blue smoke ascended from his pipe to the ceiling.

"It was too much to hope for, Parker. As I said before, the trembling of the web, but the spider remains concealed in the shadow."

"You surely do not mean your old enemy, Pons?" I cried.

"It is possible, Parker. No crime is too despicable for that scoundrel. And he would need such enormous profits as that generated by the drugs trade to fuel his infamous criminal empire. Just ring Jamison, will you? We must make sure he has not inadvertently arrested Sir Hercules or Schneider's unfortunate secretary."

8

"It was a remarkable case, Pons."

"Was it not, Parker?"

We were at lunch in our comfortable sitting-room at 7B Praed Street a week later and Mrs. Johnson had just brought the midday post up. It was a beautiful June day and the window curtains stirred gently in the cooling breeze. Pons chuckled and passed me a copy of the *Daily Telegraph*. I found a large item on the front page ringed ready for cutting out and pasting into the book in which he kept records of his cases.

"Jamison has excelled himself. At least one drugs ring has been smashed and a stop put to the traffic in that quarter. Belding himself led to some of those higher up. It was more than might have been hoped for."

"Thanks to you, Pons."

Solar Pons smiled wryly.

"Ah, Parker, you were ever generous in your evaluation of my work. In my humble way I seek to alleviate some of the ills of mankind."

"You have certainly done a good deal here, Pons," I said.

Solar Pons shook his head.

"It is just plugging holes in the dyke, Parker. There is such great profit in this foul trade that it is almost impossible to stamp out. One does what one can. My major satisfaction in this particular case is that the Doctor has been robbed of considerable profit in the matter. You will see that Heathfield, through Jamison, has made a clean sweep of the Limehouse area, and now that Gantley, Belding and the Chinese are going for trial, this will mean a considerable, if temporary, setback, in the Doctor's plans."

"I do not see how you can be so sure about his part in this, Pons?"

"One develops a sixth sense, Parker. Hullo. Here is something interesting. Postmarked Switzerland, I see."

He tore open the thin blue envelope which Mrs. Johnson had just brought up with the other letters. He studied it in silence, his eyes narrowed. Then he put it down with a low chuckle.

"Talk of the devil, Parker."

"What is it, Pons?"

By way of an answer he passed the single sheet of paper the envelope contained across to me. It bore just two lines, written in block capitals with a thin-nibbed pen.

MR. PONS—YOUR ROUND, I THINK.
WE SHALL MEET AGAIN.

F.

Solar Pons sat back at the table and lit his pipe.

"He is the most dangerous man in Europe, Parker. I would give a great deal to have netted him."

And his eyes looked beyond the homely commons of our room and gazed bleakly into the void.

The Adventure of the Agonised Actor

When 'The Adventure of the Anguished Actor' was originally published in Pocket Books' The Secret Files of Solar Pons *(1979), the name of Pons' thespian client was 'Elijah Hardcastle'. However, when the story was reprinted by Sarob Press sixteen years later in* Solar Pons: The Final Cases, *Basil Copper had inexplicably changed the actor's name to 'Cedric Carstairs'.*

It is also apparent from Basil's plot-notes *(see page 179)* *that the original title of this story was 'The Adventure of the Agonised Actor' almost up to the time he delivered the manuscript to Arkham House, even forgetting to make the correction on the Contents page and copyright information of the document.*

As he explained to James Turner in a letter dated December 9th, 1977: "I am so sorry about this. 'The Adventure of the Agonised Actor' was my provisional title and I changed it to 'The Adventure of the Anguished Actor'. I would be grateful if you would restore the 'Anguished' for the copyrighting or whatever and see that it appears in the finished work, as I do prefer this."

However, for this reprinting of the first draft, I have taken the liberty of changing the title back to the original to differentiate between the two versions. SJ.

1

"YOU CANNOT MEAN it, Pons!"

"I was never more serious in my life, Parker."

Solar Pons looked at me with tightly compressed lips. We were sitting by ourselves in a first-class railway carriage passing through the rolling countryside beyond Dorking. It was a cold winter's day and frost sparkled in the tangled grass of the fields, yielding diamonds in the hard light of the pale, wintry sun.

"Elijah Hardcastle is in mortal danger, unless I seriously miss my guess."

"Not the famous actor?"

Pons nodded, blowing out plumes of fragrant blue smoke from his pipe. He looked moodily at the landscape noiselessly passing the window, the telegraph wires making a jerky background pattern to our conversation.

"What do you make of that?"

He handed me the crumpled telegram form. The message was succinct and baffling.

THE FOURTH PARCEL HAS COME. IMPLORE YOUR PRESENCE HERE IMMEDIATELY. HARDCASTLE.

I glanced at the date. It had been handed in at Dorking the previous night.

"I do not understand, Pons."

Solar Pons looked at me sympathetically, the cold winter light making rapid patterns across his lean, feral features.

"Forgive me, Parker. When I asked you to come with me to Surrey it was in the nature of an emergency and there was little time for explanation. There are a few minutes left before we arrive at our destination and I shall endeavour to put you in possession of the salient points.

"As you have already stated, Elijah Hardcastle is the well-known stage and cinema actor. He first wrote me at Praed Street some three weeks ago, when he was on tour in the West Country. The tenor of his letter impressed me as being that of a man at the end of his tether. In short, he was in fear of his life."

I must confess I looked with astonishment at my friend sitting in the far corner of the carriage, his luggage and overcoat thrown carelessly about him. He fixed his eyes on a coloured lithograph of Broadstairs above my head and blew out another plume of aromatic smoke.

"Surely, Pons, that is one of the penalties of the actor's life," I began. "They are either idolised or loathed. And when a man like Hardcastle spreads his talents so widely, on both stage and screen, there are bound to be adherents in both camps."

Solar Pons shook his head with a somewhat mocking smile.

"It is something a little more than that, my dear fellow. And if you would just have the patience to hear me out..."

I mumbled an apology and sank back into my corner, watching the sun sparkle on the frozen surface of a stream we were passing.

"It is a bizarre business and one that intrigues me considerably."

Solar Pons leaned forward and tented his thin fingers before him.

"When he was appearing at Edinburgh in *Othello*, he received a small parcel, posted from London. It contained a skilfully crafted effigy of himself, in Shakespearean costume, lying dead with a phial of poison in his hand."

I shook my head.

"Lamentable lack of taste, Pons."

My companion inclined his head.

"You have got the heart of the matter with your usual unfailing perspicacity, Parker."

Pons was silent for a moment and then continued.

"The first parcel, which arrived some months ago, was in the nature of a warning, he felt. Nothing happened and he quite forgot the incident. But in October, you may recall, he appeared with some success at Drury Lane in a revival of *The Hound of the Baskervilles*."

"As Sir Henry Baskerville, Pons. It was an excellent performance. I saw it myself."

"Did you indeed?" said Pons with a thin smile. "About a week before the play opened he received another parcel. This time it contained a cunningly fashioned model, in coloured wax, of himself as Sir Henry. He was lying on the ground, his throat torn out, with the gigantic Baskerville hound standing over him."

"Good heavens, Pons!"

"You may well raise your eyebrows, Parker. The case presents a number of points of interest. This second parcel was also posted from London but despite all inquiries he was unable to discover anything about it, though he contacted the postal authorities. I have gathered all this from Hardcastle himself in a series of telephone conversations during his tours."

"Nothing happened on this second occasion, Pons?"

Solar Pons sat back in his seat and looked reflectively at the passing telegraph wires.

"There was an accident on the opening night. A chandelier which was part of the Baskerville Hall set in the prologue collapsed on to the stage. It narrowly missed Hardcastle and did in fact slightly injure the actor who played Dr. Watson. The chandelier was not a stage property, but one of the original massive fittings of the theatre, which is often used in opera."

"So that Hardcastle could have been killed?"

"Very easily. The police were called and found that the cable holding the chandelier had been eaten through with a powerful corrosive that would have taken about ten minutes to do its work."

"You were not called in, Pons?"

My companion shook his head.

"My services were only solicited more recently. But that is the story I had from Hardcastle. He was in a considerable state of nerves by this time."

Pons tapped thoughtfully with the bowl of his pipe on the brass door-fitting of the carriage, tipping fragments of tobacco into the metal ash-tray.

"He was in Liverpool a few weeks ago, starring in a modern thriller called *The Arrow of Fate*. This time he received a third parcel, also posted from London. It contained another skilfully contrived wax model of himself in evening dress, this time hanging from a beam."

"There was no message?"

Solar Pons shook his head.

"There was never a message of any kind."

"But something happened?"

"Most definitely, Parker. D'Arcy Stanwell, the second male lead, who was of the same build and appearance as Hardcastle, was killed on the first night as he made his entrance, just after the curtain went up."

I blinked.

"Good heavens. You think he was mistaken for your client, Pons?"

"I am certain of it, Parker. It was a combination of the lighting and the resemblance between the two men, who both wore evening dress for this particular scene. The manner of the killing was bizarre in the extreme. Stanwell was killed by a steel arrow which came from somewhere in the theatre, probably from an empty stage-box high up. It was a matinée, you see. The murderer made his escape undetected."

"But he must have had some sort of bow, Pons."

"Exactly. Which is what makes the problem so intriguing. The show closed at once, of course. And naturally the police were unable to trace the murderer."

"Why do you say 'naturally', Pons?"

"Because this case is a hundred miles outside the ordinary type of police work, Parker. You have noticed one important factor?"

"What is that, Pons?"

Solar Pons shook his head.

"Tut, tut, Parker. You disappoint me. I had thought more highly of your ratiocinative faculties."

"I am afraid I do not follow, Pons."

"Why, the warning and its execution, Parker. In each case the potential victim received a sinister warning in the shape of a wax effigy. You will remember that in the case of *Othello* he was lying dead, poisoned. But Othello himself strangled Desdemona in that distinguished work. The second warning depicted him with his throat torn out but instead a chandelier descended."

"I see, Pons!"

I sat up in my seat.

"The third time he was depicted hanging but his unfortunate colleague was shot with an arrow."

"You have hit it, Parker."

Solar Pons looked at me dreamily from under lowered eyelids.

"He was warned of his impending death but in each case the method of death was something totally unexpected. The murderer wanted to frighten, even terrify, but not to indicate the manner of death precisely or his victim might escape."

"But nothing happened after the first warning, Pons."

"There you have me, Parker."

Solar Pons pulled reflectively at his right earlobe. "Though it is impossible to prove at this distance in time I would submit that the person menacing Hardcastle's life intended some sort of *coup* at the theatre during the performance of *Othello* but was prevented by circumstances on the actual night he intended to commit his crime."

"But why did he not try again?"

Solar Pons smiled.

"Perhaps he could only be in Edinburgh for one night. There are a number of interesting possibilities. Or he may have merely intended to frighten this first time, so that the second, real attempt would be completely unexpected."

I nodded.

"And now there has been a fourth parcel?"

Pons had a worried expression on his thin, ascetic features.

"According to my client's telegram. He is currently preparing for an ambitious new play at the Negresco Theatre in London."

He looked moodily out of the carriage window at the fleeting images of the countryside.

"It is unfortunate, but could not have been better from the point of view of the person who is threatening his life."

"Why so, Pons?"

Solar Pons stood up, gathering his coat and case.

"Ah, here we are at our destination, Parker."

He looked at me sombrely as I buttoned my own overcoat.

"The play is a modern piece called *Death Comes to Thornfield*. Hardcastle himself plays the victim of a particularly diabolical murder!"

2

The day, if anything, seemed even colder when we descended at the small station near Guildford. The cab our client had engaged was waiting in the station forecourt and a drive of some fifteen minutes brought us to a handsome, Edwardian house of three storeys, standing in well-wooded grounds of about five acres. Pons was silent as our vehicle crunched over the gravel of the drive between the handsome lodges with their overhanging eaves of red tiles which flanked the white-painted gates.

We were evidently expected for the gates were open and as we drove through I could already see a white-haired man in a green-baize apron who hurried from the entrance of the larger lodge and locked the tall iron gates behind us. The drive wound up between sombre banks of rhododendron whose lighter green did little to relieve the deep shadows of the heavy pines and firs which bordered the carriageway.

But the house itself, with the pale winter sun sparkling from its well-kept façade and reflected back from a multitude of white-framed windows, had a cheerful aspect. I could see the two tennis-courts through a gap in the trees and, across the broad lawns and the rose-garden, desolate now in winter, could be glimpsed the metal framework of a diving stage and the heavy boarding covering a large swimming pool. I glanced at my companion mischievously.

"There is money here, Pons."

"Is there not, Parker. Ah, unless I am mistaken, here is our client himself."

And indeed, the handsome, somewhat florid figure of the former matinée idol was descending the steps toward us, a brace of Irish wolf-hounds at his heels. The cab ground to a stop and the driver got down to unload our baggage while the actor effusively pumped my companion's hand.

"Good of you to come, Mr. Pons! I am extremely grateful. And this is your equally celebrated friend, Dr. Parker?"

He turned to me with a winning smile and gripped my hand strongly.

"Hardly celebrated, Mr. Hardcastle."

"You are too modest, Dr. Parker. Boswell and Johnson, eh, Mr. Pons?"

Pons glanced at me, sparks of humour dancing in his deep-set eyes.

"The simile is hardly apposite from a physical point of view, Mr. Hardcastle, but I take it was kindly meant," he said gravely.

"Indeed, Mr. Pons. But come along in. It is dreadfully cold out here on these steps."

He hurried us up into the shadow of a great porch while a black-coated manservant carried our bags. During the ascent I had time to study my host properly. His features were familiar to me, of course, through cinema performances and stage appearances, but he seemed even taller and broader than I remembered. He must have been over fifty by now but was still handsome in a fleshy way and had tremendous 'presence', as those in the stage profession call it.

His eyes and his flashing smile were his greatest features and though his complexion was ruddy and florid, indicative to me of a long indulgence in alcoholic spirits, he was still a fine figure of a man and would pass for a good while yet, with skilful make-up and stage lighting.

He was dressed in a thick suit of country tweeds with a waistcoat and his theatrical and flamboyant appearance was emphasised by the gaily-coloured silk scarf loosely knotted round his neck, and tucked into the vee of a blue silk shirt. The ensemble was Bohemian and on anyone else would have looked slovenly but it suited him perfectly.

We were let in the large, tiled hall by a striking looking blonde woman of about thirty-eight, and I recognised the actress Sandra Stillwood before Hardcastle introduced her as his wife. She came forward with a smile and shook hands, while the wolf-hounds loped about the hall as though they would demolish the furniture in their boisterousness.

A shadow passed across her handsome features as she led the way into a huge drawing-room which contained many oil paintings and drawings of herself and her husband in their various stage and screen roles. Bowls of hot-house flowers were set about here and there and though a large fire burned in the stone fireplace, the room was already warm from the radiators set round the walls.

"Lunch will be served within the hour, gentlemen," said Mrs. Hardcastle. "In the meantime may I offer you a sherry?"

"Excellent idea, Sandra," boomed Hardcastle, waving away the butler, who had followed us in and now stood awaiting his instructions.

The big actor went to a silver tray standing at one end of a grand piano and which contained a great many bottles and glasses. He busied himself with pouring the sherry for us and mixing drinks for himself and his wife. Pons went to stand near the fireplace and looked at the lady of the house thoughtfully.

"What do you think of this business, Mrs. Hardcastle?"

"I prefer to be known as Miss Stillwood, Mr. Pons," the fair woman said, a faint flush on her cheeks.

She glanced across at her husband.

"I have not yet retired, though Elijah sometimes acts as though I had."

Hardcastle gave a somewhat strained smile and brought the drinks over to myself and Pons. We waited until our host and hostess also had glasses in their hands.

"Success, Mr. Pons."

"I will drink to that, Mr. Hardcastle."

Solar Pons moved over to a high-backed chair at Miss Stillwood's invitation and sat down, crossing his thin legs and looking for all the world as though he were at ease in his own drawing-room. Once again I marvelled at the effortless way in which he dominated every gathering without appearing to do so.

"I asked you a question, Miss Stillwood."

The blonde woman took a tentative sip at her drink, wrinkled her nose at her husband and pondered her reply.

"It seems inexplicable, Mr. Pons. Why should anyone want to go to all the trouble of making those wax models?"

"Why indeed?" said Solar Pons politely, his eyes on Hardcastle. "But you do not deny the matter is serious?"

The blonde woman's eyes flashed and I saw for a brief moment the dynamic beauty that had flowered to such remarkable art in innumerable films and plays.

"I deny nothing, Mr. Pons! It is damnable. Poor D'Arcy! But the whole thing seems so pointless. And Elijah is making such a fuss of the business. I keep telling him to pull himself together but he is terrified."

There was an undertone of contempt in her voice as she glanced affectionately at her husband and I saw him redden under her look.

"Damn it all, Sandra," he exploded. "It is not you who is the target, after all."

"You have a point, Mr. Hardcastle," said Pons soothingly. "We may as well get down to facts at once. I should like first to see those models you have already received. And of course, the latest parcel."

"Certainly, Mr. Pons. They are locked in the safe in my study. We will go there directly we have finished our drinks."

"Excellent."

Solar Pons rubbed his hands together and held them out toward the fire. His eyes had a far-away expression in them.

"The wrappings and enclosure were identical to the others?"

"Exactly, Mr. Pons. I have them all still."

"And again posted from London?"

Hardcastle inclined his head.

"Yes, Mr. Pons."

Before Pons could say any more there was a rapping at the door which immediately afterward opened to admit a tall, slim young man of about thirty with dark, bushy hair. He paused in some confusion but came toward the group round the fireplace at Hardcastle's command to enter.

"This is my secretary, John Abrahams, Mr. Pons. Mr. Solar Pons. Dr. Lyndon Parker."

The secretary made a graceful bow and murmured something which I could not make out but took to be a polite acknowledgement of the introduction.

"Mr. Abrahams would have received the parcels in the first place, Mr. Hardcastle?"

"That is so, Mr. Pons," said the young man, with a half-hesitant look at his employer.

"They came in the usual way?"

The secretary nodded.

"With the incoming post from the village. Simons is our regular postman and to the best of my knowledge he brought them both. That is to say, the second and fourth. The first and third parcels were received in Edinburgh and Liverpool, respectively."

"I see."

Solar Pons was deep in thought for a few moments, the only sound in the room the deep crackling of the log-fire on the hearth. The silence was eventually broken by Hardcastle's wife who put her glass back on the tray on top of the piano with a quick, decisive movement.

"If you will excuse me, gentlemen, I will see about lunch. We eat in half an hour, Elijah."

She glanced sharply at her husband as she spoke.

"Certainly, Sandra," he said somewhat defensively.

He made a wry mouth as she quitted the room, followed at some distance by the secretary.

"I am notoriously unpunctual, gentlemen. I suppose my wife must find it irritating."

He grinned and went over to pour himself another drink.

"At least I am always on stage in time for my entrances," he added. "Which is something. Another drink, gentlemen?"

Solar Pons excused himself.

"Not before lunch, if you please, Mr. Hardcastle. I am anxious to look at those parcels before we sit down."

"By all means, Mr. Pons. Come along, doctor."

We followed the big actor out of the drawing-room and into a large connecting room which looked on to the rose-garden, now austere and deserted in the bitter wind. The room was equipped as a study and the series of theatrical portraits were continued on that part of the panelled walls not given over to books. Hardcastle crossed to the natural stone fireplace over which hung an oil of himself in one of his more flamboyant film roles. He pushed the painting aside to disclose a small wall safe.

He took from it a large cardboard box and carried it over to the desk, where he placed it in front of Pons. My companion sat down behind the desk, his face keen and alert. Carefully, Hardcastle took from the box the artfully fashioned and beautifully coloured figures. There was a brief silence as Pons produced his magnifying glass and went scrupulously over them in minute detail.

"This is highly skilled work, Mr. Hardcastle. Someone has been to a deal of trouble."

"Have they not, Mr. Pons."

"Someone who follows your career closely."

"Evidently."

Pons turned to me.

"What do you think of these, Parker?"

"I agree with you, Pons," I said. "These are finely done. The threats to Mr. Hardcastle seem to me to be unnecessarily elaborate."

"You are constantly improving, Parker," said Solar Pons drily. "The same thought had already occurred to me. Let us just see what we can read from these wrappings."

Our host's flushed, handsome face had an approving expression as he went to sit on a corner of the desk, glass in hand. Pons went over the wrappings minutely and then threw them down with a grunt.

"There is little here, Parker. The paper, as you no doubt noted, is purchasable in only three major emporia in London. It would be useless to enquire in that direction as each has thousands of customers every day of the week. The lettering, in block capitals, was obviously to disguise the hand. That type of broad-nibbed pen can be bought in London or throughout the country by the thousand. Similarly, the wax seals have been made with the cheap penny stick available at any stationers. The sender has been careful not to press them down on the string and thus leave fingerprints."

Pons peered again at the lettering of each address.

"However, there is something to be read after all. The superscription has been written by a male, probably in the prime of his life but with a weak character."

Hardcastle, who had been listening to Pons' monologue with amazement on his features, cleared his throat with a loud rasping noise.

"Good Heavens, Mr. Pons!" he boomed. "You mean to say you can tell all that from a cursory glance. I came to the right shop!"

"Hardly a cursory glance," said Solar Pons reprovingly. "A lifetime's study of such matters has gone into that cursory glance, as you call it."

The big man flushed.

"No offence meant, Mr. Pons," he rumbled. "But how can you read such things?"

"Characteristics, Mr. Hardcastle." said Pons quietly. "They would be too lengthy to go into now but the human hand does not lie even when it comes to lettering of this sort. The characteristics of the weak, indecisive male are unmistakable in this script. I have written a monograph on the subject and would recommend you to peruse it."

"Touché, Mr. Pons," said Hardcastle with a wry chuckle. "You would not presume to teach me how to play Othello, and your art is just as esoteric; am I right? Well each to his last. But I'm damned impressed, I must say."

He good-humouredly drained his glass and put it down on a corner of the desk.

"What about the parcel that came yesterday, Mr. Hardcastle?"

"I have it here, Mr. Pons."

The actor had put down a second package on another part of the desk and he now passed it to Pons. He gave the brown paper wrapping a brief examination and put it aside for the moment. He took from it a small cardboard box similar to that in which the other wax models had been enclosed. From it he carefully removed a wooden plinth on which the miniature and savage drama was being played out. There was a deep silence in the room and I pressed closer to Pons in order to see the model in greater detail.

It was every bit as cunningly fashioned as the others. The unmistakable figure of Hardcastle lay on the facsimile of a patterned carpet. He was dressed in evening clothes, with an opera cloak, and his top hat lay beside him. The figure lay on its back with one leg drawn up under it. From the right eye-socket an arrow protruded; the face was distorted with pain and horror and thick blood from the wound trickled down onto the manikin's shirt-front.

It was an arresting and disgusting sight and I gazed at it with loathing. Solar Pons glanced up at me, a grim smile playing at the corners of his sensitive mouth.

"What say you, Parker?"

"It is disgusting, Pons!" I burst out. "A warped if clever mind is behind this."

"You may well be right, Parker," Solar Pons rejoined in casual tones. "As you have already observed, a great deal of skill has been expended on this. *Death Comes to Thornfield* indeed. Strangely enough this is exactly how the unfortunate actor was killed in Mr. Hardcastle's last play, though the warning took the form of a hanging figure."

He looked across at Hardcastle, whose features had grown pale and drawn. His eyes dragged themselves reluctantly from the little series of tableaux on the desk.

"There is no doubt this represents your current play, Mr. Hardcastle?"

"No doubt at all, Mr. Pons. The costume there is identical to the one I wear in the production."

"And how do you die in the piece?"

"I am strangled in the last act, Mr. Pons."

My companion nodded.

"Death by poisoning; by savage hound; by hanging; and by an arrow. It is bizarre and extraordinary."

He rubbed his thin hands together and his eyes shone.

"I cannot remember when I have been so taken with a case, Mr. Hardcastle. When does the play open?"

"Next month, Mr. Pons. I will not dissemble. My wife was perfectly right. I am terrified of this business, especially after poor Stanwell. There is something diabolical and inevitable about it. Please save me, Mr. Pons."

There was a pathetic quality in his earnest entreaty and Solar Pons held up his hand, with a comforting gesture.

"Now we know what we are up against, Mr. Hardcastle, we are forewarned. This person who menaces you obviously wants to punish you in some way in public. Therefore, we have only to fear the actual performances. I would like to attend a few rehearsals, in order to verse myself in the story of the play. And at the same time a thorough examination of the theatre would be of great assistance."

Elijah Hardcastle let out a sigh of relief.

"Nothing could be easier, Mr. Pons. I will make arrangements at the theatre."

"But be discreet, Mr. Hardcastle. I do not want any outside people to know that I am there."

Hardcastle had a startled look on his face, as Pons made a thorough examination of the wrappings of the fourth parcel.

"You do not think it could be any member of the company?"

"It is quite possible, Mr. Hardcastle. You have not yet told me anything of the possible motive."

"Motive, Mr. Pons?"

"Come, Mr. Hardcastle, every man has his enemies; especially is that true of the theatrical profession."

There were small spots of red burning on our host's cheeks now.

"Well, Mr. Pons, I must be frank with you. This matter is too serious for anything else. I have perhaps been over-fond of the ladies in my time. It is a human failing to which theatricals are particularly prone."

Solar Pons smiled thinly.

"You mean a jealous husband might be at the back of this? It is a possibility we must not overlook. Have you anyone in mind?"

Hardcastle spread his hands wide and there was something irresistibly comic about the gesture; as though his actor's vanity were saying unmistakably to us that the field was an extensive one and the suspects many. Something of this must have crossed my friend's mind also because there was a mocking smile on his lips.

"Frankness, Mr. Hardcastle. We shall be discreet about this."

Hardcastle fidgeted with the handkerchief in his breast pocket.

"There are two names, Mr. Pons," he mumbled. "I will write them down for you."

3

Gravel gritted beneath our feet as we walked along the path in the grounds, skirting the great sombre banks of rhododendron. The weather was bitterly cold and I swung my arms as I followed Pons' spare figure. He was in great form and his energetic pace had drawn protests from me more than once.

"You ate too much for lunch, Parker," he admonished me. "You are paying for it now."

"When I require you for my medical adviser, Pons," I said with some asperity, "I will inform you of the fact."

Solar Pons laughed, turning his keen, feral face to me over his shoulder as he strode onward.

"*Touché*, Parker. You are right to admonish me. But I have much to think about and my pace is but a reflection of my racing thoughts."

With that he slackened his stride and I drew level with him. It was close to dusk now and we were coming alongside an ornamental lake, the steel-grey sky reflected back from the ice on its surface. Our sombre surroundings and the vastness of the park which surrounded Hardcastle's great house seemed to me to epitomise the grim problem faced by Pons and the more bizarre aspects of the actor's situation with the unknown menace which threatened his life.

We were walking on grass and the going was downhill and my breathing slowly returned to normal. But the exercise had done me good and a pleasing warmth slowly spread throughout my numbed limbs. Pons had now lit his pipe and he puffed out streamers of aromatic smoke as we walked.

"Let us just have the benefit of your commonsense approach in this matter, Parker. You are an admirable touchstone."

"It seems very dark, Pons, but there must be an obvious explanation. The person who threatens your client's life evidently lives in London. He has been frustrated once but he most likely will strike again at the opening of the new play. As for suspects, there must be many people in Hardcastle's professional career."

The puzzled frown remained on Solar Pons' face. He shook his head.

"That is all very well so far as it goes, Parker, but it does not take us much farther."

I looked at my companion.

"I do not quite follow you, Pons."

"Motive, Parker. Motive."

Solar Pons stabbed the air with the stem of his pipe to emphasise his points.

"There has to be an extremely strong motive in all this. So far it eludes me. The skilful wax models; the obvious time and trouble they took to create; the familiarity with the threatened man's life-style and movements; the threats and the differing mode of execution; the failure of the police to uncover the murderer when Stanwell was struck down; even the foreknowledge of the forthcoming plays."

"An ardent playgoer, Pons?"

"Perhaps, Parker, perhaps."

Solar Pons paused and put his hand on my arm. We had skirted the lake, still walking on the grass, and had come opposite a small wooden summer-house which stood on the bank. It faced the water and naturally the open side was away from us but I now heard what Pons' sharp ears had already caught; the sound of voices, speaking urgently but in high altercation.

"I tell you, Dolly, I cannot do as you ask in the matter!"

"Cannot, or will not, Elijah?"

There was no difficulty in recognising Hardcastle's voice as the first but the second was a woman's; a cultured voice which denoted a proud and imperious nature. It was raised in tones of passionate anger and I saw by Pons' furrowed brow and the flash of his eye that he attached great importance to the conversation. I was about to move away but again Pons' hand was on my arm restraining me, his lips curved in a half-smile.

"There is nothing between you. Nothing, it is long overdue—we must regularise the situation!"

"You are reading far too much into it, my dear."

There was a pause and the two actors in the drama had evidently moved to another part of the summer-house for when their voices came again they were farther away and more muffled.

"I must warn you, Elijah, that things cannot go on in this manner. I do not wish to threaten . . . "

"By God, you had better not do so, Dolly!"

There was black anger in Hardcastle's voice and the wooden wall of the summer-house echoed to a tremendous crash as though he had dashed his fist against it. A moment later there came the crunching of his boots in the gravel and the huge form of Hardcastle strode savagely away in the dusk, taking the path that led from us round the other side of the lake. Pons watched until he had faded from view and then led me back to rejoin the path some way down.

"The butterflies on the Sussex Downs are gravely threatened this year, I understand, Parker," he said smoothly.

I looked at him in astonishment. Our feet gritted on the gravel path and I almost made a loud exclamation as my companion pinched my forearm.

"Indeed, Pons," I said loudly, clearing my throat.

We were almost level with the front of the summer-house when an imperious woman in furs burst from it. She came straight toward us with no attempt at concealment. I had an impression of icy beauty; of upswept blonde hair; and a manner close to tears beneath the anger.

The fur-coat and the expensive toque were utterly out of place in this country park and her blue eyes blazed as she swept past us. Pons doffed his hat and she acknowledged the courteous gesture with the faintest lowering of her eyelids. A few moments later she had gone. Pons looked after her with a quizzical expression in his face.

"Dolly Richmond has quite a temper," he remarked mildly. "I should not be surprised if Hardcastle has to keep his eyes open on two fronts during the run of this new play."

"The famous actress, Pons!" I exclaimed. "There is motive enough for murder in what we have just heard."

"Is there not, Parker. Unless I am much mistaken Miss Richmond is cast opposite our client in *Death Comes to Thornfield*."

He drew out a slip of paper from his overcoat pocket and flicked his eyes across it. A sardonic smile curved his lips.

"As I expected, Miss Richmond is not on the short list of Mr. Hardcastle's conquests. As you so sagely imply, Parker, this is a situation which merits watching."

And without referring to the matter again he retraced his steps in the direction of our host's stately home. Pons was busy on some inquiry of his own on our return and it was not until dinner that we met again. We ate in a luxuriously appointed dining room panelled in oak, and lit by antique chandeliers. The room had two fireplaces, one at each end, and the roaring flames of the liberally banked fires cast a pleasing glow across the china and silver and crystal on the table. There were just the five of us; myself and Pons; Hardcastle and his wife; and the secretary, Abrahams.

The food and wine were of excellent quality and the meal passed agreeably, served smoothly and efficiently by maids supervised by the butler who had first greeted us on arrival. Obviously, Pons said nothing of the incident at the summer-house and I had only to look at his intent face and his tightly compressed lips when I mentioned our walk in the grounds to see that he felt I might inadvertently refer to it.

After the meal Pons and Hardcastle and I adjourned to a small smoking room where we took coffee and liqueurs; later, Abrahams joined us at the request of our host and sat silent, looking from one to the other of us, as though he were secretly terrified of his employer. But Pons appeared in his element. We might merely have been weekend guests staying with old friends.

At dinner my friend had been an agreeable raconteur, keeping the table absorbed with his recitals of his extensive travels and now he discoursed knowledgeably on the theatre and the differing techniques employed by stage and cinema actors. As well as I knew Pons, I was considerably surprised at his knowledge and Hardcastle, his troubles temporarily forgotten, obviously warmed to him.

Pons had included Abrahams in the conversation and the young man, his tongue perhaps loosened to some extent by the wine he had imbibed at dinner, grew more relaxed and confident in his manner. He was a good-looking, personable young man who might have made an excellent actor himself and I had noticed that Hardcastle kept him working hard, often running about unnecessarily on quite trivial errands. It was one of his less likeable traits and I must confess I was pleased to see that he was inclined now, at the end of the day, to allow him some brief peace.

At length there was a pause in the conversation and Pons leaned forward, clouds of aromatic blue smoke from his pipe wavering toward the ceiling.

"You have not yet favoured us with your opinions, Mr. Abrahams?"

"My opinions, Mr. Pons?"

The secretary looked startled.

"On this strange threat which hangs over Mr. Hardcastle?"

"Oh, that."

Abrahams gave a somewhat placatory glance toward his employer, as though he might have some objection to the answer, but Hardcastle merely cleared his throat, an encouraging expression on his face.

"I am completely baffled, Mr. Pons. It is a dreadful business, of course, but I do not know what Mr. Hardcastle could possibly have done to merit such enmity. Perhaps it is someone mentally deranged."

"Perhaps," said Solar Pons carelessly. "Though the case has all the hallmarks of an eminently sane mind."

"Eigh?"

Hardcastle looked across at Pons with a worried frown.

"I do not quite understand, Mr. Pons."

"It is perfectly simple. Everything that I have so far learned leads me in one direction only. Toward a crystal-clear mind which is calculatedly plotting revenge."

There was an ugly silence and our host stared at Pons, his open mouth a round, blank O in his face.

"You know who is responsible, Mr. Pons?"

The question came from the secretary, whose eyes were fixed intently on my companion's face.

Solar Pons shook his head, a faint smile on his lips.

"Not yet, Mr. Abrahams. But I have some indications. I would prefer to say nothing more at this stage."

"What are your plans, Mr. Pons?"

Pons turned toward Hardcastle.

"I shall return to London tomorrow afternoon, Mr. Hardcastle.

I have learned enough here for the moment and I am convinced you are in no current danger. If the actions of your unknown persecutor run true to form, he will strike on the opening night of the new play."

The famous actor looked disappointed and sat frowning into his liqueur glass. Pons noticed his downcast mood and rose from his seat.

"I shall not be far away, Mr. Hardcastle, and you can reach me in a moment by telephone. I will be at the theatre as soon as you begin rehearsals, and we will make plans."

Our client got up too and clasped my friend's hand impulsively. "You are right, of course, Mr. Pons. You could do little by hanging about here, though I must say I derive a good deal of comfort from your presence and that of Dr. Parker. In the meantime, what do you wish me to do?"

"Report to me immediately you see anyone—friend or stranger—acting suspiciously about this estate. Be on your guard and impress on your servants the importance of securing the premises properly at night."

He raised his hand at the expression of alarm on our client's face.

"It is not that I fear anything specific, Mr. Hardcastle; it is just that we must be constantly on our guard. For example, if a message were to appear mysteriously on your desk one morning, it would be important to know how it had arrived. Securing the property would narrow down the field for speculation."

"I see, Mr. Pons."

Relief was evident on Hardcastle's face.

"Anything else?"

"Let me know as soon as you are due in London to begin rehearsals. I will meet you at the theatre. I wish to mingle unobtrusively with the company and the backstage staff. Can that be arranged?"

"Certainly, Mr. Pons. You prefer to be incognito?"

"That would be best. You may merely introduce me as Mr. Smith, a friend who is obsessed with the glamour of the theatre. I shall be able to gain a good deal of background information in this manner long before the play opens."

Hardcastle smiled.

"I see, Mr. Pons. It shall be as you wish. Abrahams will keep you fully informed."

"Excellent. And now, I am feeling a little fatigued and the hour is late. We will just pay our respects to our hostess and then retire. Come, Parker."

4

"I have just received a message from Hardcastle, Parker. The company begins rehearsals for *Death Comes to Thornfield* at the Negresco this afternoon. Are you free?"

"I can make myself so, Pons."

"Excellent, my dear fellow. In that case I should be glad of your company."

A week had gone by since our visit to the actor's home, and though it was now the end of January the bitter weather continued. But snow had held off. Pons had had much to occupy him during the past few days and, having concluded some loose ends which had been fretting him in the Alcover swindle case, had now turned his attention back to Hardcastle's affairs.

It had chafed him that there should be such a delay but there was nothing to be done and it seemed obvious, even to me, that little else could happen until the actor's latest play was put into production, if the pattern evolved by the secret persecutor continued in the same fashion.

We left our comfortable quarters at 7B Praed Street, and it was just three o'clock when we arrived at the Negresco, a palatial gilt rococo edifice in a narrow street near Shaftesbury Avenue. Hardcastle himself was in the foyer to greet us and introduced us to Ayres, his business manager, a tall, sardonic man with greying hair. Abrahams was there, standing a little in the background, but he nodded agreeably enough and the statuesque figure of Miss Stillwood came forward briskly to shake our hands.

The rest of the company was already back-stage and the house-lights were on as we hurried down the central gangway of the theatre at the heels of the actor's party. The curtain was up and a motley-looking crowd of people in ordinary clothes stood about languidly or sat sprawled in chairs on an opulent set with French windows, which represented the drawing-room of a large country house. I saw with amusement that the layout was extremely similar to that of the drawing-room of Hardcastle's own Surrey home and the fact was obviously not lost on Pons.

The actor looked back over his shoulder and seemed to read my companion's thought.

"Appears familiar, does it not, Mr. Pons? We have to do this or my wife would not know where she was."

I saw a momentary expression of irritation pass across the mobile features of Sandra Stillwood and put it down to her husband's remark but I then noticed that the tall, regal form of Dolly Richmond was standing in the centre of the stage, waiting for our party to come up.

I had never seen a professional play in production before

and the next two hours passed in a blur. What seemed chaotic to me seemed natural to Hardcastle and his company and, in an astonishingly short space of time, the players were reading their lines, the producer was lounging in a front-row seat shouting instructions and exhortations to humbler members of the cast and Hardcastle, Miss Stillwood and Miss Richmond were engaged in more dignified conferences with the producer and the play's backer.

Pons had watched all this for half an hour or so, chuckling now and again at particular pieces of business, but I had noted his deep, piercing eyes raking all round the theatre. Later, I became dimly aware that he had disappeared and when I glanced back saw that his seat was empty. From far off came the hammer of carpenters and all the bustle of a great theatre and I imagined him prowling restlessly about backstage.

I thought it best to remain where I was, as I should otherwise only disturb him, and in mid-afternoon saw his lean form in a stage box looking down somewhat sardonically upon the scene of turmoil below. The play, as our client had hinted, was an exciting affair and I noticed a sort of tension which seemed to grip the cast as they approached the climactic scene in the last act in which Hardcastle met his end in the dramatic death which gave the play its title.

I noticed a shadow at the corner of my eye and someone sat down on my right. At first I thought it was Pons but immediately picked him out in another stage box, evidently measuring the distance from it to the stage. I saw immediately what he was at and felt relief; the danger to Hardcastle, if any, would undoubtedly come from such a box though I had no doubt that the stage management would let them only to persons known to them on the opening night.

I glanced round and saw that it was Ayres, Hardcastle's business manager, who leaned across to me, his eyes gleaming.

"It looks as though we shall have a great success here, doctor, does it not?"

I hastened to agree but added a rider to the effect that it all depended on such events as had happened at Liverpool being prevented in future.

Ayres nodded gloomily.

"You're right there, doctor. It's a black business. Unfortunately there are only too many people who would like to see Elijah out of it."

I turned to him and looked at the worldly face surmounted by the greying hair so close to mine.

"Would you care to enlarge on that, Mr. Ayres?"

The business manager shrugged.

"I've told Elijah about it, often enough. There's women... and their husbands. It's always trouble in the theatre."

He made an expressive gesture with his hand as though he were cutting his own throat which I felt somewhat lacking in taste.

"Perhaps," I said cautiously. "But these situations obtain in many other walks of life."

Ayres nodded grimly.

"Correct, doctor. But you do not know theatricals. If I told you a quarter of what I have seen in my time in the theatre you would be astonished. Jealousy and yet more jealousy! It all passes belief."

I hesitated and then gave utterance to my thoughts.

"You suspect someone specific?"

The business manager gave a crooked wink.

"It would not be fair to say. But you can take it from me there is a wide choice of both sexes."

My attention was dramatically drawn back to the stage at this point by some extraordinary noises; the lights were down and the stage bathed in that mysterious half-light which one gets only in the theatre. A monstrous shadow from the French windows had enveloped Hardcastle, who, in his character as the heartless philanderer, was dying of manual strangulation. An unseen figure in a cloak had slipped a wire loop round his neck.

Pons' client was giving a magnificent performance. With his tongue lolling from his mouth and his eyes rolling, he looked an horrific spectacle as he thrashed about helplessly, emitting terrifying choking noises. Presently he dropped to the floor and was then still. There was a thin ripple of applause from the other actors and the technicians and the cloaked figure stepped forward into the light to reveal the beautiful and flushed features of Dolly Richmond. She stood there, her eyes blazing with triumph, as the curtain fell slowly.

I must admit my own palms were sore as a spontaneous burst of applause burst forth. The next moment the curtain had risen again and both Hardcastle and Miss Richmond, hand in hand, were ironically acknowledging the acclamation. I found Pons back behind me again.

"Admirable, is it not, Parker?" he commented drily. "The Thespian art has a good deal to commend it in these days of mindless and mechanical entertainment."

"They are certainly playing well for rehearsal, Pons," I said. "The effect should be tremendous on the opening night."

"That is evidently what our unknown friend is hoping for," said Pons soberly. "In my opinion this would be the exact moment; the lights down, everyone concentrating on the two dim figures. That is our Achilles heel, Parker, and somehow I have to pinpoint the greatest moment of danger and protect our client's life."

"It is a fearful responsibility, Pons."

"Is it not, Parker? But I am convinced that the opening night is what we have to fear and we must make plans accordingly."

Pons rose from his seat and drew me to the back of the theatre, which was now filled with the buzz of animated conversation.

"Let us just circulate a little, Parker. I have learned an astonishing amount of information about the lives of our client and his wife already, not to mention the other members of the company."

Pons had sparks of irony in his eyes as he looked at me mockingly. We were in the foyer of the theatre now and he led the way though the empty and deserted bar to a narrow corridor that ran down the side of the building. On one side it gave on to the emergency exits; the other wall was pierced by doors at intervals, which led back into the theatre.

"You seem to know your way around remarkably well, Pons," I said.

"I have the advantage of a plan of the building supplied through the courtesy of my client, Parker. It will be vitally important to know the layout thoroughly by the opening night."

"You are convinced the killer will strike again, then?"

"Undoubtedly, my dear fellow. The accidental death of the other actor will have made him more determined to succeed than ever."

"But supposing the whole charade were merely a mask to cover the murder which has already taken place, Pons?"

Solar Pons looked at me shrewdly as he motioned me through

the far door of the corridor into a dusty passage beneath the stage.

"You constantly astonish me, Parker. This time you have excelled yourself."

"I thought my supposition quite ingenious myself, Pons," I said with a somewhat justifiable glow of pride.

We were going up a narrow spiral staircase railed with an iron balustrade.

"I had already given that matter a great deal of consideration," said my companion over his shoulder. "To that effect I have been in touch with the Liverpool police. There is nothing at all in Stanwell's background to merit such treatment. He was an inoffensive bachelor who had few friends and his death would have benefited no one. The threat to Hardcastle is genuine enough."

He paused as heavy hammering reverberated throughout the building. Two carpenters passed at the end of an aisle, carrying heavy baulks of timber. We were evidently in the scenery store for huge canvas flats bearing the representations of Palladian temples, Arcadian scenery and sky-scrapers were stacked against massive wooden partitions. Pons put his hand against my arm as we moved down softly, and motioned caution with a finger against his lips.

There were other voices becoming sharper from among the distant hum of conversation and the cacophony of hammering.

"I tell you I have had enough of it, Hardcastle!"

The voice was a man's, thick and clotted with anger. There was not only anger but positive hatred in it.

"You must not allow yourself to become swayed by malicious and unfounded gossip, Setton."

The second voice was obviously Hardcastle's; placatory but at the same time with a hard undertone of annoyance and anger. There was a heavy crash from the other side of the flats as though the first man had stamped his foot.

"Rumour or not, it has got to stop, Hardcastle. This is my last warning. I am not a violent man but I will do something desperate if you meddle further in our lives."

There was a sneer in Hardcastle's voice as he replied.

"What would you do, Setton? I could break you in half like a rotten stick if I chose!"

"There are other ways than physical violence. Just remember what I have said. Leave Dolly alone!"

There was the rapid, staccato beat of footsteps and Pons and I drew back into the shadow. I just had time to glimpse a short, thin man with a black moustache pass the end of the aisle.

A door slammed behind him and there was a brief silence apart from the distant clamour. Then there came the unmistakable rasp of a match-head against the box. Flame grew and glowed against the end of the passageway. Hardcastle drew on his cigar, for the fragrant, aromatic odour reached my nostrils a few seconds later. Then his heavy footsteps followed his late companion and died out.

"Well, well," said Pons after a short interval. "The case grows in interest."

"You have no shortage of suspects, Pons," I said. "I thought I recognised the gentleman."

"It was Setton Richmond, the musical comedy star, Parker. As you know, he is married to Dolly Richmond and from what we heard by the lake in the park he has good cause for jealousy."

He pulled at the lobe of his ear with thin fingers, his face a brooding mask of thought.

"There is little further we can do here, my dear fellow. I think a brisk walk back to Praed Street followed by one of Mrs. Johnson's inimitable high teas will do the trick. I find that a full stomach works wonders in assisting the ratiocinative process."

5

The orchestra burst into a deafening crescendo as the overture began. I focused my eyes on the footlights of the stage as they slowly increased in intensity. Pons stirred at my side, his sharp eyes stabbing about the theatre.

"There is nothing like the final full-dress rehearsal to give the proper atmosphere, Parker."

"Indeed, Pons."

"You see that stage box up there?"

I looked up in the direction he had indicated.

"The one on the right?"

"That is the one. I wish you to go there and keep a careful watch on the stage throughout the performance, if you would be so good."

I glanced at Pons and my puzzlement must have shown on my face.

"But what am I to look out for, Pons?"

Solar Pons smiled a curious smile.

"Be particularly alert at the finale, Parker."

"The strangling scene. I see, Pons. You wish to pinpoint the vulnerable moments at which this mysterious killer might strike at the opening on Wednesday?"

"Something like that, Parker. Also keep an eye on the other boxes and if you see anything suspicious do not hesitate to shout out or cause a distraction."

I stared at my companion in amazement.

"You think this creature might be here this evening?"

"It is entirely possible, Parker. You forget that he would need to know this particular theatre, just as I myself have had to learn its layout during the past few weeks."

"I see."

Solar Pons rose and stretched himself, looking round the half-empty auditorium, which contained a sprinkling of relatives and friends of the artistes, together with technical personnel and members of the national press. So far as I could make out all the boxes were empty.

There was an extremely serious expression on my friend's face.

"You have your revolver?"

I nodded.

"Certainly, Pons. You insisted on it and I have carried it whenever I have managed to get along to the theatre for these rehearsals."

Solar Pons smiled and rested his hand lightly on my shoulder.

"You have been a tower of strength, as always, Parker. I am most grateful to you."

This was high praise indeed and I mumbled something deprecating in reply.

"What will you be doing in the meantime?"

"I shall be about, Parker. I have a few small things to do backstage yet. But it is imperative that you keep alert."

"I shall certainly do that, Pons."

I left my friend in the shadowy aisle of the theatre as the overture came to a close and made my way to the box indicated. It was strange and eerie in the half-light as I stumbled up the plush stairs and when I took my place in the box the rectangle of the curtained stage below seemed brilliant in contrast.

I took my seat on one of the comfortable upholstered chairs at the edge of the box and waited for my eyes to adjust to the light. I did not think any danger might come from those in the main auditorium; it was altogether too public and anyone behaving suspiciously would immediately be noticed by his neighbour. The cavernous darkness of the remainder of the vast theatre was another thing altogether. The boxes stretched for tier after tier to the ceiling.

Pons had ruled out the balcony as being too far from the stage to constitute a danger and in any event I soon saw this evening that there was a sprinkling of journalists and photographers spread along the front rows. I decided to concentrate on the stage boxes immediately below me and on those on the left-hand side on the proscenium. I had no doubt Pons was keeping watch backstage.

Naturally, I would watch the progress of the play itself as it unfolded before me but the difficulty was going to be to avoid getting involved in the story and forgetting to watch the surroundings. I determined to remain alert and not to let Pons down, just in case there might be something suspicious taking place this evening.

The curtain was rising on the palatial drawing-room scene and the brilliance of the lighting, the opulence of the décor and the richness of the decorations and tapestries brought a thin smattering of applause from the friends and relatives who had been invited to this preview of the play.

Several of the leading players were making their entrance and I marvelled at the metamorphosis of these somewhat dowdy individuals of the ordinary rehearsals, now transformed by rich costuming, make-up and eyebrow pencil into these colourful, larger-than-life characters who went through their dramatic paces so smoothly and effortlessly.

Only I now knew what a great deal of hard work underlay this perfection and I listened to the dialogue with more than ordinary interest and watched the gyrations of these puppets as though the entire play were something new to me. But so insidious was this spell that I guiltily withdrew my gaze from the lighted rectangle with a jerk, suddenly aware that over seven minutes had passed since curtain-up.

I glanced round the hushed auditorium but all seemed normal. The orchestra leader was in the pit, the mood music from the fifteen or so musicians delicately underlining the events being played out before us. From the additional light emanating from the stage I could see the faded gilt and plush of the other boxes. I raked my eyes over them cautiously. They were all completely empty. I had borrowed a pair of opera glasses from Ayres, the business manager, and when I had adjusted the eyepieces, I examined the boxes, the stage and its surroundings in greater detail.

Something caught my attention as I slowly scanned the stage for perhaps the fifteenth time. The first act had finished, the interval had passed, and the performance was now more than halfway through the second act. Absorbing though the performances were—and Hardcastle himself was outstanding, as were his wife and Dolly Richmond—I bore in mind the importance of the service Pons had entrusted to me and I was ever mindful of the great faith he had in my abilities.

Now, as I brought the glasses past the stage curtains, a faint smudge of white caught my attention in the shadow. I brought the glasses back, adjusted the focusing ring to give even finer detail on this new subject. I was considerably startled to see that someone was standing silently in the wings, obviously watching the course of the drama. I was certain it was not one of the actors because they would never reveal themselves to the audience in that way.

The smudge of white I had noticed resolved itself into the fingers and knuckles of a hand which was clutching the edge of the curtain. Nothing more. The thin wrist was cut off by the fold of the material. There was something so sinister and brooding in the presence of this silent watcher at the edge of the stage that I was greatly agitated and for a moment considered descending and seeking out Pons.

Then a moment's reflection convinced me of the folly of this course. It was obviously my duty to observe without doing anything, unless there was any evident danger to our client or the people in the theatre. And if it did transpire that some prompter or stagehand was merely standing in the wings out of idle curiosity I should look foolish indeed. No, it would be better to keep careful watch and make perfectly sure before I acted.

The hand disappeared before a good many minutes had passed but I nevertheless continued my careful watch of the theatre; giving my attention principally to the stage and its surroundings; the boxes I could conveniently keep under observation; and the audience in the auditorium, of course. There was nothing else suspicious that I could see and I therefore naturally concentrated on that side of the stage on which I had seen the hand.

The second interval passed and the third and final act of the drama of *Death Comes to Thornfield* commenced. There was a deep hush of concentration from the audience in which the voices of the actors came up to me powerfully reinforced by the acoustics and crystal-clear. Hardcastle was certainly a magnificent actor and he put everything he possessed in the way of talent and personality into the finale of the drama which was now inexorably mounting to its striking high-point.

This made it difficult for me to concentrate on the stage and when I again refocused my glasses on the left-hand side I saw something that gave me cause for the gravest concern. In addition to the hand which was now back in its old position there was an evil-looking bearded face which was staring at Hardcastle and his three companions on stage with rapt attention. I reached into my inner pocket with my disengaged hand and sought the butt of my revolver.

I put it down on the ledge beside me and then, when I had made sure that the intent, bearded figure was still immobile, the profile of the face just clear of the curtains, I put down the glasses and threw off the safety catch. When I again raised the glasses to my eyes I saw that the situation had changed. There were now three objects in view; the clenched hand holding the fold of the curtain; the face; and a black, shiny object which seemed like the barrel of a rifle or shotgun.

The matter looked extremely serious. I glanced at my watch. There were just ten minutes to the big scene in the finale in which Hardcastle was strangled with the wire noose. Pons and I had timed the play on so many occasions over the past weeks that I almost felt I could myself act as prompter. There was no time to lose if I were to avert a tragedy. I jumped to my feet, seized the revolver which I held close to my side and quitted the box.

As I ran down the corridor outside, which led to the staircase connecting with the ground floor, I could hear the orchestral music rising to a crescendo. The moment had almost come. I opened a wrong door at the rear of the stage and was immediately accosted by a little man in a blue serge suit who put his hand to his lips. I showed him my letter of authority signed by Hardcastle and his expression changed. When I had whispered my requirements he motioned me toward a small set of railed steps which evidently led up toward the stage area.

I tiptoed quietly up the ladder and as I did so the stage lights were lowered, the two spotlights emphasising the area near the windows in which Dolly Richmond was to strangle Carstairs. For one strange moment I wondered if the jealous, passionate actress might indeed strangle her lover in a paroxysm of rage and this thought so startled me that I stumbled and almost fell.

It was dark back here and I moved forward slowly until my eyes had adjusted to the lower intensity of the lighting, my right hand holding the revolver ready. The clear, emphatic tones of Hardcastle as he made his final speech in the supposedly empty drawing-room, unaware of the hooded figure behind him, were ringing through the theatre. I estimated I had less than a minute to go. The orchestra was silent except for an insistent, high-pitched crescendo from the violins and, masked by this, I covered the last few yards to the side of the enormous stage.

I could see Pons' client clearly, the spotlights holding him in an eerie yellow glow. Behind him were the big French doors and, uncannily realistic, the artificial "moonlight" from special lamps spilling in behind and making patterns of the window bars across the floor. The conductor of the orchestra was visible in the faint glow of the lowered footlights and there, right before me, the tense, expectant silhouette of the bearded man, so intently fixed on the drama being played to its horrific conclusion.

I paused for a moment, irresolute. The decision was a difficult one. The man in front of me might be perfectly harmless, yet I had a tremendous feeling of some impending disaster. On top of that Pons had warned me to keep alert and act if I saw anything suspicious. I could now only wait for this last minute or so until the climax of the play approached and see what this bearded stranger intended to do.

Hardcastle had paused in his soliloquy and was circling the stage, his movements tense and predatory. There was an expectant hush in the auditorium still and I could see the pale ovals of the scattered faces of this extempore audience in the glow of the footlights. I took my attention from the man in front of me for a moment and looked up at the boxes, but the reflected light from the stage made it difficult to pick anything out.

The violins of the orchestra were emitting throbbing notes of menace and Hardcastle had ceased his pacing, was slowly drawing back in front of the French windows again, the curtains of which I knew contained the figure of Dolly Richmond armed with the wire noose. My own tension was mounting too in this highly melodramatic atmosphere and I longed for the play to be over, when my responsibility should be ended.

In this novel situation where so many unexpected things could happen I was feeling a little out of my depth. I tightened my grip on the butt of the revolver at my side as Hardcastle began his last vocal musings as he expressed his thoughts to the audience. I moved in closer to the curtains, conscious that the man in front of me was slowly raising the black barrel of the weapon he carried. I had not been able to see it before as his back was to me, his body blocking the view. The stage lighting shimmered on the gloss of the barrel and I slowly raised the revolver, conscious of a sick feeling in the pit of my stomach and a dry-throated nervousness which was affecting the whole of my body.

The orchestral accompaniment was rising to a crescendo and I could see the intent, strained face of the conductor as he worked up the musicians to the finale. Hardcastle had finished his speech and behind him the hooded figure which concealed the famous actress was drawing nearer. The noose was slipped quickly round the throat and Hardcastle began his terrifying choking noises.

I was momentarily distracted and lowered the revolver. But at the same time the bearded man in front of me was galvanised into action. He turned and instead of threatening Hardcastle as I had expected, he hurled his rifle into the orchestra pit. There was a loud clatter and a peculiar whining noise. As I blundered forward, revolver raised, the man with the beard evaded me and sped across the stage like lightning. He cannoned into Hardcastle and the girl and the whole group went down with a tremendous noise.

At the same moment there was a streak of light across the spotlights and something struck the back of the stage with a tremendous crash. I did not wait for any further explanations but hurled myself forward at the bearded man as the auditorium exploded into uproar. I seized the legs of the attacker and attempted to drag him off Hardcastle as the house lights went up.

I was stupefied as the thin man's beard came off in my hands to reveal the mocking face of Solar Pons.

"My dear fellow," he said ironically, "if you will kindly remove your not inconsiderable weight from my person I should be much obliged to you."

"Pons!" I stammered. "I thought you were the person who sent those figures to your client."

Pons shook his head as I helped him to his feet.

"I felt it best to take advantage of the dressing room facilities while I was treading the boards," he chuckled. "The persons I suspected knew me too well. I realised you were behind me and trusted to your sense of self-control not to queer my pitch. Nevertheless, it was a close-run thing."

He gestured to the back of the stage where the head of a steel-shafted arrow was buried deep in the wooden flat of the scenery.

"Good heavens, Pons! Did you know this would happen? I thought we had to fear only the opening night."

"I suspected something of the sort, Parker. Which was why I asked you to be alert. But just give me a hand with Hardcastle and Miss Richmond, will you?"

The great actor and his companion had remained on the floor as though stunned during this exchange but now the stage was beginning to fill with people and Hardcastle had found his voice.

"What the hell do you mean by it, Mr. Pons? You have ruined the performance!"

"Something else might have been ruined if I had not intervened," said my companion dryly, indicating the arrow.

Hardcastle turned white and he and Miss Richmond exchanged frightened glances. Pons was casting sharp looks toward the front of the stage but now he relaxed somewhat.

"What were you doing with that shotgun, Pons?" I asked.

"Tut, Parker, it was not a gun but an ornamental walking cane," he said carelessly. "You no doubt mistook the smooth ebony of the shaft for a gun-barrel in the half-light. I threw it into the orchestra pit to put our friend off his aim."

"Orchestra pit, Pons?"

Solar Pons gave an enigmatic smile.

"Certainly, Parker. I saw quite early on that it provided admirable cover, particularly as the marksman would have to be close. And he could afterwards go out by the small entrance beneath the stage."

"I do not understand, Pons."

"It would not be the first time, Parker," said Solar Pons mischievously. "It came to me when I counted sixteen players instead of fifteen. A violin case makes an excellent place of concealment."

"I cannot make head or tail of it, Pons," I complained.

"Let us just take things slowly, Parker," said Pons as the secretary Abrahams helped Hardcastle and Miss Richmond to their feet.

"You may have wondered why I was talking so much about the case and the dangers of the first night about the theatre. That was merely part of my design. There is no place like the theatre for gossip and by this simple stratagem I hoped to put them off their guard. Ah, Inspector, there you are!"

I was stupefied to see the unprepossessing form of Inspector Jamison, our old acquaintance of Scotland Yard, coming up on to the stage.

"You have the warrants, Inspector?"

"Yes, Mr. Pons. I have left them blank as you requested."

"What does this mean, Pons?" I said.

"It means, Parker, that a nasty little drama is drawing to its close."

He kept his eyes fixed on the front of the stage all this time, oblivious of the buzz of conversation about us from the solicitous group which surrounded Hardcastle and Dolly Richmond. I confess I was puzzled by his attitude but I was even more surprised when he turned to me and said casually, "Come, Parker, we will be better placed at the front of the house. You had better come too, Jamison."

"As you wish, Mr. Pons. I have men posted in the foyer of the theatre and at the exits, as you suggested."

I turned to my companion with a dozen queries on my lips but he instantly silenced me with an imperative gesture. He led the way to the front of the stalls, where most of the seats had been vacated by the rush of people on to the stage in the confusion following the firing of the arrow. Pons' alert manner and the way his piercing eyes darted about indicated that he was very much on the lookout for something.

The orchestra conductor, a handsome-looking man with a flowing mane of white hair, emerged from a small door at the side of the stage and engaged in conversation with Hardcastle and Miss Richmond. The other members of the orchestra were slowly filing out now and I could see the secretary, Abrahams, coming up toward us, together with the business manager Ayres and other members of the theatrical company.

"Music has great charms, Jamison," said Solar Pons irrelevantly, "and as we are told, soothes the savage breast."

"Beg pardon, Mr. Pons," said the Inspector obtusely.

"For example," said Solar Pons calmly. "There are all types of instruments but some from which it would be difficult to coax a tune."

"I don't follow, Mr. Pons," said Jamison.

Members of the orchestra were still brushing past.

"A bow is of little use without a violin," said Solar Pons crisply.

He struck suddenly like a snake. A tall, slim man with a white face and a shock of black hair fell heavily to the floor as Pons arrogantly thrust out his foot. He started up with tremendous speed, his violin case falling at his feet. I moved forward in astonishment but I was too late.

Pons had the fallen man's hair in his hands. The wig came away instantly revealing a soft mass of blonde locks. The woman's voice was harsh and sibilant with hatred.

"Damn you, Mr. Pons!"

As I turned from this astonishing spectacle I saw that the violin case had fallen open and from it protruded a shining bow made of silvery steel set in velvet among a nest of metal-tipped arrows.

"Here is your man, Jamison," said Solar Pons exultantly. "Or rather woman. It is no use struggling Miss Stillwood. The drama is over."

Jamison jumped forward and secured the angry actress. Hardcastle fell back against the edge of the stage, his face shocked and ashen.

"Sandra! You don't mean it was you . . . ? All along?"

The woman's face was white with fury and she almost spat the words out.

"I have hated you for years, Elijah! And I was sick of your constant affairs. If it had not been for Stanwell edging forward that night in Liverpool we would have been rid of you."

"We?"

The voice was that of Inspector Jamison's.

"Of course, Jamison," said Solar Pons languidly. "Mrs. Hardcastle was not alone in this matter. You had best fill that second warrant in also, Inspector. In the name of Gordon Venner."

Abrahams' face was a mixture of fear and surprise. He ducked away but Solar Pons brought him down with a well-aimed kick behind the knee. He gave a howl of pain and then Jamison was on him and I heard the click of handcuffs.

There was an instant hubbub as all the people in the theatre gathered round. Pons looked at Hardcastle's shaken features and from him to the blazing eyes of Dolly Richmond.

"We cannot talk here, gentlemen. I suggest we leave the explanations until a more private occasion."

"This whole thing is ridiculous!" broke in Sandra Stillwood imperiously. "I demand to know the charges."

"Murder and attempted murder will do to be going on with," said Pons.

6

"You will remember, Parker," said Solar Pons, blowing out a streamer of blue smoke toward the ceiling of our sitting room at 7B, Praed Street. "You will remember that when Elijah Hardcastle first called me in I continually spoke of an outside menace threatening the actor. There was a very good reason for that."

I looked at my companion in amazement.

"You suspected Mrs. Hardcastle and the secretary from the beginning, Pons!"

"Hardly that, Parker," Solar Pons corrected me. "But from the very nature of the sinister incidents surrounding the family I knew it had to be very close to him indeed. The person who was sending the parcels had to know his movements intimately; even what plays he was in and the theatres where they were being presented. Furthermore, the model work was done with such skill and the whole thing planned with such sadistic pleasure that it immediately directed my mind to three things."

"Three things, Mr. Pons?"

Inspector Jamison screwed up his eyes as he stared at my companion in puzzlement from the other side of the table. It was the following day and both Sandra Stillwood and the secretary had made full confessions before being committed to cells to await a proper court hearing. Jamison had just come from Scotland Yard to join us for lunch and now we were enjoying coffee and liqueurs while Pons explained his reasoning.

He stabbed the air with the stem of his pipe to emphasise the points.

"Firstly, the models were so exquisite that they indicated a high degree of skill on the part of the modeller. This was so unusual that the perpetrator should not have been too difficult to trace. Secondly, the way the whole affair was planned—both to warn and terrify the victim—indicated great hatred. They say murder begins at home and I at once began to look at Hardcastle's domestic circumstances."

"And the third thing, Pons?"

My companion looked at me quizzically.

"Hatred, subtlety and the atmosphere of a cat playing with a mouse. I saw a woman's hand at every turn. I was assisted in my deductions almost immediately after our arrival. It had not escaped my attention that Elijah Hardcastle was hardly the ideal husband, to borrow another theatrical allusion. His numerous affairs and the scandals concerning his various mistresses were the talk of the town. His attractive wife, Sandra Stillwood, was a fiery, jealous and impetuous woman as one has only to see from the public newspapers.

"I knew she would be the last person to sit down under such treatment. Furthermore, Hardcastle was a wealthy man. I already had two good motives for his death; jealousy and greed. I looked for a further ingredient, for I knew that no ordinary skills were involved. Assuming Hardcastle's wife to be the prime mover, then she had to have an accomplice. The secretary was an obvious starting point for my assumption. He was good-looking and had not been with Hardcastle all that long. In a brief conversation with Mrs. Hardcastle I learned that she had herself introduced him to the household."

"Remarkable, Mr. Pons," Jamison mumbled.

Solar Pons chuckled.

"Elementary, my dear Jamison. So far nothing but logical deduction and simple observation. But I also saw a number of glances pass between Mrs. Hardcastle and the secretary. Such things are unmistakable to the trained observer. I rapidly came to the conclusion that she and Abrahams were lovers."

"And you let me go on thinking that Dolly Richmond or her husband might have been responsible," I grumbled.

"Not at all, Parker," said Solar Pons sharply. "Those were entirely your own completely unjustified assumptions. You were working altogether on the wrong premises. Oh, there were other suspects enough in the circle surrounding the couple, I give you. But the thing was crystal clear to me almost from the beginning. Method and motive were the things to which I now applied my attention. I was convinced that I had seen Abrahams before and that he was not in the Hardcastle's household under his own name.

"The face seemed familiar and when I returned to London I applied myself to my cuttings volumes. I soon found what I was looking for, though the name beneath the photograph was that of Gordon Venner. He was a somewhat obscure artist and stage designer who had been given a London exhibition some years ago. The photograph in my file showed him with a beautifully modelled maquette and it became obvious that his was the skilled hand responsible for the gruesome little tableaux despatched to my client. And it was he, of course, who put the corrosive on the chandelier cable during the performance of *The Hound of the Baskervilles*."

Pons blew out a cloud of blue smoke toward the ceiling and turned to the Inspector.

"All this was, of course, by way of suspicion and not at all conclusive. I had to trap the pair in the act and that required some finesse. In the meantime I telephoned Inspector Jamison, Parker, and he put some inquiries in hand. He found that Venner had disappeared from his London studio some months ago and when I put the dates together I found that his disappearance coincided with the employment of Hardcastle's new secretary."

"But would not your retention by Hardcastle put them on their guard, or at least make them abandon their plan, Pons?" I put in.

"Ordinarily, Parker, but I was relying on two factors. The first was by putting the couple completely off their guard. I gave it out that I expected any danger to come on the opening night. Therefore, as I conjectured, they moved their murder attempt forward to the final dress rehearsal. And secondly, I also made it plain by my conversation and actions that I believed the menace to come from someone outside the family. I had given a great deal of thought to the method of murder and felt that as the warning and the method had always differed they might for the actual attempt again try the bow and arrow."

"Why was that, Mr. Pons?"

"It was silent, swift and sure and they had a ready method by which they could get close to the intended victim, Jamison. I had seen enough of the Hardcastles at close quarters to realise that Sandra Stillwood and Venner were very much in love with one another and that her hatred, jealousy and greed in equal proportions would be enough to keep her fixed in her murderous course, despite my presence on the scene."

"But what about the parcels, Pons?" I put in. "They arrived from distant places when Mrs. Hardcastle was with her husband. And she was in the play with him last night."

Solar Pons shook his head.

"We shall find nothing difficult about that, Parker. Venner stayed in Surrey on numerous occasions, to take care of Hardcastle's business affairs. All the parcels were posted in London. Nothing simpler than for him to come up to post them; it is only half an hour's journey by train. As to Mrs. Hardcastle's part in the plot, I had noticed from perusal of scripts that she was always off-stage when these murderous incidents occurred. Last night her final appearance was some twenty minutes before her husband's strangulation on stage. Ample time for her to retire to her dressing room, disguise herself as one of the musicians with the steel bow concealed in the violin case and take her place at the far end of the orchestra, in the shadows. It took some daring but it was quite simple."

Solar Pons tented his fingers before him.

"I have examined the stage myself and it would have worked like this. There is another small emergency door beneath the stage which leads to the orchestra pit. She would have undoubtedly used this and there is a small space which is in darkness, near the side of the stage, in which she concealed herself. The cello player sat with his back to her and she was also concealed completely from sight by the bulk of that instrument. She had only to take her place five minutes before the final scene with small chance of detection."

"Remarkable, Mr. Pons!" interjected Jamison again.

Solar Pons shook his head.

"It was a fairly routine matter but one which required considerable patience over the past weeks. I had noticed early on that there were fifteen members of the orchestra and I discreetly checked with the theatre authorities to make certain that this was so. Last night, I disguised myself in order to render myself inconspicuous, but even so I was almost taken unawares. Fortunately, I noticed that there were sixteen members of the orchestra and the hiding place of the assassin was revealed."

"Despite your modesty, it has been a remarkable affair, Pons," I said. "I assume that after Hardcastle's death and the escape of the murderer, Mrs. Hardcastle would have inherited."

"And a discreet marriage would have taken place between herself and Venner in a year or two, Parker."

"Instead of which, considerable terms of imprisonment await them both," said Jamison. "Once again I am indebted to you, Mr. Pons."

He got up to go and shook hands with us. We waited until his heavy footsteps had descended the stairs, followed by the slam of the street door.

"What will happen to them, Pons?"

"Mrs. Hardcastle will be lucky to escape the rope but she is a brilliant and attractive woman, Parker. My guess is that, as Jamison surmises, they will both draw heavy prison sentences."

"And Hardcastle will be free to marry Miss Richmond when her divorce comes through?"

Solar Pons stared at me, his eyes dancing.

"Your romantic instinct is running wild again, Parker. I have warned you of that tendency before. I shall be very much surprised if your prediction comes true."

He went to stand at the window, frowning down at the street.

"There is just one point I am not clear about, Pons. Why would Hardcastle himself not have recognised his new secretary as Venner the designer?"

Solar Pons shook his head.

"You do not know the theatre, Parker. I said Venner was an unsuccessful designer. Though brilliant. Brilliancy and success do not always go together, unfortunately. Venner was obscure. I know that he has not designed for any major London production. Hardcastle is a famous and successful actor who appears only in major plays and films. Their paths would not have crossed. Incidentally, Venner served a short term of imprisonment some years ago, in connection with an art fraud, which is why his photograph was in my files."

"And the fact that nothing happened after the first warning, Pons?"

Solar Pons smiled enigmatically.

"I had not forgotten that, my dear fellow. I made some inquiries of the L.M.S. On the date in question, when the performance of *Othello* was being given, there was a major subsidence of the line in the Midlands which completely disrupted and for a time cancelled the train services between London and Edinburgh. For that reason Venner was unable to travel to Scotland to help in his mistress' scheme. Without his support she had no option but temporarily to abandon the plan as being too risky to attempt on her own. Ironically, it was something like the situation in one of Hardcastle's major films two years ago."

Pons traversed the room and languidly looked at the clock.

"Talking of films, Parker, there is a new Valentino at the London Pavilion. Are you free to go? He is no great actor but he has a certain animal grace which I find irresistible."

The Adventure of the Persecuted Painter

This "Sherlock Holmes case" originally appeared in the 1997 anthology The Mammoth Book of New Sherlock Holmes Adventures *edited by Mike Ashley. Despite featuring the characters originally created by Sir Arthur Conan Doyle, it could just as easily have been a Solar Pons adventure.* SJ.

1

IT WAS A dreary evening in early March when I returned to our familiar rooms in Baker Street. I was soaked to the skin for it had been raining earlier and I could not find a cab, and the dark clouds and louring skies promised a further downpour. As I opened the door to our welcoming sitting room, which was in semi-darkness, a familiar voice broke the silence.

"Come in my dear Watson. Mrs. Hudson will be up with a hot meal in a few minutes, as I had already observed you from the window, my poor fellow."

"Very good of you, Holmes," I mumbled. "I will just get into some dry things and rejoin you."

"It must have been very damp down Hackney way," my friend observed with a dry chuckle.

"How could you possibly know that, Holmes?" I said in some surprise. He burst into a throaty laugh.

"Because you inadvertently left your engagement pad on the table yonder."

When I returned to the sitting room the lamps were alight and the apartment transformed, with the motherly figure of Mrs. Hudson, our amiable landlady, bustling about laying the table, the covered dishes on which were giving off an agreeable aroma.

"Ah, shepherd's pie!" said Holmes, rubbing his thin hands together and drawing up his chair.

"You have excelled yourself this evening, Mrs. Hudson."

"Very kind of you to say so, sir."

She paused at the door, an anxious expression on her face.

"Did your visitor come back, Mr. Holmes?"

"Visitor, Mrs. Hudson?"

"Yes, sir. I was just going out, you see, and he said he would not bother you now. He said he would be back between six-thirty and seven-thirty, if that was convenient. I hope I have done right."

"Certainly, Mrs. Hudson."

Holmes glanced at the clock over the mantel.

"It is only six o'clock now so we have plenty of time to do justice to your excellent meal. What sort of person would you say?"

"A foreign-looking gentleman, Mr. Holmes. About forty, with a huge beard. He wore a plaid cape, a wide-brimmed hat and carried a shabby-looking holdall."

I paused with a portion of shepherd's pie halfway to my mouth.

"Why, you would make an admirable detective yourself, Mrs. Hudson."

"Kind of you to say so, sir! Shall I show him up as soon as he arrives, Mr. Holmes?"

"If you please."

Holmes was silent as we made inroads into the excellent fare and it had just turned seven when he produced his pipe and pouch and sat himself back in his chair by the fire.

"A foreign gentleman with a beard and a shabby case, Homes," I said at length, after the debris of our meal had been cleared and the room had resumed its normal aspect.

"Perhaps, Watson. But he may be an Englishman with a very mundane problem. It is unwise to speculate without sufficient data on which to base a prognosis."

"As you say, Holmes," I replied and sat down opposite him and immersed myself in the latest edition of *The Lancet*. It was just half-past seven and we had closed the curtains against the sheeting rain when there came a hesitant tap at the sitting room door. The apparition which presented itself was indeed bizarre and Mrs. Hudson's matter of fact description had not prepared me for such a sight.

He was of great height, and his dark beard, turning slightly grey at the edges, now flecked with rain, hung down over his plaid coat like a mat. His eyes were a brilliant blue underneath cavernous brows and his eyebrows, in contrast to the beard, were jet-black, which enhanced the piercing glance he gave to Holmes and myself. I had not time to take in anything else for I was now on my feet to extend a welcome. He stood just inside the door, water dripping from his clothing on to the carpet, looking owlishly from myself to Holmes, who had also risen from his chair.

"Mr. Holmes? Dr. Watson?" he said hesitantly in a deep bass voice.

"That is he," I said, performing the introductions.

He gave an embarrassed look to both of us.

"I must apologise for this intrusion, gentlemen. Aristide Smedhurst at your service. Artist and writer for my pains. I would not have bothered you, Mr. Holmes, but I am in the most terrible trouble."

"This is the sole purpose of this agency—to assist," said Holmes, extending a thin hand to our strange guest.

"Watson, would you be so kind? I think, under the circumstances, a stiff whisky would not come amiss."

"Of course, Holmes," I said, hastening to the sideboard.

"That is most gracious of you, gentlemen," said Smedhurst, allowing himself to be led to a comfortable chair by the fire.

As I handed him the whisky glass his face came forward into the light and I saw that he had an unnatural pallor on his cheeks.

"Thank you, Dr. Watson."

He gulped the fiery liquid gratefully and then, seeing Holmes' sharp eyes upon him, gave an apologetic shrug.

"Forgive me, Mr. Holmes, but if you had been through what I have experienced, it would be enough to shake even your iron nerve."

"Indeed," said Holmes in reassuring tones. "Pray do not apologise, my dear Mr. Smedhurst. I observed when you first entered that your cape and trousers were covered in mud, as though you had fallen heavily. You have come all the way from Dorset today, I presume, so the matter must be serious."

Our strange visitor gazed at Holmes open-mouthed.

"I did indeed have a nasty fall in my anxiety to catch my

train. But how on earth could you know I come from Dorset?"

My old friend got up to light a spill for his pipe from the fire.

"There was nothing extraordinary about my surmise, I can assure you. Watson and I attended your exhibition at the Royal Academy last summer. The extraordinary oils, water colours and pencil sketches of those weird landscapes remained long in my memory..."

"Why, of course, Holmes..." I broke in.

"And the exhibition catalogue, if I am not mistaken, gave your address in Dorset and said that you habitually worked in that fascinating part of the world," Holmes went on smoothly. "But you have a problem, obviously."

"Yes, Mr. Holmes. I thought Dorset was fascinating at first," went on Smedhurst bitterly. "But no longer after my experiences of the past two years."

"But you called earlier and then went away. Why was that?"

A haunted look passed across the bearded man's face.

"I thought I was followed here," he mumbled, draining his glass. He eagerly accepted the replenishment I offered him.

"You are among friends, Mr. Smedhurst," Holmes went on. "Pray take your time. You are staying in town, of course."

"At the Clarence, yes."

"An admirable establishment. Which means you are not pressed for time this evening?"

"No, sir."

The haggard look was back on our visitor's face. "For God's sake, Mr. Holmes, help me! This ghastly thing has appeared again. Both my sanity and my life are at stake!"

2

There was a long silence in the room, broken only by the distant clatter of a passing hansom. Holmes waited until our visitor had regained his calm and then gently asked him to continue. Draining the contents of his second glass of whisky with one fierce gulp, Smedhurst plunged straight into his story.

"I had grown tired of London, Mr. Holmes, and felt the need of country air. There was also a young lady with whom I had forged an attachment. We had met at one of my exhibitions and I had escorted her to several functions in London. She lived at Parvise Magna, a small village in Dorset, so when I went down I searched for a suitable dwelling in the area. I soon found what I wanted. It was an ancient cottage and needed a lot of repair but stood in its own land about a mile from the village. It had belonged to an old man, Jabez Crawley, who had let it go to rack and ruin, and who had died the previous year. However, I negotiated a fair price with a local lawyer who had handled Crawley's affairs, and moved in. At first, all went well and when my renovations had been completed I was extremely happy."

Here Smedhurst paused and flushed slightly. Holmes leaned forward in his chair, a gentle smile softening his austere features.

"You had come to an understanding with this young lady?"

"Exactly so, Mr. Holmes. A Miss Eveline Reynolds, a very charming person."

"I can well imagine, Mr. Smedhurst," I put in.

Holmes' smile widened.

"Ah, there is your romantic streak again, Watson."

"Well, Mr. Holmes," our visitor continued, "as I have indicated things went well. Admirably. I had my studio on the first floor of the cottage and was turning out good work. Eveline—Miss Reynolds, that is—was a frequent visitor to the cottage and I also visited her home. She is an orphan and lives with an elderly aunt, the latter making me welcome enough. The first indication that something was wrong occurred a few months after my taking up residence. I returned home from a visit to Eveline one evening to find the premises in some disarray. Things had been moved from their familiar places, there were muddy boot-marks on the stairs, and some canvases in the studio had been disturbed."

"In other words a search had been made," said Holmes, a gleam of interest in his eyes.

"Exactly, sir. To say I was extremely annoyed, let alone alarmed and dismayed, would not adequately describe my feelings. I lit every lamp in the place and made a thorough search but found nothing."

"The front door had been securely locked?"

"Certainly, Mr. Holmes. I would never leave my home in that lonely place without first making all secure."

"Perhaps your domestic help . . . " I put in.

Smedhurst shook his head.

"I have a woman who comes in twice a week to do some cleaning and cooking but she arrives only when I am there."

"No one else has a key?" said Holmes.

"Not that I am aware of, Mr. Holmes. There is only one key, an enormous thing more suited to the Bastille. The lawyer explained that the old man was terrified of being robbed and insisted on one key only and had a special lock fitted."

"And the back door?"

"Firmly locked and bolted."

"Nothing was stolen?"

"I made a thorough inventory but nothing was missing, so far as I could make out."

"Did Miss Reynolds have a key?"

Again the vehement shake of the head.

"I offered to have one made for her but she did not wish it. We both felt it might compromise her."

"Quite so," I put in.

Holmes got up to knock out his pipe in the fender, his face alive with interest. "Hmm. This is intriguing. There is more, of course?"

"Much more, Mr. Holmes, but I will be as concise as possible. The next thing that happened was strange noises around the house. Heavy footsteps as though someone were on the prowl. Then the front door latch would be tried. That was the most frightening thing of all, Mr. Holmes. In a lonely cottage, late at night, all sorts of thoughts pass through one's head."

"Quite so."

"And then there were ghostly tappings at the window. I can tell you, Mr. Holmes, that by that time my nerves were considerably on edge. These things continued for some months. In the interim Miss Reynolds and I had become engaged to be married."

I was about to offer my congratulations when I was arrested by the warning look on Holmes' face.

"You told your fiancée nothing about these unnerving incidents?"

"Certainly not."

"You did not investigate these happenings?"

"I did, Mr. Holmes. I have a very powerful hand lantern and I lit that and went outside. But I left the front door open, so that the light spilled across the garden, and I never moved more than three yards from the door."

"You were very wise, Mr. Smedhurst. Someone was evidently attempting to lure you from your home."

Smedhurst turned white and caught his breath with a little gasp.

"I had not thought of that, Mr. Holmes. This happened on several occasions, but I could never find anyone though there were occasional traces of boots in the mud when the weather was wet. Thank God, all these activities stopped when spring came."

"Obviously, Mr. Smedhurst. The person who was trying to frighten you could not carry out his activities during light spring and summer evenings."

"But what is the point of all this, Mr. Holmes?"

"Hopefully, we shall see in due course," said my companion.

"Well, with the cessation of these manifestations, I regained my spirits somewhat and Miss Reynolds and I formally announced our engagement. In the meantime I visited the lawyer and in a roundabout way asked whether the former occupier of the cottage, Jabez Crawley, had ever mentioned anything out of the way there."

"And what was this gentleman's reaction?"

"Oh, he simply asked me a few questions about faulty drains, draught and damp and so forth and then queried whether I wished to sell the cottage."

Holmes clasped his thin fingers before him and sat studying my client's troubled face for a long moment.

"Last winter the things began again," said Smedhurst. "Only

it was worse this time. Not only weird noises, footsteps and tappings, but one evening a fortnight ago a ghastly face like crumpled parchment appeared at the parlour window. I had left the curtains drawn back and you may remember the severe weather in February, so that there was a rime of frost on the panes. I caught a glimpse only for a moment but it turned my soul sick inside. A hideous white idiot face like a dwarf. I sat slumped for what must have been an hour without stirring outside. Nothing else happened or I should not have been able to answer for my sanity."

"You may well say so. But you have other troubles also, Mr. Smedhurst."

The bearded man looked startled.

"I have heard that you can work miracles, Mr. Holmes, and that you can almost see into people's minds."

Holmes gave a short laugh.

"Hardly, Mr. Smedhurst. But I know a deeply troubled man when I see one. There is something beyond all this business, is there not? Something connected with Miss Reynolds?"

Smedhurst half-started from his chair and gave a strangled cry.

"You are right, Mr. Holmes. There has been a growing estrangement because of all this. She wanted to know why I had changed but I did not want to involve her..." He broke off and buried his head in his hands.

"Now I hear that she has taken up with a young man who has come to live in the village..."

Holmes put his finger to his lips and then laid his hand on our visitor's shoulder. "All may yet come right, Mr. Smedhurst. Do not despair."

"I have not told you the worst, Mr. Holmes. Last night

someone tried to shoot me as I stood outside my cottage door. It was dusk and the shot missed me by inches. I have never been so frightened in my life."

"Perhaps a poacher with a shotgun . . . " I began.

Smedhurst stood up abruptly, trying to control the trembling that shook his frame. "No, Dr. Watson. I know a rifle shot when I hear one. That bullet was meant for me!"

"Why did you not call in the police, Mr. Smedhurst?"

"We have only a sleepy village constable, Mr. Holmes, and I had no evidence."

Holmes was on his feet now.

"Is there an inn in this Parvise Magna of yours?"

"Yes, Mr. Holmes, the George and Dragon."

"Good. If you will telegraph for rooms we will accompany you to Dorset in the morning. I take it you would wish to come, Watson?"

"By all means, Holmes. I will just warn my locum that I may be away for several days."

"Admirable! Your revolver, Watson, and a packet of cartridges in your luggage, if you please. We have no time to lose!"

3

It was a bitterly cold day with a fine drizzle when we left for London the following morning and after several changes found ourselves on the Somerset and Dorset Railway, in a small and uncomfortable carriage which seemed to be carrying us into a bleak and inhospitable landscape. We had the compartment to ourselves and our client, evidently exhausted from his trials of past days, sat huddled in deep sleep in a far corner. Holmes sat smoking furiously next to me, the fragrant emissions from his pipe seeming to emulate the black smoke our funny little engine was shovelling over its shoulder as we wound our interminable way into the gathering dusk.

"Well, what do you make of it, Watson?"

I shrugged.

"Pointless, Holmes. An old cottage ransacked, ghostly manifestations and then a murderous attack."

"But it adds up to a definite pattern, my dear fellow."

"If Mr. Smedhurst has the only key to the cottage, how could a marauder gain entrance without breaking a window or something of that sort?"

"Ah, you have taken that point, have you? There must obviously be another. Or someone must have manufactured one."

"But for what purpose. Holmes?"

"That remains to be seen," said he, his sharp, feral face alive with interest.

"What I cannot understand," I went on, "is why, if someone has a key, they have not been back."

Holmes gave a dry chuckle.

"That is simple enough. He has satisfied himself that the object of his search will not be easily discernible. He may wait for the owner himself to discover it."

"Or scare him away."

Holmes nodded approvingly.

"Excellent, Watson. You have hit the nail on the head."

And he said not another word until we had reached our destination. This proved to be a somewhat ramshackle halt with a plank platform and I thought I had seldom seen a more desolate spot. Several oil lanterns beneath the station canopy were already alight and cast grotesque shadows as they swayed to and fro in the rising wind. But a closed carriage, which Smedhurst had already ordered from the hotel, was waiting and once our client had shaken off the terror which had overtaken him on the train, he quickly took charge of the situation and we were speedily rocking through the approaching dusk to our journey's end.

I was surprised to find that Parvise Magna was not really a village but a small town composed of a broad main street, long lines of stone-built cottages and larger houses; no less than two inns; an ancient church; and a covered market.

"Things are looking up, Holmes," I said, as the cheering lights of our substantial hostelry, the George and Dragon, came into view.

It was indeed a comfortable-looking inn, with blazing log fires, and when we had quickly registered and deposited our baggage with the manager, Holmes looked inquiringly at our client.

"There should be an hour or so of daylight left. Would that be sufficient time for me to visit your cottage?"

"Oh, indeed, Mr. Holmes. It would only take twenty minutes to get there, providing we can retain the carriage."

After a brief word with the manager Smedhurst led the way round to a side yard where the equipage was still waiting, and then we were driving swiftly out of the town and up into the winding fastnesses of the blunt-nosed hills. Presently we stopped at a place where an oak finger-post pointed up the hillside.

"I think we can walk back," said Holmes, giving the driver a half-guinea for his trouble, much to that worthy's surprise and gratitude.

"It will give us an appetite for dinner," Holmes added.

We followed Smedhurst up a broad, zig-zag path, just wide

enough for a horse and cart, that eventually wound between large boulders. It was an eerie and desolate place and I should not have cared to have spent one night there, let alone made it my permanent abode. I whispered as much to Holmes and he gave me a wry smile. There was still light enough in the sky to see our way and in a short while we came to a large stone cottage set back in a rustic enclosure that might once have been a garden.

Our client then produced a massive, wrought iron key which, as he had said, might have served for the entrance to the Bastille, and unlocked the stout iron-studded front door. Holmes and I stood on the flagstone surround until Smedhurst had lit lamps within. The parlour was a huge room, with an ancient stone fireplace surmounted by a bressumer beam. The furniture was comfortable enough but the stone-flagged floor gave it a dank atmosphere, though Holmes seemed oblivious to such things. He went quickly to the large windows which fronted the room.

"This is where you saw the apparition, Mr. Smedhurst?"

The tall man gulped.

"That is so, Mr. Holmes. The nearest one."

I waited while my companion examined the glass carefully. Then he went outside and I could hear his staccato footsteps going up and down. When he reappeared, his face was absorbed and serious.

"Then the flagstone surround which appears to run round the entire house would not have shown any footprints."

"That is so, Mr. Holmes."

"Let us just examine the rest of your abode."

Smedhurst lit lamp after lamp as we toured the ground floor, which consisted of a simple toilet; a corridor; a store room; and a kitchen, which was primitively equipped. We went up a creaky wooden staircase to the first floor, where there were three bedrooms and a huge apartment equipped as a studio, with northern lights and canvases stacked against the walls. Holmes went over to stare at a grotesque charcoal sketch of distorted trees and bleak moorland, set all aslant by the near-genius of the artist.

"Presumably this room is the reason you bought the house?"

"That is so, Mr. Holmes."

"Very well."

My companion suddenly became very alert.

"We have just time to see outside before the light completely fails."

He led the way downstairs at a rapid pace, Smedhurst and myself having difficulty in keeping up with him. We rejoined him on the paved area in front of the cottage.

"So your phantom made off in this direction?"

He pointed in front of us to where the paving gave out into a narrow path which wound among bushes. Again the haunted look passed across Smedhurst's face and he went back and re-locked the front door.

"Yes, Mr. Holmes."

"Let us just see where this leads."

By the yellow light of the lantern which the artist carried and which cast bizarre shadows before us, we traversed the path and presently came out on a cleared space which appeared to be floored with some hard substance difficult to make out in the dim light.

"Ah!"

Holmes drew in his breath with a sibilant hiss, as a vast black pit composed itself before us.

"A quarry, I presume?"

"Yes, Mr. Holmes. I know little of such matters but I understand it was where they cut Purbeck stone with which they built houses thereabouts. It has not been in use this fifty years. It is not within my land, of course. My boundary ends just beyond the paved area and is marked with a post. I have not bothered to have a fence erected."

"Quite so."

Holmes was craning forward, looking intently into the forbidding depths before us.

"This place looks decidedly dangerous."

"Yes. It is over a hundred feet deep. A sheer drop, as you can see."

"But an ideal spot into which your phantom might have disappeared."

Smedhurst gave us a startled look in the yellow light of the lantern he carried. There was a leprous glow on the far horizon and I was in a sombre mood as our small procession made its way back to the cottage. Smedhurst unlocked the front door and extended his hand in farewell.

"Will you not join us for dinner and stay the night at our hotel?" I said.

He shook his head.

"I do not care to be about after dark in these parts, gentlemen. But I will join you at the 'George' tomorrow."

"About midday," Holmes replied. "I have a few calls to make in the morning. Until then."

As we walked away we could hear the grating of the lock and the ponderous shooting of bolts at the great front door. At that moment I would not have changed places with our client for anything in the world.

"What a grim place, Holmes," I said as we walked swiftly back through the gloom toward the faint glow that indicated the welcoming streets of Parvise Magna.

"Ah, I see you lack the artistic temperament, Watson," said Holmes.

Our footsteps echoed unnaturally on the uneven, rocky surface of the path and dark clouds obscured the moon, only a few faint stars staring out on the horizon.

"I prefer 221B, Holmes," I said.

My companion chuckled, a long chain of sparks from his pipe, which he had lit on his way down from the cottage, making fiery little stipples on his lean, aquiline features.

"I certainly agree there, my dear fellow."

4

The next morning I was up early but Holmes was earlier still for I found him at breakfast in the cheerful, beamed dining room, where a few sickly rays of sun glanced in at the windows. When we had finished our repast, Holmes jumped up swiftly and made for the door, hardly leaving me time to collect my overcoat from the rack and follow somewhat protestingly at his rear.

"We have very little time, Watson," he said as I caught up with him in the surprisingly busy street.

"Firstly, we must just lay a call upon Mr. Amos Hardcastle, the lawyer, and see what he has to say about this matter."

We had only some three or four hundred yards to go and when we had neared the brass plate which indicated that gentleman's office, Holmes took me aside and pretended to study the contents of a saddlery shop window.

"Leave the talking to me, my dear fellow. My name will be Robinson for the purpose of this business."

I had scarcely time to take this in before Holmes led the way up a dusty staircase to where a stout wooden door repeated the legend on the brass plate outside. A distant clock was just striking the hour of nine but the office was already astir and Holmes opened the door without further ado and I followed him in.

An elderly woman with grey hair rose from her desk in the dingy outer office and welcomed us with a wry smile. When Holmes had introduced himself as Robinson and explained that he would not keep Mr. Hardcastle more than ten minutes, she nodded and crossed to an inner door, tapping before entering. There was a muffled colloquy from behind the panels and then the door opened again. The solicitor was a man of heavy build and late middle age, who wore a snuff-stained waistcoat and gold pince-nez. His white hair fell in an untidy quiff over his forehead but his manner was cheerful enough and he asked Holmes and myself to sit down opposite his battered desk.

The room, which was lit by two large and dusty windows, was piled high with papers on the far side while the area behind Hardcastle's desk was stacked with labelled tin boxes from floor to ceiling. Holmes, in his persona as Robinson, said that Smedhurst was thinking of selling his cottage and that he, Robinson, was thinking of buying it. He had come down with myself to view the property but had found that Smedhurst had apparently gone away for several days. He wondered if the lawyer had a key to the house so that we could have a look at it.

A cautious, professional look immediately settled on the lawyer's face.

"Dear me, Mr. Robinson, this is the first I have heard of it. Have you any written authority for what you say? This is merely formality you understand, my dear sir, but I'm sure you realise..."

"Certainly."

I was even more astonished when Holmes produced a crumpled letter from the pocket of his Ulster and passed it across to Smedhurst's solicitor. He scanned it cursorily through his pince-nez, biting his lip as he did so.

"All seems in order, Mr. Robinson," he said as he handed it back.

He turned to the massed japanned boxes behind him and went down them rapidly. He took one from the end of the piles and rattled it as though he expected to find something unpleasant in it.

"Here we are."

He put it down on his desk, brushing the dust from the top of the box with a frayed sleeve. He opened it and went through a pile of yellowing papers. After sifting about for what seemed like an interminable time, he shook his head.

"I am so sorry to disappoint you, Mr. Robinson, but I have nothing here. If I remember rightly my late client was a very retiring sort of person and inordinately frightened of burglars, though what he could have had of value up there was beyond me."

He chuckled rustily.

"Some years ago he had the front door lock changed. It came with a massive single key, which he always retained on him. I have no doubt Mr. Smedhurst has it still. My regrets, gentlemen."

Holmes rose with alacrity and extended his hand to the lawyer.

"It was just a possibility. I am sorry to have disturbed you."

"Not at all, not at all." He waved us out with a smile and as soon as we had regained the street I turned to Holmes.

"Where on earth did you get that letter?"

My companion smiled.

"Forged it, my dear fellow. I thought it might come in useful. I have a passable talent in that direction which has served its purpose from time to time. Now we must interview the young lady, which might be a more delicate matter, and then I shall warn Smedhurst to make preparations for his departure."

"Departure, Holmes?" I said as we walked rapidly down the busy street. "I am all at sea."

"It is not the first time, old fellow," said he with a wry smile. "But hopefully all will be made plain in due course."

We walked several hundred yards and then turned at right-angles down a small alley, lined with pleasant old stone-built cottages. He stopped at the third on the right and opened a wrought-iron gate which gave on to a minuscule garden, where withered plants struggled for existence at this time of year. A motherly-looking lady in her early sixties opened the front door to his knock. She looked surprised, as well she might have.

"We wish to see Miss Eveline Reynolds on a most important matter. Please do not be alarmed, dear lady. A short interview will be greatly to her benefit."

The cloud gathering on her face disappeared immediately.

"Please come in. My niece is in the next room sewing. Whom shall I say...?"

Holmes leaned forward and whispered something in her ear. I saw a surprising change come over her face.

"I am sure she will be pleased to see you in view of what you have just told me."

She ushered us into a charmingly furnished oak-beamed parlour where a slim, golden-haired girl of some twenty-eight years was sitting at a sewing frame. She got up suddenly as we entered and looked inquiringly at her aunt.

"Please don't be alarmed, dear. These are friends of Mr. Smedhurst."

"Ah!"

The girl could not suppress the exclamation that rose to her lips. The aunt had silently withdrawn and Miss Reynolds came forward to shake hands formally, beckoning us into easy chairs near the welcoming fire.

"You have news of Aristide? I have been so worried about him . . . "

There was such a pleading look on her face that I saw a dramatic change in Holmes himself.

"This is an extremely difficult matter, Miss Reynolds. But I am afraid we are forgetting our manners. I am Sherlock Holmes and this is my friend and colleague Dr. Watson. I have asked your aunt not to reveal our identities and I would ask you to do the same."

He held up his hand as the girl started forward in her chair.

"Please let me continue. Mr. Smedhurst is in some great difficulty and he has called upon me to help him. Am I to take it that your engagement has been broken off?"

The girl bit her lip. "It is nothing of my doing, Mr. Holmes. He has changed over the last year or so and become evasive. He no longer confides in me. He has taken to drinking rather heavily and now he has grown that ridiculous-looking beard!"

Little red spots of anger were starting out on her cheeks.

"Forgive me again, my dear young lady, but Mr. Smedhurst appears to think that you have transferred your affections elsewhere."

The girl stared at Holmes in astonishment and then burst out laughing.

"You must mean Mr. Jacob Ashton. He is a young Australian who came to the village a long while back. He is a surveyor by profession. My aunt and I occasionally lunch or dine at the George and Dragon and we made his acquaintance there. He is in practice here, but we are friends, nothing more."

"Ah, that is good news indeed, Miss Reynolds," said Holmes, rising abruptly from his chair. "I cannot confide in you at the present moment but you may be sure that all will yet be well between you."

"Ah, if only I could believe you, Mr. Holmes!"

"You may. And I might add that he was thinking only of you in his present troubles and did not wish you involved."

The girl shook hands with us warmly, and after Holmes had again asked her not to reveal his identity, we left the house with its occupants more cheerful than when we had arrived.

"Now for Smedhurst, Watson. I must prime him as to his role in our little drama. Ah, there is our man himself!"

He had just noticed our client's reflection in a shop window and, turning, we saw that he was making for the George and Dragon. We followed as quickly as possible, catching him at the entrance, where Holmes had a muffled conversation, before following him into the crowded restaurant. A waiter hurried forward as we sat down to order our meal when Smedhurst gave an exclamation and said, "Why, there is young Ashton at the table yonder."

Holmes leaned forward and put his hand gently on our client's shoulder.

"You have no need to worry. Miss Reynolds and Ashton are merely friends."

With a muffled apology he rose from the table and I was astonished to see him make straight for the surveyor, who was lunching alone at a side table. He bent over, presumably to introduce himself and then beckoned me across.

"Please forgive this intrusion, Mr. Ashton, but I understand you are a surveyor. Myself and my friend Mr. Watson are hoping to buy a cottage down here and have found exactly what we require. Mr. Smedhurst, who is lunching with us, as you have perhaps noticed, is anxious to sell and we wondered whether you would be kind enough to undertake the survey?"

Ashton, who was a pleasant-looking man of about thirty with black curly hair, seemed embarrassed, I thought.

"Certainly, Mr. Robinson," he stammered. "But this is the first I have heard of it. Miss Reynolds did not mention it."

"It was a sudden decision," said Holmes smoothly. "Mr. Smedhurst is going to London for a few days this evening, but is leaving the key of the cottage with us. I have the address of your office. And now, I have interrupted your lunch long enough."

Ashton got up to shake hands with the pair of us.

"Honoured, my dear sir," he said with a smile. "My hours are from 9:30 a.m. until 6:00 p.m., unless I am out on survey. I look forward to seeing you soon."

"I cannot see, Holmes . . . " I began as we regained our table.

"I seem to have heard you say that before, Watson," said my companion with a disarming smile. "I think the oxtail soup and then the steak will do admirably in my case."

And he talked of nothing but trivial matters until the meal was over.

5

"Now, you understand the procedures I have outlined to you, Mr. Smedhurst," said Holmes as we regained the street. Our client nodded.

"I will leave Parvise Magna this afternoon, in daylight, with my luggage and make sure my departure is noted in the town, both by pony and trap and by train. I will give out that I am going to London for a week to see an aunt and make myself conspicuous on the platform. I will stay away for three nights. I will leave the cottage key behind a big boulder about thirty feet from the front door. You cannot miss it, Mr. Holmes. There is a fissure at the back and I will place it there, well concealed."

"Excellent, Mr. Smedhurst. Now there is just one thing more."

"What is that, Mr. Holmes?"

My companion gave him a thin smile.

"Shave off your beard. Miss Reynolds does not like it."

I spent most of the afternoon reading in the smoking room of the George and Dragon, while Holmes was away on some errand of his own. Presently he rejoined me and we both noted with satisfaction the departure of Smedhurst as his pony and trap clattered down the main street on its way to the station. As gas lamps began to be lit in the street outside Holmes rose from his deep leather chair, his whole being tense and animated.

"I think you might fetch your revolver, old fellow. We may

need it before the night is out. I have some provisions in my greatcoat pocket so we shall not go hungry."

"In that case I will bring my whisky flask," said I.

A quarter of an hour later we left the hotel and made our way inconspicuously through side streets, as though taking an innocuous afternoon stroll. Though there was still an hour or so of daylight the sky was dark and sombre as we cleared the outskirts of Parvise Magna and a pallid mist was rising from the drenched fields which skirted the rounded hills. We were both silent as we continued our walk and presently Holmes turned aside to avoid approaching our client's cottage from the front. When we could just see the roof of the property through the bare branches of leafless trees, we diverged from the path and in a few moments found ourselves on the overgrown track that led to the quarry. It was a grim place at that late time of day and we both paused as though possessed of the same impulse, and gazed down over the hundred-foot drop.

"An awful spot, Holmes."

"Indeed, Watson. But I think there is a more agreeable approach yonder."

He pointed forward and I then saw what appeared to be a white thread which turned out to be a shelving part of the quarry that led downward in gentle slopes. Our feet gritted on the loose shale and after we had descended about halfway my companion gave a sharp exclamation.

He led the way across the face of the quarry to where a dark hole gaped. It was obviously man-made and perhaps provided shelter for the quarrymen in years gone by. I followed him in and saw that the cavern was about ten feet across and some twenty feet deep. There was a narrow shelf of rock on the left-hand side, about five feet in.

"Hulloa," I said. "Here is a candle, Holmes." I bent closer.

"And recently used, I should say, judging by the spent matches which are perfectly dry and not wet as they would be had they been there a long time."

Holmes came to look over my shoulder.

"You are constantly improving, my dear fellow. You are not far out."

He went back into the rear of the cave which the failing daylight still penetrated.

"Someone has made a fire," I said, as he stirred the blackened ashes on the rough floor with his boot. "A tramp has been living here, perhaps."

"Perhaps, Watson," he said, as though his thoughts were far away.

Then he stooped to pick up a small clip of cardboard from the remains of the fire. I went across to see what he had found. I made out the faint white lettering on a blue background: CARROLL AND CO.

"What does it mean, Holmes?"

"I do not yet know," he said reflectively. "Time will tell. I think I have seen enough here to confirm my tentative theories. In the meantime we must get back to the cottage before it is completely dark."

And he led the way up the quarry at a swift pace. He put his finger to his lips as we drew close to our destination and bending down behind the large boulder our client had indicated, he brought out the massive wrought-iron key. It was the work of a moment to open the cottage door and relock it from the other side. The key turned smoothly so it was obvious why Smedhurst's mysterious intruder had been able to gain entry so easily.

"Could we have a light, Holmes?" I whispered.

"There is a dark lantern on the table yonder, which I observed on our previous visit. I think we might risk it for a few minutes to enable us to settle down. If he is coming at all tonight our man will not move until long after dark. I have baited the trap. Now let us just see what comes to the net."

I could not repress a shudder at these words, and I felt something of the terror that Smedhurst had experienced in that lonely place. But the comforting feel of my revolver in my overcoat did much to reassure me. I lit the lantern, shielding the match with my hand, and when we had deposited our sandwiches and made ourselves comfortable in two wing chairs, I closed the shutter of the lantern so that only a thin line of luminescence broke the darkness. I placed it beneath the table where it could not be seen from the windows, and after loading my pistol and securing the safety catch I placed it and my whisky flask near at hand as the light slowly faded.

What can I say of that dreary vigil? That the dark cloud of horror which seemed to hang about the cottage that night will remain with me until my dying day. Combined with the melancholy screeching of distant owls, it merely emphasised the sombreness of our night watch. Holmes seemed impervious to all this for he sat immobile in his chair, for I could see his calm face in the dim light that still filtered through the parlour windows. Presently we ate the sandwiches and, fortified with drafts of whisky from my flask, I became more alert. Several hours must have passed when I became aware that Holmes had stirred in his chair.

"I think the moment is approaching. Your pistol, Watson, if you please."

Then I heard what his keen ears had already caught. A vary

faint, furtive scraping on the rocky path that led to the cottage. I had the pistol in my hand now and eased off the safety catch. The clouds had lifted momentarily and pale moonlight outlined the casement bars. By its spectral glow I suddenly saw a ghastly, crumpled face appear in the nearest frame and I almost cried aloud. But Holmes' hand was on my arm and I waited with racing heart.

Then there was a metallic click and a key inserted from outside began to turn the lock. I was about to whisper to my companion when the door was suddenly flung wide and cold, damp air flowed into the room. We were both on our feet now. I vaguely glimpsed two figures in the doorway and then Holmes had thrown the shutter of the dark lantern back and its light flooded in, dispelling the gloom and revealing a dark-clad figure and, behind him, the hideous thing that had appeared at the window. A dreadful cry of alarm and dismay, the pounding of feet back down the path and then the horrible creature had turned the other way.

"Quickly, Watson! Time is of the essence! I recognised the second man but we must identify the other."

We were racing down the tangled pathway now, stumbling over the rocky surface, but the white-faced creature was quicker still. I discharged my pistol into the air and our quarry dodged aside and redoubled its efforts. Then we were in thick bushes and I fired again. The flash and the explosion were followed by the most appalling cry. When we rounded the next corner I could see by the light of the lantern which Holmes still carried, that the thing had misjudged the distance on the blind bend and had fallen straight down into the quarry.

"It cannot have survived that fall, Holmes," I said.

He shook his head.

"It was not your fault, old fellow. But we must hasten down in case he needs medical aid."

A few minutes later we had scrambled to ground level and cautiously approached the motionless thing with the smashed body that told my trained eye that he had died instantly. I gently turned him over while Holmes held the lantern. When he removed the hideous carnival mask we found ourselves looking into the bloodied face of young Ashton, the surveyor, whose expression bore all the elements of shock and surprise that one often finds in cases of violent death.

6

Holmes' hammering at the knocker of the substantial Georgian house at the edge of town presently brought a tousled housekeeper holding a candle in a trembling hand to a ground floor window.

"I must see your master at once!" said Holmes. "I know he has just returned home so do not tell me that he cannot be disturbed. It is a matter of life and death!"

The door was unbolted at once and we slipped inside.

"Do not be alarmed, my good woman," said Holmes gently. "Despite the hour, our errand is a vital one. I see by the muddy footprints on the parquet that your master has only recently returned. Pray tell him to come downstairs or we shall have to go up to him."

The housekeeper nodded, the fright slowly fading from her face.

"I will not be a moment, gentlemen. Just let me light this lamp on the hall table."

We sat down on two spindly chairs to wait, listening to the

mumbled conversation going on above. The man who staggered down the stairs to meet us was a completely changed apparition to the smooth professional we had previously met.

"You may leave us, Mrs. Hobbs," he said through trembling lips.

He looked from one to the other of us while anger and despair fought for mastery in his features.

"What is the meaning of this intrusion in the middle of the night, Mr. Robinson?"

"My name is Sherlock Holmes," said my companion sternly. "Your friend is dead. We must have the truth or you are a lost man!"

Amos Hardcastle's face was ashen. He mumbled incoherently and I thought he was going to have a stroke. I put my hand under his arm to help him down the last few treads and he almost fell into the chair I had just vacated. He looked round blankly, as though in a daze.

"Jabez Crawley's nephew dead? And you are the detective, Sherlock Holmes."

"Tell us the truth, Mr. Hardcastle," said Holmes, a smile of triumph on his face. "Or shall I tell the story for you?"

Something like anger flared momentarily in the lawyer's eyes.

"My client . . . " he began but Holmes cut him short.

"Must I repeat; your client is dead. He tried to kill Mr. Smedhurst. That makes you an accessory."

The lawyer's face turned even whiter if that were possible. "I knew nothing of that," he whispered. "Did you kill him?"

This to me.

I shook my head.

"No. He fell over the edge of the quarry."

"I will have you disbarred for unprofessional conduct and you will stand trial for criminal conspiracy and accessory to attempted murder," said Holmes sternly. "It was unfortunate for you that I recognised you by the light of the lantern."

"I beg you, Mr. Holmes!"

"The time is long past for begging. Let me just try to reconstruct your dishonest sequence of events. I am sure you will correct me if I am wrong."

Holmes sat down in a chair opposite the crushed figure of the lawyer and eyed him grimly.

"Let us just suppose that old Jabez Crawley did not leave a proper will. Just a scribbled note or two, leaving the cottage to his nephew in Australia, his only surviving relative. And supposing he had hinted that there was something valuable hidden there, without indicating its whereabouts. Money perhaps, bonds or the deeds to properties. There were two keys to the cottage. There had to be or you and the nephew would never have gone there and made searches while Mr. Smedhurst was out. But that is to run ahead. Am I correct so far?"

The old man nodded sullenly. He looked like a cornered rat with his hair awry and his muddy clothes.

"You wrote to the nephew in Australia at his last known address. You got no reply, I presume?"

"No, sir. More than eight months had passed and I surmised that young Ashton had either died or moved to some other country."

Holmes smiled thinly.

"You had many fruitless searches at the cottage in the interim—without result. So you sold it to Mr. Smedhurst and pocketed the proceeds. You are a pretty scoundrel, even for a provincial lawyer."

Hardcastle flushed but said nothing, his haunted eyes shifting first to Holmes and then on to me.

"After a long interval you got a reply from the nephew. Your letter had gone astray or been delayed. All this is fairly elementary."

"I think it quite remarkable. Holmes," I interjected. "I had no idea . . ."

"Later, old fellow," he interrupted. "So young Ashton made his way here and you gave him all the information at your disposal without, of course, telling him that he was the rightful owner of the cottage and that you had sold it and kept the money."

One look at the lawyer's face told me that once again my companion had arrived at the right conclusion.

"You worked out a plan of campaign. The nephew would try and sow a little discord between Smedhurst and his fiancée, in the most subtle way, of course, at the same time keeping an eye on Smedhurst's activities. Then the pair of you invented the series of ghostly happenings. When you drew a blank there and further searches threw no light on old Crawley's secret, you resorted to stronger measures, with the apparition at the window, and then, finally a short while ago, the attempt at murder."

The old man wrung his hands.

"I can assure you, Mr. Holmes . . ."

"Well, that is a matter between you and the police," said Holmes curtly. "We must inform them about the body in the quarry and the circumstances first thing in the morning, Watson. It is almost dawn, anyway."

"Of course, Holmes."

I glanced at my pocket watch and saw that it was almost

4:00 a.m. I felt a sudden weariness following the events of the night.

"What about the cave in the quarry?" I asked.

"That was clear as crystal, Watson. When carrying out his dangerous masquerade, Ashton needed a refuge and an opportunity for a ghostly disappearance. He found the place near the cottage which suited his purposes admirably. When he had made his escape and was sure no one had followed, he lit the candle and tidied his clothing. Perhaps he cleaned his shoes if they were coated with mud."

"But the fire, Holmes?"

He gave a thin smile.

"Why, simply to burn that huge papier-mâché carnival mask, Watson. The fragment of label unburned, reading Carroll and Co., showed that the mask had been bought from a well-known Soho emporium specialising in such things. Obviously, Ashton had bought a number of them."

"Yes, but how would he take them to the cottage, Holmes?"

"Why, probably in a large paper bag. No one would take any notice when he passed through the town in broad daylight. The early hours were another matter. He could not risk taking that mask through the town to the house at dead of night in case he were seen; he might even have been stopped and questioned by the local constable. Hence the fire. Correct, Mr. Hardcastle?"

"You are a devil, Mr. Holmes," was the man's broken reply. "But you are correct in every detail."

We left the shattered figure of Hardcastle huddled on the chair and walked back toward the centre of the town.

"How did you come to suspect Ashton?" I asked.

"There was the irony, Watson. It could have been anyone in

Parvise Magna. But then the idea grew in my mind. Ashton was young and personable; he had come from Australia soon after the ghostly manifestations had appeared; and he had attached himself to Smedhurst's fiancée."

"Remarkable, Holmes."

"You do me too much credit, my dear fellow."

"I wonder what the secret of the cottage is?" I said.

He shrugged.

"Only time will tell. Otherwise, a very curious affair."

7

And so it proved. Some weeks later I came to the breakfast table to find Holmes smiling broadly. He passed a cheque across to me and my eyes widened as I read the amount above Smedhurst's signature.

"Our artist has struck lucky at last, Watson," he said. "His letter is full of news. He has shaved off his beard and is reunited with his fiancée."

"Excellent, Holmes."

"And there is more. Just glance at these two newspaper cuttings."

The first related to the preliminary police court proceedings against Hardcastle, which Holmes and I had attended, and his subsequent striking off the legal rolls. The opening of the inquest on Ashton, which we were also required to attend, had been held in camera due to the involvement of Hardcastle in these proceedings also, and had been adjourned *sine die*. Therefore there had been no reports of these proceedings in the Dorset or national newspapers. During the inquest a high-ranking police officer had informed Holmes that a sporting rifle with one spent cartridge in the breech had been found at Ashton's home, together with a number of carnival masks.

The second cutting was even more sensational than the first. It was a lurid tale of an artist who had discovered £20,000 in golden guineas in a series of tin boxes beneath the oak flooring of his studio. There was no mention of Holmes, as I had expected, and the report merely concluded with the information that the discovery had been made by a carpenter carrying out work for Smedhurst.

"And here is something for you, Watson."

Holmes passed across a small buff envelope. That too was from Smedhurst and was an invitation to his wedding celebrations a month hence. I glanced up at Holmes' own invitation on the mantelpiece.

"Will you be joining me, Holmes?"

My companion gave me an enigmatic smile.

"I think not, Watson. Marriage is a very uncertain and risky business. But you may give the bride and groom my best wishes and a suitable gift from Garrards if you will."

And he reached out for his violin.

SPECIAL THANKS TO Basil and Annie Copper, Peter and Nicky Crowther, Michael and Sheryl Smith, Thomas Gianni, Val and Les Edwards, Gary Gianni, Randy Broecker, Bob Byrne, Mark Maddox, Allen Koszowski, Bob Eggleton and Michael Marshall Smith.

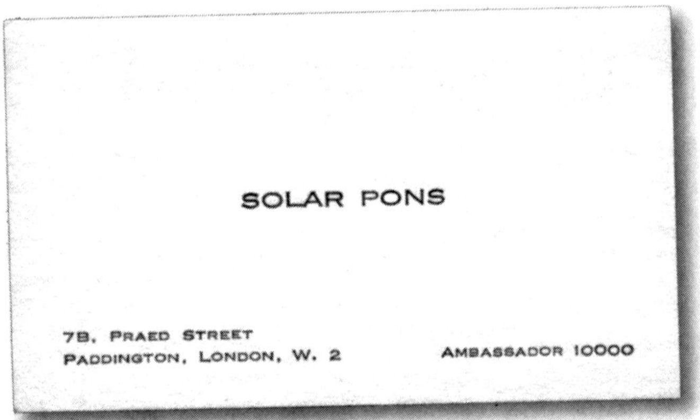

SOLAR PONS

7B, PRAED STREET
PADDINGTON, LONDON, W. 2

AMBASSADOR 10000